FROM ROCK A SONG

PART 2

The Shady Way

V. E. Bines

TERRATENEBRA - THE WESTERN MOUNTAINS

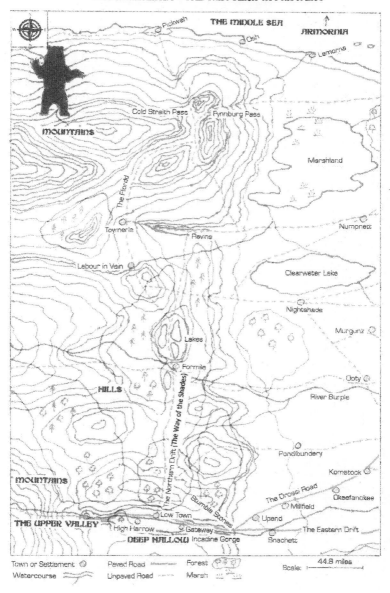

THE MIDDLE SEA

ARMORNIA

Pickwah
Osh
Lemorna

Cold Straith Pass   Fynnburg Pass

MOUNTAINS

Marshland

The Fiend

Toymeria

Ravine

Numpnett

Labour in Vain

Clearwater Lake

Nightshade

Murgunz

Lakes

Formile

HILLS

Ooty

River Burple

The Way of the Shades

Pondibundery

Kornstock

MOUNTAINS

The Droasi Road

Okeefanokee

Millfield

Low Town

Upend

THE UPPER VALLEY

High Harrow   Gateway

DEEP NALLOW Incadine Gorge   Snachett

The Eastern Drift

Stumble Stones

The Northern Drift (The Way of the Shades)

| Town or Settlement | Paved Road | Forest | Scale: | 44.8 miles |
| Watercourse | Unpaved Road | Marsh | | |

TERRATEDEBRA - THE KYMER LEVELS

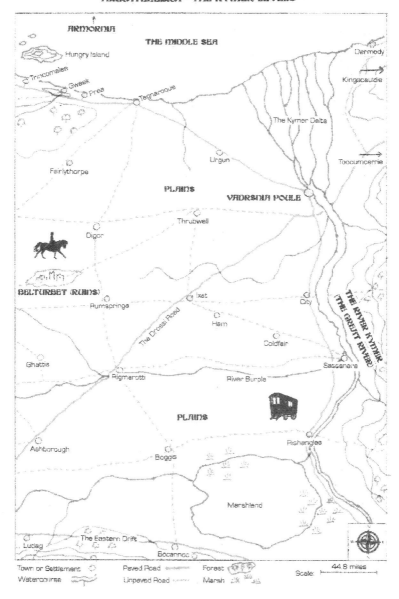

Contents

Characters in alphabetical order   7

Synopsis of Part 1 – The Valley   11

Chapter one   21

Chapter two   36

Chapter three   58

Chapter four   80

Chapter five   98

Chapter six   123

Chapter seven   135

Chapter eight   148

Chapter nine   169

Chapter ten   194

Chapter eleven   216

Chapter twelve   233

Chapter thirteen   255

Chapter fourteen   280

Chapter fifteen   305

Chapter sixteen   321

Chapter seventeen   344

Chapter eighteen   363

Chapter nineteen   382

Chapter twenty   **403**

Chapter twenty-one   **421**

Characters in alphabetical order

ALARIC (THE GRANDE STUPENDO) – age: 54/55. Actor manager. Captain of the strolling players known as the Ixat Instipulators.

ANN (HILDA HANNAH ARBERICORD) – age: 17/18. Tom's daughter. Formally a servant and attached nibbler (Nablan) at the Justification Inn in the valley of Deep Hallow. Shared a wet nurse with Dando. Has inherited *The Gift* which means she has the power to work what is commonly known as magic. Is in love with Dando.

BECCA (PEEPO) – age: 61/62. Drossi showgirl and boarding-house keeper. Comes from Armornia. Jack's friend.

CAROLUS – Tallis' horse.

CRISTIN – age: 32. Kidnap victim at Toymerle who, once released, helps care for Tallis.

DAMASK – age: 17/18. Dando's twin sister. Strong willed girl who rebels against the role assigned to all Gleptish women. Has an affinity with travelling people, particularly the Roma. Is promiscuous.

DANDO (THE LORD DAN ADDO) – age: 17/18. Until disinherited, second son and heir to the head of Clan Dan, the most powerful Glept family in the valley of Deep Hallow. A gifted cook and talented dancer. Is in love with Ann.

DR. RAYMOND SPOON – age: 28/29. Physician to the Pickwah army. Comes from Armornia.

DUKE – age: 20. A gypsy boy. Damask's first lover.

FOXY (EVERARD TETHERER TRULY, alias CAPTAIN JUDD) – age: 27/28. An unattached nibbler (Nablan). Found in the wild - a feral infant of unknown origin. Brought up by a goatherd on the borders of Deep Hallow. Formerly worked at the Justification.

GAMMADION (GUBBO THE GREAT) – age: centuries old. A powerful but corrupt wizard. The stealer of the Key.

HIRAM HOWGEGO – age: 80/81. A wealthy businessman. Jack's grandfather.

HORRY (HORACE) – Dando and Ann's baby son.

JACK HOWGEGO – age: 22/23. Gay grandson of Vadrosnia Poule's biggest shipping magnate. After being kidnapped has been blinded by the Cheetah in revenge for perceived wrongs done to his brother and himself by Jack's grandfather. Falls in love with Dando.

JORY TREWITHIK (THE GREAT LEADER) – age: 32/33. Self-appointed ruler of the city state of Pickwah and Commander-in-Chief of its army.

KRULL – age: indeterminate. Gigantic soldier in the Pickwah army.

MILLY – age: about 14 or 15. Damask's maid. A little black girl who was a child prostitute until rescued by Dando from a brothel in the town of Gateway. Idolises the one who saved her.

MEENA – Milly's cat.

MOLLYBLOBS – Damask's pony. *Borrowed* by Dando.

MURDOCK – Head gardener on the Witteridge Estate.

PHYLLIS – A very old donkey

PNOUMI THE MOG – age: hard to determine. Travelling showman from the far east whose exhibit is called *King Pnoumi's Cat Circus*.

PRIMO – singer backed by the Posse.

PUNCHINELLO – age: 47/48. Actor with the Ixat Instipulators.

RALPH – Tallis' dog.

RHYS – age: 51/52. Leader of the Labour-in-Vain expeditionary force.

SEVERINE – age: 18/19. Actress with the Ixat Instipulators.

SQUINANCY – age: ancient. Old woman who is the presiding genius of Pickwah Fortress.

TALLIS (PRINCE TALLISAND) – age: late middle. A lonely man who had spent most of his life on a quest for a mysterious object known as *The Key*. A musician.

THE CHEETAH & THE PANTHER (THOMAS and NICHOLAS MERRICK) - outlaw brothers, once legitimate business men, who specialize in holding people to ransom.

THE GOPHER – age: 68/69. Member of the Toymerle Shrine laity. An expert on all things to do with the oracle which is reputed to be the voice of Rostan, the god of the Earth's core.

THE GREAT ONES (AIGEA, PYR, ROSTAN, BRON ETC.) - alien immortals of mainly hominid origin whose original purpose in coming to earth was to retrieve the Key and dispatch it to its intended place in the cosmos but who, once here, were seduced by the notion that, with the Object in their possession, they would have absolute power over the planet's inhabitants.

THE OLD ONES – alien immortals of mainly non-hominid origin. The original visitants from deep space who brought the Key down to earth.

THE POSSE – an up-and-coming pop group consisting of members Winnie, Fynn and Matt.

TOM (THOMAS TOSA ARBERICORD) – age at his presumed death: 36. Ann's father. Cobbler and attached nibbler to Clan Dan, but also the high priest, the Culdee, of the Nablan race.

WITTERIDGE OF WITTERIDGE ACRES. – age: 75/76. Owner of a large estate on the south coast of the Middle Sea.

OTHER CHARACTERS WHO ARE REFERRED TO IN BOOK TWO BUT WHO DO NOT APPEAR

AZAZEEL (THE DARK BROTHER) - Pyr and Aigea's unnatural issue. Originally one being with his brother Pendar.

DANTOR (THE LORD DAN ATTOR) – age: 21/22. Dando's spectacled elder brother who becomes the next Dan when his father dies.

MARTHA BERINGARIA ARBERICORD nee BIDDERWADE – age at death: 19. Attached nibbler. Tom's wife. Ann's mother. Died in childbirth.

MORVAH – age when she and Tallis part: 30. His mother.

PENDAR – (THE BRIGHT BROTHER) Pyr and Aigea's unnatural issue. Originally one being with his brother Azazeel.

POTTO (POTTO POTUNALIUS APPLECRAFT) – age: about 71. Attached nibbler. Dando's manservant in Deep Hallow and substitute father.

THE DAN – age at death: 48. Dando's father and head of Clan Dan, the premier family in the valley of Deep Hallow.

<u>Synopsis of Part 1 – The Valley</u>

<u>Chapter 1</u>: Pyr and Aigea, two incorporeal beings posing as gods, are voicing grave doubts as to their continuing tenure of a small rocky planet, favourable to life, orbiting a minor star in the arm of an unremarkable spiral galaxy. They have been granted foreknowledge of a boy who may hold their fate in his hands although he is as yet unaware of the fact. On that same planet, a lonely man, a knight errant of sorts born out of his time, has been travelling for many years and at a certain point along his route arrives in the valley of Deep Hallow accompanied by his dog Ralph and horse Carolus. He puts up at an inn strangely titled *The Justification*. In days gone by his mother told him he could claim the soubriquet *Tallisand, Prince of the Lake Guardians, Keeper of the Key,* but if he is a prince, it is a prince without a people, and as for the Key that disappeared long ago. At the inn he makes the acquaintance of the innkeeper, a Mrs Humpage, and is attracted by a fair-haired servant girl that he is informed belongs to the subject nibbler (Nablan) race *'oo do all the donkey-work roun' 'ere.*

<u>Chapter 2</u>: Tallis, his horse and his dog are provided with food after which he retires to his room. Here he encounters another Nablan, a young man with an extremely truculent attitude, who brings him hot water for his bath. Tallis goes to bed but cannot sleep. Lying awake he thinks back to the beginning of his journey and his reasons for undertaking it.

<u>Chapter 3</u>: Tallis recalls his childhood in a poor mountain village far to the south. Despite their poverty his mother insisted that she had been born a king's daughter, one of a people who guarded a Treasure in the form of a Key which had the power to change the world when it was turned but was of such potency that there were few who could remain close to it for long without suffering the consequences. It was given into her nation's keeping by Pyr, known, among other things, as the Sky-Father, the Master-of-Winds and the Lord-of-Heaven. He had turned it for the present Age-of-Thought after having persuaded Aigea, the putative earth mother, to surrender it by professing his eternal love for her and suggesting they create an offspring of pure spirit between them. (Several thousand years before, this supposed goddess had also turned it, bringing about the Second Age, the Age-of-the-Heart). Tallis' mother explains that she was seduced by a

corrupt wizard named Gammadion who, although he was supposed
to be acting merely as errand-boy for another, persuaded her to steal
the Key on his behalf because he believed it delayed ageing in
whosoever held it, the more so the longer it remained in their
possession. As soon as she does what he asks and the Treasure is
surrendered, the lake beside which her people live vanishes and their
kingdom is destroyed. The nation's citizens set out to recover what
they have lost leaving Morvah along the way in a mountain fastness
to bear and raise her son. When Tallis reaches the age of fifteen she
tells him that it is his duty to follow and find his people, to mend
what his father has undone and bring back the Key so that the Land
of the Lake can be restored.

Chapter 4: Precipitously Tallis is launched on his quest when his
mother begins to fear that the villagers are filling his ears with a
different account of his origins and that he will no longer believe
what she has told him. In the last act of her life she packs him off
down the road and then relapses into a trance out of which, according
to a strange voice that issues from between her lips, she will never
awaken. At this point Tallis' recollections are interrupted by the noise
of falling rain and the sound of an argument taking place below his
window between some unknown persons and the obstreperous
Nablan whose acquaintance he has already made. Day is dawning
and he hears the Night Hymn to the Father being sung. At last he is
able to fall asleep.

Chapter 5: In a luxurious house in the center of one of the small
valley towns, a member of the ruling Glept elite, the Lord Dan Addo,
lies abed in the grip of a nightmare. This dream involves two
narratives, one of burning which has its source in actual events, while
the other concerns an enormous and threatening tunnel under the
world. On waking, Dando, second son and heir to the Dan, a
powerful clan chief, decides he must play truant from school and go
on an expedition in an attempt to exorcise this recurrent dream.
Despite having all the trappings of wealth and position (expensive
clothes, opulent living quarters, numerous subordinates) the boy is
not a typical scion of the philistine Gleptish aristocracy – among his
passions are a fascination with books and cookery. The year is now
well into its ninth month and it is the morning following Dando's
seventeenth birthday. As he sets out astride the Dans' great black
thoroughbred Attack and singing to himself (a somewhat ear-
tormenting sound!) he dwells on his recent experiences as a military
cadet - an Outrider - in the town of Gateway which lies at the

entrance to the valley. Whilst there he has heard a scandalous story
concerning his own father to the effect that he once married a nibbler
woman who bore him a son. This has particular relevance for Dando
as he also loves a Nablan girl, and it is for her sake that, the previous
year, he refused to swear the oath of allegiance to his people which
required that he put their good above all others. That is why he is
currently residing in the little town of High Harrow instead of in
Gateway or at Castle Dan, his clan's ancestral home, having been
sent there, in deep disgrace, to study estate management. During his
stay he prepares a meal for Father Adelbert, one of his teachers, and
this worldly foreign priest is greatly impressed by the quality and
originality of the dishes on offer. In fact Dando has been developing
his culinary skills since a small boy and by now has reached a
professional standard.

Chapter 6: On his way to the extreme western end of the valley our
truant finds himself amid a confusion of lanes on the south side of
the River Wendover. Here he has a strange encounter with a
supernatural being in the form of a black dog. This is one of a class
of elementals who came from outside the earth long ago carrying a
Treasure they had stolen, (the very same Key that Tallis is seeking),
and who chose to establish their hegemony on this particular planet.
These entities, the Old Ones, are occasionally visible to the human
eye and Dando has been blessed or maybe cursed with the ability to
see them because of something which happened to him when he was
no more than a child. He hates this hag-ridden side to his life and
yearns to be normal, as he imagines everyone else to be.
Nevertheless, because of the confrontation, he is prompted to think
back to his beginnings and to face up to harrowing memories which
he is usually at pains to suppress. These concern a mentor named
Tom, the Dans' Nablan cobbler, who was also, unknown to his
masters, the high-priest or Culdee of the Nablan race and the
intercessor between his people and Aigea, the earth goddess and
object of their worship. Tom's daughter Ann shared a wet-nurse with
Dando when they were babies and later played with him and with his
twin sister Damask. In due time they became childhood sweethearts.
Although the Lady Damask's people, the Glepts, ostensibly worship
the Sky-Father, she decides, at the age of six, that she would like to
pray to the Mother on behalf of one of her sick friends. While Tom is
away the three children go to his workshop where, as the young
Glepts have discovered, an image of Aigea is hidden in an annex
behind a dresser and Dando is elected to conduct the ceremony. He is

thus brought to the attention of the immortal who recognises him as the one with a destiny to fulfil which if achieved might prove a threat to her own existence. A few months later, when he is just seven, she lures him away with ill intent to her shrine in the Upper Valley, the Midda as the Nablans call it, and he would have perished if Tom, who guessed the goddess's intention, had not rescued him. Because the cobbler has gone against her will in saving the little boy he incurs the wrath of his mistress.

Chapter 7: Three years of foreboding on Tom's part pass before Aigea engineers his quietus. Blamed for the death of the Dan's youngest son he is condemned to burn as a witch within the bounds of the immortal's holy shrine. Before the cobbler's arrest Dando falls ill and only learns what has happened to his friend once he recovers from the blood-poisoning he has contracted due to his sister's tattooing techniques. Subsequent to Tom's immolation he is plagued by bad dreams identical to the one that has spurred him into setting out on his present journey. His solution, both then and now, is to go to the Upper Valley which is at the heart of the nightmare and *face his demons* as he puts it. At twelve years old when he and his twin make the trip he ventures close to the immortal's lair and as a result the dreams cease; he cannot understand why they should have returned now after so long an absence. Before Tom's presumed death Ann disappeared off the face of the earth. In fact she had been spirited away by other Nablans to live with her maternal grandmother at the Justification Inn. Desperate to find her, Dando searches high and low, including, once he has become an Outrider cadet, in the brothels of Gateway, but without success.

Chapter 8: Reaching the Midda which contains the flat-topped mound known as Judd's Hill Dando brokers a pact with the Mother: *If I can walk round the edge of this hill and back to my starting point without straying, the dreams will cease for good and I will go free.* He is vouchsafed many visions as he makes the circuit which are intended to lure him into the centre where the Mother lies in wait, but he successfully resists these temptations and completes the course. Despite this the goddess still tries to do away with him, using her power over the forces of nature, and he only escapes by cutting one of his wrists and giving some of his blood to the earth, thus tricking the deity into believing that his life has been forfeited. Groggy and traumatised he returns to the place where he left the horse only to find that Attack has panicked and fled, laming himself in the process. When he discovers his steed cowering beside the cliff that surrounds the Upper Valley he leads him back across many miles to Castle Dan but does not yet feel ready to face his father's wrath. Instead he leaves the horse in safe hands and continues on foot all the way to High Harrow on a rainy night, arriving, soaked and exhausted, in the early hours of the morning to be greeted by his faithful servant Potto.

Chapter 9: The unattached nibbler, Everard Tetherer Trooly, nicknamed Foxy, whom Tallis has already encountered in his room at the Justification has no idea as to his origins. He has been brought up by a goatherd on the border of the Dans' estates and does not venture down into the valley proper until well into his teens. When his sense of adventure leads him to the little settlement of Low Town in the centre of Deep Hallow he immediately falls foul of some Outriders, and, not understanding what is expected of him, is beaten for showing insolence to his betters. The military cadets, and by association the whole Gleptish race, earn his undying hatred for being responsible for this outrage. At the age of about eighteen Foxy leaves the valley and pays a visit to the Delta City, Vadrosnia Poule, which is situated near the mouth of the Kymer River. In this cosmopolitan metropolis he picks up revolutionary ideas and returns to his birthplace eager to launch a rising of the Nablar against their oppressors. He intends to do this by recruiting Tom the cobbler to his side. When the Nablan high priest is condemned to death he turns his attention to his daughter Ann who he hopes will eventually step into her father's shoes and, in order to protect her, goes to work at the Justification Inn. He is determined to keep his future priestess inviolate and is greatly disturbed by the fact that she loves the Dan's second son. While on one of his many poaching expeditions he sees Dando pass by on his journey to the Upper Valley and for a moment has the opportunity to kill him, thereby ridding himself of this obstacle to his ambitions. Inexplicably he fails to do so. He is also concerned that another member of the aristocracy, the Lord Yan Cottle, has designs on Ann, or Hilda as she is known at the Justification. The girl is just too beautiful for her own good.

Chapter 10: Pyr taunts Aigea over the failure of her latest attempt to do away with Dando despite the fact that it was very nearly successful. At the inn, where he is jokingly referred to as *Sir Knight*, Tallis wakes in the late afternoon and begins his daily practice on the kuckthu, the musical instrument by which he earns his living. As he plays he recalls the time when he came by the ancient proto-harp in the first place. On quitting the mountains of his birth he was lucky enough to be taken in by a philanthropist named Guyax who ran a commune. Abandoning his quest when it was suggested that the events his mother recounted told of something that had happened not recently but in the far distant past Tallis stayed with him for several years, married his daughter Prudence and only went back on the road after the romance turned sour. With great generosity he was given the kuckthu when he left. Since then he has practically traversed the length of a continent and in the process crossed from the southern to the northern hemisphere. Leaving his room preparatory to eating an evening meal he finds Ann asleep on the stairs and recognises her as the girl who attracted his attention the previous night. Inadvertently he startles her and she retaliates by unleashing the latent magical powers she has inherited from her father. These act like a blow and send Tallis sprawling. Refusing to acknowledge that anything out of the ordinary has occurred he persuades himself that he must have been taken temporarily ill. It is a fact that through age and infirmity he is beginning to feel the need of a companion on the road and he actually unbends enough to ask the innkeeper for advice. She tells him that a hiring fair is taking place in High Harrow on the morrow where he might be able to recruit someone suitable.

Chapter 11: Since puberty Damask has been confined to the women's quarters of Castle Dan which are ruled by a phalanx of aunts, robbing her of the freedom she and her brother enjoyed in their childhood when she mixed with gypsies and travellers and roamed unsupervised throughout the valley. Constantly under the surveillance of a spy network of servants her way of life is severely curtailed until Dando brings her a small black girl named Milly, a child prostitute he has rescued from a life of exploitation whilst searching the Gateway brothels for Ann. Milly becomes Damask's maid and together they embark on a series of adventures in which Damask reacquaints herself with one of her lovers, a gypsy boy named Duke. On the day Dando visits the Upper Valley Damask is informed, late at night, of his misdeeds and, leaving her apartment at the castle, goes to investigate. She finds that the great horse Attack has indeed been injured while in the care of her brother and that Dando, to her horror, has apparently run away rather than face the music. The next morning she tries to get in to see her father on his behalf but is prevented by the mercenary soldiers with which the clan chief has surrounded himself.

Chapter 12: Meanwhile Ann has been leading her usual down-trodden existence at the Justification, slaving away from morning to night. She is finding life increasingly difficult because as she gets older and nearer to sexual maturity the magical potential she is heir to is becoming more and more difficult to control; since her father's death she no longer has someone to guide her in its use. She is especially apprehensive because Yantle (the Lord Yan Cottle) is threatening to take her as his *pet*, his concubine, and she fears she will employ *the gift* as it is known to protect herself. To utilise the power for her own benefit even if it means the difference between life and death is something her father told her she must never do. In the three years that elapsed between incurring the anger of the Mother and his unmasking Tom attempted to pass on knowledge, both old and newly acquired, to his daughter. He spoke of Dando and his intuitive feeling that the boy had some world-altering task to perform. He also warned her that a Culdee should never take a lover because his/her partner will incur the jealousy of the goddess. When young, however, he did not follow his own advice and in fact fell in love with and married Martha, a woman of the Nablan race, only to lose her when she died giving birth to his child. He also tells Ann of what he has recently become aware, that the gods, the Great Ones, who hold the world under their sway actually originate elsewhere: they first arrived on the earth pursuing the previously mentioned Old Ones, and are in fact usurpers. These extraterrestrial newcomers started out as creatures of the flesh just like the occupants of Deep Hallow but, through an inevitable evolutionary process, left their physical bodies behind in the same way that a butterfly sheds its chrysalis. All intelligent beings in the universe have the potential to follow a similar path and are given the epithet *dancers* once they have *Crossed Over*. After their apotheosis they achieve immortality and are able to move unfettered among the stars. Pyr and Aigea, the Sky-Father and Earth-Mother, are two such lifeforms, as are, in a different sense, their unnaturally engendered children Pendar and Azazeel. Both offspring, who were originally one being, vanished soon after their creation, and it is a commonly held belief that, if they still exist, it is in the shadowy places deep below ground. Humans have progressed far enough up the ladder of life to be capable of casting off the cycle of death and rebirth, and Tom does not fully understand why they are rarely able to do this. He suspects, however, that the difficulty may lie with the Treasure that was brought by the aliens from somewhere in space and which, as previously stated, has taken on the appearance of a Key. The planet has been locked into a form of stasis by this Thing-of-Power and, although not it's original brief, it now determines, when turned, the nature of each new age. The fates of any beings who have held or manipulated it are inevitably linked to its ultimate destiny. Despite the Key's maleficent influence there are infrequent occasions when earthlings can make the already mentioned mutational transfer to a new type of existence. If an exceptional individual, whose mind has reached a certain level of spiritual awareness, lies close to death they may be able to overcome the interdict and achieve a *Crossing* before the end arrives. One day, so he has heard, when the curse is lifted, the whole human race will follow their example and then... *the great rocks will sing and the little rocks frolic like lambs.*

Chapter13: The next morning Tallis is up betimes in order to set off for High Harrow. He omits his usual morning prayers to the Lord-of-Heaven because of a feeling that the immortal has abandoned this valley and the ones who dwell therein and has shut his ears to their pleas. On arriving at the town's civic centre he leaves an account of his requirements with the town crier and then goes to wait at the King's Head Tavern for job-seekers to appear. Potto rouses Dando and tells him it is time to go to school but he rejects the suggestion and then sleeps through until noon. On waking he skips lunch and leaves the house, crossing the river to the fair. Here he listens to the crier's message and decides that applying for the job as Tallis' companion could provide the answer to all his problems. He meets the *knight*, as he has become known, at the hostelry but the traveller's first impressions are not favourable even though, as well as offering his services, Dando promises to provide supplies for the journey and a pony to carry them; in fact the man is intimidated by the boy's obvious breeding and status. Dando returns, disconsolate, to his base at the Dans' town house only to be arrested by his father's men and escorted back to the castle. Tallis waits out the afternoon in High Harrow but receives no further applications for the position he is offering and so returns to the Justification. Later that night, going downstairs to use the privy, he finds several people in the inn yard including Mrs Humpage. They have been woken by the arrival of the Lord Yan Cottle accompanied by one of his servants. Yantle, as already explained, has had his eye on Ann for some time and wants to appropriate her for his own amusement but has been frustrated by the innkeeper's lack of co-operation. As a last resort he has come to abduct her by force and commands his man to fetch her from the hovel out back where she lives with her grandmother. The henchman returns dragging the girl along with him. Tallis intervenes despite realising that Yantle has one of these new-fangled weapons that he has only come across once or twice before – namely a gun. His life is suddenly in deadly peril until Ann, stretching out her free hand, cries "STOP!" As the gun fires it flies to pieces and Yantle falls mortally wounded. "Witchcraft!" a voice whispers in the ensuing hush. By threatening Mrs Humpage's life Tallis manages to rescue the young magic-worker from an inevitable reckoning and then flees with her insensible body across his saddle-bow towards High Harrow.

Chapter14: Dando spends the night in a cell in the Punishment Yard at Castle Dan and the next morning is taken before his half-mad father. The Dan tells his son that his patience has finally been exhausted and that the miscreant is to be relegated to the lowly role of priest; he will fill the post of house chaplain, a greatly despised position. Dando is conducted down to the cleric's quarters in the bowels of the castle and later goes through the ordination ceremony after his head has been shaved in order to conform to tradition.

Chapter 15: Aigea, examining the time-lines, believes that Dando is going to quit the valley in the near future and presumes that he has learnt what posterity holds in store for him. Pyr replies that although this latest idea of hers is complete nonsense, the fact remains that, if he does decide, for some reason, to leave, their potential nemesis will be far more vulnerable when out alone in the world than he is now and they will stand a much better chance of dealing with him there. Tallis, by now implicated in what appears to be sorcery and murder, understands that he and his charge's only hope of escaping from the valley is to seek out the young aristocrat who offered him assistance. After hiding by the River Wendover during the hours of daylight he finds his way to Castle Dan and makes contact with Potto. He is worried about Ann who has been completely comatose since the events in the inn yard. Meanwhile Foxy, who was elsewhere at the time of Yantle's death, returns to the inn and discovers what has taken place. He immediately sets out to track the runaways. Passing through High Harrow and on up the valley he realises that those he is pursuing took a turning towards the castle, but then loses the trail in the encroaching darkness. Potto, having talked to Tallis and learnt what has happened at the Justification confesses to his master that he knew of Ann's whereabouts all along. Dando goes to meet the traveller and is reunited with his long-lost love, following which he eagerly agrees to be true to his promise and provide everything needed for the road. When he makes clear his intention of becoming part of the expedition however Tallis does not welcome the idea. At a loss to think of any other way to persuade the man to change his mind Dando suggests that he should become the paladin's squire, something he has read about in books and family records, but in so doing does not explain that there is normally a commitment on both sides. The idea of having such an aristocratic youth at his beck and call appeals to Tallis' vanity and so he agrees. Dando swears an oath of fealty to the man. He then turns his attention to the task of getting everything together for the journey including *borrowing* Damask's pony Mollyblobs to carry the baggage. They set off northwards, the direction Tallis has been following all his life, and travel up a little-used track known as the Way-of-the-Shades. Dando and Ann - the girl having by this time recovered - walk close behind their leader holding hands. "Where in the world do you think we're going?" Dando asks her in a whisper and then, "to tell the truth I couldn't care less where we go." To himself he adds, *so long as I'm with you.*

Damask and Milly, understanding that Dando has up sticks and left the valley, are both equally keen to follow, Damask because she sees this as a great opportunity to escape from her restrictive way of life, Milly for the simple reason that she thinks of the young man as her saviour and so worships the ground he walks on. In the absence of Mollyblobs they harness Phyllis, an ancient donkey, to their dog cart but then, instead of going north, mistakenly head east down the Incadine Gorge and so, without realising it, soon diverge from the way that the others have taken.

Foxy returns to the castle once it gets light, resumes the pursuit and, through his tracking skills, discovers that the fugitives have taken the northerly route. At the same time the Dan is told that his son has absconded and, through his mercenaries' persuasive techniques, learns from Potto the direction in which he is heading. Reaching a spur of the moment decision the clan chief sets out, determined to recapture his errant offspring. Foxy, as he hides amongst the rocks halfway up the valley side, sees a troop of soldiers approaching with the Dan at its head. For him this man embodies all the injustices that have been heaped upon his people throughout the generations. He failed to kill the son but now that he has the father in his sights he is determined that there will be no hesitation. He draws his bow and with deadly accuracy sends an arrow winging its way towards the clan chief's heart.

When you realize that what you don't understand
Is the only thing you can be sure of,
Then wisdom is yours.

Chapter one

Dando put his arm about Ann and swung her round so that they were both looking down into the valley. "Say goodbye," he said.

For the past half an hour the travellers had been climbing the steep northern wall of Deep Hallow following the path that ascended, first, from east to west across the face of the hillside, before reversing around a hairpin bend and mounting from west to east, gaining about thirty feet on each traverse. To and fro they plodded, gradually making their way upwards. Tallis, the *knight-errant* as some at the Justification Inn had jokingly dubbed him, went ahead leading the horse Carolus while Ralph the dog followed close behind and Dando and Ann brought up the rear, Dando holding the rein of the pony Mollyblobs. Although the track was taking the easiest route to the top, the gradient was in fact quite steep and Tallis had to stop frequently to catch his breath. The two young people, hand in hand, waited patiently below him. Not once did he turn to acknowledge their presence; he seemed to have forgotten that he was not alone. In contrast, when they halted, Ralph dropped back to the youngsters' side in order to be petted and made a fuss of; it was not an indulgence that often came his way from his master. As they climbed, the atmosphere began to change. Tallis felt a deadening, muzzy sensation lifting from his brain that he now realised had been with him ever since he entered the valley. He seemed to be able to think more clearly up here. Dando and Ann took deep breaths of the pure clean air and sniffed the wind which, blowing from the east, got progressively stronger as they gained in height. This was the world's wind that was buffeting them and Dando imagined he could hear, carried on it, a million voices, a million million voices, fleshed and fleshless, raised in a kind of planetary harmony. He and Ann were leaving their place of birth for the first time.

As the boy and girl paused once more for Tallis to ease his overtaxed lungs Dando looked up and saw a notch on the skyline not far above them, where the track disappeared over the top of the hill into the lands beyond. It was at this point that he drew his companion's attention to what lay to their rear and instructed her to take her leave. The day was overcast and extremely dull and below, undisturbed by the blast, a kind of brown murk hung above the valley floor, obscuring detail. The Justification Inn was somewhere down there, the hostelry where Ann had slaved for seven years and Tallis had stayed for just three nights. Not far distant lay the small town of High Harrow in which Dando had made intermittent attempts to play the part of a dutiful son and failed dismally. Away to their left, the border town of Gateway stood at the top of the Incadine Gorge where he had begun the military training that had come to an abrupt halt soon after his sixteenth birthday, while, almost beneath their feet and hidden by a swelling in the hillside, brooded the formidable and oppressive bulk of Castle Dan. Here the two Gleptish children, Dando and his twin sister Damask, and Ann, the Nablan baby, had begun their lives. Also in this place Dando had recently been shut in a cell overnight, had had his head shaved and had been coerced into taking priestly vows. Off to their right, behind a rocky barrier, lay the upper valley with its holy shrine where Ann's father had been put to the fire.

"Do you think we'll ever come back?" Dando asked. Ann shook her head. "Do you mind?" She shook it again. "Well then – adieu, ciao, s'long – fare thee well my motherland, it's been good to know you - I don't think." He came to attention and gave an ironic salute but Ann stretched her hand out in what appeared to be a blessing. They both turned back to the path just in time to see Tallis, Carolus and Ralph vanish from view. They hurried to catch up.

As they topped the hill and stepped down into the shelter of its crest the wind dropped. Up here they were out of the valley's ambience and looking around at the still hangers that climbed the slopes on either side of the gully which they had now entered, there seemed to be no evidence that it might still be continuing to exist a few hundred yards to the rear. Without the wind the sounds of their progress became audible: the jingling of harness, the clip-clop of hooves, their own footsteps crunching on the gravelly track. Everywhere else there was deep silence apart from the sudden lonely cry of a bird of prey, high in the air. Dando wondered how many small timid creatures were lurking in the undergrowth and noted their passing.

After they had covered another mile or so an embryonic stream joined the road, flowing in the same direction that they were taking, proving they were slowly descending. All morning Tallis trudged doggedly forward while behind him Dando and Ann swung their linked hands high in the air, tugged each other to and fro, fooled around, whispered confidences, renewed a bond that had been seven years in abeyance. At last Tallis looked back, but not at his companions. He was judging from the position of the hazy sun whether it agreed with his watch. Deciding that the midday hour had already come and gone he called a halt near a small pool. While the horses dipped their muzzles in the cool water Dando dug out mugs that he had had the wit to provide when gathering provisions at the castle and distributed some biscuits and an apple each to stave off the pangs of hunger. They ate and drank in silence in that silent place. On Tallis' part, ingrained habit, instilled by years of solitude, ruled out casual conversation or exchange of pleasantries. The young people, sitting close enough to communicate by touch, respected his taciturnity. Soon they were back on their feet and the afternoon passed in much the same way as the morning, without incident. The stream left them to flow away eastward but they were soon joined by another, this time babbling down to meet them, meaning they were climbing once more. The landscape became increasingly rocky but there was still a fair covering of trees. Towards evening the youngsters began to lag a little. Although stronger and more energetic than their leader they had not got Tallis' iron-willed stamina, learnt over a lifetime of journeyings. It was a surprise when they rounded an outcrop to see, ahead of them, the southerner ensconced on an area of level ground, unloading Carolus and spreading out his bed roll.

"We'll camp here," he said. It was a good choice but Dando immediately saw the intrinsic drawback of the pitch.

"There's no privacy," he objected, "we need somewhere where there's some privacy for Annie, cos she needs a place where she can get out of sight if necessary; where she can wash herself and dress. We should try a bit further up... my lord," he added, suddenly remembering that, as Tallis' squire, he was the one who should be receiving orders rather than issuing them. But the other did not notice the lapse; he was no more used to being a master than Dando was a servant.

"Oh yes," he said, taken aback, "I suppose you're right."

They searched further up stream and came upon a clearing with some conveniently placed bushes.

"How about this?" asked Dando.

"The ground's too damp," replied Tallis the expert. Eventually they found a spot that fulfilled all their criteria. Dando set to work to build a fire as the gypsies had taught him; it would be needed that night, the air was distinctly nippy. Tallis began to unload the horses but the young man soon took over after asking the other if he could borrow his fire-lighting equipment. He tried several times to strike a spark but did not seem to have the knack. In the end it was Ann who got the fire going as she had always done when they were together at the cottage, bringing into play all her expertise learned at the Justification. Having tended to Carolus and Mollyblobs Dando began on food preparation, a simple task for the first night or two as he had brought along leftovers from the Dans' banquet that he had discovered in the castle's main kitchen. Meanwhile Tallis, finding himself redundant, took down the kuckthu and began his evening practice session. Dando put a pot of water on the fire and made tea. He laid out the food on a flat rock over which he had spread a horse blanket. There were legs and breasts of roast chicken, hard boiled eggs and slices of the chef's deservedly famous terrine. With these he provided mixed salad leaves, tomatoes and a bowl of cold cooked potatoes coated in mayonnaise as well as crusty bread. For dessert he had managed to bring along a blackberry and apple tart and with it some stiffly whipped cream. When they had eaten their fill he noted with satisfaction that there was enough remaining for another session the following day. Tallis ate his share in quiet amazement; in all his time on the road he had never had a meal as good as this. Dando and Ann rinsed the utensils in the stream and then sat and listened while Tallis began to play again.

After a while Dando noticed that Ann, whose head had been in close proximity to his shoulder, had fallen asleep against him. He carefully extricated himself and, picking up her discarded cloak, went and made her a bed on the other side of the fire. He then returned, lifted her gently and carried her to her rustic couch, bending down to loosen her clothing.

"What do you think you're doing?" The voice was unexpected and peremptory. Dando stood up and turned to find Tallis behind him, his sword unsheathed.

"She's asleep," he said in alarm, "I was trying to get her ready for bed without waking her."

Tallis, absorbed in his music, had not noticed Ann's slide into unconsciousness or Dando's solicitude for her welfare. The first thing he was aware of was the sight of the girl prone on the other side of the fire and the boy in the act of undressing her. In Dando he suddenly saw an accomplice of the potential abductor at the Justification, another Gleptish nobleman exercising his droit-du-seigneur. He was back in the inn yard hearing Yantle order *go and fetch her.*

"Leave her alone," he commanded. "Take yourself over there. Hilda, Hilda!" Ann came back to startled life to find Tallis standing above her looking down anxiously. "If you wish to disrobe and put your night things on we'll be down by the stream," he told her. "Let me know when you're ready."

Ann turned towards Dando but he just shook his head and walked away, following Tallis. She was left alone, realising something had happened to sour the evening's pleasant atmosphere but not sure what it had been.

Dando and Tallis shared sentry duty overnight. Tallis had not forgotten Mrs Humpage's concerns about robbers and highwaymen: *you've no idea how thick they've become round the valley recently* she had said. So far they had seen no sign of a living soul but you could not be too careful. When Dando's watch ended he bedded down and then lay awake for some time, thinking things over, perturbed at what had occurred. He did not understand Tallis' distrust. Eventually he drifted off and immediately began to dream. It was not the recurring nightmare of burning that he hoped against hope he had exorcised for good, instead it was a very strange narrative that did not seem to come from within himself like most dreams do but invaded from somewhere beyond. This was the gist of it:

He appeared to be in a huge dark hall, a throne room, full of winds. There was a mighty potentate on the high throne who spoke with a voice borrowed from the wind.

"Greetings young pilgrim – you go to seek a great treasure?"

Dando was compelled by he knew not what to answer "Yes," although he had no knowledge of a treasure.

"And will you bring it here when you have found it before anything?"

Again he had no choice but to answer "Yes."

"And will you vow to become my squire and take me as your liege lord?"

At this third question Dando was roused to defiance and made a great effort to oppose his puny will to this great one.

"I can't, I'm already Master Tallisand's squire." There was a great blast of air, a bellowing, and he jerked awake.

The next day Ann led Mollyblobs while Dando walked with hands in his pockets keeping well away from her, a frown on his face.

"What's the matter?" she asked in concern. "be you cross with me?"

"No, no. Nothing to do with you. It's Master Tallisand. He doesn't trust me," nodding towards the man who was some distance ahead of them.

"What do you mean?"

"He seems to think my intentions towards you are less than honourable. Of course," with a grin, "he's right!" Ann was relieved to see him smile.

"He be a loner," she explained, "a friendless man. He don' unnerstan' folks like you an' I." Timidly she tried to put her hand through his arm but he shrugged her off.

"Better not," he said.

They talked in low voices about their lives during the time they had spent apart.

"You know, I never forgot you," said Dando, "not even for a moment."

"I never forget you either," replied Ann, "although I try to."

"You tried to forget me? That wasn't kind! Why?"

"I'm not good for you."

Before he had time to think Dando remarked, "That's what my sister says."

"Oh," answered Ann. She lapsed into silence. Dando could have kicked himself.

Halfway through the morning they saw their first sign of life. A small settlement clung to the hillside on the road's left hand side. From it a track descended, crossed the path they were on and made off into the hills eastward. This was to set a pattern. It was only where there was access to the east or west that they came across human habitation; the Way-of-the-Departed, the Shady Way as it was known, wending its lonely passage northward, did not attract the dwellings of human kind. The village they passed seemed empty, perhaps deserted. They felt no desire to enter its narrow streets; there was a slightly eerie air about its unpopulated state.

A little further on they came to a parting of the ways. Having reached a region where increasingly precipitous hillsides were the norm, a large crag now stood squarely in their path. The track split in two at its foot giving them the choice of either a left hand or right hand road. Tallis got out his compass, mystifying the youngsters, and tried to determine which route was closest to true north but found there was nothing to choose between them; one path veered slightly to the west of the bearing, the other an equal distance to the east; whether they joined up again further on or went off in completely different directions they had no way of knowing. Dando stood back staring up at the smooth face of the rock and noticed indentations just below the summit.

"Look," he said. "There's a carving of some sort on the left hand side. It's probably meant to be a letter of the alphabet, although it looks more like a key." The other two travellers also directed their gaze upwards towards the place that he indicated. Faint and greatly weathered but unmistakably the work of man, a symbol had been incised into the cliff face.

"They must have let themselves down from the top to do it;" reasoned Dando, "quite a feat. I wonder what it was meant to represent. Perhaps to show which way to take."

"Yes," said Tallis dreamily, like a man in a trance, "it's to show the way – the left hand road."

Dando and Ann frowned at one another.

"But who...?" began Dando, only to find he was talking to thin air. Tallis had started forward impetuously and was already leading Carolus around the western side of the outcrop. The two youngsters had no choice but to follow.

During the rest of the day Tallis stepped up the pace. He seemed strangely excited about something and several times the young people heard him muttering to himself but could make nothing of what he was saying. For the first time Dando began seriously to ask himself where they were headed and to wonder about the mental health of the master to whom he was bound.

When they came to a halt that evening the young man managed, after much perseverance, to light the fire himself; he realised it was an essential skill for anyone living in the wild and must be mastered. They finished up the leftovers apart from some cream and a few eggs and Dando thought ahead about meals to come.

"I've brought the essentials," he explained to Tallis, "but we can add stuff we find along the way: fungi, roots, leaves, nuts, fruit, that sort of thing. If we want meat we'll have to hunt." Tallis looked doubtful; eating had never been this complicated when he had been on his own. They were among ancient deciduous woodland and had camped beneath a magnificent oak with a huge gnarled trunk. Dando and Ann sat on separate exposed roots to listen to Tallis playing, Dando wary of getting too close to the girl in case Tallis should have another strange turn as on the previous night. When they bedded down Ann took the position closest to the tree, behind which she could retire if needs be, while Dando and Tallis moved to the other side of the fire and arranged their lookout rota.

Sometime after midnight Dando was on watch. The fire had died down but the embers still glowed, occasionally emitting faints clicks, snaps and pops and an intermittent fountain of sparks as a log collapsed. The sky was full of stars and through the tracery above he could see the thin rind of a waxing moon. Around him the woods were silent apart from the faint sighing of wind in the branches; it was an extremely quiet land this northern wilderness. Gradually a small sound invaded his consciousness coming from nearby; he became aware that Ann was crying. He looked towards Tallis. In the dim light his master was just a hump on the ground muffled up in his cloak. Dando went and stood beside him listening to his breathing: it was regular and even; he seemed to be asleep. Dando crept round the fire to where Ann was lying.

"What's the matter?" he whispered

There was no answer, only a slight increase in the loudness of the sobs. Dando longed to kneel down and take his little love in his arms, but a strong intuition told him that this was not what was required.

"Why are you crying?" he asked again.

"I kill a man," came the muffled response.

"Who would have killed Master Tallisand so I was told," Dando countered. The weeping continued and he leant back against the tree giving her room, content to wait.

Eventually Ann raised a tear-stained face to his.

"I never cry," she said, wide eyed with astonishment, "not even when..." She buried her face in her arms and gave way to a fresh outbreak of sobs. Still Dando forbore to interfere. She was going through some sort of emotional crisis he realised, had perhaps reached a turning point that had precipitated this storm and the tears might be healing. Give her a little more time and then he would be able to comfort her. But this was not to be, because, suddenly, they were violently interrupted by an intrusion from beyond the firelight. Out of the darkness an arrow came whistling, grazed Dando's skin just above the wrist and pinned his sleeve to the tree. The arrow was followed by a short, stocky, furious figure that stumped into their midst, bow in hand. Dando felt blood welling once more, close to the location of his previously self-inflicted injury. Ann, forgetting all about her troubles, leapt up and stood in front of her beloved groping behind until she made contact.

"Foxy! What be you a doin' of?!" she cried.

At this juncture Tallis woke up, took in the scene, and jumped to entirely the wrong conclusion. What he saw was Dando holding Ann in front of him as a shield against the red-headed nibbler he remembered from the inn.

"What's going on?" he demanded.

"He were a-gooin' ter bawda the gel!" said Foxy indignantly, answering in Dando's stead and extracting another arrow from his quiver. Tallis drew his sword.

"He don'!" "I w-wasn't!" cried Ann and Dando in unison.

"Step away from her," Tallis ordered his squire, choosing to trust Foxy rather than this recently acquired subordinate.

Dando took hold of the shaft of the arrow pinning his sleeve and unsuccessfully tried to pull it out of the tree. "I can't," he said.

Foxy strode forward and thrust his face close to his victim's, the light of battle in his eyes. He seized the arrow and tugged it free enabling the boy to move apart from Ann and stand rather forlornly on his own, blood dripping from his fingers. But Ann, who had stayed put despite everything, tore a strip off her skirt. "His arm need bandaging," she said, her cheeks still streaked with tears. "Don' 'ee try an' stop me Foxy."

Foxy looked at her in surprise; he had never seen his protege like this before; she was in the process of taking charge of the situation; what had happened to her since their last encounter? The girl instructed Dando to sit down, which he was glad to do, while she went a few yards off and came back with a handful of leaves. "Knitbone," she said. She knelt beside him and pushed up his sleeve to examine the damage.

"Bring some water and a clean kerchief," she ordered. Tallis meekly obeyed. Ann attended to Dando's injury while Foxy stood over them an arrow fitted to his string. A furrow had been gouged across the boy's arm, fortunately on the outside. Ann cleaned it while masticating the leaves to a pulp. These she pressed into the wound before covering it with a pad made from the handkerchief and binding it up. Dando gazed at her downcast eyes, the lashes within inches of his own and felt the warmth of her breath on his cheek. He was bewildered and a little faint – things had happened so fast that he had been left behind somewhere along the line. At the same time he was cursing himself for forgetting, in the rush to get ready to leave, that most essential of items – a first aid kit. Ann finished her bandaging and sat back on her heels.

"All right," said Foxy, "now get away from he or else it'll be the worse for your fancy man." He still had his bow and arrow at the ready. Ann got up and went to sit on the other side of the fire. "An' you Glept, you keep away from she if you know what be good for you!"

Foxy and Tallis conferred together.

"I come to take her back with I," said Foxy, gesturing in Ann's direction.

"But she can't go back to the valley," protested Tallis, "they're searching for her. They think she practised witchcraft." He still could not totally believe what he had witnessed two nights before. "She'll do better to come with me until I can find her somewhere to stay."

"But things hev changed back there since you left an' I won't be taking she to the inn - I got a place o' my own. We'll lie low until the fuss die down."

"I ain't a-gooin' back wi' you, Foxy," piped up Ann, "I want to stay wi' the knight. I'll goo north along o' he."

Foxy was again confounded. He had never credited the girl with any independence of spirit. "Well," he said, "I ain't a-gooin' ter leave 'ee."

Tallis heard this announcement with a degree of secret rejoicing. He turned to Dando. "I think it would be best if you returned to your castle, young man. I don't believe I require your services any more." He had the powerful Nablan on side now, he did not need the allegiance of this high-born boy. The news struck Dando like a blow and rocked him back on his heels.

"Oh," he cried, "but I made a vow. I swore to defend you what ere befall. I can't leave you now - I would be breaking my promise."

"I don't hold you to your promise," said Tallis.

Again Ann interrupted. All three men turned to her in astonishment.

"He give you all you need for this journey, "she said. "He give you the pony, the food, the fodder, the cooking pots, the harness, the clothes. He went agin' his own folk for your sake – you can't send he back."

There was a long silence. Eventually Tallis turned to Dando and said stiffly, "You can come or not as you choose. But you're not to go near her, do you take my meaning?"

Dando remained silent but nodded in acquiescence. He sneaked a look of gratitude in Ann's direction and her eyes glowed in reply.

Ann sat primly on her side of the fire, elbows tucked into her sides and knees together; Foxy leant on his bow, employing it as a staff, and counted his arrows; Dando nursed his arm; Tallis replaced his sword in its sheath and tidied his bed roll. After the intense emotions and high drama of the last few minutes they were all feeling a sense of anti-climax. A sizeable chunk of the night remained to be passed before morning arrived. Tallis cleared his throat.

"You can all go to sleep," he said, "I'll stand guard. You (to Foxy) can bed down there if you like (pointing towards the spot where Dando had previously been lying), you (to Dando) had better go over there. No – further – further..." Dando was banished to the outer limits. Foxy lay down after ostentatiously drawing his knife and making sure that any onlooker was aware that even in sleep he was well protected. Ann, after a moment's hesitation, disappeared round the back of the tree and then came and composed herself for rest. Tallis wrapped himself in his cloak and sat up to keep watch. Dando, well away now from the others, made himself as comfortable as possible on the chilly ground. He shut his eyes and waited for sleep to overtake him but an hour later was still wide awake. In his loneliness he was feeling extremely sorry for himself. His arm was hurting and he realised that, by being thus ostracised and cold shouldered, he had become an outsider, no longer a member of Tallis' charmed circle. Going over what had taken place he thought he had cut a poor figure. He had behaved like a wimp, allowing others to take the lead rather than being himself the instigator. He could not help but imagine how his sister would have acted in similar circumstances: she would have charged in regardless of risk and thrown her weight around; she would not have allowed herself to be humiliated as he had been. But how else could he have behaved? He had sworn to obey the traveller in all things, but the traveller had not sworn to protect him as he would have been obliged to do if the pledge of fealty had been properly performed according to ancient custom; it was his own fault for not explaining the ceremony clearly to Tallis, and the inevitable outcome – the usurping of his place by the new arrival – served him right.

This Foxy, he had seen him once before. It had been a long while ago, down at the Justification, when he - a mere twelve years old - had been looking for Ann. The young man had obviously been working in the stables and had caught Dando's eye. At the time he had felt himself to be the focus of personal animosity where this individual was concerned and had been aware that in the Nablan's opinion he was persona non grata. He had been greatly puzzled as to why this should be. But now, only this morning, he had been given a clue to the mystery. Ann had been telling him about her life at the inn.

"Foxy look arter I. He bring me food and stuff. He be there all the time I were there. He know who I be. He wou'n't let anything bad happen to me."

Dando saw he had reasons to be grateful to the fiery-headed Nablan.

"Did you tell him about you and me?"

"I tol' Granny. She want to know all about my time at the Castle. Foxy used to listen."

"Are you two... you know... courting?" It took all his courage to ask this question. In his heart of hearts he could not be more sure that he and Ann belonged irrevocably to one another, yet he could see that in the eyes of the world it would be highly likely that after seven years apart she would have found someone else. He had to face the possibility.

"No, o' course not! He don't think o' me like that. He want me to be like Dadda. He want me to stand between the people an' she up at the hooly place. I tol' he I cou'n't do that but he don't take no notice. He never lay a finger on me all the time I knowed him."

Ann was convinced that Foxy felt no physical attraction towards her but Dando was not so sure; he had seen for himself the man's proprietary attitude where the girl was concerned, his jealous possessiveness. From the unattached-nibbler's point of view Ann was his woman, there was no doubt about that. Also he knew that the man hated him; he had seen it unmistakably in his eyes when he had thrust his face close to Dando's own. He thought he was beginning to understand why.

Then there was Tallis. He could not help but wonder if the southerner would have involved himself in the risky rescue at the Justification if the witch in question had been a hook-nosed crone. Dando was starting to get the feeling that he had two rivals in love and rivals who had far more opportunity to press their suits than he himself had at present. *Oh, Annie, Annie – please stay true to me, don't desert me!* Thoroughly miserable he groped inside the pack Potto had provided looking for a handkerchief. His hand delved through underclothes, toiletries and other sundries until right at the bottom he came upon something that felt like a small money bag. He pulled it out and opened it, holding it up to the new moon in an attempt to see what it contained. Something glinted within. Strange to relate, in gathering necessities together for the road Dando had not considered his need, as a traveller, for such an important item as money; throughout his life the wherewithal had always been there when required, handled and provided by underlings, never in short supply and therefore little regarded. Even when rescuing Milly from the Spread Eagle he had just had to ask for the required sum and it had been handed over without question. Now as he tipped coins, gold coins, into his palm he realised he was looking at what must have been a fortune in the eyes of the donor of the horde. These were Potto's savings, he could not be more certain, a sum painfully accumulated over a lifetime of occasional meagre tips and the odd stint of paid labour fitted in after a day's mountain of unpaid work; this was the nest egg put by against the time when the servant would be too old to be of value to his masters. Slowly Dando returned the coins to the purse, gazing unseeingly before him. It was almost beyond his power to comprehend the magnificent generosity of this gift. One thing he knew for certain was that he was totally unworthy to receive it. He found the rag he had been looking for, blew his nose and wiped his eyes. He was no longer feeling hard done by, in fact he just knew how lucky he was to have been so loved. He tucked the offering inside his clothing close to his heart, put his head down and fell asleep.

Selling Dr Good's
From the tailgate of a van.
Such is the roving life.

Chapter two

The town of Gateway presented a bottleneck to transport entering or leaving the valley. The morning after the fair ended was particularly busy, the road alongside the river extremely congested. All vehicles, of whatever size, had to pass through the little berg's narrow high street and some of the showmen's huge wagons carrying dismantled carousels, helter-skelters and ferris wheels practically scraped the upper stories of buildings as they passed. The tight squeeze was a particular problem when the leviathans met conveyances coming in the opposite direction so a jam inevitably occurred and for a long spell nothing was able to move; the traffic piled up. Damask and Milly, in their little carriage, dwarfed by the caravans and carts that surrounded them, came to a halt far back outside the town and had no choice but to sit and wait while Damask seethed with impatience. This way they would never catch up with Dando. The three travellers with only horses to encumber them had probably managed to slip through side alleys in Gateway and be well down the gorge by now on their journey to the plains. Alongside her desire to confront her brother, Damask was also eager to find the tribe of gypsies - her adopted tribe - that had left the valley not long before. Ever since she was a child its members had been coming to Deep Hallow each year without fail, but during her last visit to the camp, where she had gone to bid them farewell before they departed for the winter, a doubt had been cast over their likely return next season.

"This summer not good," Duke her comrade had explained. "Boys, men punished for what they not do. Thieving from houses, thieving of animals, killing of animals – not us – no, no. We think not come here no more. Roma always get blame for other people's badness."

Damask had know Duke since she was five and he was seven. She could hardly remember a time when he had not been part of her life. The two of them had been friends and then more than friends. Her first sexual experiences, her experiments in love making, had been made with him, as had his with her. Now he had reached the age of nineteen and was expected to take a wife from amongst the well-protected Roma girls; but Duke had other ideas.

"You marry me," he said to Damask not long before the tribe's exodus. "I take you with me. I be good man for you."

Although she had had lots of liaisons up and down the valley this was Damask's first proposal of marriage. She was sorely tempted. But she had had plenty of time to witness the sort of life led by Roma women; it was narrow, restricted. However fond she was of Duke she was not ready to give up her freedom for a second time having once gained it. She refused him. But once the gypsies had left the valley she began to regret her decision. The thought that she might never see the young man again was unacceptable. Now that she was leaving Deep Hallow herself she saw her chance to gaze upon his face once more and maybe give him a different answer. There was a certain urgency involved in tracking him down. If she was not quick about it she might discover that he had already been persuaded to look elsewhere.

The queue of traffic in which they were trapped edged forwards a few yards bringing them level with a red-wheeled yellow caravan. The two girls gazed up at its side on which was written a legend in multi-coloured illuminated script.

"Wot does that say?" enquired Milly.

"It says *King Pnoumi's Cat Circus*," replied Damask.

"Cat *Circus!*" emphasised Milly scornfully, "wot are the girls supposed to do, jump through 'oops?"

They had imagined that the owner of the vehicle was sitting at the front in the driver's seat, behind his horse, but now a laugh came from above them and a head poked out of the rear door of the caravan.

"They do jump through hoops," it said. "Risten." They did as they were bidden and heard a faint chorus of mews issuing from within the wagon. "Pussies," said the head, "my chi'dlen. They could be yours," directing its gaze at Damask, "if you come over here."

This head was singular to say the least. It wore clown's make-up, but under the grease paint Damask thought she could detect extensive scarring. Milly gripped her arm and when she looked her way indicated her strong objection to the idea of accepting the invitation. There was another laugh and the caravan owner came out onto the rear step, proving that the head had a body; a body that was a mite on the short side and sported a long fur coat. Gripping the doorway with one hand the man made a low and precarious bow.

"Velly preased to meet you gir's," he said in a strangely accented voice, having apparently penetrated Damask's masculine disguise with ease. "Pnoumi the Mog at your service."

Damask saw that the clown make-up took the form of a cat face, even down to whiskers glued in some ingenious manner on either side of the nose plus fur-covered ears on top of the head. This was a feline clown. A long thin pigtail hung behind.

"You go down to the Kymer?" asked Pnoumi.

Damask shrugged. She felt hostility emanating from her companion and she was inclined to trust Milly's instincts, but at the same time she was fascinated by the bizarre outlandishness of this exhibitionist, by his sheer foreignness.

"Where are *you* going?" she asked.

"Mi'fie'd, Dlossi, Trincomaree, Toocumca'ie, Pickwah, Kingscau'die, Tagnaloque, Sassanala, Ixat - maybe even *Over-the-Blook*. I go where people pay to see my pussies do their tricks. You come acloss and meet them?"

"No!" muttered Milly seizing her arm.

"Both come," said Pnoumi generously, but at that moment something became unstoppered up ahead and the line of traffic that the girls were in started to move. The yellow caravan was left behind and they did not see it again for quite some time.

It took them another hour to get clear of Gateway, but soon they were making good progress down the Incadine Gorge on the road parallel to the River Wendover, little Phyllis the donkey stepping out gamely. At lunchtime they stopped to buy some hot pies at a roadside stall, (unlike her brother Damask had thought to fill her pockets with money), and climbed up away from the highway to eat them, leaving Phyllis to graze on the verge. They sat watching the various conveyances negotiating the passage along the eastern drift and pretty soon a familiar wagon trundled past.

"There 'e goes," said Milly, "'im an' 'is pussies. Merow, prrrp, sppt!"

"That's very good Milly," said Damask admiringly; she herself had no talent for mimicry.

"We 'ad a cat at the Spread Eagle," said Milly by way of explanation. "She woz always 'avin' kittens. We called 'er Dulcie. I used to talk to 'er like that an' she'd talk back."

"Tonight we must try and find where Dando and the other two are staying," said Damask. "They won't have got much further than the bottom of the gorge. I think there's a village called Upend just beyond the Stumble Stones. I reckon it'll probably be there."

They watched more showmen's caravans making their way towards the plains. Damask looked on in envy.

"If I had one of those I'd be set up for life," she said. "That and a good strong horse. You could go where you wanted and stop where you wanted. It'd be simply fabulous. Think what you could do."

"But 'ow would you earn money to live on?" asked Milly.

"Oh, there are ways."

"Not that way," said Milly.

The best part of the day was already over by the time they were winding through the waste of gigantic boulders and beetling cliffs known as the Stumble Stones, situated at the entrance to the ravine. These soon came to an abrupt end and a wide vista opened before them. Unceremoniously they were pitched out onto the grassy levels which stretched away into the distance, dotted here and there by the odd isolated clump of trees, herds of grazing animals and the occasional human habitation. The undulating pattern of small fields and woods with which Damask had been familiar since birth was entirely absent from this landscape. There were no hedges, no fences, no barriers; the panorama extended from where the dog cart rested to the horizon without interruption, going on seemingly forever. Damask turned back for one last look towards her birthplace before continuing. The jumble of massive rocks through which they had recently passed, effectively hid the entrance to Deep Hallow, and, if it were not for the well-worn track emerging from amongst the stones and the shallow water course which did the same, you would not have known the gorge was there. Her home had been a secretive place, she realised, a secluded hideaway, protecting its citizens from having to face the harsh realities of the wider world. As for herself she could not wait to discover what this new life she was embarking on held in store.

"There's an orfl lot of space down 'ere," remarked Milly somewhat disparagingly. "The Great River's thataway," pointing along the course of the Wendover, "an' Drossi's thataway. When you get there you're not far orf the Middle Sea. The circus used to visit the towns along the coast of the Middle Sea. I wonder if it still does? We might come across it. You'd like the circus."

"Well for now we've got to find ourselves somewhere to stay. Where's Upend would you say?"

"Down that way - the Drossi road," said Milly indicating a turning off to the left.

"OK. Come on then – best foot forward Phyllis".

The village, when they reached it, consisted of two rows of houses flanking a very wide thoroughfare, at the end of which could be seen an extensive network of pens and fenced off areas, the site of the monthly livestock market. Halfway along the street stood a modest hotel, the Hand in Hand.

"Let's try there," said Damask.

They pulled up outside the hostelry and noticed for the first time that Phyllis was looking weary. Her head hung down and her sides heaved.

"You stay here," said Damask to Milly, "and I'll see what I can discover."

Inside the building she could find no-one to ask at first. Eventually she ran a woman to earth who seemed to have some authority.

"We're trying to locate our friends - a middle-aged man with a large chestnut horse, a boy with a dappled grey pony and a young fair-haired girl. Are they here by any chance?"

The woman frowned and glanced up a flight of stairs leading to the first floor.

"I haven't seen anyone that fits that description. They may have been in the bar, I couldn't say – but if so they've been and gone."

"Perhaps they're staying a bit further on. Where's the next inn down the road?"

"Nothing until you come to Millfield."

"And how far's that?"

"About twenty mile or so."

"Twenty miles!" Damask was appalled. They could not ask Phyllis to undertake another twenty miles that night. They would have to remain where they were. "Are there two beds available? We'd like to take a room. We'll need a meal, stabling for our donkey and somewhere to put the dog cart."

"Two and six per person," said the woman, "shilling for the donkey. You can take your vehicle round the side."

Damask drove the exhausted Phyllis into the yard at the back of the hotel, only to be met by a sight that had become rather familiar over the last few hours: there was the yellow caravan again and there was the cat clown busily erecting a temporary stage against its side.

"Hello gir's," he called, " you rike to meet my pussies?"

"I don't think so," said Damask. The donkey was unhitched from the cart and led into a small stable nearby where a young lad took her in hand, saw to her needs and presented her with a manger full of oats. She sniffed the offering then turned away, seemingly too tired to bother with food.

"She don' look good," said Milly.

"Oh she'll be all right by morning," replied Damask with misplaced optimism.

Returning to the yard they were again hailed by the showman.

"You watch my pussy-cats do their act this evening? Velly, velly good dispray. Come, I'r intloduce you."

"Oh, what the hell," said Damask and walked over, much to Milly's disgust.

Pnoumi opened the back door of the caravan and led the way inside. The interior was softly illuminated by a lantern hanging from the ceiling and by its light she could see that the whole place was crammed with cats. A pungent smell permeated the air, although the place seemed fairly clean, all things considered. Some of the animals were in cages against the walls but the majority were sitting up on high shelves or on cushions strewn along two bunks that ran down either side of the caravan. Others were on the floor which was littered with feeding bowls and trays filled with earth. There were two posts fixed vertically on which the cats had obviously sharpened their claws. As Pnoumi entered several jumped down and came to greet him, weaving in and out of his legs while the air throbbed with a chorus of purrs.

"My chi'dlen," he said with obvious pride, "let me intloduce you – all have names that people in this country will understand. That Clissie," pointing to a black cat, "he's the oldest. And that one Tinker – he's his son. That Jimmy," a black and white feline, "and that Glimalkin," a white cat with small patches of black and ginger. "That Dinah, that Freya, that Si'kie, there Jeoffly, Alice, Zana, Perce, Jim, Ju'es, Daisy..." One by one the clowder were all individually named. "They velly clever cats – velly good show. I don't charge, just send round the hat at the end."

Damask nodded, she had never been much of an animal lover, unlike her brother.

"Do you sleep in here with them?" she asked, repulsed by the idea.

"No, no. Up flont – my bed behind here," banging on the end wall, "but this prace good to sreep in." He pushed cats off one of the bunks sending them flying left, and right. "Big enough for two. Me, Pnoumi the Mog – you velly fine woman – I would rike to make babies with you. Have you made babies before? I good at making babies, you never met a man rike me. You tly – it velly nice. We make babies – but I know ways to stop babies comin'."

"No thanks," said Damask.

"I give you good time."

"No thanks," repeated Damask

Pnoumi advanced towards her, his clown face grinning like the fabled Cheshire Cat. He endeavoured to put his arms around the girl but Damask, after retreating a step or two towards the entrance, placed her hand in the middle of his chest and gave such a vigorous push that he lost his balance, fell backwards and sat down in one of the dirt trays on the floor. He gazed up at her, his expression no longer quite so amiable.

"You not a nice rady. You reave my calavan now, prease."

"OK, glad to," said Damask and let herself out of the door which Milly was just about to open from the other side having heard a thump and feeling concern for the welfare of her mistress.

"Are you orl right?" she asked anxiously.

"Yes, fine, fine."

Later that evening Damask and Milly stood at the back of a sizeable crowd of onlookers in the inn yard, most sitting cross-legged on the ground, and watched as the cat circus went through its paces. It was a remarkable performance. Damask's acquaintance with cats was fairly tenuous, but she had inevitably been brought into contact with Dando's big old ginger tomcat Asbo and learnt some of his ways. Asbo was a cheerful affectionate creature, attached to his master, but independent and self-sufficient like the majority of felines. If you happened to call him, there was no guarantee that he would appear on the dot, even if he were nearby; he came in his own sweet time and at his own pleasure. Often, if you were lucky, he'd turn up ten minutes later, strolling leisurely into view with an enquiring look on his face as if to say *I heard through the grapevine that you were in need of my company. I hope there's an important reason for this because I really have more urgent things to attend to.* The show they witnessed behind the Hand in Hand stood all previous assumptions about the nature of the species on their head. Either Pnoumi's cats were a special breed, entirely untypical of their race, or else he was a trainer of pure genius.

A mechanical organ announced the commencement of the entertainment. The curtain opened to reveal a series of little platforms set at different heights. From first one side of the stage and then the other cats came running, leapt up the stepped apparatus and then down again, disappearing once more into the wings. Once all of the cats had introduced themselves in this fashion nine stayed put on the platforms, facing the audience, and sang a song, or at least that's what it sounded like as they mewed and caterwauled in unison for a few minutes. Using the platform above them as a pawhold they then reared up and executed a series of graceful bows, the cat on the topmost platform managing the trick unsupported. After this the platforms were removed and a miniature carriage emerged with a fine black cat in the traces and several more taking their ease in the curricle. The females were clearly distinguished from the males by the fact that the ladies were decked out in flowery big-brimmed straw bonnets while the gentlemen wore toppers. This little vehicle did several revolutions of the stage before vanishing. Pnoumi then came on wearing a garland twined around his artificial ears and carrying a number of hoops and a torch. Cats jumped through the hoops which were lifted progressively higher and higher. The torch was then brought into play and the same antics were repeated only this time through circles of flame. Now cats appeared with other cats riding on their backs and then briefly with a third tier on top of that. Cats came on walking, or even dancing, on their hind legs, then the whole company began leap-frogging over one another until the entire stage was alive with sinuous interweaving bodies. Finally a supremely athletic cat crouched down, gathered itself together and executed a huge jump from a standing start, incorporating at its height a double somersault. The curtains swept together to tumultuous applause, only to part again revealing Pnoumi covered in cats from head to toe. His troupe were sitting on his head, on his shoulders, on his extended arms and clinging to every part of his anatomy. This strange fur enveloped vision managed a low bow in answer to the applause without dislodging a single one of his little passengers apart from a pure white cat who, lying trustingly on its back in his large hand, allowed itself to be lifted high in the air, thrown skywards and caught the right way up before being tipped onto the ground. The other cats then jumped down, paused a moment to look the spectators over, before trotting off as the curtains closed for a second time. A musical interval followed during which the hat went round and then a young woman stood up to sing. Just a few notes convinced Damask it was time to retire.

"Well," she said to Milly as they made their way towards bed, "I've never seen anything like that before. What did you think?"

"It woz orl right, I suppose," said Milly grudgingly.

"Worth a few bob," replied Damask who had contributed to the growing pile in the hat. "Gotta keep the pussies fed, you know."

When they went to retrieve Phyllis and the dog cart the next morning there was no sign of the cat circus caravan, it must have moved out in the night. Phyllis seemed not much better for her rest and was swaying slightly on her feet, a fact that Damask resolutely refused to acknowledge. The stable boy informed them that she had not eaten.

"Which way shall we go?" asked Milly.

"Well we'd better carry on to Millfield and see if the three of them put up there overnight. By the way where do the Roma usually camp round here when they're about?"

"There's a place down by the river, the Kymer river I mean, where lots of 'em get together at Yuletide, but that's not for a long while yet. There won't be many there now."

At Millfield they had no luck at the Great White Horse Hotel, the grand name by which the little bed-and-breakfast establishment at the centre of town was known. No travellers answering to the description they gave had stayed there the night before.

"Perhaps they didn't stay at an inn," reasoned Damask, "perhaps they were saving their dosh. After all they've got Mollyblobs with them which means they're carrying quite a load of stuff. Maybe they've got camping equipment. Dando would probably pack some food. Where would we be most likely to find them if they were under canvas?"

"There's always loads of people travellin' up an' down the road alongside the river. You get some usin' wagons, some on' orses an' a few wiv mules and camels. The poor ones 'ave to walk of course. Lots of campin' sites."

"OK, let's go down there – you show me the way."

It took quite a bit of urging before Phyllis would move; she seemed half asleep. They headed out of town, passing through a small village called Snatchet, crossed the Wendover and were soon journeying down a deserted track which stretched ahead with unvarying monotony for several miles. A steady wind, blowing from the north, sighed around their little carriage as it swept unimpeded across the savannah. Damask felt insignificant, a mere pinprick, in the midst of this huge flat landscape. Not much further along the road it began to be obvious that Phyllis was in trouble. She stumbled once or twice, then came to a halt. With a lot of urging she was persuaded to continue, but just a short while later she sank to her knees between the shafts and was only prevented from subsiding further by the harness.

Damask and Milly tumbled out of the cart and went to see what was wrong. While Milly removed the trappings Damask pulled the little conveyance away from the donkey who immediately flopped over on her side, her breath coming in rapid and shallow gasps. Damask bent down and, seizing her mane, began shaking her vigorously. When this had no effect she tried massaging the creature's cheeks and even resorted to slapping her on the nose.

"Don't. Don't!" cried Milly, "she can't 'elp it!"

"I was just trying to wake her up," said Damask, somewhat shamefaced. They both looked down at the unconscious animal totally perplexed.

"What on earth are we going to do?" agonised Damask, "we're miles from anywhere. We can't just leave her here – and there's all the stuff in the cart."

Milly squinted along the road ahead of them.

"There's someone comin'," she said.

"Thank god for that!"

Milly went on staring - her eyesight was exceptionally keen. "It's 'im," she said after a short interval, "'im – you know – the Mog."

"Oh," said Damask, "well beggars can't be choosers. Let's just hope he'll help us."

The yellow caravan with red wheels rolled towards them and came to a stop a few yards away.

"Gleetings gir's," said Pnoumi, perched high on the driver's seat. "What wrong with your rittle neddy?"

"I don't know," said Damask, "she just gave up. We need to get her somewhere where there's a vetinary. Can you suggest anything?"

"Mi'fie'd has medicine man who tleat animals; he rook after my pussies. Come, I take you."

"Millfield?" asked Damask uncertainly. "But how can we get her on board?"

"You reave her here. We bling doctor back. That best way."

Pnoumi got down from his wagon and the three of them managed to drag Phyllis onto the roadside verge and also to move the dog cart out of the carriageway.

"You gir's get in back," said Pnoumi, "no loom for you up top."

"What, with the cats?" said Damask.

"Pussies not there - I just take them down to their winter quarters."

"Winter quarters? That's a bit early isn't it?" Damask turned to Milly. "Milly perhaps you'd better stay here and keep an eye on Phyllis and the stuff in the cart until I get back."

"Not on your nelly," replied Milly, radiating suspicion from every pore, "I'm not goin' to leave you on your own – you might need 'elp!"

"Oh, all right."

Pnoumi opened the back door to the caravan and ushered them in. Climbing up into the interior they heard a bang and a clunk behind them as the door was slammed shut and a bar dropped into place. Pnoumi passed the tiny side window on his way to the front and the wagon rocked and swayed as he climbed into the driver's seat. Then the caravan began backing up and swinging round before setting off smartly along the road it had already traversed.

"Hey, hold on," cried Damask, "this isn't the way to Millfield! Stop, stop!" She banged on the end wall but Pnoumi either did not hear or chose to ignore her. Meanwhile Milly went to the door at the back and tried unsuccessfully to push it open.

"Can't shift it," she said without much surprise.

"What's he playing at?" asked Damask and again banged on the front wall.

"Look," said Milly. She indicated the two bunks which were no longer cushion strewn but had been made up with sheets and blankets, a bed each. The cushions were piled up at the far end. She fished under one of the bunks and brought out a chamber pot. "Just wot you always wanted," she commented sardonically.

"You mean he had all this planned?" gasped Damask, "I can't believe it. How could he have known? I mean how did he know Phyllis would collapse?"

"Because 'e made it 'appen," said Milly.

"You think he slipped her something back at the inn?"

"Yers – that's wot I fink."

"Hell and damnation!"

"Course I don' know 'ow 'ee knew wot road we'd take or that there'd be no-one else about – praps that woz just luck on 'is part."

Damask searched for something she could use as a battering ram. The scratching posts caught her eye and employing all her strength she managed to tear one from its base. Then using it as a club she began to belabour first the door and then the sides of the interior until she had to stop for want of breath.

"God's teeth!" she said, "this place is strongly made! They must have used some really tough wood – fully matured oak I shouldn't wonder."

The two girls sat back on the bunks and stared at each other while Damask tried to make sense of the situation.

"What's his game?" she asked, "what's he up to? Is all this so he can have his wicked way with us? Are we going to be his private harem?"

Milly shrugged. "Praps," she said, "or somethin' worse. But I reckon 'e's just out to make some money. I reckon 'e's goin' to sell us – maybe to a cat house but more likely to one of the slave farms down south. They pay a good price for 'ealthy workers."

"Is he heck!" said Damask indignantly, "not while yours truly has her wits about her!"

"'Ee'll make you," said the worldly wise Milly wearily. "'You'd be surprised. They've got ways - 'is sort. You won' 'ave no choice in the matter.'"

"Really? I find that hard to believe. But if it's the case, then what the bloody hell are we going to do?"

At the rear of the caravan, let into the door on the left hand side when viewed from the interior, was a cat flap that had been fixed firmly shut. Around about midday the vehicle came to a halt, there was the sound of unlatching and food and drink appeared through the aperture. Damask jumped up and banged on the back door shouting "Open up! Open up!" There was no reply. Milly bent down to examine the food but Damask pulled her away.

"If he gave Phyllis a Micky-Finn he may be trying to do the same to us. Don't touch it."

"Not even the water?"

"No, don't touch it."

"But we'll 'ave to drink sometime."

"By then I'll have worked out a way to get us out of here."

Acting on this intention she sat down with her head in her hands and gave herself to concentrated thought as the caravan lurched into motion once more. By the time it began to get dark and the wagon pulled off the road for the night she felt she had a fairly watertight plan. They heard someone pass down the side and then, to their surprise, the back door opened a crack and Pnoumi peered in. Damask leapt towards the gap but the door was slammed and barred before she could reach it.

"D'you see?" she said, "he was trying to find out if we were out for the count."

"Well," said Milly, "'ave you thought of anyfink we c'n do?"

"I've got an idea, but it'll have to wait until later, till he's gone to bed and it's really quiet. You must do your cat impression Milly. Make him think there's a cat in here with us – one that he's overlooked. Make it sound as if it's in trouble. We must put some cushions on the bunks under the blankets so's it looks as if we're in bed."

"But will 'e 'ear me?"

"Well *we* heard the cats from outside. If we're lucky and if he thinks we're asleep he'll come in looking for his critter. I'll be behind the door and you can hide under one of the bunks. You'd better take your clothes off."

"Wot! I should coco!"

"Don't be silly," said Damask impatiently, "if you've got no clothes on he won't be able to see you because of the colour of your skin. But you must shut your eyes too if he bends down. Then when he's far enough inside I'll grab him and you can come out and give him a wallop – with this," she wrenched the other scratching post from its moorings. "We'll both wallop him until he surrenders."

Milly looked doubtful. "Will it work?" she wondered.

"It's got to," said the pragmatic Damask.

They made up the bunks with cushions to look as if they contained bodies and then sat on the floor to wait until all sound of movement behind the front wall had ceased. It was hard to keep awake after their eventful day. Eventually on the other side of the partition they heard the unmistakable noise of movement as Pnoumi climbed into what they hoped were his sleeping quarters. It was very dark in the back of the caravan. Silence reigned. Damask waited for what she though was about ten minutes and then patted Milly on the shoulder. The little girl took off her clothes and gave them to Damask who put them at the foot of one of the bunks before moving to her position beside the door. Milly squeezed under the left hand bunk. For about a minute nothing happened. Then a tiny sound broke the stillness. Somewhere in that huge, pitch-black, unfamiliar space an infant cat was calling for its mother. There was a long pause and then the cry came again – piteous, pathetic, desperately lonely - "Mew, mew, meeeew." Startlingly loud in contrast to this threadlike piping, the creaking of wood indicated activity behind the front wall. The caravan rocked as Pnoumi descended from his roost and his passage could be heard as he came round to the rear door. The cat flap was unlatched and the light from a lantern shone through it. "Pussy, pussy," came the call. There was no reply. Carefully and quietly the cat flap was shut and then, very cautiously, the door opened a smidgen and the lantern was held high to light the interior. "Where are you, my dar'ing," Pnoumi whispered. A minute squeak answered him. Pnoumi swung his lantern towards the left hand bunk, then to the right hand one. He spoke again in what must have been his own tongue and the kitten answered as plainly as it was possible for a little creature to do, "Here I am, come and save me."

Pnoumi climbed onto the step and then into the interior. He took one pace forward and then another. Damask slammed the door shut behind him and flung herself at his legs. Clown and lantern went flying, the lantern landing upright on the floor and continuing to burn. Milly scrambled out from under the bunk and brought the scratching post down hard across Pnoumi's shoulders. Meanwhile Damask regained her feet and then threw herself on top of the man, her knees in the small of his back. She hit him over the head with her post. Pnoumi yelled, made one attempt to free himself and then gave up. "Don't! Prease!" he pleaded. Damask was surprised to find that she was the stronger of the two; her adversary seemed very small under her hands and frail. Milly, naked as the day she was born, danced around waving the scratching post, not realising that the battle was already won.

"Hand me that sheet," commanded Damask, panting and pointing at the bunk. "Let's see what he really looks like under all this paint. Hold his hands down Milly." She lugged the clown over onto his back and began scrubbing at his face. Pnoumi moaned and cried. The make-up came away but so did a lot more than she bargained for. What she had thought was solid flesh peeled off as easily as if a snake were shedding its skin. A head was revealed sans hair, sans eyebrows, sans nose, sans lips, sans almost any recognisable facial feature.

"Ug!" cried Damask and started back in shock, while Milly, appalled, let go of the clown's hands and scrambled to her feet. Pnoumi dragged himself away from them out of reach and lay, beyond the circle of light, whimpering like a beaten child.

"Let's get out of here!" cried Damask. "Bring your clothes!"

They burst precipitously from the rear door, slammed it shut and dropped the bar into place. Milly hastened to get dressed while Damask, staring around at the nice normal night-time scene, did her best to forget what she had just witnessed. Eventually she pulled herself together sufficiently to recollect the chain of events that had led them to this place.

"We must get back to Phyllis," she said. "Do you know where we are?"

"That's the way we come," said Milly pointing along the dark road.

"Do you think we can see enough to go back in the caravan? I don't want to hang around."

"Well, we'll 'ave to find the 'orse first."

The horse was hard to locate but was eventually discovered asleep only a few yards away. They hitched it to the wagon and then climbed up into the driving position behind which were situated Pnoumi's living quarters. Damask poked her nose through the door and hit her head on another lantern hanging from the ceiling.

"I can't see a thing. Do you know how to light this?"

Milly turned a knob, the lantern sprung to life and Pnoumi's arrangements were revealed. A lot of the space was taken up with bags of dried biscuits, presumably food for the cats. There was a tiny cooking stove, a cupboard for clothes and a crossways bunk against the back wall.

"Shh," breathed Damask. They listened to see if there was any signs of life from the rear of the caravan but all was quiet.

"Look," said Milly, "'ere's 'is paint pots." She had found a box containing the clown's make-up but also a collection of strange little objects made of rubber. These were spare prostheses, noses, ears, and other less identifiable appurtenances.

"Ye gods," said Damask, "I thought I had it pretty bad in the women's section of the Castle, but fancy having to put all this on every morning."

"Praps 'e never takes it orf," said Milly.

They felt their way back along the track, retracing their route by a mixture of luck and good judgement, the lantern swinging from one of the shafts. Fortunately there were not too many junctions along the way and as it was getting light they passed a shepherd who put them on the right road to Millfield. Damask found that managing such a large vehicle as the caravan was quite a different experience from driving the dog cart. From daybreak onwards they began passing other traffic. The route was far busier than it had been the day before.

"I know why," said Milly, "the seventh day is a rest day for people round 'ere. Somepthin' to do with the River God. Yesterday they would all have been takin' it easy."

"What do you think the horse is called?" wondered Damask.

"Ast 'im," said Milly with a jerk of her head towards the rear.

Damask pulled a face. "I don't want to even think about him or what he looks like," she commented, but then immediately began to do just that. To divert her mind she remarked on Milly's talent and the fact that without it they would still be prisoners. "You were terrific Milly," she said, "I could have sworn there was a cat in there with us."

"You mean to say there wasn't?"

Damask looked confused.

Milly grinned. "Mew, mew, meeew," she repeated "poor 'ittwl tyke."

For a while the only sound was the clip-clop of hooves and the creaking of wheels, then Milly spoke her musings out loud.

"After all we don' know what 'e really meant to do wiv us. Praps 'e just wanted to keep us as 'is pets like the pussies."

"Yeah, *pets*," said Damask, thinking of the context in which the word was used back in the valley.

"I don't mean like that – I mean like wiv 'is pussies."

"Well we don't know what he gets up to with them in the middle of the night."

"Don't be filthy," admonished Milly, struck by a virulent attack of prudishness.

Eventually they recognised that they had reached the stretch where Phyllis had collapsed.

"Somewhere along here," said Damask, "Yes there she is... oh..." Before she got down from the wagon she knew what she was going to find. The donkey was indisputably dead. As she approached, flies and a couple of crows flew up from the corpse.

"Don't look Milly," she called. The dog cart was still there but its contents was missing. During the hours that they had been absent passers by had obviously helped themselves to anything they fancied. The little carriage had been stripped bare; even the harness and wheels were gone.

"Well," said Damask, "that's that. Good job I've still got some cash. We'll have to carry on in the caravan."

"But where are we goin'?" said Milly, "Wot are we goin' to do wiv 'im?"

"We'll go back to Millfield. There may be a magistrate there. We could hand him over, and the wagon, and maybe get some monetary compensation if they believe our story. I'm sure what he did was against the law. Then we can carry on astride the horse – he owes us that."

Travelling along the single-track road towards town was a tedious business because whenever they met a sizeable vehicle coming the other way, a farmer's cart for instance, they had to move over onto the verge to let it pass. The delay was so long as they made room for an enormous pantechnicon pulled by four oxen that they had time to get down and stretch their legs. Its bulk, obscuring everything further up the road, meant that they were unaware, at first, of the approach of a platoon of soldiers marching roughly in step, with a dispirited group of women and children following along in the rear. As they came into view Damask noticed that they appeared to be unarmed and that the man pacing in front was familiar: four mornings ago he had been on guard outside the Dan's apartment and had prevented her from going in to see her father.

"Quick Milly," she breathed, "get back on board!" but it was too late. An incredulous expression on the soldier's face as he approached told her that she had been recognised. After a moment spent gathering herself together Damask was equally surprised - how come the Dan's mercenaries were here at such a distance from Deep Hallow?

"Halt!" cried the man in front. The formation came to a ragged stop. Damask and Milly found themselves the focus of many pairs of curious eyes.

"Hell's bell's!" chipped in a voice from halfway down the column, "it's the chief's sister – wot's she doin' 'ere?"

"Run away I reckon."

"Yeah," said a third voice, "an' there's her little whore – the nigger tarty-pants."

"Wot you doin' 'ere?" barked the officer brusquely, the second time Damask had been on the receiving end of his insolence.

"That's none of your business," she replied haughtily trying to hide her fear.

"Maybe not, but I fink your family might be interested. Why are you away from the valley?"

"I might ask you the same question," replied Damask.

"That's easy to answer. The new Dan saw fit to disband us. Di'n't need our services so 'e said. 'E'll regret it. We'll like as not end up in Pickwah - they're cryin' out for our sort over there. But I reckon the boss'll be interested to know 'is sister is wanderin' around by the Great River dressed up as a fella wiv only a little call-girl as chaperone. If we present you to 'im, might even get our killin' tools returned."

Damask was completely bewildered.

"What do you mean, *the new Dan*?" she said.

"Oh – di'n't you know? Your pa 's gorn an' snuffed it. 'E ain't in the lan' of the livin' no more. There's been a change of leadership."

"I don't believe you."

"It's true right enough," and the man grabbed hold of her wrist. "You'll find out when we take you back there – an' get a reward for deliverin' you safe into the 'ands of your elder brother."

There was a sudden scream from Milly. Absorbed in the exchange between Damask and the freebooter she had been unaware that one of the other soldiers had crept up behind her until he seized her round the waist.

Damask struggled hard to escape. "Let me go!" she panted

"We'll take you back to the valley," said the officer, capturing her other arm and gazing approvingly as his comrade lifted Milly's skirt, "but we might make a little detour on the way."

"Unhand them!" The voice was commanding and loud enough to fill an auditorium while remaining, at the same time, honed to perfection and beautifully modulated. All the participants in the altercation on the road looked round to discover that a convoy of vehicles escorted by men and women afoot had crept up on them while their attention was distracted, and that these newcomers had come to a halt and were observing them at relatively close quarters. From their exotic, flamboyant appearance the band of travellers seemed to be entertainers of some sort. The man who had spoken was larger and more colourful than his companions.

"Unhand them!" he repeated.

"Mind your own business mate," said the platoon leader angrily, "this ain't none of your concern."

"On the contrary, I think it is. There seems to be a case of mistaken identity here. You appear to be trying to detain two of our company who are merely going about their legitimate pursuits. The young woman in the masculine attire is our principle boy and the dusky maiden wearing the gypsy costume one of our character juveniles. I think it would be wise if you removed yourselves from their vicinity and took yourselves off down the road – toute suite."

It became apparent to the platoon that a number of the men confronting them had staves in their hands and a few were carrying swords, while they were weaponless. The officer let the indignant Damask go free while Milly's captor reluctantly made up his mind that he would be well advised to postpone his plans for her indefinitely. It did not take the rest of the soldiers long to also decide that discretion was the better part of valour. Sullenly and with a bad grace they filed through a gap that had opened in the actors' ranks and straggled off into the distance, no longer in step, occasionally looking back as if hoping that the situation might have changed.

The girls' saviour swept off a large tricorn hat with a great froth of an orange feather attached to it and made a deep obeisance.

"Your servant mesdames," he said, "the Grande Stupendo, rescuer of damsels in distress, throws himself at your feet. May I have the honour of knowing whom I am addressing?"

Life holds both happiness and sorrow.
Once this truth is accepted
The world no longer threatens.

Chapter three

Lying asleep at a considerable distance from the others and from the fire Dando was dreaming again, but this time of warmth. He was out in the open beneath a bright blue sky in a sun-drenched field of corn. This was a huge field in which he found himself, one that stretched to the horizon in all directions. It was a golden sea of rippling, tossing seed heads, and like the sea, waves, driven by the wind, troubled its surface. He felt he was in the midst of the source of the bread of life; this field was large enough to feed the whole world. Oddly, he was reminded of the proving dough that, in his early years, had inspired him to take up his craft. At a distance, and at a slightly higher elevation, he caught sight of Ann's slender figure. She had her back to him, but at that moment, as he identified her silhouette, she turned and pointed ahead of her from her vantage point at something she could see but he could not. She beckoned and began to walk away. He followed, running his hands through the heavy ears of corn that rattled against his fingers as he passed. When he reached the place where she had been standing he would know what awaited him.

Back on the road in the waking world the following morning he found that he had been relegated to the rearmost position. As usual Tallis led the way while Foxy took up what he obviously considered to be his rightful place next to Ann leaving Dando to trail along behind with plenty of time to think his own thoughts and notice the country through which they were passing. He was not entirely ignored: every so often Ann would look back and give him an encouraging smile, an action that must have aroused Foxy's ire for by the evening he was in a foul mood.

"The woman should do the cooking," he opined as, once the fire had been lit and they had established their positions round it in much the same grouping as on the previous night, Dando set to work to prepare the meal.

"No - that's my squire's task," replied Tallis. Remembering the events at the inn, he was still somewhat in awe of Ann and had no desire to start laying down the law as far as she was concerned. Besides, the food up to now had been more than satisfactory. He would not interfere with the status quo.

In contrast to the previous evening Dando decided to create a dish based on rice using mushrooms and fresh herbs that he had gathered by the roadside earlier in the day. He tossed some onions in oil, then added the other ingredients at various stages. These included, as well as the mushrooms and rice, chopped salt fish, wild celery, lemon juice and chicken essence diluted with water which would have been stock if he had been in his own kitchen. He stirred the pot, cooking the rice gently, topping up with more liquid as necessary. When nearly done he sniffed and tasted the left-over cream and eggs that he had brought from home, decided they were still edible and incorporated them into the mix. He followed this with seasoning, then, as a finishing touch, grated cheese over the top after he had ladled a generous portion onto four trenchers. He called the others to come and start, handing the dishes round. Foxy refused to take one. "I'm not eating that muck," he grunted, having watched the preparation of the repast with great suspicion, particularly the employment of fungi. Out of a pouch at his waist he brought forth a large but extremely stale hunk of bread. Swallowing the insult to his cooking with some difficulty Dando offered a choice of accompaniments to this spartan meal. A piece of cheese and a raw onion were ungraciously accepted. Tallis and Ann enthusiastically finished up Foxy's untouched portion of the risotto. Neither would the Nablan accept an orange for dessert; he seemed to regard this fruit as dangerously exotic, despite the fact that it had been grown in the greenhouses back at the Castle.

"Eat it yourself, Pot Boy," he growled, "the Dans can keep their stinkin' fruit 'long with their stinkin' chieftain who'll really be stinkin' the place out by now if they ha'n't put him undergroun'."

"As I've no idea what you're talking about," said Dando relatively calmly but with a slight tremor in his voice, "I'm afraid I can't make any useful contribution to this conversation." He surprised an odd look of indecision on the Nablan's face. Foxy seemed about to speak but instead gave a snort of disgust before stumping off to sit beside Ann. Dando was left to wash the dishes on his own as Tallis was already deeply absorbed in his music, having previously decided that, as a knight with a squire, such menial tasks were now beneath him.

At the start of the next day the order of march remained the same: Tallis took the lead followed by Foxy and Ann side by side with Dando bringing up the rear. But then after a mile or two Foxy slipped away. One moment he was there, the next he had vanished as swiftly as might the cunning fox after which he was named. He was absent for several hours and then just as mysteriously rematerialised, taking his place once more in the little procession. As soon as he realised the Nablan had gone Dando came forward to claim Ann's hand, but she snatched it away and, pointing into the trees, mimed the loosing of an arrow. Dando understood her only too well. He fell back and trod in her footsteps a few paces behind. He was no longer rewarded by the smiles of yesterday; Ann seemed to have decided that a show of warmth towards him only made the situation worse. At least he hoped that that was the explanation for her indifference.

It was evident, on his return, that during his absence Foxy had been hunting. After they set up camp he detached the trophy he had acquired from his belt and flung it down in front of Dando.

"I don't s'pose you'd know what to do with that, eh Glept?" he said.

The creature was a hare. Dando looked down at the little dead body and was reminded of his three-legged pet Puss. But this was no time for sentimentality.

"I might," he said.

Foxy watched in surprise as Dando expertly skinned, gutted and jointed the carcass, reserving the heart, liver and kidneys. He had been soaking some beans all day in a water skin, intending to use them somehow or other in the evening meal. He went down to the stream to rinse these and get more water. Once the fire was well alight he put a spoonful of oil in the cooking pot and browned the hare joints all over. Onions were also fried, after which he added carrots, various dried flavourings, black pepper, the beans, the inevitable finely chopped salted fish, a small amount of orange juice, water and one of his treasures – some juniper berries. This mixture was left to simmer over the fire for about an hour and a half while they drank tea and whilst he made some dumplings by combining flour, water, suet, a raising agent and salt. Towards the end of the cooking time these were floated on top of the stew after a little flour mixed with water was stirred in to thicken the gravy. He wished he had some sour cream to add richness and flavour to the dish. When it came to this meal Foxy did not turn his nose up at the food. He scraped his plate clean despite maintaining an expression of distaste on his face throughout. Dando glanced in Ann's direction while the other two were preoccupied with eating and caught her eye. He knew immediately she was proud of him and that, had she dared, she would have voiced her wholehearted approval. They both realised that Foxy's capitulation was a triumph of sorts. Our cook's spirits rose.

And so the pattern was set. Each morning their accomplished huntsman left them on the trail while he went off to see what he could kill, bringing back, as day followed day, a huge variety of game: ducks, geese, pigeons, partridge, rabbits - on one occasion a wild sheep and on another a young deer. Dando welcomed the challenge this bag represented and set himself to butcher and cook the take with as much skill as he could muster, becoming more adventurous as he gained in confidence. His other tasks consisted of caring for the horses and waiting on Tallis. Ann made herself useful by building the fire, washing and mending, clearing up, organising the baggage, ensuring they did not live in a pigsty. Foxy, having provided what he felt to be the vital ingredient of the meal, seemed to regard his job as done and so reclined at his ease while the two youngsters worked. Tallis sat apart, austere and uncommunicative, not participating, expressing himself through the kuckthu. After dark they all took their turn at sentry duty as, by this time, Ann had insisted on playing a part. During night one she and Foxy divided the watch between them while on the next it was Tallis' and Dando's shift, and so turn and turn about. Dando, for all his useful contributions, continued to be shunned. When Foxy deigned to address him it was as *Pot Boy, Skivvy* or *Scullion*, but he saved his greatest contempt for the epithet *Glept,* which he spat out with considerable venom. At first, Dando looked towards Tallis when subjected to a barrage of abuse to see if he would intervene on his behalf, but the knight, although willing enough to accept his squire's service, still regarded him with deep suspicion, and remained coldly distant and uncaring.

Despite often being on the receiving end of harassment from Foxy, and despite his ignominious position at the bottom of their small hierarchy, Dando was not unhappy. For the first time he was doing openly what he considered to be his destiny in life, and he had the daily miracle of Ann's presence to cheer him. In his inside pocket was secreted Potto's gift to remind him that, however badly he was being treated, he had worth in his friends' eyes. Foxy he accepted as a cross he had to bear and tried not to let the Nablan get under his skin. To further gladden his heart he had one ally amongst the company who made no attempt to hide his partiality. The dog Ralph was devoted to him.

On leaving Deep Hallow Ralph had taken up a position in the procession behind Carolus the horse, close to his master, like the faithful hound he had always been. On the second day, however, perhaps sensing Tallis' animosity and the boy's discomfiture, he dropped back and walked beside Dando for a mile or two until Tallis noticed his defection and called him to heel. After Foxy's arrival Ralph became more insubordinate, growling at the Nablan and on one occasion showing his teeth. He seemed to be aware of Foxy's hatred of Dando and his enmity towards Ralph's own species, a result of his frequent hair's-breadth escapes from the jaws of hounds. The dog was fiercely scolded for his hostility and his share of the food forfeited. But this had the opposite effect to that intended, for after this Tallis could not keep him away from Dando. He became the boy's shadow, padding alongside him during the day, sitting patiently nearby as he prepared the evening meal, sleeping with him at night. Tallis was greatly angered by what he regarded as a betrayal on the part of his first lieutenant but was unable to alter matters; there was no way he could insist on the dog's loyalty.

Then an event occurred which aggravated the situation. When cooking Dando became a single-minded creator and artist, totally immersed in his craft. One day he forgot himself sufficiently to start singing softly as he worked in his strange, cracked, tuneless voice. For Ralph, the observer, this was a disturbing phenomenon; it appeared to him that his friend was in trouble. He came forward, a whine in his throat, and pawed at the boy's arm. His face wore such a comically worried look that Dando could not help but burst out laughing. Now Ralph's dignity was affronted: he hated being laughed at. To mend matters nothing would do but that Dando must go down on his knees and give the big dog a hug to show that nothing was amiss and that he intended no offence. Foxy and Tallis, witnesses to this little scene, were both equally repulsed, Foxy because Dando appeared far more cheerful than he had any right to be, Tallis through simple jealousy. So Dando earned himself another black mark and became even more of a pariah.

Things might have continued in this fashion indefinitely had not something happened that Tallis was half expecting. It was the night of Foxy and Ann's sentry go and Ann was on guard. Dando was awake and lay watching her as she sat by the fire, lit by the rays of the full moon. He often took an opportunity such as this to observe her while the others were sleeping and he knew she was aware of his scrutiny although she never gave any indication that she realised his eyes were upon her. Tired and increasingly sleepy he was just beginning to dose off when he saw Ann stiffen; she had heard something which he had missed, his ears being muffled in his cloak. She sat listening tensely for a minute or two, then rose and went to shake Foxy awake as Ralph growled, his hackles raised. The Nablan sat up and Ann bent down to whisper, pointing towards the surrounding undergrowth. At that moment all hell broke loose. There came a yell from at least half a dozen throats and into the firelight rushed a number of men brandishing cudgels and knives. Foxy was on his feet in a flash. He seized Ann and threw her into the bushes and in the same instant had his axe in his hand. He turned at bay, drastically outnumbered. From Dando's point of view there was no time to think and that was perhaps just as well. The young man cast off his cloak, groped for the sword that was lying nearby and leapt to his feet. All his fencing tuition went out the window. He grasped the hilt of his untried weapon in both hands and brought it down like a club with all the force he could muster on the head of the nearest aggressor. The man's knees buckled and he sank slowly to the ground. The fellow next to him turned and before he could engage his knife Dando swung the sword sideways so that it bit deep into his opponent's neck; the weapon appeared to have a thirst for blood. Meantime Foxy and Ralph were wreaking some havoc of their own. It seemed only a few seconds before the rest of the band took to their heels with the dog and the warlike Nablan in hot pursuit, leaving

Dando standing over two prostrate bodies, shaking like a leaf, while Tallis, sword half out of its scabbard, was still struggling painfully upright. Ann crept out of the bushes and came to examine the fallen robbers. "They be dead – the both of them," she said with unemotional practicality. Dando held up his blood-stained blade and gazed at it with mixed awe and revulsion. He had just begun to clean it when Foxy reappeared and pushed the dead men face upward with his foot. He glanced sideways at Dando.

"Well done Pot Boy," he said.

"It w-wasn't me," replied Dando, grateful none the less and amazed at the approbation, "it was the sword."

Foxy laughed. "Well you stick close to that sword, bor - it be a useful brother-at-arms."

They had not got the means to bury the bodies. Foxy dragged them out of sight into the bushes but Dando could not sleep for the rest of the night knowing they were close by. He was thankful when they moved on.

The next morning he realised that the atmosphere had changed. There was a subtle difference in the other men's attitude towards him. Although he was still *Pot Boy, Turnspit, Kitchen Slavvy* to Foxy, the names were not hurled at him in scorn as previously but spoken in a joshing, almost affectionate manner. Tallis seemed marginally less remote, acknowledging his presence when he was served and even thanking him on a couple of occasions.

And this is because I took two people's lives, thought Dando ruefully, *it seems a funny way to earn respect.*

Nevertheless his existence became a mite easier. At night he was allowed to lie a little closer to the fire although always on the opposite side to that on which Ann made her bed. Things had altered and a sort of truce had been declared but he knew it would soon be broken if he was seen to go anywhere near the girl or even speak to her except when the others approved. He was becoming frustrated; it was not enough any more to have Ann a few feet away when, as a result of these prohibitions, she might as well have been miles distant. He needed to interact with her, to touch her, to assure himself of her physical presence. He needed to feel her body close to his.

In the aftermath of the assault Tallis was going over what had happened in his mind. He realised that if he had been on his own he would probably be dead by now. When the robbers had attacked, his reactions had been painfully slow. The outcome confirmed the wisdom of taking a companion with him on the road. But it had been his squire rather than the admired Nablan who had dealt the most telling blows. Perhaps he had misjudged the boy. Would the thieves be back? It was possible, although the wayfarers had proved they could give as good as they got. They must be twice as wary of an incursion now that they were a long way from law-abiding lands. They needed to look to their arms and be ready to defend themselves at all times. He discussed tactics with Foxy.

"I wish I had your skill with the bow," he told him, "it's a fine weapon you have there. Where did you get it?"

"I make it," said the other man. "I can make you one the same if you like - that's if I can find the wood – I got plenty of cord with me."

"Make me one too, Foxy," said Ann. So, after coming back from a hunting expedition without a quarry but with several stout lengths of yew wood, Foxy set to work and was no longer idle in the evenings. He fashioned a medium-sized bow for Tallis and a much smaller one for Ann. Then, on a wicked impulse, he made one of a similar size to his own for Dando, believing the boy would not have the muscle power to draw it. But Dando's superior height told in his favour and his strength and determination were greater than Foxy gave him credit for, although in the initial stages mastering the weapon was a struggle. So now, most days, before the light faded, they had half an hour's archery practice, shooting at a mark with the arrows Foxy continued to manufacture. After some time Dando and Tallis reached a certain mediocre standard on which they seemed unable to improve, but Ann just went on getting better and better until she could rival Foxy for accuracy.

Despite his companions' newly acquired skills Foxy was becoming increasingly uneasy. "What we need is guns," he said. "Someone with a gun could hev us beat afore we know what be a-doin'. Guns be the comin' thing, happen I never seed one 'till a coupla year agoo."

As the second moon since they left the valley started to wane, the weather suddenly changed. They had become used to still, cold, quiet days and clear skies for the most part, with overnight frosts and the occasional fog. But now the wind got up, clouds streamed from the west and it began to rain; it rained for days on end. The rain found its way through their layers of clothing until everything was dank and wet and they had to get used to a continual dampness next to the skin. The trees under which they camped at day's end showered water on them if even just a light breeze got up. The nights were pitch black and although the sky brightened at dawn the sun never showed its face. They longed, just once, for a nice dry cave in which to take shelter, but nothing of that sort presented itself along their route. However something was altering. The hilly uplands through which they had been journeying since leaving Deep Hallow were giving way to lower undulating country. It was a pleasant green landscape they had come to which encouraged human habitation. For the first time in weeks they began to see faces other than their own. They learnt that a short way ahead a small river crossed their path and at the crossing stood a town.

"Praps we could stay a night or two," suggested Dando diffidently, not averse to having a roof over his head once more. The idea struck a chord with the others and although neither Tallis nor Foxy had anything directly to say on the matter it seemed to be tacitly agreed that they would put up at a hostelry if they found one in the little settlement they were approaching.

It was the evening of the fifth day since they had come down from the hills and the four travellers were in the public room of the Jolly Waggoners Inn eating a perfectly acceptable meal. They had crossed the River Burple and entered the town of Formile on the northern bank. Tallis and Dando had agreed to share the cost of accommodation between them as neither Foxy nor Ann were provided with money. Now, the meal being over, Dando was chatting to one of their fellow gourmands in that easygoing confident manner that he used with strangers, as if the whole world were his oyster. Tallis, whose attitude to those he met was just the opposite to that of his squire's, marvelled at his foolishness. Albeit he listened in to the conversation.

"Are you on your way to consult the Voice?" the other man was asking.

"The voice?" replied Dando, "what's that?"

"You know – the oracle up in the hills at Toymerle. That's where anyone travelling north through 'ere is going – nowhere else *to* go."

"Do I understand," asked Tallis, butting in, "that there's no way out of the mountains to the north?"

"You want to go to the coast, you mean? Well there is a 'igh pass, but I doubt you'd get over it at this time of year – and certainly not with those 'orses of yours," he had seen the travellers arrive. "You'd do better to retrace your steps and follow the Burple down to the Great River. Then you could go downstream to Drossi and work your way along the edge of the Middle Sea till you git where you're goin' thataway. It's a lot further but it's safer and surer."

"What is it, this voice you mentioned," asked Dando, "whose voice?"

"Why Rostan's of course."

"Rostan?"

"Yes, you know – the God of Hidden Fire – the *ruler-of-the-core* as they say roun' 'ere – different from the Mother 'oo's s'posed to rule the surface."

"Of the world do you mean?" inquired Tallis.

"Yers – the 'ole bloody world."

"And does this Fire-God answer questions?" said Dando.

"If you cough up enough dough. But I should save your money, although p'raps I shouldn't be saying that. Anyway, between you an' me 'e's no great shakes – we don't pay our respects to him roun' 'ere. It's the lady who answers our prayers."

"You mean Aigea?" asked Tallis.

"No fear – the Black Queen."

Tallis and Dando had never heard of this deity.

Just two nights in a world of warmth and comfort, of hot baths and dry beds, and Tallis was already impatient to move on. When he suggested it was time to depart, Ann's and Dando's faces clearly expressed their disappointment. Foxy was impassive; he felt no need for what he termed *soft living* and was equally prepared to stay or go.

"One more night," said Tallis, deferring to the youngsters' wishes, "then we must be on our way."

Dando took his courage in both hands. "But where are we going, master?" he enquired with great trepidation. It was a question that had been on the tip of his tongue for many days past but which he had held back from asking for fear of provoking animosity.

"North," replied Tallis shortly.

"But when will we get there, where we're going?" pursued Dando, further chancing his arm.

Tallis hesitated. Often and often he had asked himself this very same question in the secret recesses of his own heart, but to hear it put brutally into words by someone other than himself brought home to him the extent of his confusions and uncertainties. Since leaving Deep Hallow he had been learning slowly and and painfully how to get along with his companions. At first their constant presence had been an infernal nuisance. He had felt inhibited and constrained, and things that he would have done openly when alone, such as breaking wind, masturbating, spitting or excreting, he had had to keep under wraps for fear of causing offence. It was foreign to him to have to consider the feelings of others, and changing long ingrained habits at his age was incredibly irksome. But no one is so set in their ways that they cannot alter, and alter he did. He even began to get some comfort from their fellowship. He occasionally found a second opinion valuable, and the thought that he did not have to rely solely on himself in a crisis was reassuring. He even, sometimes, found himself amused or intrigued by the very *otherness* of these members of the human race. There was Ann: feminine, magical, demure, Dando: dreamy, optimistic, naïve, and Foxy: intense, obsessional, a force of nature. They were all so *different* from one another. Now, being asked the questions *where* and *when* in relation to his quest, Tallis realised that for the second time in his life (the first time had been during his stay in Gregory Guyax's commune) he had an opportunity to share the weight he carried and maybe confide some of his tale to uncritical ears.

"It all started with the Key..." he began.

"You mean the key symbol we saw carved on the rock?" interrupted Dando.

Ah, the symbol on the rock. What a leap of hope he had felt when he saw it. Never before, in all his journeyings, had he had such a clear indication that he was on the right track. But why had this sign been vouchsafed to him so late in the day when he was growing old and beginning to doubt his ability to continue?

"My Dadda tol' I about the Key," Ann suddenly contributed, "we keep the Key for the Mother until her husband come an' stole it."

Tallis looked at her in hostile surprise. "That must certainly have been a different key," he objected, "the Sky-Father never stole the Key, if that's who you mean by *her husband,* it was his by right."

"Don't let's argue," interjected Dando quickly, making an effort to defuse the situation and keen for Tallis to continue. "Tell us your story, master."

Dando and Ann settled themselves at the knight's feet on the tavern patio while Foxy sat nearby, whittling wood, interested despite himself.

"A long way from here," began Tallis anew, "there was once a people called the Lake Guardians. They had a great treasure in their keeping..."

Throughout the third day at the inn he spun his tale, while the others listened spellbound. The afternoon was fading into evening by the time he concluded with the words "...and so I found the valley which I had been promised, your valley, and put up at the inn with the strange name – the Justification."

After he had ceased speaking his listeners held their peace for a long time until he added "...and that's why I travel north," realising as he did so that he had answered neither the *where* nor the *when* of his quest.

"At the Castle," offered Dando somewhat shyly, "there was a r-room full of books. I read most of them. They were very old. There was one that had the beginnings of a poem. Your story reminds me of it because you talked about a *king,* and a *treasure* and a *stranger* and so does this poem. Do you want to hear it?"

Tallis gave him a quizzical glance. "Fire away," he said.

Dando stood up and cleared his throat. "I read it many many times - this is how it goes:

The King sat on his golden throne
Drinking the blood red wine,
'Welcome stranger to our feast,
Take what you will of mine.
What's mine is yours,' the monarch said,
'As all here must agree,
For you shall sit by my daughter dear,
And we shall merry be.'
The stranger sat by his daughter dear,
The next day he was gone,
And with him a prize greater by far
Than any man has won.
'Oh who will bring back my treasure so rare?
And who my daughter dear?
For ill-luck shall fall on this land of ours,
If the treasure be gone from here.'
Then up spoke...

That's as far as it went," said Dando, "the page was torn and the next few pages were missing. Then after that somebody had written something in another hand – all the books were hand written – something about being justified in remaining behind because the people were sick and needed time to recover before journeying on. They would follow after or maybe wait for someone to return. It was hard to read – the book was in pretty poor shape."

"Until the King returns – the King," said Tallis excitedly. "Don't you remember you said *Until the King shall return* when you made your vow."

"But that's just our way of putting things," replied Dando uncomfortably.

"Why do you think you have an ancient tavern called The King's Head in the middle of your town when you don't have a king? What's the history of your people?" asked Tallis urgently.

"Well I don't really know – it wasn't something we talked about, although the book room was called The King's Vault. The nibblers call us *incomers*."

"And you call yourselves *Glepts*," said Tallis. "Don't you know that that word just means *stranger* in the tongues of the south? I was often called glept on my travels. Why haven't you got a proper title?"

"The Incomers come from the south," interjected Ann. "an' they worship the Sky-Father but he don't care about they – he be angry wi' they. They shouldn't 'a stayed in the valley."

"Yes," said Tallis as if this was the clinching piece of evidence, "I felt it – he wasn't there!"

Tallis stared at Dando with incredulity. One of the things he had been looking for all his life, the idea he had been groping after in the valley of Deep Hallow, where his mind had all the time been muddied and clouded, now became crystal clear. His mother had told him to find his people and he *had* found them. In fact he had passed through a portion of them unawares and had left them behind, apart from the one who was standing in front of him at this very moment. Anger welled up.

"That sign on the rock," he accused, "it was left by those who went ahead for the ones they thought would follow. But you didn't follow – you stayed in the valley – you broke your promise and the god abandoned you."

"W-what do you mean?" stammered Dando, all at sea. From Tallis' tone of voice he understood he was being condemned for some heinous crime that he had not even known he had committed. Ann jumped up and put her hand in Dando's.

"It weren't his fault," she cried, "it happen long ago – long, long ago. It weren't he - leave he alone! Anyway," she added as an afterthought, "he's come now ha'n't he, so he ha'n't broken his promise."

Dando looked bewildered. "You think my people are your people?" he said

---

"Oy!" The shout came from the throat of Foxy who had dropped what he was doing and was pointing menacingly towards Dando and Ann's linked hands. He drew his knife and made stabbing motions in the air. The two young people leapt apart as if they had been stung. Tallis stared unseeingly at his three companions, his mind racing ahead as his world view shifted, dissolved, reformed, incorporating the astounding new discoveries he had just made. In the end he focussed on Ann.

"How long ago was it that they came into the valley?" he asked her.

"A long long while agoo. It were at the time of the Culdee number twenty six an' my Dadda, he be the seventy an' four."

"So," said Tallis. He shook his head. At last he was being forced to acknowledge that a vast age had passed since the stealing of the Key. "So it was all a delusion," he said. "She wasn't really there – it was just her fancy."

Ann, by some presentment, knew what he was talking about.

"Dadda tol' me," she said, "when some people die an' they move to another life, they c'n take their memories along. Your ma be like that – she tol' the truth – maybe she even chose to return to the earth to tell you her story when she could 'a' gone free. There be no need to fret."

Tallis thought long and hard, then looked up at Ann and gave her one of his very rare smiles. "We'll consult that oracle in the mountains," he said. "and ask it where the Key is to be found. If this Rock-God really has a repository of secret knowledge then perhaps at last I'll be able to tell you *where* we're going and *when* we're going to get there."

The weather improved, they loaded the horses with fresh supplies and were soon back on the trail. In no time at all they entered a region of lakes and fells where the road wound between water and hillside, making the most of the only available strip of level ground. When they stood at the south end of a lake looking north they sometimes glimpsed distant snow-covered peaks beyond the high land at the other end, floating like mirages in the sky. Then came another parting of the ways. A valley opened on their left and a path took off in that direction. At the junction stood a signpost, but it had been defaced, they could not read what had been written.

"This is the correct road – and the road to the oracle I believe," said Tallis as he directed his steps away from the northward-leading track into the side turning. The others followed with doubt in their hearts, but discovered, a few miles further on, that the way swung slowly round until they were heading in the direction that the compass needle indicated once more. Perhaps Tallis, after a lifetime of travelling, had an instinct for the correct bearing.

With the better weather had come an increased lightening of mood, at least superficially. Everyone seemed happier in their minds, even Foxy. This may have been down to the fact that they all knew their destination by now, at least in the short term, and in the long term they understood the *why* of their journey if not the *where* and the *when*. The relaxed atmosphere manifested itself in a spontaneous outbreak of exuberance on the part of the three younger people.

To see Dando cook was like watching a one man ballet: there was the graceful economy of movement, a repetitive pattern traced between fixed points during which the absorbed concentration of the perpetrator brooked no interruption; it all added up to a sort of poetry in motion. Although apparently lost in his own world as he practised on the kuckthu Tallis must have been subliminally aware of this culinary minuet because he began unconsciously to fit the rhythm of the tune he was playing to the boy's actions, and Dando, in his turn, began deliberately to keep in time to the music. It was not many minutes before he was dancing in real earnest. Next Ann got up and, flinging out her arms for balance, started twirling on the spot, her fair hair flying out around her head. Most surprisingly, Foxy, not to be outdone, began to jig to and fro, and in no time at all was capering round like a satyr at a bacchanal. Tallis, realising what was happening, moved from one lively reel to another without a break until the dancers eventually collapsed from sheer exhaustion. This hooley became a regular feature of their evenings.

On another night Ann was talking to Tallis about her life at the Justification when Foxy interrupted. "O' course, as she say, Hild and I work for our living," he contributed, "not like this toffee-nosed layabout," with a thumb over his shoulder towards Dando who was standing behind him listening. In a moment of madness Dando, who happened to have a pan of cold water in his hand, tipped it over

Foxy's head. The nibbler swung round and with his heel expertly hooked the boy's feet out from under him, sending him sprawling. He then rose dripping and walked away. Dando got up and ran after him, leaping on his back, bringing them both down. A wrestling match followed which Foxy rapidly won so that Dando found himself pinned to the ground with the Nablan's knee in his midriff.

"Pax! Pax!" he cried, holding up crossed fingers. Foxy let him go and they both scrambled to their feet grinning. Tallis watched this scene with bemusement; male bonding had never been part of his experience. What curious creatures human beings were.

Out hunting, Foxy was thinking of Dando. He was surprised to find he almost liked the lad. The high-born Glept seemed harmless enough taking all things into consideration, although a bit of a nance. They might even have become pals in a father/son sort of way but for Ann's inexplicable passion. What by the Holy Mother's tits did she see in the boy? Foxy could not understand the appeal. But then women had always been a closed book to the self-sufficient nibbler. Although he did not like to admit it because it meant that the outcome of his plans for her became more nebulous, as far as he was concerned Ann was an enigma, he did not understand the way her mind worked or what made her tick. Despite the fact that he felt Dando could almost pass muster under other circumstances, the boy's presence here was a continual thorn in his flesh because of Ann's partiality. Recently he had had a demonstration of just how strong her feelings were. Ever since he had joined the travellers he had been trying to persuade his little priestess, when he got her alone, to return with him to Deep Hallow, but it was obviously because of her attachment to Dando that she was reluctant to comply.

"Don't 'ee fret girl," he told her, "things ha' changed in the valley. I'll see no one harms 'ee."

"How changed?" Ann asked.

"You'll see when we get back. They be a-waitin' for 'ee. There'll be such a welcome because of who you are an' what ha' happen."

Ann regarded him sceptically, not understanding. On another occasion he urged her to: "Come back wi' I. Everythin's altered there since you left. You won't believe your eyes. It'll be ours again, now those duzzy rascals ha' been taught a lesson."

"I don't know what you mean Foxy – you ha' to explain."

Foxy decided to take the plunge.

"It be that ol' witch-finder – he won't be botherin' you no more."

"Are you talkin' about the boss? I don' un'erstan'. Tell me Foxy."

"I settle his hash for him," said Foxy and did the classic throat-cutting gesture. Ann's eyes widened.

"Are you tellin' me he be dead? Are you serious?"

"'E be a goner right enough – I'm not lyin' girl."

"An' you did it? Oh Foxy!" She looked at him with such an expression of horror that he was completely taken aback.

"What's wrong?" he cried but Ann just shook her head and turned away.

"It were the best thing for he," urged Foxy, rushing into words, and then, "it be quick," thinking she might be squeamish. But that was not it – something else was bothering her. From then on she refused to listen when he tried to persuade her to leave the travellers. If he suggested that they return to the valley an echo of the initial consternation she had shown appeared in her eyes. Recently, because he had no knowledge of his own relationship to the Dan, he had decided that it must be because the man he had killed had been her sweetheart's father and that meant that everything awry in their relationship could be blamed on Dando. Basically, when it came down to it, the boy was the root cause of all his failures. Concealed in his hiding place overlooking the rabbit warren he was about to raid Foxy pulled an arrow from his quiver and spat his frustrations onto the ground.

Ann was standing sentry duty in the small hours armed with Tallis' time piece: a repeater watch. Soon she would wake Foxy who would take the last shift before morning. Everything appeared peaceful enough. Thin broken cloud was drifting slowly overhead illumined from above by the waxing moon; *the floor of the gods* was what she had heard some people call this beautiful sight, shortened occasionally to *the dancing floor*. An infrequent puff of wind lifted her hair but was not strong enough to stir the branches of nearby trees. At a distance she could hear the endless song of the little stream that skirted their camp site. Dando had been watching her up until about an hour ago, at which point he had shut his eyes and fallen asleep. She knew she had Dando to thank for the consideration with which she was being treated by Tallis, indeed by all three members of their little band. If it had not been for his intervention on their first night on the road, his sensitivity to her needs, the thought would never have occurred to the others that she required some private space to which she could retire when she needed to undress, to relieve herself or deal with personal hygiene. She thought of him with gratitude and tenderness and hated the way the other men had behaved towards him. *"He be worth ten o' they,"* she avowed internally. It brought her enormous joy, at moments such as this, to realise that she was holding his safely in her hands, that she was standing between her loved-one and any danger that might threaten. However, there were occasions in which she feared that she herself might be helping to intensify that danger.

When she had taken up a position at his side as Tallis rejected him on Foxy's advent she had made a fundamental mistake. "You can't send he back!" she had cried, speaking with enormous indignation, supporting her childhood sweetheart, letting her heart rule her head, when it would have been far better to have allowed things to take their course. In that event Dando would be safely away from her by now, away from her inadvertent ability to attract the immortals attention through her possession of the gift. Foolishly she had intervened on his behalf, with the result that they were now within yards of each other twenty four hours a day, only Tallis' and Foxy's vigilance keeping them apart. *She be out for his blood,* Dadda had told her, speaking of his mistress, and *he ha' a hard an' a dangerous road to travel.* She also remembered the ominous words: *If you lie wi' the man it will be he that she hurts as well as you,* and the heartfelt advice: *You stay away from men, my hinny - don't 'ee bring sadness on yourself like I did.* The wretched truth was that her presence was inimical to Dando's welfare, a fact of which both she and apparently his sister had long been aware There was no question that she loved him - it was incontrovertible that she had lost her heart many years ago – and for that very reason she ought to keep him at arms' length and leave him for good and all as soon as humanly possible, however painful that might be.

Was she a priestess? Did she belong to the Goddess? She could not be sure. She had the gift it was true, but she had not been dedicated to the Mother as all previous Culdees had been. Since their departure from Deep Hallow she had left behind the sense of being watched, the feeling of jealous possessiveness that she had lived with in the valley. Out here she felt free, as if it were the goddess herself that had been left behind. But surely the Earth Mother's reach extended far beyond the confines of one small valley – wasn't she supposed to govern the surface of the whole world? Soon they would come to this new seat of power, this Place-Of-The-Voice they had been told about dedicated to the Rock-God who ruled the fiery depths of the earth. Might this not be another source of danger for her dear lad? She felt anxious and afraid.

It was time to wake Foxy, but for a short spell she sat lost in her own musings remembering the past. Although she had only just attained seventeen her life had already encompassed two dramatic changes of fortune. The first had been the switch from her felicitous life at Castle Dan to the back-breaking drudgery at the Justification Inn, where she learnt what it truly meant to be born a nibbler. Then there was the abrupt shift to her present unfettered wayfaring existence. She was sure Dadda had had foreknowledge of this: *You have far to go, sweetheart,* he had told her. Tears came to her eyes at the thought. She could cry for her father now, and often did so, secretly, in the depths of the night. Although she did not understand why, it seemed to be also thanks to Dando that she could grieve properly for the first time.

She thought about the power that she had inherited. She was beginning to get a feel for how to tackle this monster that had taken up residence inside her. At the time of the month when it was at its most potent she was starting to ride it, to get the upper hand. It was like breaking in a dragon to the saddle she realised, accustoming it to bit and bridle, acquiring the skills to sit securely astride its back as it soared and plunged. Left to its own devices it only understood destruction, but with her hand on the reins she could channel it towards creation or at least positive change. She began a few surreptitious experiments when the others were not looking. Touching a nearby branch she intuited next spring's leaves already latent within the bud. Taking hold of the dragon of power as she

would a bow she notched an arrow of intent to its string and let fly
the missile towards the tiny green coils that were waiting their time
to unfurl. Like a musical crescendo the immature autumn buds
swelled, hardened, split and burst asunder; then verdant foliage
exploded into the cold night air. This grew, unwrapped, spread,
smoothed until, as a grand finale, the whole bough clothed itself in
its spring finery. She did this twice, then desisted. It seemed unfair to
the tree to force it to put forth tender growth when it was still autumn
and winter's blackening frosts were yet to come. There were other
ways she found she could harness the gift: sitting on watch in the
small hours she discovered she could call up mists or disperse them
by altering the dew point of the air and when doing the washing she
was able to change the temperature around the clothes on the line by
a degree or two so that they would dry more quickly. She even, for a
few seconds, managed one of Dadda's illusions: a cloud of multi-
coloured butterflies danced in the dusk under the trees. This
tremendous increase in her confidence was also obscurely due, she
felt, to Dando's presence.

Dadda had not tried to teach her the sort of party tricks he
occasionally practised, but he had passed on to her a huge quantity of
information in the three-year breathing space he was given before his
arrest. One story stood out and had particular relevance at this
present time.

"The Chief, when he were a lad," Tom narrated, "came
back from the far end o' the valley havin' taken to wife one o' our
people. He were called Dando then although his older brother was
now head of clan. She were called Paulina, the wife, an' she had their
little baby wi' her. The chil' were named Dickon. Dando built them a
home up by the Fannon Waterfall an' he virtually lived up there wi'
them. But then his brother did away wi' himself and Dando had to
become chief. He cou'n't go to the cottage he had built any more, or
only very rarely. No one else went there either except to take
supplies. The woman had put herself between the two peoples by
marryin', she belong to neither one side nor the other, an' neither
would own her. Because the cottage were only visited once or twice
a month it were at least three weeks before Paulina's body were
discovered in the water, the pool at the foot of the fall, dead an'
rottin'; of the chil' Dickon, a boy of five by now, there were no sign.
Some say she were done away wi' because she betrayed her race, but
I don' think so. It were a very hot summer that year an' I reckon she
went a-swimmin' in the pool an' maybe caught a cramp or became ill

- I believe she were expectin' again - an' then there were no one nearby, except the boy, to pull her out. They say it broke his heart - Dando, or the Dan as he had now become. But what happen' to the chil'? I talk to Valentine, the goatherd, the one who brought up a Nablan to be his boy. It were the winter after the summer when Paulina died that he took the child in – he were runnin' wild so he tell me. When one of ours goes wi' one of theirs the babes always favour the Nablan side they do say. I believe that the goatherd's boy be the boss's son. They called him Foxy 'acos of his red hair."

Ann considered her long time protector. Foxy had believed her distress at what he had told her about the clan chief's death was centred on Dando, that she was aghast because he, Foxy, had made away with the boy's father. "All you care about is that cutchy Glept!" he had cried, "you don' un'erstan' what I've done for the Nablar - for your own people!" That had been very close to the truth but not close enough. For once it was not Dando's plight that had appalled her, it was concern for Foxy himself, for this unaware parricide, that filled her with horror.

Oh Foxy, she thought now, *you hater of Glepts. What would it do to you if I tol' you Dadda's story?*

It was the next night, and because keeping watch through the hours of darkness was very tiring, Ann was looking forward to uninterrupted sleep while Tallis and Dando took their turn. After bedding down she had just got soundly off into dreamland when she was hauled back to consciousness by someone shaking her shoulder. As she opened her eyes a hand was clamped over her mouth, and, after a start of alarm, she relaxed as she saw Dando kneeling above her.

"Come," he whispered, "We've got something to settle." When he was sure she was fully awake he removed his hand allowing her to reply.

"What something?" she asked, shaking her head slightly.

"Shhhhhh," he said, finger to lips, eyes flicking anxiously towards the other sleepers. "Come - please come. We need to talk... Please Annie."

This was what she had been dreading. Knowing he would not desist until she did what he wanted she got slowly to her feet.

From chicken to caviare,
From walk-on to starring role,
Such is an actor's hoped for trajectory.

Chapter four

"Your servant mesdames," said the showman, "may I have the honour of knowing whom I am addressing?"

Damask decided to answer grandeur with grandeur.

"You are speaking with the Lady Damask," she said, "daughter of the Dan of Dans, chief of the most illustrious clan in the valley of Deep Hallow. This is my maid Millicent."

"Millicent," murmured Milly, "that sounds like a bit of orl right."

"Please accept our heartfelt gratitude," Damask continued, "for your assistance in resolving an unpleasant situation."

"Not at all my lady, not at all," replied the thespian, "think nothing of it. Always happy to oblige the fairer sex. Are you travelling in our direction? That vehicle of yours appears somewhat familiar. Last time we encountered it it was being driven by a trainer of felines."

"Where's the Mog?" interjected another player.

"In the back," replied Damask

"Under duress?" enquired a showily dressed man, who also possessed beautiful locution. Damask frowned, looking puzzled.

"He means, has he no choice in the matter?" put in one of the women.

"He tried to kidnap us!" said Damask indignantly.

"And you got the better of him?" The company shared a laugh.

"He wouldn't have done you any harm," said an individual in cap and bells, "he just likes to collect pretty things, being so ugly himself."

"What happened to his face?" asked Damask, horrified anew as she remembered what she had seen.

"Everyone knows that story. His old caravan caught fire. The fire started at the back by the door. Pnoumi opened the door to let the cats out but they wouldn't venture through the flames."

"But, when we watched the show, they jumped through flaming hoops."

"That's just a trick – didn't you realise? - done with lights and mirrors. Anyway, many times he went inside bringing them out by twos and threes. He didn't stop until he'd rescued every last one. By that time his skin had been virtually burnt off. It's a wonder he survived."

"Oh," murmured Damask and Milly together, somewhat subdued.

"We're travelling to Millfield to stage a theatrical performance tonight," the impresario informed them. "If you care to follow us we can offer you our protection and also free tickets to our humble divertissement."

"Thanks, be glad to," said Damask.

While they waited for the troupe's vehicles to trundle past she went round to the back of the cat-circus caravan, removed the bar and pushed Pnoumi's box of greasepaints and prostheses through the half open door, averting her eyes as she did so.

"Here," she called to the man inside, "make yourself presentable."

When the last cart had gone by she and Milly climbed back into the driving seat and tagged onto the end of the procession.

The actors' heavy lumbering wagons were loaded up with props, costumes, scenery and parts of a mobile stage. Most of the company walked, as was fitting for those going under the title of strolling players. A friendly chatty girl kept pace alongside Damask and Milly's van, calling up to them, until Damask, finding that their voices were being drowned by the creaking of the axles, invited her onto the bench, an offer taken up with alacrity.

"I'm Severine," the girl said, plumping her large bottom down between the two of them, (there was scarcely room), "I'm going to be Columbine in tonight's production. This is my big break – I've only played small parts up to now."

From this loquacious female they learnt that her name was not really Severine but Mable, that she had run away from her parents' farm to become an actress, that she was in love with the actor who played the juvenile lead and that the company was known as the Ixat Instipulators.

"Alaric, that's the Grande Stupendo's real name, evidently liked the sound of it. According to him it means we don't go around tarring and feathering people so we hope no one tries it on us. He comes from Ixat you see and they always give us a big welcome when we go back there. We call ourselves *The Stips* for short. Have you done any acting?"

"I'd get my twin to write plays for my brothers and sisters to perform," said Damask. "We put them on at the Midwinter Festival. It was just kids mucking about really. I'd usually take the lead."

"Yes, that's what we used to do. That's where I caught the bug. The play we're doing tonight is called *The General – or the Remarkable History of Floy McLoy and the Madderhay Wars.* There's stuff about battles and a nice love story. Some of it is quite funny. We usually have four plays or more on the go at any one time – a comedy, a tragedy, something romantic, something scary. It depends on the place we're at as to which one we put on. At Pickwah, for instance, there always has to be lots of fighting. We're only at Millfield one night, then we move on to Komstock and after that to Okeefanokee. I think Alaric is hoping we might get a slot in Drossi sometime next year although of course they've got their own permanent theatre companies there."

"What is Alaric? Is he the boss?"

"Alaric's our Captain – captain of the company that is and also Captain on the stage. You know the character – he's sometimes called Ralph Roisterdoister. That old bloke over there is Pantalone – he used to play the Captain until he got too old. That one," indicating a willowy youth, "is my Harlequin. Hopeless, absolutely hopeless – doesn't know his arse from his elbow – I think I'll have to carry him most of the time. The chap in the cap and bells plays the part of Zanni – he's never out of character. He's good when he's sober. The fellow just in front here is Punchinello – you should see him when he gets into full costume and make-up. There's our leading lady, Isabella, and there's the hero of the piece, Leandro." She heaved a deep sigh.

"We're going on at the Corn Exchange tonight. We're having a run through this afternoon. It's a fine big hall – should attract lots of punters. Usually we perform in the open air - got our own stage. Oh," noticing that the matinee idol had been deserted by his female companion and was walking on his own, "I must go and have a word with Peter. 'Scuse me."

Very soon the town of Millfield appeared in the distance and the convoy pulled into a grassy field on the outskirts, where some tents had already been set up. The boy who played Harlequin, the object of Severine's scorn, nevertheless directed the traffic in an efficient manner and Damask drove the caravan into the space he indicated; the horse was set loose to graze. The actor who had earlier been pointed out as Punchinello came and lounged against the shafts.

"If you don't mind my asking," he said, "who were those squaddies that were causing you trouble? Did you know them? It was lucky that they appeared to be bereft of their weapons. Armed they would have proved ugly customers."

"My father employed them – they're mercenaries – they sell themselves to the highest bidder. He started off with just a few, but ended up with a virtual army. That was only a small contingent. If they've all been turfed out as we've been told we could bump into more of them at any time. This lot said they'll probably decide to make for some place called Pickwah."

"Oh Pickwah, yes, up on the coast; lately they've been advertising for recruits – building up their defence forces. Something funny going on there - they've closed their borders. Used to be quite a thriving tourist trade in that part of the world – the maritime hot springs you know. We did good business at the spa in the summer, but that's all come to a halt – temporary I hope. The strangest thing is they've also put out a call for magicians, the genuine article that is, not tricksters. What's that all about?" He paused to light an elegant black cigarette in a holder, then offered them round. Milly accepted with enthusiasm, Damask out of politeness.

"By the way," he added, "did you know that the back door to your van is ajar?"

"What!" Damask tumbled down from the driving seat and hurried round to the rear. The bar which should have been keeping the door closed and unopenable from inside was hanging from its chain. She must have forgotten to replace it on her last visit. She peered into the interior; it was empty; the bird had flown.

"Well," said Milly who had followed her round, "you've got wot you wanted – your very own caravan."

"But we can't keep it."

"Why not?"

"It's his home, and besides how would he manage with his cats without it?"

"Who cares."

"No really. I wonder if that Punchinello fellow knows where he's gone."

The gentleman in question was still leaning against the caravan, busy lighting a second cigarette from the first. Again he held them out and this time Damask accepted more readily.

"Where are you ladies bound?" he asked.

"I can't actually say. We've been trying to catch up with my brother and his two companions who left the valley before us but we've seen neither hide nor hair of them. It makes me wonder if they came this way at all."

"Describe them."

Damask did so.

"No, can't say I've heard word of anyone like that. But I'll ask around. If they're on a long journey, not just local, they will have been spotted. There's a fraternity of the road; travellers get to know other travellers. Newcomers stand out like a sore thumb. Someone will have noticed."

"Where does King Pnoumi keep his cats?" Damask asked.

"Oh, the Mog. He's a bit of a man of mystery. Comes from somewhere off east and sometimes disappears for months at a time. I'm afraid I've got no idea if he's got a base near here. I presume he's no longer in the back? Ah well – there you go." He wandered off.

Left alone for a while the girls had time to take stock, explore the caravan more thoroughly and discover if Pnoumi had left them any food. Damask also had leisure to think about the freebooter and what he had told her. That her father was dead, despite her initial incredulity, seemed almost certain; the fact that the mercenaries had been expelled from Deep Hallow appeared to prove it. How had he died? She wished she'd asked. She tried to imagine Dantor as the new Dan – impossible – he hadn't the cojones to step into his father's shoes. And yet he must have been the one to send the soldiers packing. What did she feel? She searched her heart for pangs of grief, for sorrow at her loss, but could detect nothing. It appeared she was completely indifferent - an unnatural daughter. But then, she had never been close to her parent, not even when he had taken an interest in his twins as babies. She had always come second to her brother in her father's estimation; it was Dando who had been his favourite, the one who basked in his especial goodwill, and who consequently had been the one to suffer when that goodwill was withdrawn. Dando had loved his father. Oh well, that was all behind her now: the valley, her family, the two races at loggerheads; she was done with it, thanks be to Pyr.

A little later they were approached by the Grande Stupendo himself, his former chivalric demeanour somewhat in abeyance.

"Ladies," he began in a practical manner, "I have a proposition. If you prefer, you can sit out front in the stalls this evening to watch the performance. Alternatively, how would you like to participate? Our production has several crowd scenes: women of the town, robbers, soldiers, yokels, matelots. We usually recruit from the local population but we have very little rehearsal time here. Would you care to play the crowd? We'll be having a run-through this afternoon."

"Just us?" asked Damask.

"Well, you'll symbolise a crowd - the patrons will understand - and any of the company who are not actually *on* will be able to join you. It will require a few rapid costume changes."

Damask had no need for reflection.

"Glad to," she said. Milly shook her head.

"Oh come on Milly, it'll be fun – give it a go." After a lot of persuasion Milly reluctantly agreed to take part, realising it would be difficult for Damask to impersonate a crowd on her own. "I shall feel a right wally," she complained.

At the rehearsal Damask threw herself into this particular production with enthusiasm. Quickly learning the moves required, she dragged or propelled an embarrassed Milly along with her, reciting the occasional line. The costume changes really involved nothing more than swapping one type of headgear for another: helmets for scarves, tricorns for tarred boaters, sun-hats for wimples. The way the other actors conducted themselves was an eye-opener. She was surprised that they made no attempt to insert any emotion into their speeches. They were obviously saving dramatic nuances and histrionics for the actual performance; the rehearsal was just an opportunity to test their memory of the text and stage directions. The man identified as Zanni had an even more casual approach than his colleagues; his lines were thrown away in a barely audible mumble. It was a while before Damask could work out what character he was playing; he seemed to be taking the part of a minor earl in the train of the hero of the piece and to be providing some sort of comic relief. When he stood behind her in the final act she detected a strong smell of alcohol on his breath.

"Can I borrow a copy of the play to study?" she asked as they wound up the run-through. She retired to the caravan, book in hand, and began to learn all their cues by heart, in the process memorising a great deal of the content of the work. She read some of it out loud to a sulky Milly whose whole attitude conveyed her conviction that they were making a BIG MISTAKE! Outside she could hear Alaric's raised voice; he was ticking somebody off.

The scenery and props had been taken across to that evening's venue soon after their arrival. About an hour before the performance was due to start the actors got into costume and make-up and paraded from the campsite into the centre of town. Walking among them Damask felt exhilarated and excited to be on the receiving end of cheers from the local populace. Even Milly perked up. "It's like the circus," she said.

The first half of the entertainment went swimmingly, the audience seeming to enjoy themselves. It was not a new play they were presenting, in fact it was an old favourite and the locals were already well acquainted with the plot. They applauded the familiar speeches and laughed dutifully at the punch lines of the jokes. But then came an unexpected disruption. In the interval a musical interlude had been arranged. Standing with Milly in the wings Damask watched with interest as three young men that she remembered seeing camped near where they had parked the caravan set up a drum kit on stage and unpack instruments. Harlequin, the member of the company nearest in age to the musicians, stepped through the curtain to introduce them.

"Ladies and Gentlemen, for your delectation, all the way from Vadrosnia Poule, for one night only, at great expense, I give you the Posse!"

"The Pussy?" said Milly, "is 'e bein' rude?"

"The Posse – the Posse," said Damask, "shush!"

As the group launched into their first number she realised that there had been no need to shush Milly, the band was loud enough to drown out any competing sound. The drummer created a tremendous racket right from the start and the other two boys, playing a piano accordion and a saxophone in ways that she had never heard them played before, were not to be outdone. Several of the spectators stuck their fingers in their ears, and a few of the more sensitive among them got up and walked out. Alaric was beside himself.

"Get them off, get them off!" he roared, "we're going to loose our audience!"

The cacophony continued for another five minutes until the hall's manager put an end to the session by bringing the curtain down.

"Sorry boys," he said to the indignant musicians, "time is of the essence – our licence doesn't extend beyond eleven, Got to get on with the play."

"Thank the Lord for that," said old Pantalone, "I couldn't have stood much more of it."

"Oh, you don't understand," replied Leandro, "that's the latest thing up on the coast. They call it *Raz*, short for *Raschmusik*. All the bands are into it this year."

"Well they can keep it!"

The play resumed. Both company and audience, somewhat flustered, tried to recapture the atmosphere that had been generated in the first half, but it was an uphill struggle. The assault on their senses that had taken place during the break had put everyone on edge. Damask got the feeling that they were just waiting for something else to go wrong and sure enough it did. The actor know as Zanni, under a cloud for obvious reasons, had mumbled and hiccuped his way through the earlier acts while Alaric glowered. Eventually, in a scene in which nearly everyone was on stage together, he failed to come in on cue.

"Haste thou from the battlefield..." hissed the prompter.

The actors looked round, searching high and low; Zanni was nowhere to be seen. There was a nasty pause.

"Haste thou from the battlefield, my Lord," suddenly declaimed Damask, stepping forward (fortunately she had her soldier's helmet on). "Your army is massing at yonder castle. The Lady Margaret awaits her victorious hero."

The company turned to her in surprise but quickly picked up the baton and carried on; it was unlikely that the audience had even noticed the contretemps. And so for the rest of the performance Damask took the part of a minor earl and even managed to get a few laughs along the way. Milly was left to play the crowd on her own which she did reluctantly but adequately.

The production was rapturously received. After three curtain calls the actors retired glowing with satisfaction and Damask was thumped repeatedly on the back for saving the day, or so they claimed. The Grande Stupendo came forward, smiling benignly.

"My dear young lady, you have hidden talents. As a convincing male impersonator you could become our next Zanni. The position's open if you wish to take it – that rascal has tried my patience once too often. What do you say? – we're off to Komstock tomorrow – three nights."

"I can't come without Milly," said Damask.

Alaric looked doubtful.

"She's very good at make-up," said Damask, "and knows all about costume." (This was stretching things a bit). Milly stood open mouthed as her future was mapped out.

In a matter of minutes all was settled to everyone's satisfaction apart from Milly's and also Severine's who looked put out; this had been her first night in a major role and now her thunder had been thoroughly stolen. Later as they walked back to the campsite through town Milly gave voice to her objections.

"I fought we woz goin' after the Lordship – an' wot about your travellin' man? - an' wot about returnin' the caravan?"

Damask appeared ill at ease.

"Well we don't know where Dando's gone, so we're just as likely to come across him if we stay with this lot as not. And we don't know where Pnoumi is so the same applies."

"An' the gypsy?"

"Oh – well..." she waved her hand vaguely in the air.

Back in camp they were invited to share a meal with some of the other actors. Afterwards Damask made her excuses to Milly.

"You go to bed. I've got someone I want to see – I'll join you later."

Milly nodded resignedly and made her way back to the van. She knew her mistress pretty well by now and was not expecting to set eyes on her any time soon.

"Hi," remarked Damask. She had crossed the field to where the small tents that they had noticed on arrival were pitched. "I really enjoyed your performance this evening."

"Oh yes? - you and who else?" replied a boy with a dark fringe and a long aquiline face. The Posse were sitting around a fitfully flaming fire with their instruments, gloomily extemporising. The accordion player had swapped his squeeze box for a guitar. "We should have guessed our stuff wouldn't go down well in the boon docks."

"Well I thought you were good," said Damask. "I'm Damask by the way."

"How de do. I s'pose we've gotta introduce ourselves now. I'm Winnie – that's Fynn," pointing to a fluffy-haired youth with delicate features and a slightly hooked nose; he looked no more than fifteen, "an' that's Matt, our drummer," this was an oval-faced, bleach-haired boy with a cold hard unsmiling stare, "he hardly ever says anything." The other two nodded in greeting.

"You really liked our stuff? In fact we played *Raz* tonight 'cos we've lost our lead singer although dance music's not exactly our sort of thing. We've actually got our own style – an' our own songs. - when we've got someone to sing them that is. Do you sing?"

"Yes – sort of," said Damask cautiously.

"You want to have a go?"

"Could do."

"Well try this then – it's called *Caroline*," and the boy launched into an uptempo number, speaking the words, while the saxophone provided the tune.

I'd like to bomb you from above,

With a crossbow bolt of love,

Girl o' mine.

I'd like to murder you with kisses,

Then you'll surely know what bliss is,

Caroline.

"Did you write that?" asked Damask

"No, everyone's singing it in Drossi at the moment. The second verse goes:-

I'd like to bind you in a knot,

Just to prove I love you lots,

Girl o' mine.

Then I'll caress you with my kris,

Write my name on your midriff,

Caroline.

Go on, have a go," and he repeated the demonstration. Damask took a deep breath and tentatively combined words and melody in a clear mellow contralto.

"Hey," said Winnie to the others, "get a load of this! Go on – sing it again – you can change *girl* to *boy* and *Caroline* to... er..."

"Peregrine?" suggested Damask.

The piece continued through several more verses, all on the same theme, which she sang after Winnie had provided the words. The performance ended to a chorus of approving whistles.

"How about a frail as our lead?" asked Winnie of the others. This did not go down too well. His mates subsided into an ambivalent silence.

"What happened to your singer?" Damask asked.

"Went a bit crazy on the Paradise Sauce."

"Paradise Sauce?"

"You know – Dr Good's. What? You never heard of Dr Good's Elixir? Laughing Linctus? Cures everything from cold feet to smallpox. Well – for an hour or two at least."

Damask looked around and noticed a small vehicle by the tents, similar in size to the late lamented dog cart.

"Where's your horse?" she asked

"He's the horse," said Winnie pointing at Matt, "after all they *are* his drums. Fynn and I push from behind."

"Where are you from? Where are you going next?"

"Drossi – but the scene's far too crowded there at the moment. Snachet tomorrow – then off to the Kymer. Hey, you want to hear the real McCoy? Come on guys, let's give her a blast."

The boy called Matt got several more drums out of the cart and Fynn picked up his saxophone. Winnie swapped guitar for accordion. A jam session got under way. After about half an hour they paused for a quieter interlude as Winnie played something introspective, contemplative and classical on the guitar ("That's what I'm really into but there's no call for it.") and then flung themselves enthusiastically back into full forte mode.

"Stop that infernal racket!"

"Put a sock in it!"

During a slight lull in the proceedings the other occupants of the field at last managed to make themselves heard.

"Pack it in now boys," came a slightly more conciliatory woman's voice, "it's getting late – we want to go to bed."

The squeeze box died with an expiring groan and the drummer brought his set to a close with a paradiddle and a flourish. Only the saxophone continued on in a minor key, sobbing out its heart into the night until it came to a natural ending. Silence reigned. Milly slept all alone in the caravan that night; Damask did not return.

The next morning the company had girded themselves for the road and were already moving out when Milly walked over to where the Posse were camped.

"Majesty, majesty," she called.

In response movement could be detected inside one of the tents and after about five minutes Damask emerged, somewhat ruffled, adjusting her clothing. She turned and stuck her head back inside.

"Bye bye my soul. See you in Drossi."

There came an unintelligible mumble in reply.

"Wot do you mean *see you in Drossi*?" said Milly as they hurried back to the cat-circus caravan. "I fought we woz sticking wiv this lot now."

"Well," said Damask rather sheepishly, "the Stips are aiming to end up in Drossi next spring, so we will too if we stay with them. We might come across the Posse while we're there – you never know."

Milly cast a cynical look in her direction.

"Anyfink in trousers," she said.

"You don't know what you're missing," said Damask

"Yes I do," replied Milly with a frisson of disgust.

92

For the next few weeks the two girls became members of the acting troop and crisscrossed the plains with them as they followed a tortuous route through the towns on the Levels, gradually making their way towards the delta. Not surprisingly things did not go altogether smoothly. Damask had certainly been flavour of the month after the performance at Millfield, but her credit with the company's rank and file began rapidly to diminish as they became better acquainted. The other actors started to get the impression that she was a show-off, a clever clogs and too big for her boots. Having been put on the payroll, they opined, such a newcomer - and a totally inexperienced one at that - should have displayed a proper humility in the presence of theatrical veterans such as themselves. Instead, she put several people's backs up with her patrician airs, and earned Severine's eternal enmity by being seen coming out of Leandro's (Peter's) caravan in the small hours. There was even a suspicion that she had something going with the Grande Stupendo himself; he certainly seemed very favourably disposed towards her. Zannis usually specialised in valets and jesters but Alaric generously put other roles her way, parts that the company felt should have gone to one of the regulars. However they could not fault her performances; she seemed to have a natural gift for comic timing despite her equal facility for rubbing others up the wrong way. Her companion they looked on more kindly, and were soon happy to hand over responsibility for their make-up to the young girl. Milly should have been pleased to find her skills thus appreciated but instead she spent her days fretting and fuming, convinced they were wasting time and were being diverted from their main purpose of tracking Dando down. Therefore, when, sometime later, Damask announced that she would have to leave the troupe, nearly everybody breathed a sigh of relief.

"Your travellers have been detected," Punchinello told her one evening, "they're on the Northern Drift between the Lap-of-the-Mother and Formile – an elderly man with a chestnut horse and a large grey dog, and a young man and woman with a dappled pony, the boy dark, the girl fair. But there's a fourth with them – a red headed fellow – spends his time hunting."

"The Northern Drift? Where's that?" asked Damask.

"It's a road running south/north up among the hills – I've occasionally heard it called the Way-of-the-Shades; not many people use it apart from pilgrims – it's got a bad reputation – pretty lawless country. But if you want to rendezvous with them you'd better head westward and follow the Burple upstream – downstream it meets the Kymer at Sassanara. If you're quick you'll maybe get to Formile ahead of them."

"Well, I don't know..." said Damask reluctantly.

"It might be as well to warn them not to go any further north. People travel that way to visit Rostan's shrine at Toymerle – not many at this time of year of course – but those that have gone recently haven't returned. I've heard stories about ransom notes being received."

"Well, I'm not really sure..." began Damask again, but Milly, who had been standing by, opened her eyes wide in concern at this last piece of information and if it had been at all possible she would have turned as white as a sheet.

"Oh majesty!" she cried, "do you fink 'e's in danger?"

"No, of course not," said Damask, but there was a note of uncertainty in her voice.

"I'll get some food in," said Milly, suddenly frantically busy, "we c'n go tomorrow mornin'." Her absolute determination to leave brooked no opposition and her uncompromising conviction that no alternative existed seemed to settle the matter.

They hitched up Pnoumi's horse, which someone along the way had told them was called Shingai, said their goodbyes, and, with a hastily hand-drawn map sketched by a helpful Punchinello, set out to rendezvous with the River Burple and follow its course against the flow, a route which would take them away from the plains and into the mountains.

The road beside the rushing, tumbling river was narrow and sometimes very steep. Shingai had trouble hauling the caravan up the precipitous inclines. Damask and Milly got out and walked on either side in order to lighten the load, but progress was slow. Milly bit her nails down to the quick, hoping against hope as they rounded each bend that this time they might come in sight of the town they were making for. Damask paced beside the caravan in a gloomy reverie, becoming more and more convinced as each mile took them further from what she thought of as civilisation, that she was doing the wrong thing. At last they saw buildings and a bridge ahead; Formile lay on the other side of the stream.

The little burg contained only one establishment that could claim the status of an inn. The girls found somewhere to park their vehicle and then went to enquire after the travellers at the Jolly Waggoners. The news they were given was exactly what they did not want to hear. Yes, said the innkeeper, he recognised the description of those they were after and especially of the horses. Yes, they had stayed there but they had up sticks and left over a week ago. Where had they gone? He could not say. One of his customers had chatted to them in the dining room he believed; he would try and find him for them. Damask and Milly sat twiddling their thumbs until, sometime later, the landlord returned with another man in tow.

"I talked to one of your friends," this individual told them, "a very pleasant young gentleman. The party seemed intent on travelling north. I told the older gent that the passes would be shut at this time of year, but when they set out a day or two later they went by the Northern Drift. If they've gone to the Voice at Toymerle they'll be coming back the same way I should think, although there are a couple of tracks going east further along – one comes out of the hills about level with Drossi, the other not so far up - but they're both pretty hazardous and particularly difficult for horses."

"This Toymerle," said Damask, "we heard that people have been disappearing who've gone that way. Is that true?"

The two men glanced at each other.

"Certainly not," said the innkeeper emphatically, "no truth in that at all – it's just someone spreading malicious rumours – trying to ruin our trade. Although Rostan isn't worshipped around here we do our best by the pilgrims and they show their gratitude in the most practical manner. We see that the road is kept safe."

The other man nodded vigorously in agreement, but Damask thought they both looked rather uncomfortable, almost shifty in fact.

"Well thank you," she replied, "we may wait for a day or two to see if our friends return or we may decide to follow them. Can we eat in your hostelry while we're here?"

"Certainly, certainly and we have some comfortable rooms if you wish to stay."

"That won't be necessary – we've got own accommodation."

"You won't get your caravan up the Northern Drift," put in the second man suddenly, "far too narrow – it's little more than a foot path."

"Oh – I see. Well thank you."

Damask and Milly partook of some excellent food at the road house and then walked back to the parking lot having also been given food for thought.

"I d'n't believe 'im," said Milly, "we've gotta go after 'em – 'for they gets into trouble."

"I believed them about the caravan," said Damask, "when you saw what the road was like along the river."

"Well we've gotta go after 'em," said Milly, "wiv or wivout the caravan."

"I'm not going without the caravan or the horse," said Damask, "remember what happened to the dog cart."

"Can't we leave 'em wiv the inn people?"

"I wouldn't trust them further than I could throw them, and besides they'd expect to be paid."

"Well, I'm goin' to go after 'em."

"Milly! - you can't go alone!"

"Why not?"

"You just can't."

They reached the caravan in silence and it was not until they were climbing into their bunks that Milly spoke up once more.

"I'm goin' to go after 'em tomorrow."

"No Milly."

"Yes."

"Milly, you're just a kid – you can't go wandering around in the wild on your own, I won't let you."

"Do I b'long to you then?"

"No of course not."

"I b'long to myself?"

"Yes of course."

"Then I'm goin'"

There was another long silence.

"I won't wait for you," said Damask.

"See if I care!"

The next morning Damask took Milly into the town's shopping centre, neither of them inclined to talk, and bought her some warm clothes, a satchel and a small knife. They acquired provisions from the Jolly Waggoners to place in the satchel and then Damask divided what remained of her money between them. She put her arms around the little girl, briefly hugging her.

"Tell him I'll catch up with him sooner or later," she said. "Tell him... no, never mind."

She swung Milly round until she was facing towards the northern perimeter of the town, gave her a slight push in that direction and watched as she walked away. After that, trying to ignore the fact that she was feeling both conscious-stricken and blameworthy, she returned to the caravan, hitched up Shingai and set off back along the road they had already travelled, heading down once more towards the plains and the Great River.

The west wind on the field,
You and me my love,
We move in the same way.

Chapter five

"Come, please come – I need to talk to you. Please Annie."

His eyes were dark shadowy pools with a glint of moonlight on the surface. The stark monotones of the lunar ascendancy gave his features a desperate angularity that they never displayed in daylight. Ann got reluctantly to her feet. "It be too dangerous as things are," she murmured. Dando took hold of her hand and tried to lead her into the trees. When she resisted he repeated his plea, "Please, Annie, please."

She reached up and pulled his head down to her so she could whisper in her ear. "If we want to be together," she confided, "we'll have to change things so they won't notice."

"Well ok – but how?"

"I c'n make them stay asleep."

"You can?" (too loudly).

"Shhhhhhhhh."

Ann sat down cross legged, facing the comatose men, and began swaying slightly from side to side like a snake charmer, meanwhile softly singing something that sounded like a lullaby. Her hands made gestures in the air which were halfway between beating time and the miming of a caress. When she came to the end of the song she sat still for a moment or two before getting up and saying in a normal voice "They won't wake 'til I break the spell." The two moved away from the fire, Dando glancing sideways at Ann with a mixture of scepticism and awe.

"How do I know it's for real?" he whispered.

She was indignant. "You try an' wake 'em! I know what I be a-doin'. Dadda taught I that years ago. They'll only come to themselves without the gifted individual's assistance if there's a crash, like a clap of thunder, or if danger threatens."

"Oh, right."

He led her a little way up the stream they were camped beside to a flat grassy area. Ann saw that horse blankets had already been spread on the ground.

"You're s'posed to be on watch," she said.

"I can watch from here."

"What d'you want to talk to me about?"

"This," and he tried to put his arms around her. She pushed him away. "No."

"Why Annie?"

"It be too dangerous."

"I don't understand."

"I'm not good for you."

"You're always saying that but it doesn't make any sense."

"Dadda tol' I - She be jealous. The Culdee sh'n't marry. She bring about my ma's death."

"But you're not the Culdee."

"I don' know," she said miserably.

Again he tried to embrace her and again she fended him off.

"Sit, at least," he said, pulling her down onto the blankets and placing himself close beside her. "Do you realise," pushing his nose into her hair, "your name is inside mine – D–An–do – it's sort of symbolic." She shook her head vigorously, softly whipping his face with her tresses. He drew back and laughed. "You don't need to worry about that old phony – Aigea, or whatever she likes to be called. I've got her number – I know how to handle her now."

"Be quiet - you don' realise what you're sayin'!" and then, "There's somethin' *I* wan' to tell *you* – two things."

"Oh, OK – go ahead."

"Dadda tol' I a story about the boss; about how he took a wife from our people..."

Dando interrupted. "Yes I know about that. It's you and me only a generation earlier."

"An' they had a little chil', an' then the woman got drownded in the pool an' the chil' disappeared."

"Yes I know that."

"Well Dadda think he know what happen to the chil'."

"Go on."

"There be a goatherd. He took in a boy - one o' ours – not long after the woman died, an' brought he up. Dadda think that that boy be the boss's chil'. It be Foxy."

"Foxy?"

"Yes."

Dando scratched his head, an amazed expression on his face. "You mean that Foxy...?"

"Yes."

"And therefore Foxy would be..."

"Yes."

"Bugger me!" In his astonishment he borrowed one of Damask's more common expletives. "Does he know?"

"No."

A delighted and mischievous smile spread across Dando's face. Ann looked at him nervously. "You mu'n't tell 'e."

"Why not?"

"'Acos... just 'acos."

Dando grinned, but seeing the look on her face his grin faded. "What's the matter?" Ann shook her head; a dark shadow seeming to have enveloped her.

"What's the matter?" he said again, and then fiercely, "has someone been bothering you?"

"No – it's not that."

"You said you had two things to tell me." She laid a hand on his arm and gazed anxiously up at him, all her soul in her eyes.

"Your dadda be dead, my love."

"Dead! What do you mean?"

"He be dead, the boss – shot wiv an arrow."

"Where? - How?"

"He were comin' after 'ee; someone shot he on the northern path."

"Coming after me?" Dando looked stunned, trying to take this in. After a pregnant pause he asked, "how do you know?"

"Foxy tol' I."

"Who was it?" Ann did not reply.

"Do you know who did it?" She remained silent and turned away. Suddenly he had to have an answer

"Ann - look at me – who was it? Who did it? Do you know?" With an unreadable expression she glanced sideways at him and then nodded almost imperceptibly. Dando, always a bit slow on the uptake, frowned in puzzlement for a moment, then, managing to put two and two together, made four for once in his life.

"It was him wasn't it!" he cried, "it was Foxy!"

Ann, her eyes full of tears, nodded again. Dando's whole body went rigid. He blanched, then opened his mouth to speak, to say something vital, but for a full minute was unable to articulate. Then he burst out with, "He's going to pay for this! I'll kill him!" He seemed about to leap to his feet and carry out the threat there and then. In fact he did scramble up and felt for his sword but realised he had left it back at the camp, lying beside his bed. Ann tried to catch hold of his arm in order to drag him down again.

"No, sweetheart, no." Instead she hung on to his leg as he panted from fury and shock, preventing him from leaving. After a while his breath slowed and he stopped trying to pull away.

"Listen, sweetheart," she said, "you mun take it no further. Your dadda he kill my dadda and then Foxy, he kill his own father. Let that be an end to it. He be your brother, Dando."

In a series of vivid flashes Dando saw images of both the Dan and Foxy. He saw the loving parent he had known during his infancy, then he saw the imposing leader sitting in the position of power at banquets, religious ceremonies and inter-family parleys. He saw Foxy as he had looked five years earlier when he had first set eyes on him at the Justification. He saw the Dan as he had appeared in the Hall of Oaths in Gateway and as he had last seen him in the Dans' chapel. He pictured the devoted father who had played with him as a child and then the one who had turned irrevocably away. He saw Foxy the archer with his great bow pulled back, an arrow fitted to the string, a marksman's expression of total concentration on his face. He stood looking down sideways, biting his lip. At last he fell to his knees and his shoulders slumped in acquiescence.

"Oh Annie," he said.

Ann, also kneeling, put her arms around him and he buried his face in her shoulder. She stroked his hair which had grown back sufficiently to cover his scalp in curls. "Don't tell 'e," she whispered.

A long while later Ann reminded him, "It be time to break the spell."

They walked back to the camp hand in hand.

"Will you come tomorrow?"

"Not while I be on watch."

"Well, the next night?"

"Maybe."

Ann stood over the two sleepers who appeared not to have moved a muscle since the charm was cast and clicked her fingers. "You c'n wake he now," she said, pointing towards Tallis, and went to her bed.

As the land of hills and lakes through which they were travelling came to an end, the road began to rise in a purposeful manner. From this point on, however far the path descended on one stretch it always climbed to a greater extent on the next. Rushing streams replaced the still waters of the meres and rewarded Foxy with some sizeable fish. The hillsides became bare and scree covered. The wayfarers were not keeping an account of the distance travelled but were probably averaging little more than ten miles a day. This was because there were times when they made no progress at all as on some days Tallis was unable to continue. Either through weariness or lack of willpower the older man had periods when he could not even rise from where he had bedded down for the night. Hours would be spent in complete enervation. But then the next morning, although apparently still exhausted, he would be prepared to carry on. As they gained in height, however, his vigour seemed to return and he looked eagerly towards the mountains that stood like a wall across their path.

It was Dando's watch. Once again he woke Ann and once again the spell for sleep was cast. On the blankets that he spread she allowed him to sit next to her with an arm about her shoulders, but when he tried to become more amorous she repelled him.

"No, no – I tol' 'ee – no."

"But why Annie?"

"It's her – she be jealous – she could hurt 'ee. You don' realise. Have a mind for what happen when we were little. Back then Dadda knew she want to do 'ee harm but he d'n't fully understan' why." Dando remembered the grotesque totem that had lurked at the rear of Tom's workshop, long since destroyed. "We've left her behind surely. She's back there in the valley – not out here in the world."

"She be greater than you think. She rule other places besides Deep Hallow."

"Listen Annie – if there's a risk I'll take it. On my head be it – it's not up to you."

"But what do 'ee wan'?"

"You know what I want; I want to make love to you – the whole hog, the full works. It's what's meant to happen – you know it – I couldn't be more sure."

"But what about babies?" This was a last desperate throw in her attempt to postpone the inevitable; she knew she could not hold out against him for much longer. But Dando had an answer ready. Not for nothing had he been an Outrider cadet in Gateway for two years. Whilst, at that time, he had strictly maintained his celibacy his fellow cadets were busy having their way with the local nibbler women. It was commonly asserted that such unions between the races always proved infertile, but secretly everyone knew that this was not the case. To maintain the deception and avoid such unpleasantness as forced abortions or surreptitious infanticide one had to take precautions. At the start of his first year, along with his cronies, Dando had been handed the items by which he could protect himself although he had never had cause to use them. "Oh, leave that to me," he said patting his pocket where the condoms were stashed, "you don't need to worry."

"Take your clothes off Annie."

"But it be cold."

"Please, I want to see you."

"Well, what about you? I will if you will."

"Oh – ok."

They began divesting themselves of several layers of not terribly fragrant garments, hopping on one leg and then the other, scattering their cast-offs round about them, until they stood naked in the frigid air. Ann wrapped her arms around herself, teeth chattering.

"Come on," said Dando, already aroused, "lie down – we can get under the blankets. Now then – we're going to do this in a civilised manner."

At this they were both overcome by mirth (*I'm laughing!* thought Ann in amazement) following which Dando started tentatively to explore the girl's body. She was at first reluctant to allow him these liberties and administered a sharp little slap to his naughty hands, but he turned on her such a comically pleading look, like a puppy begging for a treat, that she could not help but laugh again, and then of course she was done for: with a sigh and a shrug she let him go where he wished. When she began to return the compliment and touch him in his more intimate places he quivered like a nervous young colt and captured her hands. Defensively he held them immobile for some time before carrying them to his lips. He kissed her fingertips then gently folded them in towards the palm, after which he released her while conveying earnestly with his eyes alone that he placed himself entirely at her mercy. Once more she laughed. Dando making love she found irresistibly funny and therefore irresistible.

At the start Dando was careful and considerate. "Is this right? Am I doing it right? I'm not hurting you am I?"

"No, no – don' 'ee worry."

But after a while he found his body had a will of it's own and he was swept along helplessly either to triumph or disaster. It did not seem to matter if the sex went wrong. They collapsed into giggles and tried again or else just lay in each others arms, stoned on happiness. What could not be denied was that by the time the light of morning started to creep into the eastern sky, the thing was a fait acomplis; they had both of them lost their virginity with all that that might entail.

Heading into the mountains the travellers soon gained sufficient altitude to look back over the lands they had traversed from a high vantage point. To the younger members of the party the distant view emphasised the fact that, even at the slow pace they were being forced to adopt, they had come a vast way from their beginnings, and if they ever wanted to go back it would be a journey of weeks rather than days to effect a return. Foxy in particular felt a sharp pang of home-sickness. As he stared towards his point of origin he was made acutely aware of something that up to now had been just a vague ignored abstraction – that such a return might never be possible.

On one particular evening clouds were louring as they made camp; the sky had taken on a greenish tinge and seemed to be threatening bad weather. They tucked themselves, plus the horses and the dog, under an overhanging cliff in what was virtually a cave, to get as much shelter as possible. All night long the gale raged but they were safely out of the blast. When they awoke the next morning the world had been transformed. In previous days they had experienced a few sleety flurries, a smidgen of hail, but now they opened their eyes onto their first heavy snowfall of the winter. The wind had died and the dawn sunlight tinged the brilliant scene a delicate pink. It did not even feel cold. With a whoop Foxy leapt out from the shelter and almost disappeared into a feet-deep drift. The others followed more cautiously, treading the transforming whiteness that had blanketed the landscape. Dando scooped up a handful of snow and threw it at Ann. In no time at all a snowball fight was under way; even Tallis joined in. Later they bound cloths around the horses hooves to prevent them slipping on the ice and then set out, the knight leading. He seemed to have an instinct for picking the easiest and safest route, the places where the snow was not too deep to impede progress. By the end of the day a thaw had set in but they all realised that this fall was just a rehearsal for what might await them in the future.

Every other night when he was supposed to be on watch, Dando woke Ann, she wove her sleeping spell and he led her away to make love. The conditions, below freezing for the most part, necessitated the construction of a nest with cloaks and blankets in which they could snuggle together. An hour or two of bliss followed. Then Ann was always the one to remind Dando that the time had come to rouse Tallis. She frequently had to bring home to him that unless he did so they would betray themselves, for to her chagrin her lover seemed completely careless of the consequences should they be found out. In actual fact he was purely and simply drunk with joy and could hardly be held responsible for his actions. To Dando it appeared that his passion for Ann had moved onto a higher plane: he was walking permanently two feet above the ground and felt that each and every love song ever written (the happy ones, that is) had been written for him. It was almost impossible not to reveal his exultation to Tallis and Foxy; he wanted to shout it to the world, wanted everyone and everybody to share it with him. As it was he could not even share it with the person closest to him. His dearest wish was that Ann should join him in his personal seventh heaven but sadly this was not to be. She was his partner in the ecstasy of the moment but then fell away into a fog of anxiety and self-reproach. He knew the things that were concerning her but considered that the strength of their devotion should negate such scruples; after all, *love conquers all* don't they say; surely everything could not help but turn out all right.

Because Ann was worried that Dando would give them away she acted towards him with coldness and hostility during the day, refusing even to meet his eye, hoping to put a damper on his ardour and to divert any suspicions. The thought of Foxy discovering what was going on was a nightmare that haunted her every waking moment; she hardly dared imagine what his reaction might be. She also knew she was doing exactly what Dadda had warned her not to do. And of course there was the spell for sleep - she was misusing it. When Tom had taught her the technique (she had been very young) he emphasised that it was to be employed as an aid to healing wounds, both mental and physical; he had not intended it as a cover-up for deceit. She felt ashamed. Yet despite her concerns, when Dando came for her, always a hour or two after she had lain down, she never refused to go with him; she loved him far too much to turn him away, and besides, what he wanted she also wanted, the happiness she experienced when they soared together was worth all the angst.

Sometimes as they lay side by side, post coitus, they fell to talking. Along with trying to share some of her worries Ann listened to Dando's confidences and where appropriate offered advice.

"I've been having some funny dreams," he explained, "but not like I used to have in the valley. These seem to be put in my brain from somewhere else"

"Tell me."

"Well there's one that happens in a huge field – you're there – you're going to show me something on the other side of a low hill but I always wake up before I find out what it is. Then there's one in an enormous dark hall – there's a sort of lord on a throne. He keeps asking me questions about a treasure – he seems to think I'm going to bring it back to him. But it's Master Tallis who's looking for a treasure, isn't it, not me."

"What's he like, this man on the throne?"

"I can't see him properly but he's got a voice that sounds like the wind, and the hall is full of winds."

Ann thought, firstly, of the sky deity and then of the destination for which they were bound, this shrine of Rostan, the God-of-the-Core that they had been told about. "You shou'n't go to this oracle place," she said.

"Why on earth not?"

"'Acos there be somethin' about 'ee, my bonny lad, that makes them angry and afraid, the ones that are spoken of as immortals."

"Oh no – not again. Why is everybody always trying to nanny me? I'm not a baby you know."

She forbore to make the obvious comment.

Another time as they cuddled in the small hours, sharing the warmth of their bodies, Ann said, "This Key that the knight be a-lookin' for, it mus' be the same one Dadda tol' I about."

"Why do you think that?"

"Well he say it were stole by a powerful wizard, jus' like in the knight's story. He tell me it rule the years an', when turned, brings in each new age. In the old days it was believed that if the time for a turning was missed the world would get sick and maybe start to die. Well, now that ha' happened - no one know where it be any more an' the time for the next turning ha' come an' gone. He tol' me he think it be comin' true - what they believed."

"Really? The world seems all right to me apart from the fact that the weather has been really weird over the last few months."

"No, there *is* a difference. When spring come there don' be so much blossom on the trees an' the birds sing less. When did you las' hear a cuckoo?"

"I can't remember."

"An' those long-distant flyers that goo on journeys, they don' come back no more, an' creatures babes an' people's babes be borned poorly like as not, ha'n't you noticed?"

"No, not really." Dando thought back to his last impressions of the valley, gathered the previous summer. Yes perhaps, after all, it did appear that nowadays nature had turned parsimonious and was rationing her gifts: one cuckoo per spring if you were lucky and fish in the river that made news because of their rarity. He remembered tales of when it was nothing to hear four cuckoos calling at the same time and if you lay in a field ten skylarks would be singing overhead. Sometimes Potto had reminisced about the time when, under the water, fish had swum in shoals and over it had flown multitudinous flocks of migrating birds. In those days every stretch of country had had a black speck above it, high in the vault of the heavens, ready to stoop and come hurtling down, a thunderbolt with talons, while foxes had shouted hoarsely under every hill and the woods were sonorous with owls. And the flowers – oh the wild flowers! – fields so full of poppies that they seemed to be running with blood!

"You may be right," he said.

"I think your dadda's baby that die were a sign."

"Well let's hope that Master Tallisand finds the Key – then it can be turned by someone and everything will be put back to the way it once was."

"But not by you!"

"No, of course not – why should you think I'd be involved?"

"I don' know but..." and she went on to recount much of what Tom had told her during their last days together concerning the future destiny of the human race and the curse under which he believed the world was labouring. "...an' he say that if it ever be got rid of from the earth – he mean the Key - then the world'll be so happy that even the stones will start to sing."

"You could do that."

"Me?"

"Yes – you've been priested." They were lying together one evening after she had woven the spell and she was beginning to think that perhaps the task could be shared.

"No, I couldn't."

"Why?"

"I can't sing, remember, anymore than stones can."

"Anyone can sing."

"I can't."

"Aaaaaaahhh." Ann sang a note.

"Arghhhhhhh," responded Dando, making a noise rather like a parrot being strangled.

"Mmm. Do you trust me?"

"Yes."

"P'raps I could mend it if you'd let me. Do you want I to try?"

"Yes please."

"I never done anythin' like this before."

"I trust you."

"Well – take off your woolly then. Open your shirt."

When they stood breast to breast Ann's head fitted neatly under Dando's chin. She laid her ear against his chest, listening. "Help me Dadda," she prayed

Yes, it was surely her inherited powers that told her that there was something out of kilter within the boy's body that a slight correction might be able to put right.

"Sit down," she commanded. Dando sat on a log. Ann put her left hand round the back of his skull and her right hand on his throat. It was at this point that her father would have invoked the Mother Goddess - that was always a part of the ritual - but Ann did not wish to attract the attention of any of the immortals. Instead she whispered again "Help me Dadda," and shut her eyes.

Dando waited patiently to see what, if anything, was going to happen. He was just beginning to think that there would be no discernible outcome to this witchery when, for a moment, Ann's right hand seemed to glow red hot. He could not help flinching away but made no determined attempt to escape. Then the pain was gone and a warm tingling sensation started in his neck, spread to his chest and up into his head. He waited, expecting more, but instead Ann said "That be it," and released him.

"That's it? That's all there is to it?"

"Aaaaaaahhh," sang Ann and looked at him invitingly.

"Aaaaaaahhh," sang Dando.

"Aaaaaaahhh," on a different note.

"Aaaaaaahhh. Pyr be merciful! I can sing!" He seized Ann and whirled her up into the air, dropping her down into a bear hug, "thankyou! thankyou!" and then gave voice operatically to the full extent of his lungs, "I CAN SING!"

"Shhhhhhhhh!"

"Ha! You mean to tell me your spells don't work? Pull the other one!"

"They won't if you make that hullabaloo."

"Annie – you're a marvel!" Ann glowed.

All the next day pink marks resembling four Nablan digits were visible on Dando's throat, much to Tallis' and Foxy's bemusement.

Ann taught Dando to weave the sleeping spell. She instructed him on the focusing of the mind, in the same way that Tom had once done when teaching her, and explained the process by which one blanks out distractions. She showed him how the hand movements should be performed, how the body should move and how to know when your objective has been fully achieved.

"It hardly matter what you sing 'cept it mus' be quiet an' restful, somethin' mothers sing to their babes be best. If the ones you're tryin' to spellbind don' be asleep you hev to do the singin' inside your head – it be a bit harder."

Oh can ye sew cushions was Ann's favourite lullaby but Dando went back to his own nursery days and tried *Rock-a-bye baby, Mockingbird* or the haunting *How many miles to Belturbet* – all rhymes Doll had sung to him when he was a little boy. After a few nights of practice Ann yielded her place to him by the sleeping men and with an encouraging smile gestured for him to proceed. He sat down and brought his consciousness to bear on a single point as he had occasionally done spontaneously when out alone in the valley. Thought slowed and almost ceased. He began to hum, the movements of his body becoming a natural extension of the music. After what seemed a huge time lapse he felt a hand on his shoulder.

"You can stop now my love – it be in place. Don' 'ee send *yourself* to sleep."

Later Ann said to him, "It come easy to 'ee. It's a shame 'ee don' hev the real power – you could hev been a great conjur. I c'n teach 'ee some other bewitchments, things Dadda shew me, things anyone with a quiet min' can do."

Dando thought back to a day when his mentor had stepped into the breach.

"It was Tom who first taught me how to concentrate my thoughts – that time when I was being bothered by spooks – there's a way to shut them out – he understood all about it. I hardly ever see them now, but I could if I wanted to."

"You know," said Ann, "lately I sometime feel I hear Dadda speaking to me. Do you think that be possible?"

"Well – who can tell."

It was at this stage of their journey that, for several nights, the travellers got the impression that they were being shadowed by wolves. Each evening they heard their eerie cries away off in the darkness. They never actually caught sight of the animals and as they climbed higher they appeared to leave them behind. They were now not far off the winter solstice. Tallis looked back anxiously at the sun where it hung so low in the southern sky, even at midday. Was darkness going to permanently envelop them? Would the Lord-of-Heaven, who had the day-star in his care, fail to ensure its return?

"It's said that he goes into the Underworld at this time of year to look for the Wayward son," he remarked.

"Yes," said Dando, "at home now we'd be choosing the Year-Child to tempt him back again. They'd be putting up decorations and sending out invitations all over the valley. The kitchens would be getting food in to prepare for the feast." He suddenly felt rather sad that he was not going to be there for this year's celebration.

"What form do your ceremonies take?" said Tallis

"Well it starts with the children, the ones twelve and under that is; it's really their festival. It's something we used to look forward to all summer..."

How clearly he remembered being part of it as a youngster. An hour or two before midnight on the shortest day of the year the smaller children, having been woken from sleep, would gather in a bedroom behind closed doors. There, with the help of one of the mothers and with great merriment, they would deck themselves out in all manner of finery, tinsel and streamers. Ivy and mistletoe would be wound into wreaths and garlands along with any other green and growing thing that they had been able to gather during expeditions earlier in the day. On the stroke of midnight the doors were flung open and they would issue forth, torches in hand, and in their midst, born on a litter in the place of honour, the youngest of them, preferably a baby of the year just ending. A strange silent house awaited, apparently abandoned, doors and windows flung open to admit the cold heavy darkness. Then one of the revellers, in a clear voice. would proclaim the joyful news - "Behold a child is born!" An answer would be given out of the apparent desolation in a lower more subdued key, "Hope of the world." Straightway a carol would strike up and the procession would move from room to room lighting lamps and lanterns, shutting out the night, restoring warmth and brightness. Like pale ghosts the older members of the household would emerge from the shadows and shower gifts on the baby and his entourage. All the shrines in the house would be visited and the child presented to each in turn. Dead candles would be rekindled and another joyful hymn sung. The Dan would give his blessing. Finally the company would sweep into the great hall. The Yule log which had been smouldering angrily under piles of dust and ashes would be raked clear and would burst fiercely into life. Rows of steaming salvers would be carried from the kitchens, the boards would be loaded to groaning and the feasting would begin.

At the age of thirteen Dando was no longer qualified to play his part with the youngsters in the bedroom. To be out in the dark empty house instead of with the gay company inside the sleeping quarters affected him strangely. Supposing one year the door opened and behind it was no Year Child but just coldness and silence? To let winter into the stronghold even for an hour or two seemed a dangerous practice, and, who knew nowadays, if Lord Pyr would deign to drive the malevolent season out from beneath the roofs of this particular valley?

"Yes, we do somethin' like that at the inn," said Foxy. "Every year they get in a good crowd. A lot o' 'em drink theyselves unner the table – you should hear the singin'!"

"Well we'll have to have our own little celebration," said Tallis. "When is the due date do you think?"

"Five days to goo," said Foxy. No one asked him how he knew this and in fact when the significant day arrived, celebrating the solstice was the last thing on their minds.

Someone ascending a hillside often gets the impression that the summit is well within reach when in fact it is still a great way off. This was the experience of the wayfarers as they penetrated deeper into the mountainous fastness. They saw peaks ahead, apparently quite near, but when the path reached what they thought was the final crest they found that over it a further climb awaited. On one occasion, topping a ridge, they discovered that a wide defile, one might almost have called it a glen, stood between themselves and the mountain proper. This was a discouraging sight but also intriguing because, below them, tucked between the hill they stood on and the heights ahead, were obvious signs of human habitation. A sizable village composed of low-roofed buildings stood in the midst of a series of corrals, in one of which they could see a flock of sheep and in another some spectacularly horned cattle. Their route was going to take them through the middle of this settlement built for the most part of timber, pearly-grey with age. In the centre, rising above the other roofs, stood a more substantial structure, probably a temple or church. As they descended, some figures came out of the first house they came to and stood barring the way.

"Halt strangers," a man cried, holding up his hand, "where are you bound?"

Foxy unslung his bow and pulled an arrow from his quiver. Dando and Ann did the same.

"We travel north," said Tallis, "do not seek to detain us."

"Do you go to the Voice at Toymerle?"

"Yes, that is our intention."

"In that case you would be well advised to change your plans."

"Where we choose to go is our business," said Tallis. "All we ask is free passage through your village."

"Those who have travelled north recently have not returned, while lodging with us here in Labour-in-Vain we have most of the shrine's acolytes. I would suggest, before you pass on, you listen to what they have to say."

"For my part I would advise you to get out of the road and let us through," said Tallis, putting his hand to his sword. "We have no time to talk."

"If you go any further you could be sealing your own death warrant."

The men stood stolidly in the path and gave no indication that they had any intention of moving. "The way is forbidden," shouted someone from the back.

"P'raps we ought to allow these *acolytes* or whatever they're called a chance to put their case," said Dando the conciliator and earned angry glances from both Foxy and Tallis. "It wouldn't hurt to hear their story," he persisted.

The villagers' spokesman apparently decided to try appeasement. "We mean you no harm," he interjected, looking in Dando's direction. "We can offer you a meal and maybe a bed for the night if you'll let our guests explain matters."

Despite this attempt at peacemaking neither Tallis nor Foxy showed any willingness to change their stance or hide their distrust and there things might have stalled if something had not happened to interrupt the stalemate. A horseman came galloping through the village from a northerly direction and reined to a halt in a swirl of dust.

"The Cheetah and a large group of his men have left the shrine," he cried. "They went east and then turned down the Northern Drift – I shadowed them as far as I could. They'll be taking the Ixat road to the plains I shouldn't wonder. It looked like a raiding party. If you want to put the plan into operation now's the hour. You could be in charge and ready to defend the place by the time they return."

"In that case we'd better get moving," said the man who up to that moment had been blocking the wanderers' passage. "You Evan - you report to the chief. Put out the word," and turning to his companions, "get everyone back to Bryn's. Tell them to bring their weapons."

The group scattered in all directions. Tallis and his party were left standing in the road, completely forgotten. They stared at each other in mystification and then moved cautiously forward. As they penetrated the settlement people emerged from houses on either side and ran to and fro on various errands but nobody took a blind bit of notice of the travellers. They reached the centre of the little burg and stopped to look around.

"Don't you think we ought to find out what all this is about?" said Dando. "After all – it might be important – for us I mean."

"There be the church," said Ann pointing across the town square towards a large building on the other side. "It be one o' his." Outside the house-of-worship a group of people in two differing types of clerical garb were talking. They appeared to have emerged in reaction to the heightened activity in the village.

"P'raps they'll be able to help us," said Dando and walked over. Tallis and Foxy followed reluctantly as an elderly dried-up little man detached himself from the group and came towards them smiling. Dando considered it was not his place to be their mouthpiece and deferred to Tallis. The man seemed about to ask a question but Tallis pre-empted him.

"We are intending to travel to the Rock-God's shrine at Toymerle," he said, "have you anything to say on the matter?"

"Oh you mustn't do that, no no, not if you value your lives," replied the ancient, "it's a den of thieves now. Bandits attacked us there back in the summer, drove our poor clergy out of the sanctuary and kidnapped Bishop Cadman. You certainly mustn't go. They've occupied the place and are using it as a base for their evil doings. Any travellers in that direction are waylaid. They rob and kill them or hold them to ransom if they think someone might pay for their release. They've taken possession of the Holy of Holies and are committing all sorts of blasphemies and sacrilege so we've been told." "Your clergy," asked Tallis, "are they the ones that serve the oracle?"

"Yes that's right. Since the raid they've been forced to live down here and throw themselves on the mercy of the sky-god's priests. We're managing the best we can and waiting for the day when the townsfolk of Labour-in-Vain retake the shrine. They're on our side you see because it's important to them. They make a good living by being on the pilgrim route. We've promised to reimburse them, to give a reward to anyone taking part, once the treasure cave has been recaptured."

"Treasure cave?" Tallis and Foxy both pricked up their ears. Tallis was reminded of the particular treasure he was in search of while Foxy thought of money to finance the buying of guns.

"But surely," said Dando, "the robbers will have taken any treasure?"

"We don't believe so. To penetrate the defences of the cave is nigh on impossible without knowledge and we've heard they've been putting some poor people to the question to get at the secret. That means they haven't yet found a way in."

"Are your priests inside the church?" asked Tallis. "May we enter?"

"Well..." Their informant's friendly attitude seemed suddenly to vanish. "Yes - you may – but not her," pointing at Ann, "women are not allowed."

"But in the sky god's churches surely women are permitted to sit at the side?" said Dando.

"Some women – but not her sort."

Ann appeared to understand the other's hostility. She drew her cloak closer around her and turned away.

"If she can't enter I'm not going in either," said Dando, "I'll stay here with her."

"No you won't," interjected Foxy in a threatening manner.

"I be all right," said Ann. "You goo. I'll jus' set here an' take care of the dog an' the horses." She was adamant that she would be none the worse if they left her behind.

The little man seemed satisfied that an awkward situation had been resolved and was again all smiles. "I'm called Gopher, because that's what I do," he said eagerly, "I'll show you round."

Within they discovered that the interior of the church had been turned into a dormitory. Mattresses were ranged along each wall and various personal possessions were scattered haphazardly across the floor. It was only at the far end where an image of the god stood almost roof high that the building was still being used for worship. A man in a dark habit approached them.

"This is Father Sion," said the Gopher, " Prelate of the Chamber of Audience. These foreigners wish to meet the keepers of the shrine, my Lord."

"Oh yes?" said the cleric, "and what is your business?"

"I believe your order is famous for tending an oracle," said Tallis on a note of suppressed excitement, "which I've heard described as a Voice – the Voice of none other than the *God-of-Fire*, otherwise known as the *Lord-of-the-Core*. In all my travels I have never come across such a thing before. I would dearly like to consult this augur if you could explain to me how it is done. I have ample available funds if a fee is required."

The priest, gimlet eyed, looked down his nose at Tallis.

"I'm afraid you've come at just the wrong time. The Voice does not move around at our convenience – it is tied to the underground flue from which issues what is known as the Breath. It is only in that particular place that the *conveyor* - the name we give to someone who takes on the role of intermediary - is inspired to speak prophecies or answer questions, and that place is being held at this very moment by a bandit known as the Cheetah and his men. I'm sorry I can't be more helpful. Of course you could always travel up to Toymerle on the chance that the robbers will let you into the underground chamber out of the goodness of their hearts. They might if you ask nicely enough."

Tallis realised that behind the freezing politeness he was dealing with a very angry man and that some of that anger was being directed towards himself for want of a more legitimate target.

"But aren't you going to try and retake the shrine?" asked Dando. "That's what your servant told us."

"The citizens of Labour in Vain, not us," said the prelate. "Toymerle priests renounce violence at ordination, more's the pity. And now if you'll excuse me..." He turned away.

"Come an' look at this," said Foxy who had wandered away during this interchange in order to explore the church more thoroughly. He led them to a pedestal on top of which was placed an ornate box with a glass lid. It presented the appearance of a sort of reliquary, and when they peered inside they were confronted by a small piece of grey-coloured flesh.

"Yuck!" said Dando. "It's a thumb. Who did it belong to I wonder?"

"Our poor dear bishop," came the reply. They found that Gopher had reappeared beside them after going off on some business of his own. "Bishop Cadman is being held prisoner at Toymerle. They asked us for a ransom, but how on earth did they think we were going to pay it? Our wealth, such as it is, is hidden up there in the treasure cave – down here we're poor as church mice. They sent further messages, each more threatening than the last, and then we received that," pointing to the box. "Now they say that unless we pay up they'll send us the other one. That's the sort of devil he is, this Cheetah - absolutely ruthless. Woe betide you if you fall into his clutches; woe betide our poor bishop and woe betide anyone else he may have in his power."

"They're going," said a voice from the back of the church. One of the men who had been standing outside had come in with news. "Straight away, while the bandits are absent and as soon as they can get everyone together. Strike while the iron's hot is the watchword. They're saying that it's twenty pounds for all who volunteer, to be paid out once they've recaptured the treasure-house."

"I'll have a word or two to say about that," said the Prelate of the Chamber of Audience, alias Father Sion. "Where are they gathering?"

"In Bryn's corral."

"Come brothers," to other clergy who were standing by, "we must consult with them before they leave. And you," he said as he passed Tallis, "now's your chance to get to speak your piece to the god if that's what you so desire. There'll definitely be a reward for those who hazard the venture 'though I can't promise twenty pounds."

"Shall we go?" said Dando his eyes bright with excitement. "It'd be wicked – real hand to hand fighting perhaps." Since his brush with the raiders, despite his initial horror at the killings, he had begun occasionally to wonder if he had the makings of a warrior.

"I'm willin'" said Foxy, lofting his bow and pinging the string.

"Well," said Tallis more cautiously," I'm not too sure. I certainly don't want to delay or turn back now when we've come so far, although I don't think we should get involved in combat. Perhaps it would be better to wait for them to return. Let's go to the meeting place and see what's being planned."

They exited the church but came face to face with Ann who was sitting patiently outside.

"Oh, of course, there's Annie," said Dando realising he had forgotten all about his soul-mate and experiencing a cold douche of reality. "Did you hear the news? We've been asked to go along on this expedition to liberate the shrine. I don't think you ought to come."

"She can't come," said Foxy, "it be too risky. Women jes' get in the way when there's a scrap in the offing."

Tallis nodded in agreement.

"But we can't leave her behind," said Dando, " unless we find her somewhere to stay and pick her up later."

Ann's eyes sparkled with indignation.

"It be I that decide what I be a-gooin' to do – not you!" she said, looking directly at Dando.

"Oh, right."

"An' if you're gooin' I be a-comin'!"

"Oh OK – if you say so."

"I be better at shootin' than you."

"Right."

"Don' 'ee try an' stop me – nor you Foxy."

The three men exchanged glances. They knew they had been thoroughly put in their places and assumed a sheepish air.

"But you shou'n't goo," added Ann to Dando as if she had suddenly become aware of the implications.

"Oh," said Dando, blushing slightly, "don't start that again."

Just outside the village a motley group of citizens of all shapes, sizes and ages had assembled. There were men, women and even a few children; Tallis estimated about a hundred. They bore a catholic selection of arms ranging from ancient swords to bill hooks, from pitchforks to kitchen knives. One or two rode donkeys and mules but the majority were afoot. In the centre of this huddle stood a giant of a man with a bushy black beard accompanied by two younger males of equal stature who were obviously his sons. As Tallis' party arrived at the corral this person was in the middle of outlining a plan of action.

"...and we'll stop about a mile short, near the Drossi turning. Then Evan and Dai can go ahead - they know the lie of the land – and discover whether those that've been left behind have posted lookouts. If they have we'll take them out one by one as quietly as possible, after which we'll surround the place and launch a surprise attack from all sides. I'll divide you into units of twenty and you can pick your own leaders. We'll have the place in our hands before you can say *piece-of-cake*. When the Cheetah returns he'll get a shock, I can tell you. Any questions?"

"Rhys, he knows what he's talkin' about, look you," said a man at Tallis' elbow. "He was away fightin' the furriner's wars for him before he had reached eighteen. If anyone c'n bring this off he can. Hallo," he continued, looking from Tallis to Dando and then from Foxy to Ann, "you're not from these parts then, are you? What are you doing here?"

"We're just passing through," said Dando, "my master wants to consult the oracle."

"Well, it looks like you're well equipped for battle – we could certainly do with some help in that department. The Voice is up there where we're bound. I'm sure they'd let you ask your question for free if you lend us your arms."

Father Sion was addressing the crowd.

"The priests of the shrine will be eternally grateful if you drive these sacrilegious vermin from the sanctuary. I'm afraid our vows prevent us from accompanying you on the expedition but several members of our laity are determined to go. I just ask one thing – please, no violence in the holy places. As it is, in order for the god to speak once more, we will have to carry out a thorough cleansing of the shrine to rid it of the filth with which these reprobates have defiled it. We'll show our gratitude in due course – there'll be five pounds for every man and boy, every woman and child who takes part."

The company raised a half-hearted cheer at this, tinged with a certain disappointment, they had been expecting more.

The Gopher appeared from amongst the crowd looking self-important. "You're coming – good, good. I've been asked especially because I know all the secret underground ways behind the walls of the basilica, including the location of the God's-Breath chamber. Besides that, I understand the mysteries of the treasure cave. The chief is requesting that you join him at the head of the march as you're the only ones among us with both bows and arrows - join him and me that is."

Dando looked at the others with a grin. "I suppose that means we're going," he said.

Tallis shrugged in resignation, Foxy raised his weapons into the air, Ann pursed her lips and shook her head slightly. The muster straggled out of the corral and started up the hill, forming a ragged procession. The travellers made their way to the front where Rhys gazed wistfully at Carolus. It was obvious that he was seeing himself sitting astride the big chestnut horse. However Tallis' mount was laden with baggage and was not available for riding.

"How far is it to Toymerle?" Tallis asked him.

"About a day and a half on horseback – three days afoot. God grant we make it before the raiders return. If there's enough time we'll rest for a few hours out of sight down the road before we launch our attack so that everybody's fresh. Meanwhile Evan and Dai can spy out the land."

And so, almost without having come to a definite decision and against Tallis' better judgement, our protagonists found themselves setting out in the van of a rag-tag army, uncertain of what to expect, yet feeling they were heading for what might turn out to be a small but bloody war.

How do it be that we've got ourselves into such a pickle? thought Ann as she trudged northwards following Foxy's broad back, and aware as always of Dando bringing up the rear.

Stage or screen -
Which shall it be?
Fortunes are riding on the outcome.

Chapter six

   Trying to suppress the conviction that she was betraying not only Milly but her brother as well, Damask tickled up Shingai and hurried back down to the plains with the intention of rendezvousing with the Ixat Instipulators and resuming her acting career. The two months she had spent as part of the company had been the most stimulating and rewarding of her life. For the first time she had felt she was earning her way in the world, that the bread she ate had been gained, if not by honest toil, then at least by her own unaided efforts. And she was good at it, this acting lark. If she did not actually immerse herself in the roles she was given then at least she made those roles her own, she put her own individual stamp on them. Because of this she had started to become known and recognized. Young men who sought her out in the intervals between acts and at the end of the performance told her they had come to see the show purely for her sake; she had been starting to acquire a sizeable fan base. The fact that most of the parts she played required her to cross-dress did not seem to put off her admirers.

   Having been exposed to a small dose of fame she had gained a taste for it and was not averse to experiencing more of the same. It had been a mistake to leave the troupe just as she was finding her feet; the sooner she linked up with them again the better. But where to run them to earth? She knew they were hoping to put on a show in Drossi sometime next year but that could be a long way off yet. Alaric obviously had some plan for the route they were to follow, might even have had a specific arrangement with certain venues, but if so his schedule had never come to her notice. It was something she had hardly thought worth bothering her head about and now she cursed herself for her inattention.

One thing she remembered concerning their pre-performance publicity was that bill posters were sent on ahead to announce the company's immanent arrival in a particular town or neighbourhood, so when she passed a building with a wall absolutely covered from top to bottom with notices she drew the caravan to a halt and went back to have a closer look. Running her eyes over the mass of faded and tattered paper she took in announcements of concerts, coach time tables, club meetings, a hot-air-balloon launch, shop sales, lost and found items, other rival theatrical attractions both amateur and professional, but nothing about the Ixat Instipulators. One advertisement that sparked her interest and which seemed to have been posted recently called attention to a motion picture show which claimed to be *Straight from Armornia,* trumpeting a main feature titled *An Account of the Temptation, the Grave Sins and Subsequent Redemption of Phyllida Throstlethwaite, Ingénue,* with *a host of extra attractions, some in hand-tinted colour! They Move! They Dance! They Romance!* shouted the blurb, *More Real than Real Life! You Won't Believe Your Eyes! Come One! Come All! Come Every Mother's Son! Admission - adults sixpence, children under fourteen threepence.* The site where this event was due to take place lay a little further along the highway if the road signs were to be believed.

An hour later when it was just beginning to get dark Damask started to think about halting for the night and preparing something to eat. She suddenly realised she was lonely. Although she did not like to admit it she missed Milly's pert presence; for the last two years they had spent scarcely a day apart and she was not used to being on her own. It was at this point that she became aware that the way was becoming thronged with people and, above her, stretching across the road, was a banner proclaiming *STRAIGHT FROM ARMORNIA – THE SINS AND REMORSEFUL REDEMPTION OF PHYLLIDA THROSTLETHWAITE – HERE! - TONIGHT! - 7.30 pm.* The crowd was turning into a field on one side of the road while on the other lay an area where vehicles could be parked. Damask decided that perhaps the show was worth a gander and might take her mind off her feelings of isolation.

"Where's Armornia?" she asked the man on the gate as she handed over her sixpence.

"Armornia? - it's part of Pangorland on the other side of the Middle Sea – *Across-the-Ditch* – O*ver-the-Brook*. That's common knowledge! - where 'ave you been 'idin' yerself?"

Damask walked forward into the open-air venue and found that a huge vertical silver sheet had been erected at one end of the field while around the perimeter stood a ring of flickering lamps on poles. In front, facing the screen, a large number of people were sitting in rather disorganised rows talking animatedly or eating picnics. She found a place at the back but was soon hemmed in by later arrivals. This was hardly the first time she had been in the audience for such an entertainment. Not this autumn but the one before there had been something similar at the High Harrow Hiring Fair. She and Milly had paid a visit to the tent where it was to be staged and been less than impressed by this new diversion. There had been a man turning a handle on a sort of box that projected a guttering image so dim that it was hard to make out what it was portraying. They had come away feeling they had wasted their money. But here things were very different. At the back of the crowd stood a large engine, wheezing, chugging and emitting gouts of steam. This was linked to another contraption producing an angry buzzing noise which was obviously going to be the source of the forthcoming entertainment as it was casting a large white rectangle of light onto the screen. Just below and to the left of this projection sat a woman at a rather battered upright piano trying to compete with the racket issuing from the machines.

Soon the lamps dimmed and went out; the performance began. Damask was immediately impressed. Animated faces appeared, so huge that you could have driven Pnoumi's caravan up their nostrils. A sequence of men throwing pies at each other followed, which caused great amusement, and then coloured pictures of flowers took their place that went from bud to blossom in a matter of minutes. As promised there were images of people dancing, a style of dance that was quite novel as far as she was concerned. Lastly came a distant view of a huge mechanism travelling on rails and hurtling through mountainous scenery as it trailed a long white streamer of smoke from some kind of flue. Those were the extra attractions. There was a short pause, filled by the lady on the piano, and then the title of the main feature was revealed.

They were only a short way into the narrative before Damask began to get the impression that the rather soppy melodramatic love story being presented was on a par with the novels she had been forced to read during her spell under the thumb of the Castle Dan aunts. The film was a silent one and little was left to the imagination as each scene was proceeded by a printed caption explaining the action. For example - *The Abductor creeps up on the innocent Phyllida and seizes her, while Robert can only listen helplessly on the other end of the telephone.* This sequence was played out on a split screen, the two lovers using what Damask took to be some kind of long-distant communication device. There appeared to be something wrong with the projector's speed as at one moment the movement was rushed and jerky, happening far too fast, then at other times everything reverted to slow motion as if the story was taking place in a dream. But Damask's interest was kept alive by what appeared behind the main action. She was amazed to see vehicles travelling along roads with apparently no visible means of propulsion. She saw buildings so tall that they practically had their heads in the clouds and, as a means of moving between the floors of said buildings, strange little rooms with sliding doors that travelled vertically up and down. She saw staircases that also moved and huge ships with chimneys but no sign of a sail. For a brief moment a close-up of a machine equipped with fixed wings appeared flying against a background of clouds with a man inside it at some sort of controls. At other times the frame was filled with magnificent scenery depicting water that rippled and sparkled and mountainsides covered in trees that threshed and bowed in the wind. *My God*, she thought to herself, *the Stips could never manage that on stage*.

The film was a long one, a real epic, and an interval had been arranged half way through the proceedings. As the picture faded the lamps came on round the field apparently powered by the same hard working machine that drove the projector. Damask was one of the first to get up from the ground where she had been sitting in order to stretch her legs, and as she did so heard someone shout a greeting. "Cara mia! Ragazza mia!" came the cry. A few rows in front a middle-aged woman surrounded by several children was waving in her direction. She looked behind to see who was being hailed and then realised that she herself was the object of the salutation. All at once she recognised a familiar face; the woman was none other than Nadya, Boiko and Duke's gypsy mother; the friend who at one time had been so desperately ill. Thrilled to bits she clambered forward over the intervening rows and was soon being enthusiastically embraced.

"It so good to see you Principessa," said Nadya. "How you come here? You come for celebration?"

"I'm looking for my brother but I can't find him," replied Damask. "What are you doing? Where are the others?"

"I bring little ones to picture show – give their mothers a break. Our people just along road. You come to wedding?"

"Wedding?" said Damask.

"Day after tomorrow. Big party."

Just then the lights faded and the film recommenced. Afterwards, when it had ended, Nadya roused the children – some of them had fallen asleep – and prepared to leave.

"Where you staying?" she asked.

"I've got my own van now," said Damask. "At least, it's on permanent loan. It's just across the road. Whose wedding were you talking about?"

"My boy Duke's. You come? It good thing for us." She looked at Damask anxiously. She and all of the gypsy tribe had been well aware of the decade-long relationship between the girl standing before her and her eldest son. For this reason the high-born Glept was not exactly the first person she would have chosen to be present at these festivities. However the rules of Roma hospitality demanded that Damask be invited and made welcome.

"He marry Kizzy Lee. It good thing for all of us," she repeated with a hint of pleading in her voice. "The Lees and Petulengros – lots of trouble in the past – now we make friends – the marriage is to show we forget the bad times."

"Oh, of course," replied Damask with a smile but her throat ached with regret. It appeared that Duke, her long-time lover, was about to become the property of another woman, when by rights he should have been hers. This new relationship seemed to negate a lifetime of understanding between the two of them. Well, all was not lost; the ceremony had not yet taken place.

"You've got the pony and trap with you?" she asked. "I'll follow you back. I was looking for somewhere to park for the night."

At the camp the children were reclaimed by their mothers and carried off to bed. Damask was given a right royal welcome by the Roma but there was an undertone of concern in their greetings. She searched their ranks for a glimpse of her erstwhile sweetheart but if Duke was in the vicinity he was maintaining a low profile.

Next morning Damask made an attempt to be useful by putting up decorations and arranging chairs etc. but in fact only got in the way. It was not until after midday, when she had given up looking for him, that the prospective bridegroom suddenly appeared before her, having emerged from one of the vans.

"Ciao Principessa," he said, formally shaking her hand. "It good you come to watch me get married." He smiled wanly but his eyes reproached her. She could see that he was not happy. Earlier the arrangements for the next day had been explained. The Lees were camped about a mile away. The bride would arrive soon after eleven o'clock, decked out as if for a carnival, mounted on a white charger and surrounded by her family. The ceremony would be conducted by Donka, the Petulengros great grandmother, who was qualified to do so by her seniority. The celebrations would go on well into the small hours with feasting, singing, dancing and the gypsy music that was so full of unfocused longing. The Roma were past masters when it came to a knees-up.

The evening meal having ended Damask went back to the cat-circus caravan and waited. At some unearthly hour after midnight there came a knock on the door. As she opened it a dark figure pushed past her into the interior; it was the one who, not long ago, had asked for *her* hand in marriage. Nothing was said. For a moment they stared at each other in the dim lamplight, then they were in each other's arms. A long while later, all passion temporarily spent, they found time to talk.

"Let's run away to Drossi," said Damask, "or p'raps further afield. We could go now."

"No – too late – far too late."

"Surely not."

"Her people find me and kill me," and when she opened her mouth to protest, "yes – they would. Then my family kill one of them – and then they kill someone else – they keep killing – it would be vendetta."

"We could go across the Middle Sea."

"No – far too late – too late."

They made love one last time. Then Duke got dressed and went to the back door. Damask went with him, hanging on to him, kissing him, her grief lending her dalliance an urgency which hinted at substantial distress.

"You always in my heart," said Duke, pressing his hand against his chest.

"And you in mine," replied Damask taking his hand and putting it to her own breast.

"I love you."

"Of course, my soul. This isn't goodbye. One day..."

Duke shook his head and slipped out of the caravan.

Getting through the long drawn out nuptials on the morrow proved to be an ordeal. Damask's face actually started to hurt from the fixed smile she was forced to maintain in order to give the impression that she was enjoying herself. Witnessing the ceremony itself was extremely painful and she had no appetite for the meal that followed. As soon as it was decently possible she slipped away to her caravan, hitched up Shingai and made her way back to the road. Despite her sadness she set off with new determination and a sense of purpose. The fact was she now knew where she was going. A girl who had sat next to her during the feast turned out to be a sort of theatrical nut who kept tabs on all the comings and goings of the actors she adored. The Ixat Instipulators, she informed Damask, were in the middle of a three week stint down in Sassanara. "Just follow the road east and you'll be there in a few days. I'd come too, but I'm not allowed."

Sassanara lay on the west bank of the Kymer, the Great River as it was more commonly known. Damask was prepared for the fact that this waterway would be bigger than the valley's little Wendover; any fool could have worked that out from the name. But when she finally came within sight of the flood she could scarcely believe her eyes. Surely this could not be a river, this huge stretch of water; it was more like a vast lake, a sea almost, its further shore so remote that it was nearly over the horizon. But yes, it *was* a river because the stream was in motion, flowing quite fast in fact. The boats travelling with the current were passing at a rate of knots while those sailing against it seemed hardly to move. To see this great fluid mass making its majestic way to the sea was awe-inspiring indeed.

The riverside settlement proved to be a sizeable town, a town big enough to boast its own purpose-built theatre. It was fairly late by the time Damask arrived and the evening performance was well under way. She parked her caravan near the company's familiar vehicles and went and bought a ticket from the man at the box office who warned her that she had missed most of the first half. The auditorium was fairly full, the Stips seemed to be having a successful run. Almost the first thing she noticed as she took her seat was that the company had a new Zanni. He (it was a man) was unfamiliar to her. They must have brought in someone from outside; she had grudgingly to admit that he was quite good. In the particular play they were doing that night Severine featured prominently; her career was obviously on the up and up. There was also a new Harlequin on the stage; she wondered what had become of the old one. She saw no sign of Alaric – he did not seem to have a part in this production. Perhaps tonight he was just directing – his wagon was definitely outside. When the performance finished she went back to the grassy area where the vans were parked and waited to see who would emerge. It was quite a while before anyone appeared because, as she realised, the actors had to remove costumes and grease paint and make themselves presentable within the everyday world; it was not something that could be achieved quickly.

Severine was the first cast member to appear at the stage door. She stopped short when she saw Damask's yellow caravan, then after some hesitation crossed the intervening space.

"What are you doing here?" she asked in an offhand manner.

"Just stopped by to say hello," replied Damask.

"Well, hello," continued Severine, "and goodbye."

"Oh, thanks a lot!"

"There's no vacancies," said the girl, "so you needn't think you're going to pick up where you left off."

"I don't know that that's for you to decide," said Damask.

Some other members of the troupe had now gathered round. One or two greeted her quite pleasantly although she sensed a distinctly hostile attitude from the majority.

"Where's Alaric?" asked Damask, "is he in his van?"

"If he is he won't want to speak to you," said Severine.

"We'll see about that."

Damask got down from the driving position where she had been sitting and walked across the field towards the Grande Stupendo's caravan. Just outside she was waylaid by Punchinello who sauntered into her path smoking one of his inevitable black cigarettes.

"I think I ought to put you in the picture, young lady," he said. "If you're considering rejoining us I might as well tell you that after you left last time, people began to talk, as they will, and the general consensus was that you had been a somewhat disruptive element. A company like this, living in intimate contact most of the time, needs to get along together; a certain amount of tranquillity is required for creativity to flourish. They didn't think your presence was helpful, to say the least."

"That's absolute rubbish!" said Damask indignantly.

"I'm afraid not," replied Punchinello.

"Well let's see what Alaric has to say about it!"

She dodged round him and ran up the steps to the Captain's caravan in order to bang on the door.

"Alaric, Alaric," she called, "it's Damask." There was no reply.

"Alaric," she cried again, "please can I have a word." She waited for a few minutes and then banged again.

"Alaric, Alaric," but *answer came there none.*

"Alaric, Alaric – I know you're in there." She paused, holding her breath, trying to detect some sign of movement. All that she was aware of was a sort of listening silence. Most of the company stood at the bottom of the steps viewing the proceedings with interest. Eventually, refusing to give up, she beat another tattoo on the door.

"I won't go away 'till you show yourself," she shouted. "I c'n stand here and bang all night if you like." Suddenly the door yielded and the onlookers watched in disgust as she disappeared inside.

Time passed and eventually Damask extricated herself from the Grande Stupendo's embrace and made an attempt to put her case.

"This is all very nice," she remonstrated, pulling her trousers up and her shirt down, "but what about my career? I was well on the way to becoming your star attraction a few weeks ago. Surely you want that to continue. I was bringing in the punters."

"My dear girl," said Alaric, "things have moved on since then. As you may have noticed we have managed to secure the services of Gabriel Lovejoy, well known up and down the river as a fine actor. If it hadn't been for the fact that he left his last company under a cloud he would never have agreed to become our new Zanni. There are no openings commensurate with your talents at the moment, although if you'll agree to taking bit parts for the time being something might offer itself later."

"Bit parts!" cried Damask scornfully, "you mean a bit part as your bit on the side!"

"Oh, hush, hush, my dear. Come here – don't get so upset. I know it's unfair, life's unfair..."

It was well past the breakfast hour by the time Damask left the Grande Stupendo's caravan. Reluctantly she had decided that there was nothing for it but to pack up and move on. It looked as though she was going to be frustrated in her ambition to become a leading light of the stage. Perhaps instead she would go to this Armornia place, *Over-the-Brook* as they termed it, and learn how to make one of these *movies* like the one she had seen the day before yesterday. Maybe she could become – what would be a good name for it? - a *movie star* - a *star of the silver screen.* She would go to Drossi - that's where the big ships docked so she had heard – and buy herself a passage across the Middle Sea to the northern continent of Pangorland. But then, whilst in Drossi, she might bump into the Posse (Posse – Drossi!) and perhaps become the lead singer in a band instead.

Damask left the town on the well-used track beside the river. She made her way north for several days noticing that the country was becoming more populated and that the traffic, both water born and land-based, was getting denser. She had the feeling that she was approaching the heart of the surrounding delta area. Travellers afoot, both solitary and in groups, were now a familiar sight. She paid them scant heed and as she crept up on a small man walking in the same direction as herself with pack on back and in each hand a large wicker basket she had her mind on other things. It was not until she was passing him and he had disappeared down the side of the van that she heard the sound of faint mewings coming from behind and below. Damask leaned out and looked back, guessing in advance what she would see. Yes, it was the Mog – Pnoumi the Mog - she recognised the clown make-up, the familiar cat face. The meows were issuing from the baskets. She pulled on the reins and brought the caravan to a halt. Clambering down onto the road, she walked round to the rear of the vehicle, only to find that the clown had retreated far back along the highway. He stood some distance away and gazed at her with obvious alarm.

"Don't be scared," she called, "I'm not going to hurt you. Do you want your caravan back?"

Pnoumi did not move. He put the baskets down on the ground - they must have been extremely heavy - and regarded her warily. Damask waved her hand towards the van.

"It's yours," she said. "I've just been looking after it for you. Come on – I won't bite." There was no response.

Damask re-entered the interior and looked round for something she could use as a carrier. All she could find was a pillow case. She began to fill this with her personal effects, such as they were, and the few surplus items of clothing that she had acquired since leaving Deep Hallow. She took with her all the food she had left, tied the pillow case to the end of a pool-cue she had discovered beneath Pnoumi's bed and slung it over her shoulder. Then she climbed down onto the road and, turning to the rear, found that the clown was still staring hard in her direction like a small prey animal alert to a dangerous predator and ready to flee at any moment.

"It's all yours," cried Damask again and thumped her fist against the yellow paintwork. "I'm giving it back to you. No? You still don't trust me? Oh well, I'm gone. See you in Drossi perhaps."

She tightened her belt, settled the stick more comfortably on her shoulder and took off along the road, ignoring what might be happening behind. For some time she expected the caravan to overtake her and in that case she would have attempted to hitch a lift, but when finally, after ten minutes, she stopped and looked back, the highway was empty. Pnoumi must have taken possession of his vehicle and, still profoundly distrusting her, have beaten a hasty retreat in the opposite direction.

Danger of Jabberwocks!
Every precaution should be taken
Outside the safety zone!

Chapter seven

Of all the fugitives from the valley Milly was the only one who could be called, unmistakably, a dyed-in-the-wool townie. Although, through familiarity, she did not feel a stranger on the Kymer flood plain or in Deep Hallow, her natural habitat was amongst the crowds of a city, among the terraced houses, the concrete and tarmac, the street musicians, pavement artists, lamplit bars and dives. These were the things imprinted on her subconscious, and amongst which she felt most at home. The world of nature was a complete mystery to her. During her earliest days - the period that was mainly blanked from her mind due to childhood traumas - the sky had been banished to just a narrow strip above her head between the roofs of buildings, glimpsed occasionally and little regarded. The weather, tamed and controlled with the help of umbrellas, gutters, street sweepers and sewers, had impinged on her awareness barely at all. The memory of that initial time was still there, deep, deep within, although now far beyond conscious recall. Although forcibly uprooted from her primary environment she had still never been far from the haunts of men and knew little of wild flora and fauna; the circus had contained few animals apart from a small equestrian act. She was not prepared for what confronted her when she reached the outskirts of Formile, eight days after Tallis' party had passed the same way. Although the settlement did not come to an abrupt end - for a while she noted smallholdings on both left and right – inevitably these solitary crofts finally petered out and the inimical terrain which loomed into view profoundly disturbed her. As the track turned a corner around the side of the last man-made structure she saw what lay in store. Apart from the road, there was no sign of the hand of man within this vista. Ahead stretched a glen hemmed in between imposing fells whose sides were clothed with dark impenetrable forest. The valley floor was home to coppices and thickets among which the way she was following lost itself, while in the middle distance she glimpsed the silvery gleam of sky-reflecting water. Further off were hills, hills and more hills. Strangely shaped clouds provided the sole detectable movement in this vast panorama as they progressed in stately fashion from above the heights on her left to the heights on her right. The only sound that came to her ears was a faint sighing.

Milly was seized with an urgent impulse to turn and high-tail it back to the cosy streets of Formile, to the odours of cooking and bad drains, to the comforting sounds and smells of residents living in close proximity. But of course she did not retreat – she had more gumption than that. Instead she dealt with herself sternly, handing out a reminder of the reason for her present circumstances. *He* might be in trouble, her dear Lordship, he might be walking unknowingly into great danger with no-one but herself to bring him warning. They, the travellers, had taken this route days earlier and therefore she must follow as quickly as she could and overtake them before they came to harm. She looked back once towards the lands of men, then, lifting her chin and taking a deep breath, stepped forward into the wild.

As she walked down the deserted road the surrounding silence preyed on her nerves. She needed some sort of distraction from the oppressive sense of being watched by the whole alien landscape that grew out of her isolation. Again she asked herself why she was there. Well, one thing was clear, if it had not been for her young Lord's intervention she would still be at the Spread Eagle in Gateway, or perhaps somewhere much worse. So the blame for her situation could really be laid at Dando's door and was therefore not to be regretted because nothing to do with him could be wholly bad.

She liked to remember the first time they had met at the whore house. The encounter had taken place during the weekend, but the day of rest had been no holiday for a working girl like herself. He had been her third client of the morning. The second had used her roughly and her usual sense of apprehension was heightened as she went to this new assignation. She remembered the surprise she had felt at her first glimpse of the high-ranking Glept and the answering surprise on his own face, surprise and disappointment. It had been his youth that had taken her aback; the sort of men who asked for the tenderest of flesh were usually middle-aged. Later she discovered that his reaction had been identical to hers; he had not realised that girls of her years were on the game. She started to undress but he stopped her.

"No, no – I don't want... I just want to talk. Here – put them back on."

Well, this was a turn-up for the book!

"Itwl still cost you," she said.

"Yes, yes, of course. What's your name?"

"Milly."

"Hello Milly – I'm Dando. How old are you?"

"Don't know."

"Milly – is there a girl works here – fair hair, blue eyes, a nibbler? About my age?"

"Connie's got blue eyes – she's a nibbler."

"How old is she?"

"Twenty free."

"No, she's got to be my age – fifteen. Is there anyone like that?"

Milly had shaken her head. The Lord looked downcast. He asked again, "How old are you?"

"I'm older'n ten. When Colonel Quatre bought me orf of my dad 'ee said 'ee'd 'ad me for four years an I woz wiv the Colonel for six before 'ee sold me on to Madame La Tour."

"Do you like it here?" Milly shook her head again and then whispered "Don' tell Madame, she'd take it out on me."

"How long have you been doing this sort of thing?"

"Um - a long time reely, wot wiv one fing an' anuver."

He questioned her about her early life, little of which, as already mentioned, she could recall and, in reply, she told him about the circus and then a bit about the workings of a Gateway brothel.

When he left he paid her more than she asked and promised to come and see her again. She remembered how eagerly she had looked forward to his second visit but with grave doubts as to whether he would keep his promise. But true to his word he was there on the next rest day, almost to the hour. They talked again for a while and then he asked, "Would you like to get out of this place?"

She nodded.

"Where would you like to go?"

"I'll go wherever you go," she whispered.

"Do you know how much – whatsername – Madame La Tour paid for you?"

She shook her head.

After that she did not see him for over a fortnight. She had sadly made up her mind that he was not coming back when she was summoned to the owner's private parlour. Dando was there.

"We've come to an agreement," said the madame, "you're a very lucky girl. There's not many of my ladies have had such good fortune. You belong to this gentleman now. Be sure you do your best to please him."

Outside her dear Lord lifted her up onto his horse and mounted behind her.

"It's not true what she said," he told her, "you don't belong to me. You don't belong to anyone." They rode out of town. She did not ask where they were bound.

Milly had not yet learnt ways of telling the hour without a clock. She walked on for what seemed a fair number of miles and for a longish period. Eventually she began to feel peckish. The road crossed a small stream on a bridge comprising one large slab of stone. Scrambling down the bank in order to drink she scooped up some water in her cupped hands and sipped. She pulled a face. Plain water was not her cup of tea at all. In fact that was just what she felt she could have done with at this juncture – a nice hot milky cup of tea. She made her way further along the road looking for a place to sit and eat and in the end turned off into the trees where a fallen trunk provided a suitable perch. She took an inventory of the food in her satchel. There were several packets of flat bread, a speciality of the

Jolly Waggoners, cheese, a spiced sausage, short-bread biscuits, dried fruit and chocolate. That was about it, apart from a few liquorice sticks and humbugs that Damask had purchased for her from a sweet shop before they parted. Earlier that day she had asked herself how far she would have to travel and how long it would take her to reach her goal. It behoved her to be as abstemious as possible she decided, to eat just to sustain life and no more. Was there anything along her route with which she could supplement these meagre rations? Near where she was sitting she noticed an extremely prickly bush bearing some rather shrivelled berries. She picked one and popped it into her mouth. Again she pulled a face. This roadside bounty was horribly sour she discovered. She took a couple of bites from the sausage and ate two pieces of bread, then finished the repast with a humbug. She still felt hungry.

As she ate she had her ears peeled for any suspicious noises, much as if she was a soldier on sortie behind enemy lines. The harder she listened the more she was aware, in the calm that prevailed that day, of strange little rustlings and whisperings, both near and further off. By the end of the meal she was in such a state of tension that when a large beetle fell into her lap from the branches above she almost screamed. Instead she leapt up and shook it out of her skirt with a shudder of revulsion, not taking her eyes off the insect until it had scuttled away into the undergrowth. The sense of being in hostile territory increased and she got the feeling that she had to keep as quiet as possible to avoid being detected. It was with reluctance that she stepped once more into the road. She felt exposed away from the shelter of the forest but at the same time feared its dense shadows, impenetrable to the eye, which might be providing cover for some creature that intended her harm.

Oh, if only Damask were here! Milly was pretty sure that, in a similar situation, her mistress of the last two years would not have allowed herself to get into such a silly panic when away from her familiar stamping ground. If she had had Damask's presence beside her it would soon have boosted her courage. From the start the child had been impressed by the older girl's forceful and imperious manner. The Glept's total self confidence and certainty that she was right were qualities that Milly imagined a queen might possess. In fact she *was* a queen in the little girl's eyes; after all wasn't she called *Principessa* by the gypsies. But Damask had not seemed to care if her brother was in trouble or not; she had been more concerned about that blessed caravan. And yes, it was true, the caravan would have had to be left behind in Formile if they had both journeyed onwards together; the roadway was not wide enough to accommodate it. Despite the fact that they had had a sharp disagreement, she did not bear a grudge. In truth she rather regretted the abrupt way in which they had parted. It was just that, given a choice between the twins, she was bound to favour Dando.

Sometime later she stopped again for rest and refreshment away from the track but still within sight of it. It was as she was having this second snack that she heard something that was not a part of the ambient sounds that surrounded her. Hooves! People! Her impulse was to rush back onto the highway and hail these oncoming travellers. Caution prevailed however and on second thoughts she remained where she was. She was suddenly struck by her loneliness and vulnerability, far from assistance, if the newcomers proved unfriendly. Two men came in sight through the trees heading in a southerly direction, mounted on stocky workmanlike ponies. They were bearded, shaggy-haired and rather dirty. They also seemed to be armed to the teeth. Milly shrank back into her hiding place and watched them pass. They looked like outlaws or bandits she thought. Where were they going? Surely not to the town? Such desperadoes would not be welcome in Formile. If the road was home to such folk she was going to have to be twice as vigilant.

It became apparent to her that the light was fading. Her first day in the wild had nearly reached its end. The air was turning blue and very chilly. She remembered with longing her cosy little bed in Damask's apartment and also the comfortable bunk in the cat-circus caravan. She wondered if she ought to attempt to find somewhere to wash but just the thought made her shiver. Instead she stamped down some bracken in a clearing to try and create a place to sleep, and lay down feeling cold, hungry and unclean. It soon became obvious that even a short nap was going to be out of the question. Every few minutes she raised her head listening, listening, straining her ears. Any noise at all made her jump and look round nervously. When something, hidden in the undergrowth and apparently quite large, passed within yards, snuffling and grunting, she leapt to her feet. She was not to know that her night-time visitor was probably nothing more than a curious hedgehog. Milly had never climbed a tree in her life but now she spent the rest of the night wedged uncomfortably in a fork between the trunk and one of the lower branches of a young ash. She had plenty of time to think about her situation and tried to cheer herself up by going over every minute she had spent with Dando since their first meeting, meanwhile reminding herself that she would soon be with him once more. But of course, now he was reunited with his sweetheart, he might not even be pleased to see her.

The next day proved to be sunny with some warmth in the air. When she came across a pleasant grassy slope beside another stream she saw no harm in sitting down for a while and eating a mouthful or two of her provisions. Also a few minutes stretched out on the grass would not hurt. When she awoke, having been dead to the world, the sun was in a different part of the sky, the shadows were lengthening and she realised she had been asleep for several hours. Well, if she was unable to sleep at night but could do so during the day, she might as well walk throughout the hours of darkness. So as long as she was able to see the road dimly in front of her that is what she did.

The track began skirting the edge of a series of large lakes, following a course between the water margin and hillsides to which clung dense hangers. Milly slept in the morning, ate when the sun was at its highest and then walked until it began to get dark. She rested for an hour or two and then walked again until she was too tired to continue. The great lochs beside which she had no choice but to travel she found both impressive and also slightly eerie in their quietness and hushed presence. What was the purpose of all this water? The only similar expanses that she had glimpsed as the circus progressed from one town to another had been the Middle Sea and the Great River, and they were always dotted with ships, a useful highway for the people living beside them. These lonely upland meres seemed to exist purely for themselves or for what they contained within their depths. Sometimes, staring across the breadth of a lake, she noticed an arrow-shaped ripple progressing rapidly along its length, suggesting that some large creature was swimming just below the surface. She watched nervously as it passed her, many hundreds of yards out, wondering what would appear if it turned and came in towards the shore. Most nights were never so inky black that she could not get a sense of the road's direction ahead of her, but on one occasion it was certainly dark enough for her to completely miss the left hand turn by the defaced signpost that the group she was following had taken. So, once again, as at the start of her journey in Deep Hallow, the paths of pursued and pursuer began to diverge.

During the day, like the travellers she was attempting to overtake, Milly saw mountains in the distance, up amongst the clouds, and wondered why they gleamed so brightly and how far off they might be. Surely they could not be a continuation of the land on which she was presently stepping; they were too much like a vision from another world. The lakes were soon left behind and the road began to climb. And with the change in the landscape's topography came a noise in the night that froze her blood. A few hours after sunset an unearthly singing would start up, sometimes coming from two directions at once, as if messages were being passed. It sounded like the howling of dogs, but wilder and more abandoned. Night after night she heard it echoing amongst the hills and it kept pace with her on either side of the road until she felt she was being stalked by ghosts; any confidence she had gained by coming unscathed this far went up in smoke. She no longer dared to walk after nightfall. Instead she spent the hours of darkness in the only place where she felt safe – up in the trees. For several days and nights she barely slept. Once or twice she thought she caught a glimpse of them, whatever they were: she saw several hunched grey shapes in the twilight slipping like a line of shadows through the distant brush. Then came a night when pandemonium broke loose as an almighty row erupted. The howlers were present, off to her left, all giving voice at once, but there was also something that roared, something bigger and fiercer so that a mortal conflict seemed to be in the process of playing itself out. Almost as quickly as it started the cacophony died and peace was restored. Milly clung to her tree, whimpering in terror, her head spinning from stress and tiredness. But the next day her persecutors were absent, and then also on the next and then the next. She hardly dared to believe it but they seemed to have been driven off – but by what or by whom?

She had been forging ahead as fast as she could, keeping her intervals of rest to the minimum, counting off the miles. Surely she should have caught up with Dando and his companions by now? With the old man and laden horses she did not imagine they would make rapid progress. Since her sighting of the two armed bandits she had only encountered travellers on one other occasion and then it had been the same two men returning along the road, only this time with a third – bound - slung across one of the saddles. As before she had hidden and they passed by – but where were they making for? She had no idea. Her food was now virtually exhausted. Besides her tiredness she was being plagued by a growing hunger. If she did not arrive somewhere soon where she could replenish her stocks she would be in real trouble. A waste of rocks and rushing streams surrounded her, beyond which rose beetling cliffs with the occasional dark cavern at the base. In her imagination the entrances to these caves looked like the portals to a monster's lair. For several days there had been snow on and off. She preferred to be on the move if possible because if she stayed still for more than an hour she became chilled to the bone. One morning the road descended a slope with a corresponding rise ahead and at the bottom of the dip she discovered another road running east-west across her path. She dithered at the crossroads for sometime looking at the three choices presented to her. In the end she decided that the ways to left and right were narrower, more overgrown and more forbidding than the one she was currently following, so she rejected them and continued north but with an unhappy feeling of uncertainty.

A day or two later the track she was on breasted a hill only for a gully to come in sight below her through which a wide hurrying stream flowed eastward; you might almost have called it a small river. Its course was impeded by numerous boulders and shelves and there was a lot of white water where it tumbled amongst them. As she looked down from her vantage point she saw that the track crossed this watercourse by means of a series of flat-topped rocks quite widely spaced. These were going to be difficult to negotiate for someone of her size, and maybe perilous. She descended to the bank and assessed the situation. Yes, it looked doable. It was too far for her to step from one rock to another with her short legs, but she thought she would be able to jump if she kept a cool head and did not lose her balance. She made sure her boots were tightly laced and the straps of her satchel properly adjusted. Then she sat down on the bank and sucked her very last humbug while her tummy rumbled.

Oh well, she said to herself, *in for a penny in for a pound.*

She rose, went a few paces back, took a short run up and leapt across to the first rock. Mmm - child's play, easy-peasy - but the following jump would have to be done from a standing start. She gathered herself together and sprang forward landing squarely in the middle of the next rock. Now she was well out into the stream with foaming and frothing water all around. Five more stones to go and then there would be the final leap onto the opposite bank. It was not really so difficult. She counted them off as she jumped until she stood on the seventh with just a fairly wide channel to negotiate before reaching dry land. She squinted across the gap, measuring the distance. *Sink or swim*, she thought, *or hopefully come safe to land. I'm going to do this.*

She prepared carefully for her last jump, prematurely congratulating herself on completing the course, when something totally odd and unprecedented happened in front of her eyes. A large brown bush on the bank ahead, half hidden amongst other vegetation, suddenly acquired an unplantlike momentum and rose up into the air like larva erupting from a fissure. As it lifted it took on the shape of a huge animal standing on its hind legs, towering up at least ten feet, and having attained its full height it emitted a strangely familiar pulsating roar from its white-toothed jaws. Huge front paws with black claws flailed the air, after which, swaying from one leg to the other, it came down on all fours, aggressively displaying two fine rows of gnashers for her benefit. Milly, shocked and fearful despite being well out of range, recoiled instinctively, took a step backwards and tumbled into the freezing, foaming water.

Suddenly she was looking not down but up at the stepping stones as they rapidly receded into the distance while she was swept downstream with her head just above the surface. Then the current swung her round and she submerged, breathing water up her nose and into her lungs. She hit something, turned a somersault and again had her head above water. As she coughed and spluttered it grew dark, she saw a rocky wall rushing past before she sank once more into the depths. Everything went quiet, her ears were full of water, and she knew for certain that she was going to drown. Then the darkness came to an end, bright light burst upon her and she was aware of a wide expanse ahead, above which were the trailing branches of a tree. She had just enough presence of mind to grab hold and cling to a branch while, with fits of coughing, she tried to clear her waterlogged passages. The surface here was calm, she was in some kind of backwater out of the current, and the shore was quite close by. She pulled herself from branch to branch until all at once there was oozy mud beneath her feet and she was able to half crawl half scramble onto the river's grassy side. Limply she lay gasping and choking until she realised that if she did not move soon she was going to die, not from drowning, but from cold; her whole body felt numb and her blood seemed to be coagulating.

She got to her feet, took off her wet clothes, wrung them out as best she could and put them back on. Her satchel was somewhere down stream, she had parted company with it amongst the rapids. She tried jumping on the spot to get her circulation going, then realised that the best way to warm up would be to start walking and continue her journey. Staring round, wondering where she was, the full impact of her situation came home to her. The road was gone, it was somewhere up the culvert and when she looked in that direction she understood why it had turned dark when she was in the water. The river here was wide and smooth-flowing, but just above where she stood it came rushing forth from a narrow gap carved into the hillside that might almost have been termed a small ravine. She must have been swept down through this rocky, shadowy place until she found salvation in the shallows beyond. It took only a little exploration to convince herself that it was quite impossible to return that way, the water filled the whole couloir from side to side. Anyway, she was not anxious to retrace her steps, the monster might still be waiting for her by the stones; it had been the river, she realised, that had saved her from its jaws. She looked up at the hill which stood between her and the Way-of-the-Shades. Could she get back to the road by climbing? No, impossible - on this side it was a sheer rock face, even overhanging in places. She would have to try further along.

She noticed a small slowly-ascending combe leading roughly northwards, down which tumbled a tributary of the stream in which she had nearly drowned. Perhaps if she followed this watercourse it would lead her to where she wished to go. During the many days she had been away from civilisation Milly had acquired a certain amount of bush craft. By now she had begun to see that there was a correlation between the position of the sun and the time of day. She vaguely remembered learning that the sun rose in the east and set in the west. If you understood that and also that it travelled between the two extremes through the southern sky, you could get an idea of direction. Now, estimating that it was about midday, she worked out that the gully she proposed to climb ran more-or-less on the same bearing as the road she had been following. If later she came across an opening to the left she might, if she were lucky, regain the highway once more.

Without further ado she set out, but soon found that deprived of a track or even a footpath to follow it was very difficult to make progress. Several times she had to retrace her steps and try another route when she came up against an unclimbable shelf of rock or a mass of impenetrable vegetation. At least she soon got warm and her clothing began to dry, but after hours of struggling with the wilderness she felt thoroughly disheartened. She did her best to deny one of the reasons for her low mood, the conviction that she was completely lost, but could not ignore the other, the terrible gnawing pain in her gut that was already sapping her strength. That night she could not face the climb into the trees but instead curled up under a bush, hugging her stomach, too miserable to care if ravening beasts were prowling nearby.

For two days she stumbled onwards in this way, always trying to turn in her desired direction but always frustrated, finding her passage blocked by steep non-negotiable hillsides. The way she had chosen led up towards a saddle of land which was followed by a gradual descent. Rugged country awaited her and the mountain peaks, which had again come into view, were now much closer and no longer looked like mirages. On she trudged until over a second rise she came upon a dramatic change of scene practically at her feet. The land in front of her ended abruptly, there was an edge where earth and vegetation gave way to a great gulf of air, before another cliff, misty and remote, rose, facing her, from invisible depths. She had come upon a wide sheer-sided gorge smack across her path and now had no option but to turn either east or west, for straight ahead was out of the question. At last she had the opportunity to go left it she wished, but even more exciting was what she saw running parallel to the chasm just a few feet away from the margin. A track lay there – a man-made way - a sign that she was not the only benighted human being to have penetrated this godforsaken country! She descended to the road and looked along it in one direction and then the other. Of course it was too much to hope that there might be a fellow traveller in sight, she was beginning to think she was never going to set eyes on another human being again. But then, as if to give the lie to this conviction, she heard what was unquestionably a male voice coming from beyond the rim, from out of the canyon. It was not far off, this voice, and was born clearly to her ears. She found such a phenomenon hard enough to accept, but even stranger and more bizarre was the fact that the person seemed to be singing. She stood still and listened. Yes, it was a man and the song was a sea shanty. Milly recognised *What shall we do with the drunken sailor*, and when that came to an end the voice started on *Bully in the Alley:-*

"*Help me Bob, I'm bully in the alley,*

> *Way hey, bully in the alley,*
> *Help me Bob, I'm bully in the alley,*
> *Bully down in Shin-Bone Al..."*

Milly remained rooted to the spot, unable to move. She felt totally conflicted. On the one hand she craved human contact after such a long time in isolation; on the other, weighed against this, was her deep suspicion of all men (all men with one exception), and especially unknown men on their own, encountered in lonely places. Eventually, with great caution, she crept towards the lip of the cliff and, going down on hands and knees, peered over.

If a fellow human is brutalized
Then their pain is mine,
We are one in suffering.

Chapter eight

Soon after leaving Labour-in-Vain Rhys' army entered a frigid world. The members of the troop were now experiencing temperatures that remained permanently below freezing both night and day as, at some point in their ascent, they had crossed the snow line. Tallis looked with concern at Foxy's bare arms and feet.

"You need to cover up," he warned, "otherwise your flesh will rot with the cold; I know what I'm talking about."

"I be all right," said the Nablan, "I be used to it. I never wear shoes in all m'life."

"But you've never been at altitudes like these before, have you?" said Tallis.

"We get hard winters in the valley," retorted Foxy.

Ann had on a fine pair of boots provided by Doll, and Dando of course was equipped with the boots made by Tom which had given him not a moment's discomfort. The two of them were well served in the footwear department. When it came to their clothing it was a different matter. What they were wearing had seemed perfectly adequate up to this point in the journey, but now the harsh conditions made them pull their cloaks more tightly around them and wish they could add another layer.

"You'll find some all weather gear at Toymerle," said Rhys who was walking with them in front of the little force and listening in to their conversation, "that you can borrow or buy if you're intending to carry on into the mountains after our campaign is brought to a successful conclusion. They're well supplied at the shrine; they have to be, living so high all year round."

"Has the oracle always been there?" asked Dando, keen to pick Rhys' brains - he seemed to be a knowledgeable and well-travelled man.

"Goodman Eidolon, a sage of the ancient days, was told about the cave by a troll at the start of the second age, and revealed its location to his disciples so that all could share in the new dispensation and communicate directly with the God-of-the-Voice." Rhys sounded as if he was reciting a lesson learned by rote.

"And is this Voice God the same as the one you name the Master?" queried Tallis, somewhat confused.

"No – when we say the Master we mean the Master-of-Winds – that's what my people and the people to the north of here call the Sky-God. He's not the same as Rostan - Rostan is the God-of-Fire and rules the core of the earth just as Aigea rules the surface. The two of them are said to be constantly at war. My people worship the Master but not Rostan or Aigea. All the same we assist the pilgrims that pass through Labour-In-Vain."

"My countrymen pay homage to the Father-in-Heaven," said Dando, "only we call him Pyr - Lord Pyr."

"Mmm – I've heard that name before but I thought it came from very far to the south. Where do you live?"

"Deep Hallow."

Rhys shook his head.

"Some people used to call it the Lap-of-the-Mother, or so I've been told."

"You come from the Lap-of-he-Mother and yet you worship the Master?! Things must have changed a bit in that part of the world!"

"The pilgrims stand in the basilica to ask their questions," interrupted the Gopher at this point from where he had also taken up a place at the head of the little army, "and they think they hear the god speaking. Very terrible the sound of it is too, that's why they call it the Voice – it's tremendously loud and echoes all around. But the answers are really given by the Conveyor in the Breath Chamber.

The voice in the basilica is just one of our priests speaking through a tube in the rock. The god's words are passed on to him. Trade secrets you know," and he tapped the side of his nose.

"Can you tell us anything about the Key?" asked Dando of Rhys. Tallis looked at his squire in alarm and shook his head. Despite his need for guidance he did not want everyone to know their business.

"The Key? What do you mean? The Key of the Ages?"

"Yes I suppose so,"replied Dando, more cautiously.

"Well there's a song that they sing around Trincomalee – how does it go..."

> *"For the first turning a debt was owed,*
>
> *The fates of man and beast were sowed.*
>
> *The second time that the Key was turned*
>
> *The ways of life on earth were learned.*
>
> *On the third turn of this fateful Key,*
>
> *Our minds were oped that we might see.*
>
> *On the final turn the bells will toll,*
>
> *To usher in an age of gold..."*

"The Key is turned at the opening of each new age but some say it wasn't turned right at the world's outset – that it came later from some remote place beyond the stars. There's a belief that men discovered it lying temporarily lost and turned it to their detriment at that time. The first two lines are about that. Then comes the age of the heart – hers," he pointed downwards. "And then follows the age of the mind – that's the Master's. The age of gold is just pie-in-the-sky I think because we're still in the third age; who can tell what follows and when the change will take place. I don't really know what it means by *a debt* although, if it was a member of our own species that turned it at the beginning, maybe we sent humanity and the whole of life on earth off in the wrong direction. There's another song that tells about how - *The Key was stolen and can't be found so the age of thought goes round and round.* That's why some people say there's all this cleverness – machines and such-like."

That evening, after passing a crossroads, the expeditionary force camped in the snow beside the track and the members crowded close to a fire lit from fuel that some of the more far sighted had collected along the road. Food was shared out equally; not everyone, in their hurry to get started, had thought to pack any. Dando cooked a large quantity of vegetable stew on his own little fire, using up the last of his perishable supplies, and received a number of much-deserved compliments. When the meal was over and they were sitting making the most of what was left of the main fire's warmth he asked Rhys about the situation at Toymerle.

"These men who have taken over the shrine, who are they?"

"Very bad men – outlaws, bandits. They're led by someone who calls himself the Cheetah. In fact there are two of them – the Cheetah and the Panther - they're brothers – and also brothers in infamy. Between them they rule the criminal underworld – piracy, gambling, slavery, prostitution, drugs – they're into all the rackets – but they specialise in kidnapping. The Panther's territory covers the Seven Sisters, that's the towns along the north coast of Terratenebra - Drossi is one of them - and the Cheetah's is in the hinterland – the Plains, the River and all the high country to the west. Did you never get a sniff of him where you come from?"

"I don't think so – I don't really know."

"You'd know all right – he smells pretty rank. You must have been well protected."

Dando realised that the Outriders may have had some purpose after all.

"And that's what they're doing at Toymerle – kidnapping people?"

"Nobody's safe on the roads these days – especially if they look comfortably off. They send out raiding parties and pick up wayfarers on lonely stretches, then ransom notes are despatched and if the wealthy relatives don't cough up immediately they start mutilating their victims. The Cheetah got chased out of his last hideout, so that's when he decided to make the oracle's neck-of-the-woods his base – good jumping off point for all stations east and pretty easy to defend. But the Panther's got an even more impregnable lair. You've heard of Hungry Island up on the Middle Sea?"

Dando shook his head.

"It's other name is the Dark Island – Trincomalee is the nearest place on the coast. People avoid it like the plague and have done for centuries. Trees grow there which have acquired a really bad reputation. They're carnivorous you see – they trap birds and insects and small mammals within specially adapted leaves and twigs that suck goodness from their quarry and then when what's left of the flesh falls to the ground it feeds the roots. But people believe that sometimes they go after larger prey – they believe that they walk, if you'll credit it, that they're actually man-eaters. As a consequence no-one will set foot on the island if they can help it. According to local myth the trees were once much more widespread and people used to worship them and make sacrifices – human sacrifices to appease them. Anyway, the Panther has bucked the trend and taken up residence in their main habitat in order to revive the practice. He's snatched some unfortunate holy man to act as intermediary and has started stringing captives up amongst the branches - suspends them by the wrists - that's how it was done in the old days. He believes that in this way he and his men can use the island with impunity - that they will be safe from offshore attack because of its reputation yet also have nothing to fear from the trees. He ties rocks to the feet of the poor wretches he sacrifices to weigh them down. That way he makes doubly sure none of them escape."

Dando pulled a face. "Not nice," he said.

"No, not nice indeed."

On the third day of their journey the scratch force reached a track almost on the same latitude as Drossi, which ran, like the one they had crossed further south, at right angles to the Ffordd - that was the name by which the road they were following was known locally. They camped just short of the crossroads around a convenient bend. Evan and Dai continued on, melting into the rocks ahead, while some of the army stretched out on the snowy ground intending to grab the chance of a quick nap before the action started. Others looked to their weapons and discussed tactics.

"Now you come into your own," said Rhys addressing Foxy, "I'm going to call on your skills with the bow if we get a report that there are lookouts around the place. Secretly and stealthily are the watchwords. We must dispatch them without alerting the rest of the gang."

"Hild be as good as I at shooting," said Foxy, pointing towards Ann and conveniently revising his earlier opinion of women and war in order that she should not be left behind with Dando. "You'll come won't you girl?"

Ann gulped and then nodded. Dando looked at her anxiously.

"I don't think..." he began but was silenced by one of Foxy's angry glares and a shake of his loved-one's head.

After about an hour the two scouts returned and gave their report.

"There's three men on watch further up the road. No-one else as far as we could see. The houses are completely deserted and there's just five or six gang members in the community hall guarding some prisoners, but we heard a lot of noise coming from the church – something going on there we think – some kind of whooper-dooper I reckon."

"Mmm," said Rhys, "that'll be a problem. We can deal with the people on watch and in the village, but how are we going to get them out of the church? No violence in the holy places the father said."

"I think I could help," offered the Gopher and outlined a plan.

"I see – well, that's an interesting idea – might be worth a try." Rhys raised his voice and addressed the crowd. "I'm going on ahead with my boys and – what's your name?"

"Judd," said Foxy.

"With Judd and his lady friend who is an accomplished huntress, and also a few of our best fighters. The rest of you can follow and wait just out of sight. When we've dealt with the lookouts I'll give the signal and we'll attack the village and make as much noise as possible. Hopefully that will draw the others out into the open. And you," he said to the Gopher, "can put into practice what you suggested as soon as the way is clear to the cavern."

"Cavern?" enquired Dando vaguely as he, Tallis and Gopher marched up the road with the main attack force. He was finding it hard to focus, preoccupied as he was with the thought that he should have displayed more guts when intervening on Ann's behalf. Because he had been so easily deterred when Foxy enlisted her to take part in the fighting he was berating himself for cowardice.

"Yes, the basilica's hidden inside the cliff," continued the little man. "At first sight you wouldn't know it was there. Within the walls are many passageways and tunnels; it's a real warren. You could easily lose yourself and never get out again unless you know your way around like me. My idea is that we could put the fear of god into the robbers inside the church if we speak through the Voice's tube. If they hear that they'll get a real fright – they won't want to hang around I can tell you. They'll think Rostan himself has come to punish their wickedness."

"But what will you say?" asked Dando.

"I haven't worked that out yet."

Dando relapsed into silence remembering the King's Vault at Castle Dan and the books he had read which came from there. In some of them words had been put into the mouths of gods and goddesses. He thought he could reproduce the grand archaic style that had been used.

"Can I suggest something?" he ventured, making a great effort to concentrate on the task at hand.

"About what?" asked the Gopher.

"About what you could say."

"Go ahead."

"Well how about something like *Beware ye evil doers! The hour of retribution is at hand*"

"Mmm – not bad."

"*Flee foul desecraters of Rostan's temple!*" continued Dando with increased enthusiasm, getting slightly carried away. "*Flee if you value your lives! Defy the god at your peril! Interlopers on the sacred ground will be cast into the uttermost circles of hell! Begone! Begone!"*

"Yers," said Gopher, impressed despite himself.

"Just an idea," Dando added, suddenly embarrassed.

"No – I think you've got something. Perhaps you'd better come along."

"And Master Tallisand?" asked Dando, remembering his duties as squire and therefore feeling he needed to stay close to the knight as the next few hours might prove hazardous.

"Well yes – if he wants to."

According to instructions the little army halted just outside Toymerle. From where they stood, half hidden behind a dilapidated barn, Dando and Tallis had leisure to examine the place that awaited them. The houses were of a similar construction to those at Labour in Vain, being of timber with low sloping roofs, here bearing quite a weight of snow. But the most impressive aspect of the settlement was the huge cliff against which the buildings clustered, and the black vertical slash, soaring almost a hundred feet high, in the face of this cliff.

"Where's the church?" asked Dando.

"In there," said Gopher pointing to the dark orifice towering over the settlement. "It belongs to the god and it was made by the gods."

A figure appeared on the road ahead and beckoned.

"OK let's go," cried the man called Bryn, "that's the signal." The force started forward.

"No, not that way," said Gopher to Tallis and Dando as they were about to fall into step, "the entrance to the tunnels isn't through the main doorway. It's fairly well concealed. Follow me."

They hugged the southern edge of the hamlet as they headed towards the cliff until they came to a smaller cave in the rocky wall which was half hidden behind a boulder. It was here, just within the opening, that they left the horses. Further inside they discovered a shelf bearing a number of lanterns, three of which the Gopher lit, handing one each to Dando and Tallis.

"Now keep close to me," he said, "so you don't get lost. We must go on foot and I warn you, it's a long way."

They set off along a low narrow tunnel walking in single file, Dando and Tallis frequently in danger of bumping their heads on the roof as they progressed. This was a true labyrinth - there were numerous passageways to choose from along the route and sometimes they came to a junction with several openings. Part of the time they were walking on the level, but at others the floor climbed steeply and Tallis began to pant. The air was fresh and cold but smelt of nothing but inorganic stone and sterile water. Dando realised they were entirely in the Gopher's hands: without him they would never be able to find their way back.

"Hark," the little man said, " we're getting near."

Somewhere dead ahead of them they began to hear a confused buzz of human voices. It sounded like a sizeable crowd. The noise rose and fell and sometimes built to a crescendo of either jeering or laughter. The Gopher shook his head.

"Wicked, wicked," he muttered and then, "shield your lanterns."

It was brought home to Dando that regular splodges of light were penetrating the passage from the right hand side. The wall had gaps. In fact the walkway they were following ran along behind a perforated stone screen, carved into a regular pattern, unmistakeably artificial. The Gopher stopped and looked down through one of the holes, sharply drawing in his breath. "Sacrilege!" he gasped. Tallis and Dando followed suit and a remarkable scene presented itself.

What they were viewing, from a high vantage point, was a huge cavern, but a cavern greatly augmented by the hand of man. In all his life Dando had never come across such a vast enclosed space. There were lights below him but they scarcely had the power to illuminate the whole of the great chamber; it stretched away and up into darkness. However, he could just about make out an enormous hall to the right with rows of columns, but whether they were natural or man-made he could not be sure. At the end of this hall were two massive doors with a smaller door, standing open, cut in the bottom of one of them. In front of him lay a gigantic circular arena with elaborately patterned walls, the patterns formed partly by nature and partly by human ingenuity. Looking to his left he could see a low alter above which were placed paintings and a bas-relief depicting what must be an episode in the Core-God's legendarium, while on the floor were intricate mosaics half obscured by wooden pews and tables. All this he took in at a glance, but the thing that drew and held his eyes was what was happening in the body of the church.

He was overlooking some kind of orgy. A large number of outlandishly dressed men and a smaller number of practically naked women were sprawled across the seats, eating, drinking, coupling and drunkenly singing bawdy songs. Another group was massed before the altar and these were the ones creating the most din. They were playing some sort of knife throwing game and each time a weapon flew through the air there was a loud cheer. Behind the altar, below the paintings, in what was obviously the most sacred part of the church, stood a beautifully carved reredos with a row of decorative projections along the top. To this screen a man was tied, his arms above his head, his wrists bound to two of the pinnacles. And it was this wooden reredos that was the target for the knife throwers. The game seemed to be to see who could strike the board nearest to the pinioned prisoner without actually wounding him. As each knife landed, closer than the last, a resounding hurrah echoed up into the roof of the chamber. Dando could see that it was only a matter of time before one of the drunken competitors became too ambitious or misjudged his aim and then blood would flow.

Dando examined the victim. Was he unconscious? His head was sunk on his breast and his eyes appeared to be closed. All he could make out was that the bandits' scapegoat was a slight young man with dark-blond hair and a pinched, starved look.

"Come on," said the Gopher, "quickly – this way."

Tallis and Dando tore their gaze away from the scene below and followed him. At the end of the passage lay a small round room with no apparent function, just an empty space within blank walls. But Joseph pointed to something that looked like the mouthpiece of a loud hailer sticking out of the rock.

"There you are – now you can say your piece."

"Me?" said Dando taken aback.

"Yes – like you did down the road. That's the Fire-God's tube – it biggens your voice – biggens it into a giant's voice – that's how we give the prophecies. Speak like you did before – if it doesn't scare them silly then I'm from Pickwah."

They could still hear the noise in the basilica coming through the stone tracery along the corridor they had just left. Tallis walked back so he could view the consequences of the Gopher's plan through one of the holes. Dando cleared his throat and, crouching slightly, put his mouth to the opening. From the body of the church came a vast sighing as if a giant were inflating his lungs. Dando drew back and the noise ceased. He realised that what he had heard was the sound of his own breath.

"They're looking worried," said Tallis.

Dando bent down again, psyched himself up and spoke.

"*BEWARE DESECRATORS OF THE HOLY PLACES! STINKING WORMS, FLEE IF YOU VALUE YOUR LIVES! ROSTAN IS A JEALOUS GOD AND WILL CAST YOU DOWN INTO THE UTTERMOST CIRCLES OF HELL!*" He paused and then breathed hard into the tube. The sounds of respiration grew into a full scale storm. "*BEGONE! BEGONE!*" he cried. "*FOUL WRETCHES TRESPASSING ON HALLOWED GROUND – YE EVIL DOERS, THE HOUR OF RETRIBUTION IS AT HAND! THIS GOD EXACTS VENGEANCE!!*"

He stood up straight, a grin on his face and turned towards Tallis. At that moment there came an enormous crash – a thunderclap inside the church. Tallis who had been looking through the tracery stepped sharply backwards.

"The doors!" he exclaimed. All three of them peered into the interior of the basilica. The great doors, which had probably not been opened for a hundred years or more, hung off their hinges and past this wreckage streamed the occupants of the church. In a matter of minutes the cavern was virtually empty apart from one or two insensible bodies.

"How do we get down?" asked Dando urgently.

"This way," said the Gopher. He led them through the room of the Voice to the top of a spiral staircase round which they hurried until they reached a door leading into the rotunda. Tallis and Gopher went towards the light-filled entrance through which came shouts, screams, the clash of weaponry and loud reports. Dando turned the other way; he had not forgotten the helpless man behind the altar. As he drew near he saw that the bound figure was a boy about his own age or perhaps a little older. The victim's head was bowed and he hung limp in the ropes. Quickly drawing his knife

Dando pressed his body against the other's to prevent a fall, then reached up with both hands and began sawing at the bonds. He was caught off guard when an incongruously refined voice spoke close to his ear.

"What are you going to do to me this time?"

Dando gathered his wits.

"I'm not going to do anything to you," he replied, "except set you free."

"Who are you?" asked the boy.

The last rope parted and the released prisoner fell forward into his arms. Dando lowered him carefully to the ground and then straightened up, able for the first time to look full into his face. He gasped and recoiled, his shock so great that he had no hope of hiding his reaction.

"Sorry," said the young man and turned his head aside.

"Who – who did this to you?" stammered Dando.

"It's what happens in this place. It's one of the *uttermost circles of hell*, you know. That was you, wasn't it? Clever trick – but how did you manage the thunderclap?"

Dando could hardly believe the calm almost cheerful tone of voice, the insouciant manner.

"But your sight!" he cried like a callow bumpkin stating the obvious, for the boy had been blinded. Where his eyes should have been there were two red weeping sockets only partly obscured by the blond hair that flopped over his forehead.

"That's what they do – if your dear mama and papa fail to make with the money they cut off bits of you and send them through the post - gives those on the receiving end more of an incentive."

"But to take your eyes!"

"Well in my case it's a little more complicated. I'll tell you sometime."

Dando looked around helplessly, horror having rendered him totally ineffectual.

"What can I do?" he asked, "there must be some sort of a priest's room where you could lie down and recover."

But the boy had other ideas.

"Don't you want to know what's going on outside?" he countered. "There was the sound of a full scale battle a few minutes ago."

Dando remembered Tallis, Foxy and Ann – especially Ann. He desperately wanted to find out what was happening to them. But he was also needed here.

"I'm not going to leave you," he said.

"No – I'll come with you – hang on," and the young man climbed to his feet and stood swaying slightly, his hand held out before him.

"Jack – Jack Howgego."

Dando took the hand and held it.

"I'm Dando," he said.

"Just Dando?"

"Yes."

He retained the boy's hand, leading him past the ruined doors and through the soaring archway of the cave mouth into daylight. He was brought up short by the scene that confronted him.

"What's the matter?" asked Jack Howgego.

"Bodies – dead."

In front of the holy place was a wide open space where the recent conflict had occurred. The ground was littered with casualties but otherwise the square stood deserted. Surveying this aftermath of battle Dando felt slightly sick. He was vividly reminded of the two robbers who had died beneath his sword and experienced again his initial appalled reaction. A warrior? No - who was he kidding? - he was not cut out to be a fighter. His hand and Jack's were still linked and suddenly the other's grip became vice-like. Dando was just in time to grab hold of him as the boy's legs buckled. He half carried him back into the church and sat him down on a chair by the door.

"What's wrong," he said, "are you ill?"

"No food," said Jack, "they starved us."

Dando's first impression of Jack had been that he was painfully thin, now he understood why.

"I'll get you something," he said.

"No, get me a blindfold to hide this," and he pointed to his face. "I don't want to scare your friends when I meet them."

"You think I've got friends?" said Dando. "Well, I'll do that but you also need to eat. You really ought to see a doctor you know."

"That'll have to wait until I get back to Drossi, there's no doctors here."

"I'll return – I promise."

Dando rejected the contaminated half-eaten food left by the bandits in the church and hurried into the settlement on his errand, threading his way through corpses and spilled blood, thankful to see that there were few of Rhys' army amongst the slain. Rounding a corner he practically bumped into the Gopher and another man coming the other way.

"Where is everybody?" he asked.

"The gang has fled. We beat them hands down! Rhys and the rest have gone after them to run them to earth. None of them must be allowed to bring word to the Cheetah."

"What Master Tallisand as well?"

"Yes."

"What about Ann, the fair-haired girl?"

"You mean the priestess – the heathen woman? She's gone with Rhys and Captain Judd - he's a fighter and no mistake. Better she doesn't come back – we don't need her sort round here. I've stayed behind to guard the holy places. This is our dear bishop, still in the land of the living, thank the lord. He's just about to set off for Labour-in-Vain – he doesn't want to be here when the rest of the gang returns. It's against his vows to engage in hostilities."

"Is there no one else left?"

"The prisoners are all down in the storerooms, stuffing themselves."

"Tell me how to get there."

The storerooms were well stocked; depriving the kidnap victims of sustenance had been just a pointless cruelty. About twenty men and women were eating and drinking with a sort of dedicated ferocity and paid Dando not the slightest heed. He noticed that one or two were missing minor body parts such as a finger or an ear but they all still had their eyes as far as he could tell. He looked round for food he could take to Jack. Here was some milk – good – the settlement was obviously home to a few dairy animals, and over there was bread as well as butter, apples, cheese and nuts – also eggs. He took half a dozen – there must surely be a stove somewhere to cook them on – and here were some oats – he might be able to make porridge. There were also flagons containing what smelt like ale, and bottles of something much stronger. He found a small barrow and piled the supplies into it, wheeling it outside into the street. For the first time he noticed that most of the house doors were open, the dwellings had been broken into and ransacked. He peered into one or two and then hit the jackpot: a fully equipped kitchen with range and a pile of wood. He pushed the barrow in through the front door, lit the stove, then, recalling Jack's first request, climbed the stairs and explored the upper story. Rhys had been right, he found heavy duty outdoor clothing hanging in a closet; if all the houses were so supplied they would certainly be able to equip themselves adequately. But in a room that, by the evidence of rag dolls lined up on top of a chest seemed to have belonged to a little girl, he found a far more incongruous item. Spread out on the bed as if ready to be worn that very evening lay, in pristine purity, a white lace dress with tiered skirt and ruffled sleeves – a party frock. Dando wondered for the first time what had happened to the ordinary citizens of Toymerle; he hoped most of them had gotten safely away when the gang took over. The white dress had a coloured silk sash that was easy to remove. Taking it with him he left the food in the kitchen and started to make his way back to the square. Halfway there he remembered the horses and made a mental note to fetch and install them in the small stable he had discovered at the back of the despoiled house as soon as he had provided for Jack.

When he returned to the basilica the boy was still on the chair where he had left him. Gopher and the bishop were at the altar end of the church; they had either ignored, or not even noticed, the pale young man sitting so quietly near the door.

"Jack, I've found somewhere where we can go – better than this."

"Did you bring me something to put round my head?"

Dando explained about the party frock.

"A dress – yes – that'd be just up my street. What colour is the sash?"

"Navy blue."

"Well – as long as it isn't pink."

Dando folded the ribbon into two lengthways and tied it round Jack's head, knotting it at the back. The ends hung down to the boy's waist.

"Shall I cut these off?"

"No, leave them, I imagine it looks quite good – sort of piratical."

Dando told him about the house with the kitchen range, then asked:-

"Can you walk?"

"I think so."

They made their way down through the little town, Dando's arm around Jack's shoulders as the hard packed snow was treacherous underfoot. Once in the kitchen he guided the boy to a chair and then set about cooking some porridge with the milk and oats, even finding a jar of honey in the otherwise plundered larder. He followed this with a cheese omelette and bread and butter.

"Don't eat too fast," he warned, "your insides aren't used to it."

They ended the meal with bread and butter spread with honey followed by an apple each and then broached a bottle of spirits. Jack sipped slowly and silently, finishing one measure and then another. All at once he bent forward over the kitchen table, pushing the dirty crockery aside, and buried his head in his arms.

"What's the matter?" asked Dando.

"It's this I'm not used to," came the boy's muffled reply.

"What?"

"You looking after me like this."

He sat hiding his face, his shoulders shaking. It took him some time to recover. When he was finally able to sit up they adjourned to the house's front parlour with the alcohol. Here Dando lit the fire, righted a few upset chairs and then invited Jack to sink into the welcome comfort of one of them, following which he went and fetched the horses.

"How did you do the thunder?" asked the boy on his return.

"That wasn't us, it came from out of the blue."

"These people you're with – tell me about them."

Dando looked at him uncertainly but then decided to comply.

"Well, there's Tallis – he's on a lifetime's journey searching for a Key. He's my master."

"Your master! - don't pull my leg! - by your voice you're pretty posh. People like you don't have masters!"

"Ah – but what I mean is I vowed to serve him as his squire – like they did in the old days. It was the only way he would take me along. Then there's Foxy, he's Nablan, but he's not typical. He's a great hunter with the bow. We didn't get on too well at first but things have gotten better lately. And then there's Annie, she's also Nablan - seventeen like me. She's very pretty."

"Ann you say – is she this Foxy's woman?"

"No," said Dando proudly and indignantly, "she's *my* woman."

"Yours?"

"Yes," emphatically.

"Oh." Jack relapsed into silence. Eventually he said, "I wish I knew what you looked like."

His companion remained quiet for sometime, amazed that he was having this apparently normal conversation with someone whom he felt should have been totally incapacitated. Eventually he was impelled to remark, "Don't blind folk read people's features by touch?"

"Do they? I'm new to this game."

Acting on the suggestion Jack reached out and Dando took his hand, knelt before him and guided it to his face. With great delicacy the young man ran his fingers over nose, eyelids, forehead, mouth, chin, hair until they came to rest cradling Dando's cheek. Then with a light slap that was almost a caress he drew back.

"You're a good-looking blighter, aren't you," he said.

Dando laughed in embarrassment.

"But does everyone wear their hair that short where you come from?"

"No – it's a long story."

"A long-haired story? I'd like to hear it."

So Dando told him a little about the situation in Deep Hallow, about his upbringing and recent history, but omitted certain emotive events such as the Dan's murder and his encounters with the supernatural. When he finished they sat drinking quietly and companionably for a while until Dando broke in with, "You said you'd explain about... you know..."

"Oh well – yes - all right. The fact is you and I are very similar in many ways. We've both had families on our backs, although in my case it's been a grandfather, not a father. My granddaddy runs the biggest import-export business in Drossi - he trades across the Middle Sea – he's a massive shipping magnate. The Howgegos have always been seafarers, it's in our blood, but granddad is the first one to make any money at it. I think Hiram Howgego's ambition - that's his name by the way - was to found a dynasty and become head of the most influential family in all the Seven Towns. But right from the outset, almost as soon as he started making plans, he received a setback. His son Giles, my father, who was being groomed to take over, was sent to sea to learn the business from the ground - or maybe you'd say the water - up. He'd just got his first captaincy and had barely had time to see me into the world, when on its second voyage his ship just vanished. No-one knows what happened. My father was lost at sea, presumed dead, and my mother left a widow. Granddad, who couldn't have cared less about *her* feelings, immediately took over my upbringing and the first rule he laid down was that I was never to board a ship. Well, being a Howgego, all I wanted as I got older was to follow in my predecessors' footsteps - still do - but I wasn't allowed, at least when he had his eye on me. By the time I reached my teens I was so thoroughly frustrated by this shore-bound existence that I cut loose and went a bit wild – well, not just a bit. Not to mince words I tried every dodgy thrill that Drossi had to offer, and to complicate matters I discovered that when it came to – how d'you say – lerve – I was left of centre..."

Dando looked puzzled. "I don't understand"

"Oh you know – on the hur – skewiff - bent. What's your word for it where you come from?"

Dando coloured. "There isn't one," he said.

" I suppose that means your homeland is one of the places that sweeps such things under the carpet. Anyway I did everything I could to annoy the old man and made no secret of my *depravity* as he called it. Poor old chap – first of all he loses his son to the deep and then he finds he's got a faggot for a grandson. In the end his patience ran out and he wrote me off as far as everyday communication goes. We've had nothing more to do with each other for the last four years although he still goes on paying my debts and ensuring that no-one afloat will employ me."

"But that doesn't explain..." said Dando.

"Oh that – yes. Well about six months ago I was living pretty close to the edge – brushing shoulders with a lot of unsavoury characters. One night out in the street someone whacked me over the back of the head. I woke up in a cart trussed like a chicken on the way to the mountains. They thought they'd hit the big time you see: they imagined they had my grandfather's most prized possession in their clutches and they had a grudge to settle; they didn't realise that by this point in the proceedings he couldn't have cared less what happened to me, in fact was probably quite relieved to have me out of the way. By *they* I mean the Merrick brothers, that's what they were called before they became the Cheetah and the Panther. At one time they were running a legitimate shipping business together. My grandfather forced them into bankruptcy and also seems to have had a hand in the Cheetah's being convicted of fraud. He spent a long time in prison. So when I was kidnapped they sent a ransom note as a matter of course, but asking for some astronomical sum, and when grandpappy didn't cough up they sent him this," pointing to his face, "and then this, as a sort of revenge for past injustice." He paused and when Dando failed to speak added, "and there you have it – the whole sorry mess." Still Dando remained unresponsive; he had been silenced by overwhelming sadness, his heart wrung with pity.

Jack flopped back against the armchair in which he was sitting, the paleness of his face accentuated by the dark blindfold. Talking had exhausted him. He needed rest Dando realised.

"There's three bedrooms upstairs," he explained to the boy, "a double and two singles. You can have the double – I don't mind one of the singles." Maybe he had spoken too emphatically, maybe there was something in the tone of his voice. Whatever it was Jack picked up on it. He smiled tiredly and somewhat ruefully. "It's alright, lad," he said, "you needn't fear I'm going to try to hit on you."

Sometime in the small hours Dando was woken by a moaning noise like the sound of an animal in pain. He waited, listening, and when it came again got up, lit a candle and went to investigate. Entering the other boy's bedroom he discovered his new-found friend in trouble. He appeared to be unconscious, but while asleep was tossing first one way and then the other as if in the grip of unseen adversaries.

"No, no, no, no," he was muttering into the pillow and then, flinging himself over onto his back, let forth an anguished cry. He seemed to be able to scream without waking himself up and so remained under the dream's dark enchantment. Dando saw that it was his responsibility to break the spell.

"Jack," he cried, gripping the other's shoulders and shaking him. Jack gave a great gasp and raised his bound head as if trying to see. He put up a hand to tear the sash from non-existent eyes. Dando caught his hand and held it.

"No, no," he echoed.

The young man fell back onto the pillows and lay breathing fast, beads of perspiration on his forehead. Dando awkwardly patted and squeezed his shoulder.

"It's not real, Jack – it was just a dream - just a dream."

"No. it *is* real – it happened – and I'm never going to be able to forget it."

After a while when nothing more disturbed the quiet room and Dando thought Jack had gone back to sleep, he got up to go, but the boy reached out as if trying to detain him.

"Don't leave me alone," he said. And so Dando climbed into the double bed and for the rest of the night the two of them lay side by side.

The landscape, dear love,
Spreads like a dark dream before us,
Full of false promise.

Chapter nine

When Tallis emerged from the basilica in company with the Gopher after the destruction of the doors, he was confronted by the scene of carnage that Dando witnessed a little later. However, on the far side of the body-strewn space, he also saw the towering figure of Rhys lecturing a number of other Labourites who were looking relaxed and vaguely triumphant, while Foxy and Ann stood by, their bows still in their hands. Apart from the corpses there was no sign of any of the gang members who had fled the church. Tallis left the Gopher to go his own way and dodged across between the fallen in order to hear what Rhys had to say. He discovered that he was urging his troops on to further action. "No time to lose!" the big man cried. "Aled, you're a good tracker, take your contingent and go north – I think some of them went that way. Mostyn, you go down the Ffordd and if you don't find anyone at the village carry on towards Formile. And you Bryn take the Ixat turning. We'll head towards V.P.," he was now addressing Foxy, Ann and his sons, "I think that's the way most of them have gone. Be careful – as we've discovered some of them have guns. Capture preferably, but kill if necessary. Remember no-one must get through to forewarn the Cheetah. Hallo," to Tallis, "another volunteer - fine - we can do with anyone who's willing. Good luck everybody."

Not waiting for a reply he set off at speed southwards, then, at the first junction, eastwards, with Foxy and a few others close behind while Tallis and Ann brought up the rear. Within half-an-hour of turning left they overtook three of the bandits and a sharp skirmish ensued. Despite Rhys' instructions about taking prisoners these men were all left for dead and they carried on swiftly down the track, Foxy's eyes glued to the ground. "There be at least six ahead o' us," he said.

The chase went on well into the night. For Tallis, already wondering if he was capable of such exertion, the pace was extremely demanding and after a while he fell further and further behind. At last he had to admit defeat and came to a halt, struggling to regain his breath. And as he stood there, his chest heaving, it was exactly as if something snapped inside his skull. The landscape whirled like a carousel, he lost his balance and fell backwards. Lying face upwards he gazed stupidly at a thin sliver of moon that appeared to be executing a crazy dance. Then the moon vanished and, with stars in her hair, Ann was looking down on him. He tried to speak, he tried to say *there's something wrong with my head,* but all that emerged was a garbled babble. After that he tried to get up but his arms and legs would not obey him. He strained against the weakness, his features distorted with effort.

"Stay quiet, stay quiet," insisted a perturbed Ann. She pulled his cloak around him and took off her own to provide extra warmth, after which she knelt by his side.

"Stay quiet," she said again.

Tallis did as he was bidden and slowly things began to calm down. A pounding ache started on the left hand side of his scull and he shut his eyes. For a while he must have lost consciousness for when he was again aware he seemed to be once more in command of his body. Ann was still sitting quietly next to him.

"I think I would like to go back to the town," he said, with just a slight slurring of his speech.

Ann helped him up. After having regained his feet he stood leaning heavily against her, using her shoulder as a crutch and testing his limbs. Slowly they made their way along the track, Tallis relying on the girl for support. It was already getting light by the time they arrived on the outskirts of Toymerle.

Leaving Tallis sitting on a low wall Ann set out through the town to look for a suitable refuge and, in one of the houses off the main square, found a room with a bed on the ground floor. She fetched Tallis, helped him undress down to his underwear and, once he had lain down, spread covers over him. She pumped some water, brought him a drink and then remained with him until she was sure he had fallen asleep. After that she could not resist going in search of Dando whose welfare was causing her concern. She did not like to think of her lover so close to the Fire-God's seat of power; the gift she had inherited from Tom gave her sixth sense an extra dimension and her intuition told her that Dando had much to fear from such places although she did not really understand why. Gathering from a passer-by that the kidnap victims were ensconced in the store she decided to drop in on them to see if they knew where the young Glept was to be found. But when she opened the door a few minutes later she discovered a room in disarray. The majority of the prisoners were lying on the floor and some had been sick. Others had apparently had an attack of the runs and the smell was indescribable. Many empty bottles were dotted here and there throughout the area and a few of the inmates were still drinking what were obviously strong spirits. A couple of women were ineffectually attempting to deal with the chaos.

All of Ann's housekeeperly instincts came to the fore, she could not abide mess, her seven years of hard labour at the Justification had marked her indelibly. She set to work to put things to rights and to clean up those who had over indulged. First of all she confiscated all the remaining alcohol and poured it into the street. Then she began washing bodies and dressing wounds – as Dando had already discovered several of the victims had suffered at the hands of the outlaws - after which she turned her attention to mopping, scrubbing and laundering. Alongside her toiled one of the women prisoners whose name she discovered was Cristin. Although obviously not used to performing such menial tasks this upper-class female was willing to follow Ann's lead, making up in enthusiasm for what she lacked in skill. It was much later in the day before things were shipshape, the hostages chastened, grateful and on the road to recovery and she was given time to remember what had brought her there in the first place.

"Ha' you seen the tall dark-haired young gent who help chase the bad men out of the temple?" she asked.

"Oh yes, we heard about that," replied Cristin. "Your boy-friend is he? If he's who I think he is I believe he's in a house along the main street with the Howgego lad. It's a good thing your people arrived when they did otherwise the gang would have done for that one altogether, although from his point of view - not that he has a point of view any longer - perhaps it would have been a blessing."

"I mus' call in somewhere else first," said Ann, explaining about Tallis and about his sudden illness. Cristin accompanied her when she went to see how the southerner was faring only to discover that he was still fast asleep. The woman kindly suggested that she should stand watch until morning to give Ann a break.

"Run along with you," she said, "I was your age once. I know what it's like to keep a boy waiting. I'd rather stay here than go back to that pigsty."

Dando had spent part of the day cooking for Jack, trying to provide food that would build up the boy's strength but not overtax his weakened digestion. Also, because, in the morning, the young man asked to go out, he had led him through the streets and found him a walking stick with which he could feel his way; Jack insisted that it should be a smart one. There was scarcely anyone else about although they did hear word from a solitary loiterer that the prisoners were still making up for lost time in the storerooms, some inevitably suffering the consequences. Later they went back to the house and sat and talked, learning more about each other's lives. There was a five year gap in their ages Dando discovered, enough for him to defer to Jack as to an older brother. It was fascinating to compare their disparate upbringings: both privileged young men, both born to wealth, the one in the remote upland valley and the other in the big city. Jack was intrigued by the fact that Dando was a twin, and had many brothers and sisters, while Dando learned a little about the sort of counter-culture to be found in a town such as Drossi.

"You'd like my sister," he said, "she always had a yen to walk on the wild side."

"And not you?"

"The situation between the Glepts and the Nablar was wild enough for me."

Dando confided some of his secret hopes and fears to this new-found friend while the boy from Drossi gave voice to his undimmed ambition to go to sea.

"They employ blind sail-makers in a few of the ships I believe. I shall have to learn how to do that."

This period of waiting in Toymerle provided a charmed interval during which they had the chance to forget harsh reality for a while. But already Dando was getting intimations of problems ahead. What was to become of Jack and who would look after him once Tallis returned and they resumed their journey? The southerner would not be prepared to linger long in this particular place he was sure and he would not want a blind man along as companion on the road: he would see him as an impediment to their progress. Inevitably, if it came to a choice, he, Dando, was bound to follow Tallis, having sworn himself to his service.

After lunch Jack stated his determination to venture forth alone.

"If I don't try I'm never going to learn."

Dando stayed behind, worrying about him and also about Ann whom he had not set eyes on for an awfully long time; he hoped Foxy was looking after her and also after Master Tallisand. If it was not for his concern for Jack he would have gone in search of them.

Jack came back after two hours still in one piece and with information to impart.

"Your friend Gopher's opened the treasure cave and, on the instructions of the bishop, who's already scarpered, is going to hand over ten pounds tomorrow to everyone who took part in the liberation. And my companions in misfortune are planning to set off for the plains as soon as they feel fit enough, although some of them seem pretty buggered at the moment. They don't want to be here when the Cheetah returns – I don't blame them – I think I may go too."

"But you're not strong enough Jack."

"Rubbish, I'm ok. If I can walk round here I can walk to Drossi and I'd better take the chance to leave while I can. Why don't you lot come with me?"

During the afternoon members of the Labour in Vain force began to straggle back into Toymerle with a few cowed bandits in tow who had been taken alive. These were shut in the community hall where the kidnap victims had been held. A start was made on fortifying the settlement by erecting barricades across streets and in the gaps between buildings. As Jack and Dando were eating dinner a knock came at the door and two men informed them that they were requisitioning furniture. The boys had to argue fiercely in order to hang on to their beds and chairs; the jobs-worths even wanted to take the range. When a second knock was heard Dando went to answer it, ready to defend to the last ditch their remaining fixtures and fittings.

"You can't have any more, you've already taken..." he began and then saw who it was on the step.

"Annie!"

The love of his life smiled up at him, her blue eyes shining, the very picture of a warrior maiden. Her wild tangle of fair hair stood out from around her flushed dirty face like a halo. She carried her bow over one shoulder, quiver over the other, the arrows very much depleted. Dando looked up and down the street - neither Foxy nor Tallis were in sight. He reached out and grabbed her into his arms.

"Oh, Annie – I've been so worried about you!"

"An' I be worried about 'ee my love."

"I'm fine, fine. Where's Master Tallis – and Foxy?"

"Foxy be still after the runaways – he goo ahead. I bring the knight back to the village 'coz he come over queer. He's took to his bed up the street. It be best if 'ee don' disturb he jes' yet."

Dando heard a snicker behind him. He turned to find Jack grinning, as if at some private jest that only he could appreciate. Much to his annoyance he suspected that Ann was the butt of the joke.

"What's so funny?" he asked belligerently.

"Nothing," said Jack, immediately straight faced. "Is this your girl friend? Introduce me."

"This is Annie," replied Dando somewhat mollified. "Annie – this is Jack, he was one of the prisoners." Jack stepped forward and held out his hand.

"Pleased to meet you," he said formally.

"Likewise I'm sure," answered Ann, shaking the proffered hand and looking towards Dando with a concerned expression. Dando frowned and put his finger to his lips.

"Don't take any notice of him," said Jack, proving that Dando and Ann were not the only ones to have a sixth sense, "I can't see and that's all there is to it, and sometimes I come over queer as well."

"She doesn't know what you're talking about," said the Glept but laughed despite himself.

That night Jack generously offered to exchange sleeping arrangements.

"Will you be all right on your own?" asked Dando

"If I make a row just shoot me – it would be the kindest thing." But the night passed quietly apart from the creaking of springs; it was the first time Dando and Ann had made love in a proper bed.

After breakfast Foxy reappeared and with angry suspicion reclaimed the girl, leading her away on the pretext that they needed to watch for the bandit's return.

"Why do you let him do that?" asked Jack when the pair had left and he had been apprised of some of the subtleties of this odd eternal triangle. Dando shrugged wearily and sighed.

"I don't think he'd rest until he'd finished me off and perhaps her too if he knew how far things have progressed. He's set himself up as a sort of guardian and the simple fact is that besides being the wrong sex I'm the wrong race as well. I don't think he wants her to have anything to do with men."

"He's in love with her himself," said Jack wisely.

"The chief reckon that the boss man be comin' back in the next few days," remarked Foxy to Ann. "He be agooin' to get a shock when he find we be holdin' the place agin' 'e."

Foxy and his protege had been sent north to establish a lookout post along the road in that direction, with the promise that they would be relieved at dusk. They climbed up the hillside to a vantage point from where they could view the track for a good distance ahead.

"I doubt he be a-comin' thisaway," said Foxy. "I hope they send word if they see he comin' from the south. I be vexed if I miss the fightin'."

"But Foxy, the knight be settin' off agin as soon as he feel well enough. I know he never bide long. He won' wan' to wait."

"Let he goo," said Foxy, "you an' me we c'n do better stayin' here. Rhys he tell me he need our strength wi' the bow."

"I goo wi' the knight," said Ann obstinately.

Foxy looked at her with anger and exasperation.

"It don' be the knight you wan' to goo wi' – it be that incomer, that son of they rascals that take our lan' away from us. He don' be worth it girl - none of they be worth it."

Ann was suddenly totally weary of all the deception, the subterfuge that she and Dando had been practising for weeks past. She decided to speak plainly for once.

"I know him all my life. We drink the same milk as babes. I knowd him longer than I knowd you. He be my sweetheart Foxy – I love he an' he love me an' he need me more 'n you do."

"That be a load of flapdoodle!" exclaimed Foxy unfeelingly, and then, "*I* needs 'ee." After a long pause he added, "I ain't a-gooin' ter back out now," following this with, "if he lay a finger on you he'd better watch out."

"No Foxy. Promise me you won' do he no harm. Promise."

"I promise as long as he keep away from 'ee."

"No, that be no good. I wan' 'ee to promise no matter what – no matter what come – else I won' be your frien' no more. Promise."

Foxy tried to hold her gaze, to stare her out, blue meeting blue, dark against light, but in the end he had to look away; in his turn he also felt a great weariness and for once in his life his determination wavered.

"I promise," he muttered almost soundlessly.

Ann's spirits rose into the stratosphere. She felt she had triumphed. It had always been taken as read by the inhabitants of the Justification that Foxy stuck by his word even if the pledge had been given in a moment of thoughtlessness, and with this response he had demonstrated a clear resolve to forswear violence. She believed – she hoped - he would not renege. It appeared that now she could go to her lover without fear of the consequences, although she realised that the Nablan would probably never speak to her again if she did. She was free at last to follow her heart's desire, yet, all through this exchange and despite her jubilation, she knew she was making a fatal mistake. She knew that she should have agreed to stay behind in Toymerle and let Dando go north alone, thus removing her dangerous presence from his side.

Tallis awoke to find the concerned face of his squire filling his field of vision. The boy disappeared, only to return, lift him gently and put a full beaker to his lips. The drink was sweet, rich and milky with a spicy taste and had some ingredient that gave it a substantial kick. Holding him in a sitting position after the container had been emptied the lad shook up the pillows behind and then allowed him to subside against them and close his eyes. Where in the world were they? Tallis felt so tired that it hardly seemed to matter. But something was niggling at the back of his mind, something that would not let him sleep. There was a thing he had to do that could not wait - a task he had to accomplish and time was running out. Groping through a thick fog he suddenly had a mental image of an asymmetrical piece of metal - an opening device - a key. He was looking for it, that was right, and he had to find it before... before what? - before he grew too old? Oh, and then of course there was the Oracle! He sat up and made an attempt to swing his legs out of bed. Immediately Dando was at his side.

"Don't get up yet master – rest a while longer. Tomorrow you'll feel better. You need to gather your strength."

"But I can't waste a moment – I must go north – north."

"There's mountains to the north and you'll need all your strength."

"I understand mountains."

"Yes – you need to recover so you can show us the way through. Rest today – tomorrow will be soon enough."

"I want to ask the god a question."

"The Gopher'll know how to do that."

Tallis eventually slept but woke several times as the day wore on. Only once, late in the afternoon, did he find Dando absent and then Cristin was standing in for him.

It was the expeditionary force's third morning in Toymerle, the bodies of the enemy had been buried in a communal grave and Gopher was holding court in the church, sitting at a table with a chest of gold at his feet. Rhys' two enormous sons were on duty at either side to keep order and see fair play. A line soon formed back to the shattered doors, composed of the victorious citizens of Labour in Vain. As each combatant reached the head of the queue they were given a handful of coins and marked with a brush dipped in stain to ensure that nobody cheated and came round a second time. Towards evening Tallis, Dando, Foxy and Ann presented themselves for their reward, Tallis walking unaided and looking much healthier. At first the Gopher, who was deep in conversation with another man, did not notice who was before him. When he did he jumped to his feet, pulled himself up to his full five foot two inches and pointed at Ann, shouting, "Get out of my church, witch!" The girl shrank down into a typical attitude of nibbler humility and turned to flee, but both Foxy and Dando held out their arms to detain her while Tallis protested, "What do you think you're doing?! - she's owed the same as everyone else! - she helped liberate your sanctuary – she risked her life!"

"Idolaters are not allowed in the holy places," harrumphed the Gopher, "except for those that are here for the benefit of the shrine."

"Well, she certainly has benefited your shrine," replied Tallis, but, mainly because Ann was desperate to leave, gave up the argument and went out into the square along with the others where they waited for nearly an hour before the Gopher emerged.

"You must understand my position," the little man began in a conciliatory manner, "I have to maintain the purity of the sacred ground. This is a very sensitive time – the god's house had been desecrated and we will have to carry out a cleansing. Any disruptive elements could jeopardise the purification."

"Annie isn't a disruptive element," exclaimed Dando putting his arm around his beloved and hugging her to him. Foxy looked askance but did not interfere.

"We try to be tolerant towards those not of the true faith," said the Gopher, beginning to hand out the gold and including coins for Ann which he gave to Tallis.

Once the business had been transacted Tallis asked, "I wish to consult the Oracle – can it be arranged?"

"What – before the purging? That could be difficult. The conditions must be right before the God will speak. Also we need a priest – there are no priests here at the moment."

"I understand there is a fee to be paid – I have ample funds – you can set your own price. I will pay in advance if you like."

Thr Gopher shook his head but with an avaricious glint in his eye. "I'd like to oblige but the conveying is always done by a cleric. Only someone in holy orders can breath the breath of the god." He went to walk away.

Dando addressed Tallis, careful to avoid catching Ann's eye.

"I'm a priest," he said diffidently, "I've been ordained according to the rites of the Church of the Heavenly King."

"Really?" replied Tallis in astonishment, "you've never told me that before." He suddenly remembered the dowdy robes the boy had been wearing at the castle when he set eyes on him during their second meeting.

"It was my father's wish," said Dando.

The Gopher turned back looking surprised and then laughed.

"So," he said to Dando, "you're not satisfied with being the Voice of the God in the basilica, now you want to be the Conveyor as well."

"I serve my master," said Dando stiffly.

"Well," said Tallis, "there you have your solution – my squire can officiate."

"No!" broke in Ann, an anguished expression on her face, "don' let 'e do that – don' let 'e Foxy!"

"It don' be up to I," replied Foxy indifferently while Dando muttered, "Leave off Annie!"

"And you'll pay whatever fee is required?" said Gopher. "Come back tomorrow about noon; I'll see what I can do."

Before it got dark Tallis, having benefited from at least forty-eight hours of complete rest, went in search of some much needed information. He made tentative enquiries at the prisoners' door and was told of two individuals among their number - a father and son - who were actually Toymerle residents. They were to be found, so he was informed, at their ransacked house where they were trying to restore things to some sort of order. It was against Tallis' nature to ask for help but in this case circumstances overruled caution.

"Is it feasible to travel north of here at this time of year?" he asked the couple.

"What? Take the road to Pickwah? No, impossible – no-one has ever gone over the pass later than the tenth month. Even our mountaineers wouldn't attempt it."

"I have experience of high country. I think I could get through where others might fail."

"If you tried you'd be found stiff as a board when the snows retreated in the spring, if we found you at all. Mind you there is the other way east-nor'-east to Trincomalee – that has been crossed in winter but not very often. The road that runs through here rejoins the Northern Drift further up and then, a steep climb after that, you'll see the Trincomalee turning leading off on the right. It goes through the Fynnburg Pass which is a bit lower and more open than the Cold Straith, the one on the route to Pickwah."

"Could I take my horse?"

"Oh no – not in a million years. There's several stepped sections – hard enough for people on foot let alone pack animals. You'll have to leave it behind."

This was a blow – it would be a wrench to part with Carolus, his loyal and long-time companion. Facing up to the inevitable Tallis went in search of Rhys, an elusive and very busy man, to crave a few moment of his time.

"We're about to travel on through difficult terrain. Could I trust my horses to your care? You can have the use of them in exchange for their keep. When I return, which may not be for some time, we can settle any expenses that may have been incurred."

"You're not staying to defend the Shrine?"

"My squire and I need to leave on a matter of some urgency. I can't speak for the other members of our party. What about the horses?"

Rhys had had his eye on Carolus from the moment he first saw him; it was not often that such a fine looking specimen came this far into the hills. To have the use of such an animal would be hugely desirable even if it was only on the basis of a temporary loan.

"I could take the chestnut off your hands," he said cautiously.

"No, it must be both or none at all."

At that moment a runner with a message concerning the fortifications claimed Rhys' attention and Tallis had to stand by while he dealt with it. When he had finished with that matter someone else arrived and he seemed about to rush off to another part of the settlement. Tallis sought to detain him.

"What about the horses?"

"Oh yes – all right. Leave them with Aled, my son. He's good with animals – they'll get well looked after."

In caring for Tallis Dando lost track of Jack's comings and goings. The boy from the Delta City was becoming extraordinarily bold, roaming to and fro through the settlement and its environs, his elegant cane sweeping the ground ahead of him. He occasionally got tangled up or took a tumble but always extricating himself successfully from these predicaments, his confidence growing by the minute. He spoke to those manning the barricades, apologising for the fact that as a lookout he would be a non-starter, but offering to act as a messenger and as a nurse to the injured when the fighting began. He soon became a familiar sight tapping his way up and down the streets, happy to accept if anyone lent a guiding hand but prepared to manage on his own if necessary. Once or twice he ventured too far and got lost out alone on the hillside. He experienced a few moments of panic but managed to find his way back by using his ears and nose, with only a few bruises to demonstrate the route's hazards. He returned to Dando every so often with an account of recent developments.

"Dando, they're going tomorrow – that lot down in the stores – at least the ones that are still on their feet. I was going to stay and help defend the place but they say they'll take me with them – I can't refuse. You'll come won't you? I know all the best bolt-holes in Drossi – all the clubs and bars – not just the gay ones. And I know all the people worth knowing. Come on man – come back to Drossi with me – we'll have a ball."

"I can't – you know I can't – I explained how things are."

"Oh yes – you've got to stay here with your sweet little Nablan girl friend who isn't even yours and your weird so-called knight-errant with a bee in his bonnet about some non-existent key. I get the picture and I'm out of it - that's very clear." Dando was startled at the bitterness in his voice.

Jack disappeared again but returned shortly with an apology.

"I'm sorry lad – I get cranky at times."

"You've a perfect right to," said Dando, "considering..."

The Glept found Jack a knapsack and filled it with food. He also helped him choose some clothes suitable for a journey from amongst the extensive supply available in the abandoned houses. Jack was very particular about the cut and the fit, the feel of the cloth and also about the colour. He was frustrated by Dando's vagueness.

"Well, it's a kind of greeny-brown I think. No it's not it's grey... This one's not quite white... Oh, and this is a sort of red – or maybe it's purple."

"Make up your mind!" exclaimed Jack impatiently.

Ever since Foxy had returned to Toymerle they had seen little of Ann. There was no repetition of the time, forty-eight hours previously, when she and Dando had shared a double bed. Instead, Dando lay beside Jack, ready to exorcise his night-time demons. Then on the fourth morning after their arrival he went with his friend and the ex-prisoners to the Drossi turning. He had made the acquaintance of Cristin and was glad that she was to be one of the party.

"We'll take care of him," the woman said, "don't you fear. We'll make sure he doesn't go awol."

Dando was at a loss for words as he and Jack walked down the short stretch that led to the crossroads. His taciturn attitude was in sharp contrast to that of his companion who chatted away cheerfully enough. When it came to parting he found himself being embraced and then, to his acute embarrassment, enthusiastically kissed.

"As I'm cutting a swathe through the Drossi talent," said Jack, "I'll be thinking of you. If you lose your eyes your other senses become remarkably acute I've discovered, including your prophetic ones. I predict that we'll meet again – I'm sure of it. Au revoir chickadee – see you anon."

That noontide Tallis and Dando walked to the church to keep their prearranged appointment with Gopher, while Ann, who had given Foxy a rather obscure feminine excuse for abandoning lookout duty, tagged along behind. Ralph also accompanied them. The dog had been missing for most of their time in Toymerle. Having become used to being continually on the move and having grown restless when faced with Tallis' and Dando's apparent inaction he had gone off on his own business, which broadly involved playing court to the local bitches. But now he put in an appearance, joining the end of the procession. Beneath the soaring cavern entrance Ann possessed herself of one of Dando's hands. She sought to hold him back and prevent him from persisting in this folly on which he seemed undeviatingly bent. Ralph too reached up and pawed at Dando's arm, whining deep in his throat. By main force the boy pulled away, an angry set to his mouth, and without looking back followed Tallis into the shadows. Ann sat on a stone ledge outside the doorway to wait for his return, Ralph at her side.

Within the church the Gopher prepared to escort them to the Chamber of Breath after a not inconsiderable sum of money had changed hands. He led the way to a concealed door at the right-hand extremity of the rotunda.

"Long way down," he advised.

Their goal proved to be quite small: a rectangular, low-ceilinged, airless cavity deep below the main cavern, approached by many flights of steep stone steps, some almost ladder-like in places. Here on the walls, lit by the lanterns' fitful gleam, were archaic images of strange beings faded with age. In the midst of the space stood a waist-high pedestal of rock with a shallow depression in the top, and at the centre of this basin a hole, the entrance to a duct, from which rose almost invisible fumes. A strange suffocating smell pervaded the cave. Both master and squire sensed the oppressive weight of rock, hundreds of feet thick, bearing down upon this little room. Even the most stout-hearted pilgrim might well suffer from claustrophobia in such a place.

"Have you your question ready?" whispered Gopher to Tallis. Tallis nodded. "Kneel down then both of you. I will recite the invocation."

"Lord of the hidden fire, of the core, of the very heart of our world, draw near, and in your infinite mercy breathe the Divine Breath into this human instrument here present, so that he may say that which you design for him to say, no more no less, and convey your Holy Word to the humble suppliant who kneels before you on this Sacred Ground. Amen."

At the Gopher's urging the petitioners rose to their feet. The little man took Tallis aside.

"I'll require your help," he murmured. "While in the power of the god he will need to be supported. There's normally two acolytes in attendance." Then to Dando, "Come here – put your face to the Source. Bend right down – stay there for as long as you can."

Dando, trying to suppress a strong intuition that he was doing something utterly stupid, bowed low over the aperture in the pedestal and took a deep breath. He was immediately seized by a paroxysm of coughing and desperately attempted to back away in order to get some clean air into his lungs, but Gopher would not allow it. He pushed the young man's head down into the fumes and held it there with surprising strength until his victim ceased to struggle.

"Come and lift him," he said to Tallis for Dando's legs had begun to give way. A small milking stool had been placed beside the font-like rock and onto this the Gopher and Tallis lowered Dando's lanky frame. The boy crumpled forward until his head hung down almost between his knees. The Gopher seized him by the hair and pulled him upright once more.

"Quick," he urged, "ask, ask! The trance doesn't last long!"

Dando's face had taken on a corpse-like hue, his eyes mere slits and his mouth hanging open. He looked stupefied. Radiating from his body Tallis sensed an overpowering alien presence that throbbed and twanged between the room's four walls and had nothing to do with the pitiful corporeal entity inside of which it had temporarily taken up residence.

"Can you..." Tallis began with great trepidation, "I mean, may I humbly beg of you to tell me where the Key – the Key-of-the-Ages – is located?"

Dando's lips did not move, his mouth remained open, but from between his teeth came a rushing sound within which one could distinguish words.

"Over-the-Brook... it is to be found within the city... he who speaks must turn it."

The sibilance died away

"But I don't want to turn it!" cried Tallis, "I want to restore it to the Land of the Lake! Can you explain what you mean by the city?"

"You can't ask twice," protested Gopher, apparently scared to death and out of his depth.

"Here," said Tallis, plunging a hand into his purse and pulling out several more coins, "I'll pay."

"Help me lift him then."

Between them they managed to manoeuvre Dando's head a second time into the fumes.

"Where is the Key to be found?" asked Tallis once more.

The rushing roaring noise, like a gale through a forest, welled up through the boy's lips but on this occasion it was hard to make out anything coherent.

"*The old man is not the one... nor will he go back... it should be taken outside...* " were the only words that came through clearly.

"Again, again!" cried Tallis proffering more money but on the third attempt nothing could be distinguished.

"That's enough," exclaimed the Gopher, *more than enough,* he added inwardly, dismayed despite himself at the sight of Dando's huddled figure slumped beside the pedestal. He and Tallis stared at the boy waiting for him to recover.

"They usually get over it pretty quickly," said the little man as if trying to convince himself. "He'll be back with us soon."

It was at least ten minutes before, to their immense relief, Dando lifted his head. This relief was short-lived. The countenance that he raised to them had a greyish tinge like the face of one whose spirit has long departed. Only his eyes – lakes of whirling amber fire – were alive, and they seemed to be turned inward onto a view of vast alien landscapes. They were no longer Dando's eyes.

"Come on lad," said Gopher, " we've got a long climb ahead. Get on your feet."

The boy gave no indication of having heard, but after a minute or two rose and stood by for further orders - an automaton waiting to be set in motion.

"He'll be all right once we're back in the fresh air - I think he's just tired out," said Tallis uncomfortably, trying to avoid looking at his squire.

As Tallis and Dando appeared in the church doorway, Gopher no longer in tow as he had stayed behind to put into operation the cleansing routine that had been ordered by his superiors, Ralph jumped up and ran towards them, his plumed tail swinging to and fro with pleasure. But as soon as the two shadowy figures emerged into the light he stopped stock still, his tail suddenly tucked between his legs. The hair along his spine rose and his head dipped, while his lips curled back into a snarl. Then he turned and fled away before halting, looking rearward and giving vent to a rumbling growl. Ann also leapt to her feet with an intake of breath, her eyes fixed on Dando.

"He's a bit under the weather," Tallis said to her apologetically, pushing the boy forward for all the world like someone returning damaged goods to their rightful owner, "perhaps you could take him to the house where I was yesterday. I don't mind moving. It's a good bed."

He seemed in a hurry to off-load responsibility for the boy's welfare and was therefore prepared to recognise for the first time that Ann might have some claim on the young man and he on her. Ann looked up into Dando's face. Strange eyes looked back at her unseeingly.

"What be wrong my lad?" she asked in a choked voice.

His lips parted but the only sound to emerge at first was a faint hiss like that of a frightened cat. Then she made our the words, *"Nothing wrong."*

She turned to Tallis as if asking permission to take him away.

"A woman's touch is what's needed now," the knight said with an apologetic smirk, "I'll leave him in your care." He paused as if to add something further but then abruptly turned and walked off into the town abandoning the two young people. Ralph still hovered in the vicinity but immediately backed away once they approached.

"Come you on my love," said Ann, "come wi' me," and, putting her arm around Dando, shepherded him through the settlement, making for the house with the ground floor bedroom that Tallis had occupied for three nights. The boy stumbled along beside her, not looking where he was going, while the dog followed at a distance as if tracking a dangerous adversary.

At the house they went indoors and she ordered the young man to sit. He subsided onto the bed staring at nothing, his body bowed as if with age. She placed herself next to him.

"Look at me my dear."

He turned and she took his head in her hands, tilting it gently towards her, and laid her forehead against his. The next minute she recoiled and sat staring at him in horror, still holding him but now at arms length. In that moment of contact she had been aware of something shifting and stirring within his frame, something resembling a pupating insect or a parasitic worm, battening on the core of his being inside the fragile outer carapace. There was a creature, a presence, that was not Dando, looking through his eyes, using his organs, possessing him, and as a consequence his mind, driven into some dusty corner, had totally lost control of his body. It could be none other than the deity who ruled this place – Rostan, the God-of-the-Core. They were alone in this humble dwelling with one of the Great Ones and Dando lay beneath his sway. She quailed in awe.

All afternoon her lover remained on the bed, quiescent, helpless, unmoving. She could not get him to eat or drink. When later she undressed him she found he had fouled himself. Foxy came to the doorway at about five o'clock, glanced in Dando's direction and went away again.

Ann sought for a solution, some means by which she could bring about a healing of this terrible affliction. Who would come to her aid - who could she call on to act in her place? There was no-one. If he was going to be saved it could only be by her and her alone. She thought of Tom and his wide knowledge of the spirit world. If she had been right about feeling his presence at various points on their journey, Dadda might be able to tell her whether the idea growing in her brain was the means to bring about a rescue or just a wild and dangerous fantasy that would lead to disaster. She went apart and sat quietly for a while, stilling her thoughts, committing to mind much of what her father had taught her.

"Do this be right dadda?" she prayed.

"It be the only way," came an answer, *"but it will bring you both to sorrow."*

Midnight, the time furthest from the light, was when she would make the rescue attempt Ann decided. Aigea's powers were known to wax at this hour whereas those of the other immortals were normally weaker. The liberation should be done when she and Dando were in intimate contact – when they were joined in all but name – and in his present state that meant only one thing. She must be there with him both in body and spirit when the crisis came, in the hope that she could restore him to wholeness at the crucial moment.

"Take heed sweetheart – we mun love one another tonight – I be so minded."

As he raised his eyes to hers she thought a flicker of comprehension interrupted his blank stare, a momentary awareness of his condition which gave birth to a fleeting expression conveying a terrified appeal for help.

"Be of good cheer, bonny lad" she said, "together we be strong."

Late in the evening she washed him and combed his hair then, as he lay face upwards, she climbed astride and began to do all the things he most liked: stroking, kissing, sucking - trying to initiate an arousal. His body and mind were disconnected, but at this point it was to the body she was appealing. When his penis rose and stiffened she took him into her and slowly he began to respond.

A great power had him in thrall and to free him she was going to have to invoke an even greater. As they interacted she began to get a better idea of the nature of this incubus that was controlling him. It was a creature of fire she sensed but the flames had been a little dimmed by the cold days and even colder nights of midwinter: Rostan ailed and was feebler at this season, and that gave her hope. Now, as she brought her lover towards his climax, she entered a mythic world in which she began to invoke Aigea, one of the few beings strong enough to oppose the Core-God's will. To bring these two deities into confrontation was really a task for a great warlock and not for a rank beginner such as herself, but unless she attempted it no-one else would. She dangled a bait.

"You want him? - look, he be here wi' I – in the grip o' your enemy – come, come."

She had had no contact with the goddess since they left the valley but now she was immediately aware of her presence deep beneath the snows, stirring out of a somnolent reverie.

"Come – here be the lad you want – yours for the taking."

She was answered. A voice clanged inside her head.

"Is that you? - I've found you at last! - and you have the child of destiny! - what luck!"

The eternal female reached out. Immediately Ann resisted, endeavouring to maintain her integrity in the face of an avid rapacious greed, and to hold Dando safe as their intercourse reached its consummation - a task beyond her perhaps. She struggled – fighting all the way – getting mentally battered in the process - working towards the one, the only possible, end.

"Come, come!" and as the man came within her and they were physically and spiritually united, so, from below, an upward avalanche, a rock-solid geyser, erupted. Using its momentum as impetus she allowed herself and Dando to be hurled forward towards a corona of flames, then with an assertion of her own volition she flung her lover's psyche and her own aside from harm's way as the two powers collided. A split second later and the languishing subterranean fire was temporarily vanquished, disappearing far into the depths. In that supreme moment Dando was set free. He shouted and leapt up, trampling her in his attempt to escape. He staggered, naked, out into the street and was violently sick. Then he groped his way back in and fell to his knees beside the bed.

"What was it? What was it?" he gasped.

Ann did not reply. She was in a chimerical region where occult events have dimension and solidarity, taking place upon a huge flat plain. Then she was back in the bedroom but stretched thin as a membrane to contain the thwarted anger of Aigea, the power she had raised. She dare not talk – dare not move even – all her strength was needed to suppress that vengeful spirit. At first she was sure her mind was about to give way, but then, from somewhere, she found the will to resist, perhaps because something or someone intervened, someone interposed themselves between her and the furious immortal; she was given space to re-establish herself in the material world where she could hold the goddess at bay.

"Annie – what happened? I don't understand!"

She turned her head to see Dando's traumatised face beside her, but a face where blood was flowing naturally beneath the skin and from which two clear dark eyes, Dando's eyes, were staring into hers. Unable to speak she held the coverlet open, smiling weakly, and he climbed into bed beside her, clinging to her like a drowning man.

It took time for both of them to even partially recover from the ordeal they had just been through. Then Dando, heaving a long shuddering sigh, croaked once more, "I don't understand."

Ann swallowed a couple of times and found her voice.

"What do you remember?"

Dando thought back to something that seemed to have happened to someone else in another lifetime.

"Master Tallisand was keen to ask a question. I said I'd breathe the Breath for him. I didn't want him to be disappointed. We went down to this poky little room – way, way down. I think I knew it was wrong. Then I woke up here with you, feeling awful – that's all."

"You be possessed – dadda tell me it happen but I never seed it before."

"And you rescued me? - Annie, I've been such a fool!"

"Praps you'll take more notice of what I say another time."

"I will – I will."

They lay silently for a while.

"How did you do it?" asked Dando.

"It were that one from down there who had 'ee in his power. I call on the ol' woman an' she come fro' her part o' the earth. She sent he packing. We were love makin' an' I take 'ee wi' me out o' her path. But Dando, she know where we be now an' she be angry wi' I acos I wou'n't let her have 'ee – like she were angry wi' dadda the time he save 'ee when you were naught but a babby – just like. I be afeared."

"Don't you worry – I'll look after you – I won't let her do you any harm."

"Oh my dear!" she said with exasperated tenderness, but laughed the while.

Dando pulled her more closely to him.

"I do love you Annie – I always have and I always will."

"I know my sweet one, I know."

"I said he just needed a good sleep," remarked Tallis to Foxy, more thankful than he liked to admit at finding Dando apparently restored to his normal self the next morning. They were getting ready to leave Toymerle. Tallis had announced that he would not stay beyond another dawn and Foxy had reluctantly fallen in with his plans. Ann seemed more anxious than ever to continue the journey and the Nablan could not contemplate parting from her. He persuaded himself that this was because he hoped against hope that he could still bring her round to his way of thinking. Today she seemed more like the old Ann he had known at the Justification. Gone was the confident warrior queen. Instead she was creeping around like a frightened mouse and in this frame of mind she would perhaps be more amenable to any suggestions he cared to make. Dando too seemed uncharacteristically subdued. He had scarcely a word to say for himself all day although he set to work willingly enough to prepare for their departure, gathering supplies - among other things Tallis insisted that they take some small shovels - finding suitable carriers, bringing a selection of outer wear for them to try on.

"I'm leaving the horses," Tallis had informed him. "I've been advised that the going is far too hard for them." "Leaving the horses!" exclaimed Dando in dismay.

"Yes, we'll have to carry everything ourselves. I'll collect them on the return journey."

"You think we're actually coming back?" asked Dando.

"No question of that – of course we are!" Tallis sounded thoroughly vexed, his emphatic response out of all proportion to the nature of the exchange.

Dando sought out Aled who, he had been told, would be his charges' new carer. He explained about their likes and dislikes, their little quirks, what frightened them and what made them happy. Then, taking Ralph with him, he went to the stables to say goodbye. After his recent experiences which, for the moment, had rendered him extremely thin skinned, he could not hold back the tears as he caressed big Carolus and little Mollyblobs for the last time. He was profoundly grateful that the only witness to this weakness was the dog. Ralph had come creeping back in the small hours, belly close to the ground, quite clearly apologising for his previous show of hostility. Now he pressed hard against Dando's leg as if inspired by a fellow feeling. Dando looked down.

"At least *you're* not going to abandon us, old chap," he said, "are you."

When it came to choosing warm clothing for the road Foxy no longer held himself aloof. He had been having trouble with his feet and Tallis' prediction of frostbite seemed to be coming only too true. For the first time in his life he had acquired a pair of boots and was endeavouring to learn how to wear them, although it was far too late to prevent some nasty burns to his toes. Walking was a painful business and put him in an extremely irritable frame of mind.

One more night spent under the roofs of the high-level settlement and then they heaved the very heavy packs onto their backs and went to bid farewell to Rhys and his cohorts.

"I wish you every success in your defence of the shrine," said Tallis formally.

"I could have done with your help," replied the Labour-in-Vain giant looking reproachfully at Foxy. The Nablan nodded and pulled a face, indicating that his departure was regrettable but unavoidable.

"Anyway," Rhys said more cheerfully, "I expect you'll be back – they tell me the mountains are rarely fit to be crossed at this time of year."

The travellers made their way to the northern perimeter, Dando and Ann walking close together for comfort, neither Tallis nor Foxy raising any objections. Part of the barricade, a fine kitchen dresser, was shifted to allow them through and they were saluted by the defenders as they negotiated the gap. A short way along the road they passed some lookouts up on the hillside, after which they were on their own. There had been a fresh fall of snow overnight and the road was barely distinguishable from the surrounding wilderness, giving forewarning of problems ahead. Nevertheless the sky was clear, the morning bright, and their spirits rose as they headed towards the high peaks, glad to be on the move once more.

"*Over-the-Brook*," said Tallis to Foxy, "that's what the Oracle said. That means across the sea, doesn't it?"

"To we it stan' for *goo free*," said Foxy, "to get away from the hounds."

Dadda had another meaning, thought Ann to herself, *to him it meant exchange one sort of life for another and, maybe, dance among the stars.*

It's hard to make it

When you're out of funds,

And raw talent's not all that's required.

Chapter ten

Damask had arrived at the start of the Green Dolphin Avenue, but of Vadrosnia Poule's towers and domes at the far end she saw not a sign, for on this particular morning the city was swathed in what was known as a *Drossi Broth*; fogs were common in the low-lying watery environment of the delta, particularly in winter. As she stood there she was informed more by her ears than by her eyes. The screech of protesting bearings, the rumble of metal-shod wheels, the shouts of drivers and the crack of whips, the tootling of horns and trumpets in many different keys advertised the presence of a huge variety of vehicles rolling by on the road. Accompanying these sounds she could hear the tramp of hundreds of feet and the hum of voices as a continuous procession of wayfarers overhauled her in the haar. No-one took any notice of the travel-stained girl wearing masculine attire and leaning against the parapet; in such a throng the individual becomes anonymous.

So, she thought, *here I am where for years I've longed to be, I've wanted this - it's no use getting cold feet at the last moment.* Joining the stream of pedestrians making their way across the grand approach, she set off towards the city's land-gate. At intervals the huge copper-clad dolphins, Drossi's trademark, materialised out of the mist, dripped gobbets of freezing water on those passing beneath and faded once more into the murk.

Gaining the city limits she purchased a street map from a convenient newsagent and looked up the way to the docks, otherwise known as the Poule. It appeared that she had to find a road running beside the main waterway and follow it to the other side of town. Her impressions of the place as she walked its pavements were of an insubstantial aqueous domain half hidden from view, wet surfaces reflecting spectral lights that gleamed in the miasma. Buildings and moving figures loomed up and then disappeared like immaterial ghosts. Occasionally the fog was suspended a few feet above her, but it always reached down to ground level over the canals and waterways where it was at its densest. Most local citizens seemed to have taken refuge behind closed doors away from its clammy breath.

As she penetrated the rather seedy area close to the quays an unfamiliar smell tantalised her nostrils. It spoke of dampness and rotting wood, of algae coated stone and stagnant locks; but in the base note of this perfume hung a tangy salty aroma that seemed to have nothing to do with land whatsoever. Because of the day's poor visibility she did not see the cranes towering over the houses which would have warned her that the harbour was close by. She found herself among ships before she realised that she had reached her destination. What immediately struck her was how *big* they were. She had been familiar with Dando's little dingy which he sailed on the Wendover or sometimes rowed on the still waters of the Broad, she had seen the boats toing and froing on the Kymer, but her imagination had failed her completely when it came to envisioning the reality of sea-going vessels. What huge trees must have been felled to provide those masts that vanished up into the fog! what acres of cotton to supply the canvas! what miles of hemp for the rigging! She made her way slowly along the wharves. The light was fading and lamps were being lit on top of iron posts embellished with the effigies of dolphins; the bollards on the edge of the quay were also in the shape of dolphins. All the ships she had walked beside so far had been wind-propelled merchantmen but now she came upon a massive, steel-hulled vessel similar to those that had appeared in the background of the moving-picture show she had recently watched. It had no masts but instead sported a row of enormous backward-leaning funnels projecting from its superstructure. She detected an unfamiliar smoky, oily stink hanging around it as she passed. The craft gave the impression of being strange, alien and out of place, as if it originated from another world entirely.

At last she came across what she had been looking for: a large wooden shed with notices affixed to the outside wall advertising times and prices of voyages. It seemed to be open for business. She went inside and asked the rather uncooperative man behind the counter whether she could book a passage to Pangorland. But here she met with a major setback to her plans.

"No such thing," said the ticket-seller brusquely, apparently getting a perverse pleasure out of dashing her hopes.

"Well how do you make the crossing then?" she asked.

"You don't," the man replied. "The authorities in Armornia are as mean as cats' meat when it comes to granting entry visas. You 'ave to be a moneybags, (you ain't one by the way, are you?), or 'ave ancestors there goin' back to the year dot before they'll let you lan'. The only boats allowed to dock from this side of the brook are those offloading cargo, an' even then they won't let the crew stray far from the quayside. You'd think we was carryin' the plague or sompthin'. There are those who try to smuggle themselves in on more unfrequented parts of the coast but the border patrols are pretty hot on illegal immigrants an' they don' just turn you roun' an' send you on your way I c'n tell you. Course we c'n do you a passage to any of the towns along this seaboard."

"No thanks," said Damask. She went outside feeling deflated and gazed absently at the notices while she tried to decide what to do. A small card caught her eye.

Rooms to let

Short stays catered for

5/- a night

Apply Mrs Wylie

25 Quay Street

It was obviously designed to attract crew members from the ships. Damask got out her map.

She paid for a week's bed and breakfast in advance. As she needed to reformulate her plans she thought she might as well give Drossi the once over in the meantime, it would be stupid to miss the chance to go on the town. The city covered quite a wide area, spread as it was over several large islands at the place where the river began to split into many channels, but it did not take long to walk from near the harbour where she was staying, over a series of bridges and lock-gates to the smart west-end quarter in which the choicest venues were to be found. She was anxious to see the sights, but soon discovered that in this highly fashion-conscious town it was a case of see and be seen. Under the scrutiny of the immaculately turned out passers-by she became acutely aware of how shabby and worn her clothes were, almost ragged in fact, and how bizarre her male attire must look. She was tired of rather unsuccessfully impersonating a boy, it would be nice for once to acknowledge the fact that she was a woman. The next day she decided to visit one of the many shopping arcades. In the window of a small boutique she noticed an exquisitely made two piece: a jacket and skirt of heavy bronze-green shot silk that looked just her size. It was the work of a moment to cross the threshold and ask to try it on, and yes, she was right, it fitted perfectly, from the narrow waisted jacket to the full very feminine skirt which ended just below the knee. Of course, now she needed a blouse, tights, underclothes, shoes and handbag of commensurate quality to complete the outfit. When she came to pay and saw the size of the bill she turned a little pale, but then stiffened her sinews and handed over the money, assuring herself that it was a good investment. Leaving the shop she retired to a nearby ladies convenience to don her newly bought attire and try to tease her unruly hair into something resembling the style she had noticed most women were wearing. She emerged a little later, her old clothes concealed in the shop's carrier bag, feeling that now she could strut her stuff with the best of them.

Her confidence boosted sky-high by the glimpses she caught of herself in shop windows, she began visiting expensive restaurants, feeling she was now dressed for such places and looked the part in her new ensemble. In the evenings she dropped in at wine bars and attended two theatrical performances in order to compare the local talent with the Stips. She took a water-born cruise that she saw advertised during which local landmarks and celebrity dwellings were pointed out and scraped up the entrance fee to various museums and art galleries. Drossi prices were well in excess of anything that she had met with in the hinterland and, although she thoroughly enjoyed herself, by the end of the week her reserves had dwindled to almost nothing. She had to face the fact that it was now time to pay another instalment on her room.

"I'm sorry, Mrs Wylie," she said placatingly to her landlady, "I'll have the money for you in a day or two."

"Tomorrow, 9.00am, at the latest," the woman replied grimly.

Come the morning she slipped out early before breakfast and spent the hours roaming the streets, ignoring her hunger, fruitlessly trying to think of ways to raise some cash. When she returned to the lodgings, well after dark, she found the pillowcase, pool-cue and her other possessions waiting for her on the doorstep. The place was locked against her and no amount of knocking produced a response. Picking up her luggage she wandered off along the spider's web of alleys that lay inland from the wharves. Each dolphin-encrusted lamppost she passed cast a spherical glow into the night through which fell a persistent drizzle that had set in after a week of fairly good weather. Although she was wearing her old threadbare coat over her new clothes the rain was rapidly soaking through and she worried that the expensive silk would be ruined. She must find shelter and somewhere to spend the night. During a conversation she had had with her landlady when they were still on speaking terms there had been mention of a seamen's mission down by the Armornia Docks. Perhaps if she could find her way there they would give her a roof over her head until the weather improved. She paused under a street lamp in a deserted alley and rummaged in her bag for the, by now, rather tattered map. Absorbed in this search she did not notice the man until he spoke.

"'Ow much?" said a gruff slightly inebriated voice.

Damask looked up to see a thick-set, tanned individual with the powerful tattooed arms of an old salt. He was obviously off one of the ships.

"What?" she said.

"'Ow much?" repeated the sailor.

Damask thought fast, weighing up the pros and cons, and decided that desperate times called for desperate measures.

"Twelve pounds ten shillings," she said, half hoping that this would be enough to discourage him, but the man accepted immediately.

"In advance," she insisted.

A dark passage going off to the left provided the ideal bolt hole. Damask led the way into it and was absent for only a few minutes. When she reappeared, somewhat flushed, she felt a great deal richer but also slightly soiled. The seaman swayed off into the night. However the alley was now far from deserted. A sinister-looking man - a flashily dressed bejewelled individual holding an umbrella - stood at the edge of the pool of light. He appeared to have been waiting for her.

"Orl right," he said, "'and it over."

"What do you mean?" said Damask.

"You're on my turf. 'And over the sponduliks if you don't want your face rearranged."

Behind him in the gloom she glimpsed two menacing figures, one of them holding a knife. This time Damask did not have to stop and think. She kicked off the dainty high-heeled shoes that, over the last few days, had been her pride and joy and ran for her life. Fortunately, a few yards further along, the alley twisted and for a brief moment she was out of sight of her pursuers. A narrow turning led off to the right. She ducked sideways, plunged into the darkness and almost cannoned into a high wall blocking the path. A dead end! There was only one thing for it. With all her strength she hurled her possessions over the almost ten foot high obstruction and then followed them, swarming up like a squirrel, as she and Dando had once done when they climbed the outside defences of Castle Dan. For a moment, reaching the narrow parapet, she teetered precariously on the coping before falling forwards into the unknown.

Although she was not aware of it Damask, in her aimless wanderings, had reached the borderland between the docks and a much more up-market residential enclave named Two-Tree-Island. The wall she had climbed stood as a barrier between the mutually antipathetic bailiwicks so she was lucky not to have encountered defensive broken glass or spikes on the top, also that her landing was cushioned by soft earth. She found herself in a garden, the garden of a sizeable house. There were dim lights shining through the windows and by these she could distinguish an outside staircase leading up to a balcony on the first floor. Retrieving her things she crept up the ascent and discovered an unlocked door at the top. Slipping within, she pulled it to and shot a bolt home that her hand fell on in the gloom. Then, looking back through the glass, she stared down into the garden, waiting to see if anyone else would appear over the wall. Suddenly she heard an abrupt clicking noise and swung round in time to see a tiny blue flame being ignited behind her. As the light brightened she was confronted by a very small person in a very large bed.

"Who are you?" asked a treble voice. A little boy, lantern in hand, was staring at her with wide eyes. Damask put her finger to her lips indicating that he should keep quiet.

"Who are you?" the child asked again, but this time in a whisper.

"Your fairy godmother," said Damask.

"Really? Oh - but you're just funning me."

"Can't you see my wand?" She held up the pool-cue.

The boy laughed in an uncertain manner.

"I need to stay here for a few minutes. Some bad men are chasing me. Where are your parents?"

"In Osh, visiting my granny."

"When are they due back?"

"Maybe tomorrow."

Here was a stroke of luck; if she played her cards right she might be able to secure a bed for the night.

"Who's looking after you?" she asked.

"My nanny and Martha."

"And did Martha teach you how to light the lantern?"

"No, my daddy did."

Damask sought to gather more information.

"What are your parents called?"

"Mummy and daddy o' course!"

"No, I mean what's their surname?"

The little boy looked baffled. She noticed a book by the side of the bed and tried a different tack. "Can you read?"

"My mummy's teaching me."

"Well, when letters come for your daddy what's written on the front?"

The child retrieved an envelope being used as a bookmark from the bedside table. "Here's one," he said. Damask perused the address: *The Rt. Hon. Cnclr. Freebody, the Garth, 105, Seventh Sluice Road, Two Tree Island, V.P.* she read.

"So your daddy's Counsellor Freebody and your mummy's Mrs Freebody?"

"Mm – I think so."

Damask noticed an old holdall on top of a wardrobe in the corner of the room. She got it down, dusted it off and transferred all her things into it, then tucked the empty pillow case and cue under the bed. The child watched with interest.

"I haven't got any shoes - can you find me some of your mummy's I could borrow?" The little boy left the room but soon returned bearing a pair of red courts. These proved to be slightly on the large size but wearable. She tidied her hair and adjusted her clothes.

"Now go and wake Martha and tell her I want to see her. Say I'm a friend of your mummy's. I'll be downstairs. By the way, what's *your* name?"

"Adrian."

Damask found the main staircase and descended to a large hall on the ground floor. At the far end she saw what appeared to be a door leading out into the street. She walked across and, putting the holdall on the floor, quickly pulled back bolts and released chains, meanwhile rehearsing what she was going to say, trying to make the role she was in the process of inventing personal to her and her alone as she had done when performing with the Stips. After a few minutes a drowsy, dressing-gown-clad woman descended the stairs.

"Oh dear," said Damask in the clipped cut-glass accent of a Dan aunt, "You must be Martha. I really do apologise for disturbing you at this unearthly hour. I've just arrived from Osh and I would have called tomorrow morning except the hotels are all full and Mrs Freebody said you could provide me with a bed if it came down to it."

The woman stared at her owlishly, stifling a yawn.

"Did someone let you in?" she asked.

Damask gestured towards the door.

"It was open and I didn't want to ring as it was so late. Fortunately I just caught Adrian looking over the bannisters. It seems he couldn't sleep – missing his mummy I expect."

"That Bert!" exclaimed the housekeeper in fury, "I'll tan 'is 'ide for 'im! It's not the first time he's forgotten to lock up! 'Scuse me mum, but can you tell me 'oo you are?"

"Why – I'm certain Mrs Freebody must have mentioned me. I'm Sarah – Bethany's younger sister. Of course you know Bethany, she's one of Mrs Freebody's oldest friends in Osh – they were at school together. The Counsellor sent me with an apology as I was coming this way. They're going to be a little late back – the old lady's had a fall. They told me to look in and let you know and to give their love to Adrian. He's a real grown up little man now, isn't he – a credit to his father. I'll tell you all the details in the morning but just now I'm dying for a bite to eat and some shut-eye. Be a treasure and get me something, will you?"

The hastily improvised meal was excellent, the feather bed even more so. It was with great reluctance that Damask rose in the darkness before dawn, crept out of the front door of Maison Freebody while the rest of the house slept, finding that it had stopped raining. She looked nervously along the canal-side path but everything appeared quiet: there was not a soul about. The area was well lit and had an atmosphere of prosperity about it. The owners of the imposing but similar houses on one side of the street were obviously on the up and up judging by the luxurious craft moored alongside the waterway on the other. Damask turned towards town and walked rapidly away, still carrying the holdall and wearing the red shoes. She hoped it would be a long time before they were missed. Meanwhile she felt it would do no harm to put as much distance as possible between herself and the scene of her recent exploits; a couple of people might be a bit too eager to make her acquaintance, namely the pimp and the counsellor, and she was not keen on encountering either of them. It was time to say goodbye to Drossi and strike out for somewhere entirely different.

By the time she reached the city centre it was getting light and people were stirring. Near the land gate she noticed a café already open for custom judging by the delicious smells wafting out onto the morning air. She felt hungry and fancied a cooked breakfast. At least now she had some money to pay for it. When she passed through the door into the warm fug of the interior she found the place already packed out. The eating area was full of excited talk and laughter from a bevy of young people sitting around tables; there did not appear to be any spare seats. She was just about to retreat when a motherly looking waitress called on her to stay.

"Don't go dearie, I'll get you a chair. I'm sure they'll shift up. It's the mid-winter festival you see – always draws a crowd – especially the goings-on in the music tent. Is that what you're here for?"

Three girls and two boys willingly made room for her. They went on chatting amongst themselves as she ordered her meal but at the same time directed inquisitive surreptitious glances in her direction, obviously anxious to know who she was and what she was doing there.

"Come far?" asked one of the boys once she had laid down her knife and fork.

"Far enough," said Damask.

"Where are you staying?"

"I'm not," she replied. "I'm on my way out of town."

"Not stopping for the show?"

"What show is that?" she asked.

The five exchanged amazed glances.

"Only the one with all the best bands this side of the brook! Here."

A girl dug out a flyer and handed it across. "It goes on all today and tomorrow. Miss it and you've lost your cred for the rest of the year."

Damask ran her eyes down the long list of acts itemised under the title *Solstice Headliners*. At first she thought she had heard of none of them and felt very square and out of touch. But what was this about halfway down? Beneath the word PRIMO, printed in very large letters, was the legend - and the Posse – printed in very small ones.

"Primo and the Posse?" she ventured.

"Oh Primo!" replied the other girl, rolling her eyes heavenwards with a sigh, "he's the main attraction tonight – the place will be heaving."

"I think I've met them," said Damask, "the Posse I mean. At Millfield a few months ago."

"You know them? Well that settles it. You're coming with us! You can blag your way into the artists' tent afterwards and maybe we'll get to meet *him*."

"No..." replied Damask uncertainly, but tempted nonetheless. She felt a sudden urge to renew her association with Winnie. "I don't think so really..."

But to her new acquaintances the matter was already done and dusted and they brooked no refusal on her part. A spare ticket was acquired from amongst their friends and they bore her over the causeway to a large common known as Parker's Piece where the festival was due to take place. The winter solstice was a strange time to stage an open-air event such as this but Damask was told that the tradition went back into the mists of time and that the new year would get off to a bad start if it were not held. There was a funfair, rings for wrestling, sites for horse-jumping and athletic contests plus numerous sales tents, food stalls and sideshows. In the centre stood a huge marquee where the musical entertainment was due to take place. Throughout the day people wandered in and out of this venue as act followed act, some obviously more popular than others. Damask got to know her new friends better: Snoz, Toofee, Bonnie, Lopside and Fancy were their names, or rather nick-names. They came from a small town called Thrubwell on a highway leading ultimately to the mountains which also passed through other places equally unfamiliar to her such as Digor and Numpnett.

"We could give you a lift afterwards," offered Toofee, "if you're going our way. Thrubwell's OK but needs waking up a bit – in fact it's hellishly dull most of the time."

"Is there any way of earning a living there?" asked Damask.

"You want a job? Well you might find work on the farms or behind a counter I suppose, and the school is always crying out for assistants."

"I'll consider it," said Damask cautiously.

"If you want to come, be sure to be at the entrance after tomorrow-night's performance. We've got a spare seat in the buggy on our homeward journey – save you a fare."

Later Damask asked, "This Primo – who is he? When I knew the Posse he wasn't around."

"Primo comes from Dermody; there he was a big fish in a small pond. It was inevitable he would move on to Drossi. Now he's one of the brightest stars along the coast."

"But how did he get together with the Posse?"

"Oh," dismissively, "I s'pose he needed a backing group and they were available."

As predicted the marquee was packed out when it came time for this particular act to perform. The lights came up on the three young men whose acquaintance Damask had already made, following which they played in a rather subdued manner, certainly nothing remotely like the way she fondly remembered from Millfield when they had attacked their instruments with such reckless abandon. After a couple of numbers Primo leapt on stage and the audience broke into wild cheering. Damask was taken by surprise – he was not at all what she had been expecting. For one thing he seemed at least ten years older than the other musicians, and secondly he looked more like a miner or a stevedore than a popular singer, dressed as he was in a string vest, workmen's trousers and sporting hair cropped to within an inch of his head. But it was when he opened his mouth that Damask saw her dream of becoming the Posse's vocalist vanish into thin air. With his strong, husky, rather hoarse voice and unadorned but topical songs Primo held the audience spell-bound – the man had charisma and to spare. The other occupants of the stage faded into the background and became mere adjuncts to this powerful performer. At the end of the set, after several encores, the applause was all for him.

"Come on," said Bonnie as the rest of the crowd started to leave, "I'll show you the way to the stage entrance." But when they got there the place was swarming with young women and a few slightly embarrassed young men all brandishing programmes and autograph albums; Damask could get nowhere near the front. Various performers emerged and were mobbed, but it was when Primo appeared, followed by Winnie and Fynn, that the screaming started. Primo scribbled his name a few times, then made a dash for a fast looking phaeton into which all three disappeared before being whisked off into the night. Damask had waved and shouted with the rest but was not sure if she had even been noticed. She preferred to believe that in the crush Winnie had not spotted her; it would be just too humiliating to think she had been seen and then ignored.

Now that the main attraction had left the fans began to drift away.

"I'm going to find the others," said Bonnie. "There's the opportunity for a drink or two before closing time. After that our lot's heading to a b-and-b in town. There might be a spare bed if you want it."

The girl set out to rendezvous with her friends but Damask remained where she was. She had seen only two members of the Posse – where was the third? It was over fifteen minutes before the silent bleach-haired drummer, a hood hiding his white locks, made his appearance. One or two girls accosted him but were rudely repulsed.

"Matt," called Damask.

The pale face turned in her direction and there was a momentary flash of recognition in the cold unsmiling eyes. He walked over.

"The up-market bird from Millfield, right?"

"Yes," said Damask.

"You doin' anyfing?"

"No."

"Let's get goin' then."

Without more ado he led her out of the field gates and down the road towards Drossi, but instead of crossing the causeway he turned left along the edge of a wide distributary in which the lights of the town were reflected. About half a mile further on he descended the bank, Damask following, to where a small boat floated on the black velvet of the water.

"Get in," he ordered.

Damask sat in the stern as the drummer shipped some oars and pulled strongly out from the shore. She wondered idly where they were headed; it was all too clear that Matt would not volunteer the information. Looking up she saw faint stars; although the temperature had fallen neither rain nor fog had returned. The distant lights grew gradually brighter until, suddenly, she was aware of a structure overhead. There was a sound of water lapping and dripping along with other noises from above her: footsteps on wood, an unidentifiable banging, music, people's voices; the up to now fresh night air became tainted by the combined smells of excrement and stale food. The boat bumped against an obstruction in the dark and Damask realised they were no longer moving. Matt was doing something with a rope.

"Come on," he said, "here's where you get off."

"I can't see," said Damask.

"The first rung's just above you. I'll guide your steps."

She realised he was expecting her to climb a vertical ladder without any idea of how high it was or where it led.

"You go first," she said.

The young man grunted impatiently and swung himself up into the darkness. If she did not want to be stranded below in the boat she had no choice but to follow. Pushing an arm through the handles of her holdall she started counting the rungs as she climbed and had got to ten when Matt, who was no longer on the ladder, reached down and hauled her over a protruding edge onto narrow wooden scaffolding. She had the sky above her once more and could dimly make out her surroundings.

She found she was in the middle of a shanty town, but a shanty town built over water. The mean little flat-roofed cabins surrounding her were located on platforms which seemed to be floating in mid air above that unreliable restless element. Rickety walkways spanned the gaps between the shacks and swayed under the weight of people's footfalls as the inhabitants passed to and fro; the place was apparently well populated. Matt did not wait to see how the climb had affected her or if she was following but immediately set off, sure footed, along the unguarded planks. Damask trailed him nervously, realising that if she took one false step she would end up in the drink. After negotiating numerous changes of direction her guide stopped before a door and flung it open to reveal a surprisingly large low-ceilinged room lit by two lanterns. Peering over his shoulder she made out a space that struck her as a cross between a kitchen and a bedroom - kitchen because there was a stove, larder, table and chairs to one side – bedroom because there were also a couple of basic-looking cots, both occupied, on the other.

"Out!" cried Matt, striding into the room and banging his fist on the table. Two startled-looking prepubescent boys, little more than children, leapt to their feet and tumbled through the door without a word of protest.

"Poor kids," said Damask.

"They take advantage – I'm not running an orphanage," replied Matt. "Here, you hungry?"

He raided the cold shelf of the larder which was situated beside the stove and retrieved a loaf of bread, some pork-pie slices, a cucumber and a jar of pickle. Damask became aware that she had not eaten since breakfast that morning and now it must be nearly midnight. Matt waved his hand at the food with an expansive gesture.

"Pitch in - you might as well - otherwise it'll just go over the side."

They shared the repast between them, eating in total silence. When it was all gone Matt brought out two small tumblers and what looked like a medicine bottle from a cupboard. He filled the glasses half full with a golden liquid and pushed one across to Damask. Before drinking she picked up the bottle and looked at the label:- *DR GOOD'S ELIXIR – STRENGTH 2*, it said in archaic characters. Turning it over she found further reading matter on the back - a long dense passage in such tiny writing that it practically required the use of a magnifying glass to be made sense of. *Highly effective,* she read, *guaranteed to cure sunstroke, scalds, hysteria, jaundice, sleeplessness, hanging, common-continued fever, gout, convulsions and freckles. Entirely relieves the symptoms of smallpox, blistered feet, digestive complaints, mumps, measles, apoplexy, cramp, sore throat, scurvy, epilepsy, quinsy, squinting and piles. A sovereign remedy against melancholy, the megrims and all ill-humours. Also recommended in the case of consumption, scrofula, tic-doloreux and water on the brain. If applied externally soothes rashes, eczemas, the bite of fleas and all other pesky varmints. Will restore hair loss...* She gave up trying to decipher the rest.

"A miracle beverage," she commented.

"Paradise sauce," replied Matt. "Comes from over there," waving his hand vaguely towards the north. "They can't bang you up for it."

Damask sipped her way through the first glass and then through a refill. A pleasant lassitude stole over her. Matt produced a box of what looked like miniature cigars, a couple of which he lit after spitting them on long pins. He handed one to Damask. Two or three puffs and her languor vanished to be replaced by a cheerful euphoria.

"Are you on again tomorrow?" she asked.

"Yes, then tour," said Matt.

"You mean you're leaving Drossi?"

"They are – not me."

"Why's that?"

"I've had enough."

"Do they know?"

"No."

"What will they say?"

"I don't give a fuck. They've sold out. They c'n go to hell as far as I'm concerned."

Damask laughed. She suddenly found it irresistibly funny that Primo and the Posse were about to find themselves all at sea through the defection of their drummer.

"You won't be popular."

"I don't give a fuck."

Matt's normal state of mind, his stock response to his surroundings, seemed to consist of a continual seething anger against the world which was only slightly ameliorated at the moment by the mind-altering substances they were sampling.

"What a grump," giggled Damask.

The boy's mouth set in a hard line and he glowered at his drink, relapsing into a long sulky silence while Damask hummed to herself and sang, *"I'd like to bind you in a knot..."*

"Why are you so cross?" she asked eventually.

Matt's eyes flicked in her direction and then away. He did not respond, preferring to top up his glass and take a drag on his third reefer of the evening.

"You're the crossest person I've ever come across," she persisted and went off into a peal of laughter at her own witticism.

"You'd be pissed off if you were born in a dump like this," said Matt breaking his silence.

"You were born here?"

"This very room."

The drugs had at last had the desired effect, the floodgates were opening, and the boy began to unburden himself, for it was patently obvious that the silent drummer needed to talk. Because she happened to be available Damask became the inadvertent recipient of his life's history, which poured out unstoppably with scarcely a pause for breath. As he spoke he fixed her with a steady unblinking gaze.

Yes, he had been born in this particular shanty town to a single mother without a penny to her name. When she acquired a few coins to rub together they mostly went on drink. She had loved him in her own way but her love had taken the form of trying to persuade all and sundry that her child was sick. This elicited charitable sympathy and gave her a certain clout among her peers. So Matt had spent most of his early years convinced he was at death's door. He had never been able to discover who his real father was but had endured a string of useless and usually violent step-fathers who knocked his mother about and put the fear of god into him. When he became big enough to try and defend the woman he got knocked about in his turn. Several times he ran away but always came back, the umbilical connection was too strong. Then, one of the succession of men disappeared more abruptly than usual, just failed to return one day, but in his going left behind something of great value - an almost brand-new drum-kit. Matt began experimenting and found his vocation. The drums saved him from drifting into the local gang culture; they gave him a purpose; he discovered some self-respect for the first time in his life. It was not long before he began to make a name for himself.

The torrent of words dried up and the boy relapsed back into his normal taciturn state.

"Well..." said Damask and then "well..." again. Eventually she added, "good for you!"

After a period of silence she went on, "If I were you I wouldn't be angry – I'd be proud."

Matt gazed at her as if trying to determine whether she was sincere. At last, for the first time since she had known him, she saw him smile, something that completely transformed his face.

"Where's your mother?" asked Damask.

The sun went in. The boy pursed his lips and shook his head; this was obviously an unmentionable subject.

In due time they got to the bottom of the first bottle of Dr Good's and Matt produced a second.

"How many different strengths?" articulated Damask, trying to read what was written with vastly unfocused eyes.

"Five, plus super."

"An' so – what you gonna do now – now you left the Posse?"

"Own band – but I'll be the front man – I'll write the songs."

"Goo' for you... goo' for you..."

I write the songs: the phrase had triggered a melody in her head and Damask hummed the tune, but whether out loud or internally she could not be sure. Time passed, maybe a considerable stretch, but as far as she could tell it was still night outside. Matt was sitting opposite her slumped sideways in his chair breathing heavily – he was to all appearances unconscious. She cast her eyes doubtfully over the sleeping arrangements; neither billet appeared big enough for two. She looked down but there were no convenient rugs; the floor consisted entirely of bare boards. Where had Matt's mother entertained her succession of lovers she wondered? She tapped the young man tentatively on the shoulder ("Wake up my presh,") but without eliciting a response. According to her personal code of honour she would normally, at this juncture, have offered her body to her host in return for hospitality, but as he was completely out of it there did not seem to be much point in trying to pursue this course of action. Perhaps later they could get it on together. She shrugged, yawned and put herself to bed in one of the cots. Almost before her head touched the pillow she was away and knew nothing more for several hours.

She woke blear-eyed and hungover with the conviction that it was late afternoon or maybe already early evening of the following day. She looked round the room and found she was alone. On the table a circle of flat-bread topped with melted cheese and sliced tomato had appeared. There was also a jar of what smelt like small beer. She waited for some time but when Matt failed to appear she allowed her appetite to get the better of her and ate and drank the offering. Having filled her belly she felt a great deal better. She looked out of the door and saw it was again getting dark. She had missed nearly twenty-four hours. She remembered the suggestion of a lift that had been made a day earlier. If she wanted to take advantage of it she would have to be at the festival site by the time the entertainment drew to a close. How was she to get back to dry land? She had no idea where the boat was. She hung on for a while longer, waiting for the drummer to appear, but then decided that if she was going to return to the show-ground before things ended she would have to leave. Putting on her still damp coat she picked up the holdall and quitted the shack.

Outside the lights of Drossi drew her. She threaded her way precariously along the walkways afraid every moment that she would miss her footing and plunge downwards. However, after a while she realised that there was no longer water below her; the rickety wooden planks had metamorphosed into mean little alleys, although the shacks that lined them, improvised out of every material imaginable, were almost identical to those built above the Kymer distributary. She was once more within the purlieus of the city and turning right it took just a short spell before she was back at the land-gate, and after that only about another ten minutes to reach Parker's Piece. To her dismay she found that people were already streaming away in droves; the extravaganza must have ended earlier than it had on the previous night. She stood at the entrance scanning the crowds anxiously with an uneasy feeling that the Thrubwell contingent might have already left. The longer she waited the more certain she became that this must be the case. The ranks of merrymakers began to thin and wagons and carts belonging to the showmen took their place. Disheartened, Damask was just about to turn away when she spotted a familiar vehicle in the procession. It was none other than the cat-circus caravan! Quickly she slipped behind a convenient ticket booth and peered out. Yes, there was the clown up on the driving seat and she even thought she could detect a chorus of mews as it passed; Pnoumi must have been at the festival all along, staging his show somewhere on site, although their paths had not crossed until now. She watched as the van turned to the right away from Drossi, taking the road up river. Giving it time to get some distance ahead she set out to follow.

Pnoumi did not travel far that night. Only about a mile down the track he pulled off the highway onto a convenient grassy verge and unharnessed the horse. Damask stopped further back and leant against a wall in the darkness, awaiting developments. Soon a light came on in the small compartment behind the driver's seat. Carrying a lantern, sack and what looked like a milk-churn she saw the clown descend and disappear round the back of the caravan, presumably to feed his cats. He was gone for sometime but then returned and climbed up to the place where his cooking facilities and bed were situated. Damask waited patiently and after about half an hour saw the light go out. She remained where she was a little longer, then got up and made her way towards the vehicle.

Putting her luggage behind one of the wheels she reached up and, nerving herself to attempt something that would probably end in embarrassing failure, hoisted herself into the driving position. Her weight caused the caravan to tilt and she held her breath while she waited to see if this would rouse the clown. Everything remained quiet. Exploring, she found that the door into his sleeping quarters was slightly open. Pushing it further ajar she slipped inside. With the lightest of touches she felt for the bunk along the back that she remembered from the time she and Milly had been in temporary charge. Yes, here it was and the man was lying right up against the rear wall leaving room for another to stretch out beside him. This was a great opportunity. Quickly she shed her clothes and climbed in, pressing her body against his. He sighed and turned towards her and in response she took him into her arms.

"Come my soul," she whispered. As if in answer his hands found her shoulders, slid down to her waist and then to her buttocks. She pressed his head against her and opened her legs.

"That's the way," she urged.

Pnoumi's body suddenly stiffened and, jerking back, he cried out in an unfamiliar tongue, trying unsuccessfully to extricate himself from her embrace, and she felt his heart beating wildly as they lay skin to skin.

"No, no sweetie-pie," she murmured soothingly, "this is what you wanted – remember? You could give me a good time you told me – we could make babies together. I'd never met a man like you – isn't that what you said?. Come on – here's your chance to prove it – I'm not going to hurt you."

She kissed and stroked him using all her not inconsiderable seductive skills in an attempt to calm him down and overcome his initial terror at finding the two of them in such close proximity. She was doing everything in her power, both vocally and physically, to persuade him to have sex, because, with that in the bag, she knew he would no longer regard her as a threat.

"Now, now," she encouraged in a honeyed tone, "everything's all right – it's fine, fine. Come on, show me. There's nothing to be afraid of."

Slowly and surely her plan began to succeed. As Pnoumi gave in to the inevitable and started to surrender to her will Damask discovered that he did indeed know how to make babies in novel and surprising ways and that, as he had originally claimed, he had the means to ensure that the babies arrival would be postponed indefinitely.

The next day Damask sat beside the clown on the driving seat as, following her instructions, they turned right into the road that led through Thrubwell, Digor and Numpnett.

"Less competition," she advised, "you'll be an overnight sensation in such out-of-the-way places. Everyone'll come and see you. And you've got a glamorous assistant now - I'll wear my new outfit." "You stay with me?" he pleaded, "you be my rittle wifie?" "Of course," she promised.

Throughout the morning they encountered hardly any traffic on this meandering byway. Not many people had reason to journey into the mountains at the dead of winter, and that was where the road eventually led. They passed a few farm carts carrying locals on their way to market but then about lunchtime two riders appeared in the distance. As they approached, Damask was able to make out their mounts in greater detail: a large chestnut gelding and a dappled grey pony. She rubbed her eyes and looked again. "Stop!" she commanded.

Surely she recognised that barrel-shaped compact little animal, the smaller of the two horses – surely it could be none other than... "Mollyblobs!" she blurted out.

She scrambled down from the driving seat and ran forward. The small dark-faced horsewoman astride the pony drew it to a halt, her eyes round with astonishment.

"Majesty!" she exclaimed. "Milly!" cried Damask.

Wending homewards,

Perhaps we may reach sanctuary

If the goal posts haven't shifted.

Chapter eleven

At about the same hour that those who made up Tallis' party were shaking the snows of Toymerle from their feet, only to plunge into deeper drifts further up the road, and Damask was walking through a *Drossi Broth* after having given Pnoumi back his caravan, Milly lay full length on the ground peering over the edge of a cliff into a deep ravine. After being alone in the wilderness for nigh on three weeks she at last had evidence that the world she inhabited was not completely devoid of other members of her own species. However this evidence came in the form of a masculine voice raised in song and, as usual, she was greatly averse to encountering any man on a one-to-one basis. Spying out the lie of the land she realised that the drop beyond the rim from which the voice arose was practically vertical until interrupted by a narrow ledge, after which it fell away again to another lower ledge partially hidden from view. It was on this second level that she glimpsed the top of a head, the source of a light tenor voice floating on the vast gulfs of air within the chasm. The singer sounded at if he was young and by his posture - sitting with his back to her, legs dangling in space - appeared to be admiring the view and nonchalantly ignoring his peril. Having progressed from the sea shanty *Bully in the Alley* through *Windy Old Weather* to *Blow the Man Down* which he rendered with full-throated enthusiasm, he stopped, coughed once or twice and remarked "Not bad - not bad at all." Milly wrinkled her forehead. He seemed happy enough, she thought; best leave him be. She raised herself onto hands and knees preparatory to retreating. In so doing she leant on a flat rock that she imagined was perfectly secure and immovable, but now, under her weight, it shifted, slid forward and shot out into space. For a moment she thought she was about to follow, but then, saving herself by the skin of her teeth, she scrambled backwards, sending a shower of stones after the rock.

"Who's there?" called a voice.

Milly froze, holding her breath, trying to pretend she had not given herself away.

"There's somebody there," cried the voice again, "you nearly crowned me! Please, I need help – I don't care who you are if only you'll just come to my aid."

Milly crept forward and looked down. The man had swung round and his head was tilted upwards, but curiously he seemed to be wearing a blindfold.

"I can't see," he called, "can you tell me how to get back up?"

Well, that was certainly true – with that thing around his eyes he certainly could not see; why was he wearing it? She shook her own head as if in answer to his question but did not speak.

"If you don't help me I'm done for," he went on, "I can either die quickly by chucking myself off this ledge, or slowly when my food and water run out."

This altered matters.

"You've got food?" Milly enquired cautiously but with an eager undercurrent to her voice.

"Ah – so there you are! Yes, I've got food. Do you want some? I'll let you have it all if you'll just show me how to get out of here. I've tried – god knows I've tried."

"Stay there," she said. "I'll 'ave to 'ave a look."

Upright once more, she began following the rim, searching for some place where he might climb, and found it about a hundred yards further along where the upper ledge dwindled away to nothing and a chimney led from the shelf he was on all the way to the top where she stood. It was a possible route, the only feasible one in the vicinity; a fit person able to see could perhaps escape that way, but for someone whose sight was restricted...? She was tempted to continue on along the path, despite the promise of sustenance, but her destination lay in the opposite direction and in the end she turned round and retraced her steps.

"Wot are you wearin' that fing round your 'ead for," she demanded.

"So as not to scare the kiddies," he replied. "Have you found somewhere?"

"Yers, but it might be difficult wiv that bandage – why don' you take it orf?"

"Sorry – no can do." He climbed cautiously to his feet. "Can you give me directions?"

"Well, I s'pose you'd better turn roun' an' face the rock – keep your toes close to the cliff. Now step sideways along this way – that's right – keep goin'. I'll tell you when you gets there."

"Get where?"

"There's a kinda crack where you could wriggle your way up. At least..." She trailed off.

"Keep talking," he instructed, edging along towards her voice. She noticed he had donned a back-pack which was probably making it more difficult for him to maintain his balance. Because that presumably held the food he had promised her she did not suggest that he leave it behind.

"'Ere you are," she called, stopping at the place she had discovered. "There's a gap in the cliff just ahead of you – c'n you feel it?"

The young man explored the recess with his hands, reaching as high as he could. He was about forty feet below her.

"It comes right to the top," advised Milly, " it's the only way up, far as I c'n see."

The boy took the pack off his back and put it on arsey-versey. Then he wedged himself into the crevice, his shoulders against one side and his feet against the other. Bracing himself he began to inch upwards. Milly realised for the first time that he was very thin, almost emaciated in fact, which made her wonder if he had the strength for this undertaking. If he failed to keep his body taut between the sides of the shaft, if his muscles weakened even for a moment, he would plummet downwards, probably missing the ledge he had just left, and plunge into the gulf below.

"Come on," she called anxiously, "you're doin' fine, you've got 'alfway up orlready."

She was surprised to realise that she was rooting for him, and not just because of what he was bringing her. The boy grunted with effort as he climbed higher, his progress painfully slow, until at last Milly was able to shout, "You're nearly here! One more shove an' you're out!"

She reached down with both hands and, seizing him under an armpit, used all her strength to drag him to safety over the edge. Once on level ground the young man lay panting, trying to recover from the huge effort he had made. Eventually his breathing became more normal and he sat up, remarking to himself, "Surprising how tenaciously one clings to life."

As soon as she realised he was safe and a free agent once more all Milly's wariness returned and she backed away giving him a wide berth. "Well," she said, "I'll be gettin' along."

Despite this she remained where she was, but at a respectful distance, watching him suspiciously. The boy rubbed his grazed elbows and then, climbing to his feet, turned in a circle as if trying to get his bearings.

"Where are you off to?" he enquired.

"That's my business."

"I was on my way to Drossi. Praps if you could point me in the right direction..." He sounded doubtful.

"'Ow did you get down there?" asked Milly, curious despite herself.

"Those I was travelling with saw some people coming up that turning a little way back – people that they weren't too keen on meeting. They started running and I did too but I ran right out into space. There was nothing beneath my feet but air."

"Well," said Milly again, "I'm goin' this way. I fink Drossi mus' be that way," pointing eastward, "bye, bye." Still she did not move.

"Are you going to Toymerle?" he asked.

"Toymerle?" Milly's ears pricked up, "joo know where it is?"

"Look here," said the boy, "I'd better explain something. Toymerle's not a good place to be at the moment. There's this robber baron called the Cheetah and I think he's just returned there. I think there might be a lot of fighting in progress."

Milly looked at him in dismay.

"But that's where *they* woz goin'" she exclaimed.

"They?"

"The Lordship an' 'is sweet'eart an' the ol' man an' another geezer wiv red 'air. 'Ave you seen 'em? Are they orl right?"

The young man frowned and shook his head as if trying to clear it

"What are you talking about," he said. "Who are you? Tell me your name."

"Wot's that to you?"

"I think I may have heard about you at second hand."

"I'm Milly," said the little girl, making a grudging concession in order to learn more.

"Milly, that's right, you're Dando's sister's maid. How amazing!"

Milly almost leapt in the air with excitement.

"You've seen 'em!" she cried, "you've bin there! Where is 'e? Is 'e all right? 'Oo are you?"

"My name's Jack. About three days ago when I left Toymerle I said goodbye to a young man of noble birth travelling with a fellow by the name of Tallisand who had been given the anachronistic title of knight, and two members of the Nablan race. They were planning on taking the road north. Would they be your friends?"

"That's 'im, the Lordship! I've bin lookin for 'im all over. We mus' go an' see if e's orl right!" Milly was hopping from foot to foot with impatience.

Jack frowned, apparently turning over the situation in his mind.

"Yes," he said, "I think perhaps we should. Before heading to Drossi I think I'll do a bit of reconnoitring and satisfy myself that they got away safely. I'd like to make sure they haven't fallen into the Cheetah's hands. By the way – didn't you say you wanted something to eat?"

And so began a strange alliance. As the two of them prepared to set off together he shared items of food with the girl. She snatched the offerings and retreated, stuffing her mouth, surprising him by how ravenously she gobbled them up. When she asked for more he realised she must be really starving and cautioned her not to eat too much at once. Discovering that she was suffering from the cold he lent her some gloves and a hat with ear flaps that he had brought along as spares, telling her that, as they neared Toymerle, they would be climbing to a higher altitude and conditions would become harsher.

"OK," he said, "shall we go?"

They started off in single file, Jack leading, and things went well for a while, but then he began to wander away from the path and stray dangerously close to the ravine. Milly watched him sceptically and only called out a warning when he seemed about to topple over. Up to now she had suspected that the blindfold around his head was just some wily ruse to engage her sympathy - a trick to put her off her guard so that he could take advantage of her. Because of this she did not understand why he was not walking in a straight line and as much as hinted that she thought he was playing some sort of devious game.

"I know what you're up to," she said, "you can't fool me."

Jack was baffled by her hostility. From what Dando had told him Milly had a heart of gold and had proved to be a thoroughly loyal lieutenant to both Damask and himself. Her present attitude seemed totally at variance with this. Could it be that she thought he represented some sort of threat?

"Don't you get it," he said patiently, "I'm blind. I'm beginning to realise I can't manage along here by myself. You'll have to lead me. If you take one end of my belt and go ahead I'll hold the other and follow."

But Milly was not about to let him get that close to her. "Not friggin' likely," she said.

Jack fumed but made a great effort to speak reasonably.

"What are you afraid of? I'm not going to try anything on. I'm not after young girls. You couldn't be safer with one of my sort. I have a different orientation."

At first baffled, Milly suddenly had an inkling of what he was talking about.

"Are you telling me you're a poofter?" she asked in amazement. "'Ow do I know that's true? 'Ow do I know anyfink you're tellin' me is true?"

"Look!" In exasperation Jack snatched the sash from his head and turned his face towards her. "Do you think I could do you any harm in this condition? I don't know where you are half the time. Doesn't this prove to you I'm not lying?"

Milly stepped backwards and stared at him horrified.

"Yers, orl right," she said in a subdued and chastened tone of voice. "Put it back on."

She took her end of the belt.

That evening, having passed the turning onto the southern section of the Northern Drift, the road that Milly had been following until her encounter with the monster, they stopped beside the path and bedded down for the night, the girl making sure they were far enough apart to rule out any inadvertent contact. Despite being on a new footing with her travelling companion she still did not wholly trust him. By this time Jack had explained the situation in Toymerle and his own plight in more detail.

"I think my fellow sufferers - the other kidnap victims I was with - saw the bandit chief coming up that track back there. He was probably returning from a raid with a gang of his men and maybe bringing new captives with him. Once the ex-prisoners spotted him they took to their heels and the outlaws took off after them - I've no idea if they managed to escape - perhaps they're safely down on the plains by now. Anyway, what's for sure is that Rhys and his army were in Toymerle at the time waiting to fight it out. I'm pretty certain that when the Cheetah got there - if he did - Tallis would have already gone north and Dando with him. That's what I hope anyway."

"We mus' make sure," said Milly with mounting concern. She had discovered that she and Jack shared a common bond in that they both cared passionately about the welfare of a young aristocrat to whom they each owed a debt of gratitude. Because of this she was prepared to look on this new companion more kindly and to tolerate his presence during their period of collaboration.

Next morning, further along the path, Jack outlined a plan of campaign.

"When we get near we must be hellishly careful," he cautioned. "We won't know who came out on top until we suss the place out. If the wrong ones are in charge we don't want to be captured. Once is enough for me – I'd rather slit my throat. Have you got any weapons?"

"Only this," replied Milly, then realised she needed to explain. "It's a knife – just a small one."

"Well, better than nothing."

They continued westward through several heavy snow showers until they reached a junction and, just south of Toymerle, turned right onto the road known as the Ffordd.

"Now comes the part where I'll be worse than useless I'm afraid," said Jack. "it's up to you. Creep forward and do a circuit of the village – stay under cover and make sure no-one sees you. There may be men on watch so you'll have to have your wits about you. I'll stay here until you return. Am I out of sight of the track?"

"Let me borrow your jacket," said Milly, "I won't show up so much."

Normally Milly's black skin would have been an advantage when carrying out a recce, but in this snowy landscape it meant she stood out like a sore thumb. The jacket was light in colour and had a hood - it would help to camouflage her. After she left it seemed to a freezing Jack that an age passed before a slight sound warned him that someone was nearby. He went rigid and shrank into himself, not relaxing until he heard Milly say, "It's me!" He reached out and the little girl actually put her hand in his before giving him back his jacket.

"I din' come across nobody," she whispered, "I bin all roun'. There's no tracks because the snow's coverin' everythin' up. I bin right to where the 'ouses start. It's strange."

"They may be in the church – that's inside the cliff," said Jack. "Did you hear anything?"

"Nuffink."

"OK – I'll come with you – but you'll have to be my eyes – I'll be the ears."

Hand in hand they walked up the road to the edge of the village. The little settlement was lost in the hush that often accompanies heavy winter precipitation. The items of furniture that had been piled between the houses, so carefully assembled a few days earlier, had either been partially dismantled or burnt, if not completely done away with. Cautiously they progressed to the centre of the hamlet and then to the soaring cave entrance that concealed the church.

"We ought to look inside," said Jack. "Can you make out where the doors used to be? Go and explore, but be careful."

Milly waded forward through the snow towards the portal but then an exclamation was jerked out of her. She had tripped over something hidden by the precipitation.

"There's somebody here – buried – they're all col' an' stiff!"

Jack joined her, kneeing down and brushing snow away.

"Dead," he said. "Who is it?"

Milly explored further.

"There's more 'n one," she said

"What do they look like?"

"'Ere's one wiv a tash – an' this one's quite young. 'An this one's a very big geezer."

"Has he got a beard?" asked Jack urgently.

"No – but this one 'as – a black one."

Jack was not satisfied until they had thoroughly explored all the ground in front of the cave and uncovered a total of eight bodies, meanwhile repeating his instruction to Milly to look inside.

She came back after a few minutes. "There's no-one as far as I c'n see," she reported.

"Do you recognise any of these?" he asked apprehensively. He had been spending the time running his hands over the features of the frozen dead, dreading to feel again the young face of which his fingers still held a memory.

"No, of corse not – if yor lookin' for the Lordship 'ee's not there. Don' you fink I would 'ave said if 'ee woz!"

He went back to the corpse with the beard and measured its limbs against his own. They were massive in comparison. "These aren't the gang members that got killed when Rhys's army arrived," he said, "I'm very much afraid that this is Rhys himself – the leader of our rescuers - and here are his sons. Dando gave me a pretty good description of what he looked like and then later I met him myself. He was a really big bloke."

"None of 'em are the Lordship's lot," said Milly. "None of 'em are old, or 've got red 'air, an' they're orl men."

"What could have happened?" puzzled Jack, frowning over the scene of slaughter. "Well, lets suppose those guarding the outskirts of the village were driven back to the church by the Cheetah, or these few anyway because I'm sure Rhys would never have run away. Maybe the rest *did* run once their defences had been breached - down the Ffordd to Labour in Vain - and when the bandits had killed the ones still standing their ground maybe they went after them. Or perhaps it wasn't until Rhys and his sons were killed that the defenders ran, after they saw their leader fall. Anyway, although the Cheetah's not here anymore he may come back once he's found the fugitives and dealt with them. What's undeniable is that, for now, there's no-one left on either side, neither defenders nor attackers, and sooner or later, if it goes on snowing, the town'll be cut off."

By this time it was starting to get dark and the conditions were worsening.

"It's late," said Jack. "Snow or no snow we'll have to remain here overnight. Come with me and I'll show you the place where Dando and I stayed. By the way, if you see a walking stick on your travels let me know; it helps me to find the way around. I've lost the one that Dando got for me when we first met."

Unerringly he let the way to the comfortable little house on the main street with the well equipped kitchen.

"We can spend the night here. This is where Dando cared for me and the horses - ungrateful sod that I am - except when he went down to the square to look after his master. He was a real star."

"'E's my Lordship," said Milly fondly, "that's the sort of fing 'e does."

"I'll show you where the storerooms are. There should be plenty of stuff left. We can stock up for the journey. There's three bedrooms upstairs... what's that...?"

He stopped still his hand raised.

"I d'n't 'ear nuffink," said Milly.

"Listen!"

They both held their breath. From somewhere to the rear of the house came a pitiful neigh.

"Gee-gees!" exclaimed Jack.

A moment later they tumbled out of the back door. A strong smell of manure assaulted their nostrils. Milly peered into the adjacent stables.

"It's Mollyblobs!" she cried in astonishment, "'an there's anuver big brown 'orse. They're in a right ol' mess. Wot are they still doin' 'ere? Why 'aven't they taken 'em?" Her voice acquired a note of sharp anxiety.

"All right," said Jack, "don't jump to conclusions," but in his turn he sounded somewhat perturbed.

"Praps they d'n't leave in time," cried Milly. "Praps they woz 'ere when..." She burst into noisy tears.

"Hush," said Jack pulling her to him and putting his arms around her while she sobbed against his chest. "The first thing we've got to do is see these are all right. That's what Dando would have done. Meantime I'll have a think and tell you what probably happened. Do you know how to look after horses?"

Between them they got the beasts mucked out, fed and watered.

"It's obvious," Jack assured her sometime later. "If they were going into the mountains they wouldn't take horses – much too steep and dangerous. They'd be fools to even try."

"But the Lordship wou'n't just leave 'em."

"No of course not – someone would have been asked to care for them – but they ran away with the rest probably, or else got killed."

Milly looked at him doubtfully as if wondering whether to accept this idea.

"I'm goin' to find out for sure in the mornin'," she said. "I'm goin' to go an' look for 'em. You comin'?" Jack pursed his lips into a sceptical pout and shook his head.

"Not a good idea," he said. "If we don't want to be snowed in here we ought to go east as soon as possible and get down to lower levels. Otherwise we're going to find ourselves trapped."

At first light Milly equipped herself for the road and set out north, giving Jack a cursory goodbye with little thought of what was to happen to him, all her concern being for Dando and her need to assure herself of his safety. Jack, pretty confident of the outcome, but anxious nonetheless, kept the little house warm and waited. It was late afternoon before there came a banging on the door.

"Who is it?" he called

"Me."

Milly came in bringing a freezing blast of cold air and a flurry of snow with her. He could actually hear her teeth chattering.

"I got stuck," she said. "It woz deep as deep an' it's getting' deeper. I 'ad to come back."

Jack opened the door to the range and she huddled over the flames shaking like a leaf while he massaged her hands and feet. For a long time the only sound was the crackling of the fire. Then, with great sorrow, Milly said "'E's gorn," but whether she meant *north* or was speaking of some worse fate that had befallen her beloved was not clear. What was obvious to Jack was her deep unhappiness. He realised he was going to have to generate sufficient optimism for the two of them.

"Dando and his friends set off long before the heavy snows began and before the latest fighting started," he assured her. "They'll be well on their way to the coast by now. We've got to think about ourselves. We must leave tomorrow morning at the latest, especially if we're going to take the horses. They'll be useful - they can carry stuff and maybe us as well."

Jack knew a few things about horses – Milly practically nothing. Using her as his eyes he ran to earth saddles, harness, blankets, panniers and supplies both for themselves and for the animals. In a shed attached to the stables they found some strange little contraptions made of thick leather with small spikes attached. Jack explored these with his hands.

"They're shoes!" he exclaimed. "Not horse-shoes but shoes for horses – to be worn in bad weather. Let's see if they fit."

Within one of the bedrooms, buried in a bottom drawer, Milly found a small cache of money that the robbers had overlooked. After some debate they decided to take it and leave an I-O-U. By the time everything was ready it was late evening.

"We'll risk another night here," said Jack. "We'd better bring some shovels tomorrow in case we have to dig our way through."

They had something to eat, then went to bed but, as far as Jack was concerned, not to rest: he was once more afflicted by bad dreams. In the morning he looked washed out and somewhat fragile.

"Are you orl right?" the little girl asked. "You don' seem quite the ticket. Shall we stay another day?"

"No, we must go now – it's still snowing isn't it? There's no time to lose."

They set out.

If it was not for the fact that the road was marked by posts they would never have kept to the track. To say the going was tough was an understatement. For a great deal of the journey's early stages Milly was up to her waist in snow and several times the shovels were brought into play. The horses stumbled, slid and complained despite their bad-weather shoes. Soon the ravine opened up on their left-hand side and the track from Formile joined them from the right. Milly looked along it in surmise.

"Wot about that way?" she wondered. "Praps, cos the weather woz bad, the Lordship decided to go back to the town where 'ee stayed once before"

"No, I don't think so," said Jack, "and anyway we might encounter the Cheetah returning a second time."

A mile or two further on the walls of the ravine became less sheer and the Northern Drift branched off to their left, continuing in its normal direction by means of some hairpin turns.

"Praps they went that way," suggested Milly longingly. "Shall we try?"

"Does the track go right to the bottom?" asked Jack.

"Yers, an' then up the uver side."

"We'd never get the horses all the way down, and if we did we might never get them out again. Besides, we'd then have to take them through the mountains. Look here Milly – when we reach Drossi we'll only have to wait for a bit and, bob's your uncle, Dando will be sure to turn up. He won't be able to keep away from Drossi – everyone ends up in Drossi sooner or later."

They bypassed the tempting northern way, Milly with great regret, and carried on along the eastern track which at last began to show signs of descending in real earnest. It took them several days to reach climes where the temperature rose above freezing for at least part of the twenty-four hours and even then it did not mean they had left the wintry conditions behind. Hail, fog, sleet and chilly rain all made progress difficult until at last the track widened and became less precipitous while the weather slightly relented. The easier going meant they could mount the horses and get along faster, although for Milly this was a steep learning curve; she had never ridden in her life before. However Mollyblobs was just the right size for her, as was Carolus for Jack, and she soon gained in confidence. She no longer had to guide her companion. Somewhere back along the road from Deep Hallow the big chestnut horse had recognised that when it came to their small equine team Mollyblobs was the boss. He was quite happy to plod along nose to tail with the little pony, following her lead, while the blind boy sat on his back letting him have his head.

By this time Milly had entirely lost her fear of Jack. She had accepted him as an honorary member of her own sex and treated him as such. She felt she could confide in him and ask his advice as she would have done with an older and wiser woman. She told him about her rescue from the Spread Eagle, a detail Dando had omitted in his conversations with the young man, about her life with Damask and their adventures down on the plains.

"The majesty wonts to go on the 'alls I fink – she woz real good at this acting lark. I fink that's why she di'n't come wiv me to look for 'er bruvver. I fink she might be back wiv Alaric an' the rest of 'em by now – although they wozn't too keen on 'er ac'chally – she tol' 'em wot was wot a lot an' got orf wiv the boss."

"She sounds like someone after my own heart," said Jack. "I could fix the acting thing for her if she came to Drossi. I'm on first name terms with several of the luvvies."

After a few more days they left the high hills behind and returned to the haunts of men. They began passing through remote villages and then small towns. Eventually they came to Numpnett and put up at an inn. They visited the high-street and in one of the little shops that sold just about everything, Jack bought a new cane along with some dark glasses and was able to dispense with his blindfold. The horses had a night of luxury in the inn's stables before they moved on.

"*Going home, going home...*" sang Jack as they rode easily side by side, exchanging a word every now and then.

"Is Drossi your home?" asked Milly, who could not remember ever having had a permanent home.

"Yes, of course – yours as well."

"Mine?"

"Of course. No-one who speaks like you could come from anywhere else."

"But I never knowd for sure where I cum from. I knowed it woz a town but I d'n't know which one."

"You, with or without your family, must have lived in Drossi at some time – there's quite a crowd of your people down in the Little Kymer district."

"Wot d'you mean – my people?"

"Your colour."

"'Ow d'you know wot colour I am?"

"I guessed," said Jack with a half-smile.

I'm going home, thought Milly in wonder, *to the big town where they have things like circuses and warm rooms and plenty of food.*

Although she had told the boy almost everything that she could remember of her early life, he had revealed very little of his own. She began to be curious about her companion. She had never met anyone quite like him before.

"Wot's it like bein' a poofter?" she asked one day with devastating frankness.

Jack laughed, unoffended.

"No different from being anything else," he said, "in Drossi at least. Other places are not so tolerant – you have to be careful – you could find yourself doing time – that is if you're lucky. Occasionally it's much worse than that."

"'Ow worse?" asked Milly but Jack just shook his head.

Soon they passed Digor and Thrubwell and were getting near to the point where their track joined the main road along the Great River.

"We'll be in Drossi by this evening," promised Jack. For the last day or two his normal flow of cheerful conversation had dried up. His mind was dwelling on how he was going to cope in a sinister lightless metropolis which would be familiar yet totally strange, and he was wondering what sort of welcome awaited him there. It was likely that a number of people, including his grandfather, would have written him off after his abduction, and to find him back in the land of the living in his present condition might be an unwelcome surprise for some of them.

"Look," said Milly, pointing along the road and forgetting for the umpteenth time that Jack could not see, "that's the sort of van that the majesty an' me woz travellin' around in when we woz down this way before. She allas said she'd give it back to the clown if she cum across 'im but we never did."

The distant vehicle came closer and Milly was able to pick out more detail, such as the type of horse in the traces and how many people were up on the box.

"'Ang on," she exclaimed, "I fink that's it! It woz yellow – bright yellow wiv red wheels. I fink that's 'er an' the clown as well. Blimey – 'oo'd 'ave thought it!"

She watched as a girl jumped down from the van onto the road and came running towards them.

"It *is* 'er," she explained excitedly to Jack, "it's 'is sister. She's wiv the clown."

She drew Mollyblobs to a halt and prepared to greet the approaching Damask.

"Majesty!" she cried, "it's you! Where've you bin? 'Ave you seen the Lordship?"

Hell's fires climb higher,
Yet it's cold despite the flames,
As cold as old age.

Chapter twelve

The field was no longer bright and sunny. The sky was overcast and an increasingly belligerent wind streamed across the surface of the crop causing the corn to flatten before the blast. In this latest dream Ann was far ahead and Dando got the impression he had been walking for hours trying to narrow the gap between the two of them. She was just about to go over a rise and out of his sight, and as so often happens when under the influence of such a chimera he felt he was wading through treacle, his movements slowed almost to a standstill. Eventually, as he reached the top of the gradient, he caught sight of her once more and saw what she was making for. He realised that this world-sized field had its limits; there was a border, a boundary at the bottom of the next downward slope, and in it a gate, just an ordinary farm gate, a few yards in front of her. On the other side he saw a far country, vague and indistinct. He was tormented by the thought that if she passed the barrier he would not be allowed to follow, despite the fact that as she came to it she turned once more to beckon him and smile. With a supreme effort he banished the lassitude that was hobbling him and crying, "Wait! Wait!" rushed through the corn desperate to arrive in time to stop her. As he ran he saw her open the gate and go through and, before he reached it, it had clanged shut behind her and she was gone.

The force with which he threw off this vision propelled Dando into a sitting position. He took great gulps of the freezing air, his eyes wide open in shock. He had been lying between Tallis and Ralph and now, distraught, he stared across Tallis' body to the other slumbering figures, trying to identify them. Yes, thank heaven, she was there, she was still there, between Tallis and Foxy; by the light of the full moon he could make out the faint gleam of her hair. With enormous relief he sank back down, filled with an unfocused gratitude. Almost every night now his dreams were of partings and loss. He knew precisely when the affliction had started; he could date it from the time she had rescued him from the God-of-the-Core. Something had changed then which he could not explain. He was only aware that an ill-defined menace hung over them now which diminished during the day and acquired weight and substance as he slept, disturbing his rest with eldritch nocturnal terrors.

They had been back on the road for a week, and the conditions were such that only Tallis had experienced anything like them before. The temperature seemed to have plunged to a new low especially at night. The air was bitter and their breath froze as soon as it left their nostrils, frost accumulating on their eyelashes, eyebrows and on the men's beards. Tallis insisted that they expose as little of their flesh to the elements as possible. He inspected their extremities regularly for tell-tale signs of damage. They obeyed him and followed his lead, even Foxy, recognising in the southerner someone who had taken in mountain lore with his mother's milk. It was absolutely vital, he told them, that they share body heat at night; modesty and social convention must go by the board. All the same, although they were allowed to walk side by side during the day, when it came time for the travellers to bed down Tallis and Foxy always managed to ensure that Dando and Ann lay apart with someone else lodged between them, even if it was only the dog. Despite the harsh inimical environment through which they were travelling they were now making fairly good progress and the going was not too hard. During these early stages of the march Tallis was optimistic and felt that if the weather did not worsen they would be able to gain the pass they were making for before many days had worn away.

Foxy had a new toy which he no longer dared to touch with bare hands as it was made of metal and would have scorched his skin in the extreme cold; nevertheless he inspected it several times a day, gloating over his acquisition.

"It be on one of the outlaw bodies," he explained, "I don' believe it hev ever bin fired. I search for more but don' be findin' any. I got the bullets too. I c'n shew you how to load it."

His prize was a pistol and it was his pride and joy; he never tired of demonstrating its mechanism and aiming it at distance objects. The temptation to discharge it was resisted however in order to conserve his ammunition. Dando, Ann and Tallis looked on in two minds. They were impressed by the firearm's powerful menace but at the same time regretted that their hard won skills with the bow seemed to have already been rendered obsolete by this new weapon.

Tallis had decided not to resume the system of watches. There seemed little point in doing so when he was confident that they were far away from others of their kind and even the wild-life at this altitude was virtually non-existent. Because of this and because of the new sleeping arrangements Dando and Ann's secret night-time trysts were perforce a thing of the past. To Dando this was barely tolerable. To have Ann so close, close enough for a surreptitious hand clasp during the day but always separated from him at night left him almost ill with desire. On one particular morning when Foxy was off on his own business and Tallis' back was turned he seized the opportunity to encircle Ann with his arm and sneak his hand within her coat, cradling her right breast. Gently she disengaged herself and moved away. Dando closed the gap, putting his arm round her waist and again pulling her to his side.

"It's about time I got the chance to hold you properly," he grumbled in a fierce undertone, sensing a resistance that he did not understand. "It's driving me bloody insane carrying on like this – it's doing my head in. Can't you work your sleeping spell?"

If he could only enfold her in his embrace, if he could just make love to her properly once more, he was sure that all his doubts and fears, the baleful feeling of foreboding that was haunting him, would disappear. It seemed so long since the last time they had gone all the way. When *was* the last time? From what she had told him it had happened when she saved him from the fire god by calling up an even greater power, but he had no memory of that at all.

"Can't you do the spell?" he asked again.

"I don' be able," she replied, a guarded look on her face.

"You can't?" he said, perturbed that she did not seem to want what he wanted. "Or do you mean won't?"

"My spells don' work any more," she said.

He looked at her disbelievingly. For twopence-halfpenny he would have thrown caution to the winds and taken her aside openly that very night, but then the thought of the deadly little weapon that Foxy had acquired restrained him. He might be putting both their lives at risk. He knew nothing of the promise Ann had elicited from the red-headed Nablan, which should have ensured that they no longer needed to hide their love. Well if *she* would not cast the spell for sleep he would have to do it for her. About an hour after they had lain down, when he felt everyone was deep in slumber, he tried cautiously to extract himself from the horizontal line-up in order to sit apart as was required when working the magic. However Tallis woke when he sensed movement – they lay side by side, virtually touching – and, his scheme stymied, Dando had quickly to think of an excuse for his fidgetiness.

"Just going for a pee," he muttered and wandered off alone, foiled for the moment from putting his plan into operation.

"Tu-whit-tu-whoo, tu-whit-tu-whoo."

Ann swum slowly up through a somniferous ocean of sleep and opened her eyes. As she surfaced, the call of an owl was lodged in her memory. She raised her head, blinked drowsily at the icy moonlit scene and summoned her scattered faculties in order to make sense of what she had heard. Owls up here? No, impossible – she must have dreamt it. But as if to give the lie to this conclusion the call came again. She looked across at her companions – they were all insensible – the concert appeared to be solely for her benefit. She turned in the direction of the sound and, on a high crag against the sky in which hung a plethora of stars, she saw the silhouette of a bird. Owls on cliffs? - they were surely more at home amongst trees in twilit meadows. She made a rough guess at the distance between herself and the stark, monolithic figure. This was an enormous bird she realised, bigger than an eagle, bigger than a vulture. It sat so still that at first she wondered if what she was seeing was just an owl-shaped outcrop atop a hill. But then the head stretched upwards and the cry was repeated - *"Tu-whit-tu-whoo, tu-whit-tu-whoo."* This was wrong, all wrong – it could not be coming from the throat of a single bird; she was enough of a country girl to know that such a call always took the form of a duet between the sexes – one voicing the *tu-whit*, the other replying with the *tu-whoo*. She tried to shake Foxy awake – he would be able to confirm her understanding - but it was like trying to rouse the Rock of Pickwah; by the time he had woozily come to and she had directed his gaze towards the crag, the outline against the sky had disappeared. The next day she did not mention what she had seen to either Tallis or Dando, but she was left with the uncomfortable feeling that her night-time visitor had been not of this world.

Each evening, on the traveller's retirement, it was Ann's habit, since the weather had worsened, to spin an invisible protective sphere around herself and her companions within which she raised the temperature by a few degrees. She found she could work the charm with just murmured words and some minute hand gestures. It meant they could sleep in relative comfort, yet the difference inside and outside the bubble was not great enough for them to notice that anything strange was happening. On leaving Toymerle she returned to this practice and it was not until several nights had passed and she had awoken twice with ice clinging to her chapped lips that she began to suspect that the spell was no longer effective. Puzzled she tried one or two other enchantments that her father had taught her - a transformation spell, mist raising, a spectral illusion – nothing worked. A day or two later she noticed that her nipples were sore, something that often happened before her monthlies. She waited for the period to start but in vain. Then on one occasion, after eating, she had to go aside and vomit up her breakfast into the snow.

For several days she tried to carry on as normal as if nothing unusual were taking place, but in the end she could not ignore the fundamental changes occurring within her own body. One morning as she trod in Dando's snowy footprints through a narrow defile she allowed the monstrous idea elbow room. *Knocked up; bun-in-the-oven; up the duff;* there were so many crude phrases for it, so many ominous expressions she had heard people use – but not about her, please not her, oh please let it not be me! She came to a dead stop, her muscles dissolving, and for several minutes froze into a state of fight or flight, the primitive base of her brain in control. Then her panic abated slightly and she was able to think coherently once more. She began to ask the obvious question – how could it have happened? Dando was always so careful... they had never run any risks... it was not possible surely... The answer hit her like a sledgehammer. When he was possessed and she had led him unknowingly down the paths of love, by force of circumstances they had had no protection! That was when she must have fallen. Tears welled up and the world about her dissolved into a smeary formlessness. Far ahead of her now Dando turned and walked backwards a few paces.

"Come on," he called, "put a move on - you're getting left behind."

That night she could not sleep. Ideas whirled in her brain, monopolising her attention, forcing themselves into the forefront of her mind. Oh, if only she had left long ago when their small band had first set out, or had let Tallis banish Dando from their company. She had known even then that gifted individuals such as herself acted as magnets to any others similarly endowed, such as the dancers, and that therefore, while she remained close to him, she would draw the Great Ones' attention to her lover. It was undeniable that she was a liability and now, after what had happened at Toymerle, the danger was all too real, in fact had been multiplied a thousandfold. If, at the start, she had been the one to leave, allowing him to continue his journey unimpeded by her presence, he might, with luck, have been able to slip through the world unremarked. Yet, at the beginning, it almost seemed as if the goddess had been left behind in the valley while the Sky-God had not yet come on the scene. As a consequence she had chosen to ignore Dadda's warnings. In truth, as she could now comprehend, her love had not been strong enough to renounce what she held most dear. In the present circumstances her father's remembered words took on an added significance: *She be a jealous god, an' she be most vengeful when the woman be expecting – if you fall pregnant that's when you both have the most to fear.* So he had wisely told her and now the thing he considered to be the greatest threat had actually come to pass. If the Mother, who was already angry with her, got to hear of it her fury would know no bounds. Perhaps she already knew – perhaps even now she was preparing to exact a terrible retribution.

Desperately she sought for some solution to the bind they were in. She had heard that there were ways to mend matters in such situations, potions, such as the gypsies brewed, that you could swallow to bring on the bleeding, but she had no clue as to what the ingredients might be, and anyway, ever since she had been old enough to understand what was meant by pregnancy she had felt that it was akin to murder to do away with even such rudimentary life. This was a child, after all, and not just any child, it was *their* child. She felt a slight stirring of maternal feeling and from this an idea was born. Perhaps it was not too late; perhaps, if she went now, he would be safe and she, in her solitary future, would still have the baby to comfort her. All ready to act on this notion she was brought up abruptly by the remembrance of their situation: there was no way she could survive alone in the hostile country that surrounded them. Anyway the others would not let her leave, they would track her down - easy enough to do in the snow. It would be no use her walking off saying self-sacrificingly *I'm just going outside and I may be some time* (a phrase Dando had quoted to her once from one of his story books), they would make sure she was brought back. Again she was plunged into despair and this was only partially alleviated by the hope that, against all the odds, when they came down from the mountains and reached habitable country there would still be time for her to take advantage of some byway or other and remove herself from his presence. Almost every night from this point on she heard the voice of the owl in the small hours. It taunted her with words inside her head: *"**Wherever you go, whatever you do (tu-whit-tu-whoo) I'll get the both of you in the end.**"*

Dando's culinary skills were no longer required. Because there was no fuel for fires in these remote regions the preparation of meals had come to an abrupt halt. The travellers were forced to exist on way-bread, dried fruit, preserved meat and cheese. They drank melted snow thawed by the heat of their own bodies. There was no need to monitor the supplies anymore as everyone was carrying their own provisions and he had no horses to tend. His one remaining job, waiting on Tallis, gave him little satisfaction as the knight seemed once again self-absorbed and rarely acknowledged his presence. Foxy, although no longer abusive and occasionally quite friendly, usually ignored him. Ann had withdrawn into herself. Twice he tried to find out what was wrong but without success. At first he conceived the notion that she was ill – a while since he had caught her heaving by the side of the track – but, when he voiced his concerns, she had dismissed them with such angry impatience that he felt he must be mistaken. At a loose end, he had plenty of time, when they were not on the road, to sit on his own and brood, only Ralph, close beside him as usual, providing an antidote to his loneliness. He agonised about Ann's attitude. She no longer returned the small gestures of affection he was able to make when they were unobserved. He was afraid she had fallen out of love with him.

"You do still care for me don't you Annie?" he said.

"O' course," she replied but with none of the extra endearments that she had been wont to employ. Her attitude dealt a knock to his self-esteem. Perhaps having been so long in his company she had at last tumbled to his true nature and he had been unmasked for the useless so'n'so he really was. He needed physical reassurance, he needed her closer than close in order to re-establish their love, but there was no prospect of that happening while they struggled through this icy terrain.

The greater the distance they came from their starting point the harder the journey was becoming, and, although they had left Toymerle in reasonably high spirits, in the last few days it had begun to snow heavily and Dando suspected that Tallis was worried. Tonight it had stopped for a while and he lay awake beneath the waning moon wondering how much further they were going to be expected to travel. He thought of the account Tallis had given them of his beginnings. He had been gripped by the narrative in the same way that he had by legends and folk tales in the books from the King's Vault. As a child it had been beguiling to plunge into that fictional secondary world and he had willingly suspended disbelief. But, always, at the end of a reading session he would look up from the page in order to re-enter prosaic reality, being careful to mark his place for the next occasion when he was able to step into the land of make-believe. Tallis' story seemed at one with those ancient fables – a procession of kings, princesses, wizards, and memories of past incarnations that were not to be met with in real life. Once before he had doubted Tallis' sanity. Now, under the sway of his present gloomy mood, he again asked himself whether he was following a madman on a journey to nowhere, a quest that had no reality but in the man's own imagination. A gust of regret that he had bound himself to the stranger swept through him. It had been a spur of the moment decision; he had sworn himself impulsively to the knight's service, and, although he had no intention of reneging on his vow, after a promise made in haste it seemed unfair that he should now have no idea how many months or years this serfdom was going to last.

Although they were joined at the hip by the ceremony they had shared he could not say that any sort of rapport had been forged between himself and his master; the man's basic personality was just as much a mystery to him as when they had first met at the King's

Head in High Harrow nearly three months earlier. In spite of this he could not claim complete indifference; it was not in his nature to be in a person's company for so long without developing feelings of one kind or another for them. Tallis he could have admired, nay loved, if only the southerner had shown some generosity of spirit and come part way to meet him. As it was the knight errant remained an enigma to the boy and Dando's attitude was consequently one of regretful ambivalence. Nevertheless the monkish traveller still impressed him with his cold asceticism as he had done right from the start when he had first glimpsed him through the secret spyhole at the inn. His initial infatuation had had time to cool but had not disappeared altogether; Tallis had done nothing so far to completely destroy his faith.

Dando turned over, sighed and buried his nose in the fur of his hooded jacket. He asked himself what was to become of them all. Although at the moment it had stopped, snow had been falling all day and the way was presenting a greater and greater challenge. Perhaps everything would end here in these mountains if they could not make it through the high country and that would provide a solution at one fell swoop to his multiple concerns.

Foxy, it seemed, had his own issues about the journey.

"For-why," he asked Tallis, "do we be allas gooin' narth when we could goo roun'?"

Tallis looked at him in surprise. "What do you mean?" he said.

"Well, the fellow at the Waggoners tol' we to goo down to Drossi an' then take the coastal highway, an' Rhys an' his friends say the same. They weren't whooly keen on we gooin' through the mountains like we be a-doin' – not in the dead of winter any road."

Tallis answered with barely concealed testiness.

"I thought you understood. I explained it back at the inn. I seek a Key and, according to the history my mother told, when it was stolen the thief fled due north, thousands of miles in a single night. Also, in my researches, I found that every myth and legend that mentions the Key-of-the-Ages speaks of it as being found in the north. And now the voice of the god has instructed me to go *Over-the-Brook* which as I understand it means to go north."

"That be all very well," persisted Foxy, not ready to give up on the argument just yet, "but if you take the road to Drossi there be many ways startin' from there to get you to where you wan' to go. I know – I bin there."

Tallis clicked his tongue as if wondering whether it was worth trying to convince this pig-headed young man of his reasons for holding to a single bearing.

"If I diverge from the northerly direction, even for a few miles, I might miss it. Don't you see? How do I know where it's hidden? For instance, when I heard of the treasury at the fire god's shrine I had hopes that that's where it might be. A temple sacred to the God-of-the-Core, surely that would be a most fitting resting-place if along the way the thief had been bested by Rostan and the Key had fallen into his hands. Back at Formile, if we had taken the advice of the man at the inn then we would never have heard about a treasure cave. As it was, in the end the Gopher assured me that nothing of the kind was to be found there, but it can stand as an example of why I have to stay faithful to my course. I must keep going straight as a dye because somewhere along that route, that northerly route, it will be found, you mark my words."

"But how be you a-gooin' to know?" continued Foxy, worrying at the subject like a terrier with a bone. "A key be but a small thing. Mayhap you hev already passed it where it lie hid. How ken you tell?" "I'll know," replied the wayfarer with absolute certainty.

Despite this forthright defence of his modus operandi Tallis was by no means as confident as he made out. In fact, over the years, his journey had been a lot less direct than he claimed. Natural and man-made obstacles had often stood in his way, causing him to twist and turn and veer away from his intended route. And soon he was going to have to deviate once more when he followed the advice of the couple in Toymerle by rejecting the Cold Straith Pass to Pickwah in order to turn north-east towards the lower Fynnburg Pass. Well, considering the worsening weather and going on his past experience they would be lucky even to make that crossing. He was greatly perturbed but did not share his anxieties with his companions.

The road they were following, the Ffordd as the Labourites called it, eventually swung eastward and rejoined the

Northern Drift (*The Way of the Shades* thought Dando with a certain frisson of dismay). Not long after that they were faced with their first really stiff climb. It was a case of scrambling to and fro across the face of an almost vertical cliff and then hauling themselves over a series of giant steps. Ann, because of her diminutive stature, had to be lifted and passed from one man to another up these steep ascents. The snow, falling once more, hid everything but the nearest landmarks and the unremitting whiteness was starting to play tricks with their eyes. They did not seem able to get enough air into their lungs, and even fairly mild exertion brought on an attack of breathlessness. After a while the day darkened and a violent wind began to try and knock them off their feet.

"Here's the other road," shouted Dando over the blast; he happened to be in the lead. The ghost of a signpost loomed up and its wording could only be made out when they stood virtually beneath it. "Pickwah and Osh straight ahead," he yelled, "Formile, Toymerle, V. Poule the way we've just come. Trincomalee and Tagnaroque off to the right. I s'pose that's where we're supposed to go."

"That's the one," replied Tallis, "east-nor'-east. We'll swing north again the first chance we get once we've left the pass behind." As the road divided and they took the right-hand option he looked back regretfully in the Pickwah direction as if for two pins he would have ignored the knowledgeable advice he had received and have attempted the more difficult crossing.

The climb was now not so precipitous but was nonetheless a long and steady haul. When the track took them close to the mountainside the wind came slamming down from above; at all other times it blew horizontally into their faces turning them into snow men and women. As it strengthened, the weaker members of the party faltered and had to be supported, Tallis by Dando and Ann by Foxy. Clinging together and bent almost double the two couples headed into the storm. Soon even the strongest of the travellers – Foxy – was finding it hard to make progress.

"It's no good," shouted Tallis, cupping his hands round his mouth, "we'll have to dig ourselves in. Over there – the drift against the rocks – get out the spades."

Under his instructions they turned aside and began hollowing out a cave in the feet thick wall of snow; it was none too soon for their stamina had been sorely tested. Tallis showed them how to pack the snow within the interior they had created to stop the refuge collapsing and then how to pile more snow against the outside to act as insulation. The five of them crept into the shelter leaving the howling gale behind and huddled together in order to conserve every last degree of heat, like rabbit kits secure in their burrow. The final remnants of daylight faded and, surprisingly comfortable, one by one they fell asleep in their sepulchre of ice.

Dando came to himself several hours later in complete darkness, roused by a stuffy lack of air. He sensed that their egress had become blocked and that someone was attacking the obstruction with a spade.

"Keep going," he heard Tallis say, "you're nearly through - just a small hole." He felt a cold draught on his face, took a few grateful breaths and drifted off to sleep once more. The next thing he knew the interior was flooded with blue light. He raised himself on one elbow to find that Tallis and Foxy, with Ralph in attendance, were both outside on a bright sunny morning and that, inside the cave, Ann's head was so close to his that a few strands of her hair had crept into his mouth. He was tempted to take her into his arms but caution prevailed. Instead he scrambled out through the hole that had been made and discovered that the wind had dropped completely.

These good conditions did not last. Although the storm had passed on and the day was comparatively calm the sky gradually clouded over, causing the light to fade. Snow began to fall once more, so thickly that they were soon climbing through an absolute white-out, making it impossible to see more than two or three feet in front of them. As time wore on and nothing relieved the absolute monotony of putting one foot blindly in front of another in an utterly formless environment the trek was reduced to a pure endurance test. Minutes and hours ceased to exist; progress became just a question of wading through ever deepening snow with the fear that finally strength would fail and all four would collapse from sheer exhaustion. No-one spoke and, although Dando and Foxy still lent a helping hand, each of the travellers was locked in their own little world. Everyone was waging their own private war against enervation, their chests aching as they panted in the harsh thin air; even the dog seemed to be having trouble. It was when night was not far off that Dando made a significant discovery, the discovery of something that might have been happening for some time but of which he had not been aware until that moment.

"We're going down!" he exclaimed.

"Yes," croaked Tallis, "it's behind us." But even as he spoke he fell forward into the snow. Dando and Foxy hurried to pick him up and with their support on either side he was able to stand.

"Look," said Ann, pointing to a rock right in their path that had emerged from the gloom, "it be a sign." Carved into the stone was an arrow pointing to the left.

"Stay there," said Dando handing Tallis into Foxy's arms, "I'll go and see."

Frighteningly fast he disappeared into a curtain of falling snow, leaving no evidence of his presence apart from some quickly filling tracks. Those left behind, listening for his return, could hear nothing but faint patterings and sighing. Then when they had almost given him up for lost he was suddenly before them once more.

"There's a cave – a real cave – and I believe there's even some wood for burning. Come with me – quickly, quickly."

The cave, and the fuel provided by who knows what generous benefactor, was their salvation. Without it they might not have survived another night. They lit a fire to cook on and were also able to have hot drinks made from Dando's chicken essence of which he still had a small bottle. Just the preparation and consuming of this simple beverage improved their mood. Tallis, despite being completely exhausted, had also received a boost to his spirits.

"They came this way – the Guardians," he said. "The carving proves it. We're still on the right track."

Although we didn't see the key symbol, mused Dando but kept this thought to himself.

Sometime during the hours of darkness the snow ceased to fall and the next morning the outlook was set fair. It appeared that, having passed the watershed, they were now under the influence of the marine environment which lay ahead. As they descended, taking things in easy stages because of Tallis' weakness, the fallen snow began to melt, then disappear. The season gave the impression of having passed from winter into spring over night, although the second month had barely arrived. At first there was no sign of man in this northern landscape. The mountains gave way to rugged hills and then to barren moorland without even a few sheep to indicated a human presence. The wind blew into their faces once more and began to carry an unfamiliar smell which only Foxy recognised.

"We be not far off the sea I reckon," he told them. "We should be getting' a view of it before too long."

Dando wondered what would happen when they reached the coast. Would they turn west towards Pickwah, east towards Vadrosnia Poule, or might Tallis want to find a boat straight away in order to put to sea? Wherever his master went he was bound to follow. But what about Foxy and Ann? Did the two Nablans intend to go their own way when they got the chance? Once he would have been absolutely certain that Ann had no other wish but to stay with him, but now he was not so sure. They seemed to be at odds with one another, almost estranged, although there had been no angry words to speak of. He desperately needed to get her alone so they could talk openly and he could discover what was wrong, but he had the feeling that she was trying to avoid what he most desired. She was acting coldly towards him and he was terrified he was losing her. He must reconnect, must communicate physically in the most basic way. He awaited his chance.

One morning as they reached the top of a slight incline their goal finally materialised. The land dipped and then rose again to a ridge at some distance, but this upland was broken directly in front of them by a deep combe, a large notch in the range, through which they caught a glimpse of an undifferentiated blueness that stretched all the way to a vague horizon.

"There it be," said Foxy, pleased to have his prediction confirmed, despite the fact that he was no expert, having only encountered the tidal reaches of the Kymer River up to now. "That be it – the Middle Sea. There could be houses below here – we'd better set a watch tonight."

As they made their way downwards they came upon a much larger road which ran at right-angles to the one they were following.

"I reckon this be the coastal highway," said Foxy, "if we turn along it we'll end up at some town or other. I think the place called Trincomalee be not far away."

"No," said Tallis, " We'll keep straight on - I want to get to the sea."

They crossed the thoroughfare and continued in the same direction, entering the mouth of the aforementioned valley and passing through a little wood of stunted wind-twisted trees. On emerging from this coppice they found themselves standing just above a collection of rude dwellings that tumbled down, one below the other, to a rocky coastline. At this point Tallis felt the need to sit for a spell to regain his strength as he had begun to do fairly frequently now that the mountains had been left behind, and while he rested the three young people scrambled up the side of the declivity to the crest of the ridge in order to get a better view of their surroundings. Up on top everything was bright and airy with a vast cerulean expanse spreading itself out below them. The pungent smell of wet sand and rocks, of seaweed and shellfish hung in their nostrils and over the edge of cliffs not far from where they stood came the sound of surf. All around gulls were calling. "I never knowed it be so big," said Ann awestruck.

Dando looked to where sky and sea met. Somewhere on the other side of all this water there was another continent so he had been told, but if true it was distant enough to be hidden by the curve of the earth. Little ships were plying to and fro across the aqueous expanse and far to the west a long shadowy shape with a swelling on the left hand side heaved itself above the horizon.

The Dark Island – Hungry Island, he thought to himself remembering what Rhys had told him. Foxy raised his nose much like his namesake and sniffed the air.

"Lan'" he said, "I smell lan'. There be lan' over there," gesturing towards the skyline.

They returned to Tallis and all four made their way down the twisting main street of the coastal village – so steep that in places it was stepped - to a small harbour where one or two fishing boats were anchored and another was just unloading an extremely modest catch. To their right, on the far side of the harbour wall, lay a pebbly beach where small waves broke and withdrew and where a few sailing dingies were drawn up. Tallis walked out along the top of the wall and stood gazing in fascination at this alien environment, the main element of which stretched away, continually in motion, until it merged with the sky from which it took its colouring. In all his travels he had never seen anything like it. At last he tore himself away and turned back towards the seafront. It was long past midday and they would soon have to start thinking about a place to sleep.

"P'raps we could stay here," suggested Dando eagerly. "Shall I try and find out?"

There was a group of old men sitting on the quayside wall who had been watching them intently. Dando walked over. He came back quite soon with news.

"That gentleman says we can use his daughter's cottage tonight if we like. She's off visiting relatives and her husband's at sea. He wants to know how much we'd be prepared to pay."

A price was fixed and the retired sea-dog got shakily to his feet and led the way to a tiny dwelling halfway up the main street. "There be two bedroomz upstairs and two downstairs," he said, "you c'n yave one each, zee. An' there be a kitchen o' course. Privy out t' back."

"Is there a shop?" asked Dando, "We're a bit low on food."

"Oy c'n let 'ee yave sompthin'," replied the ancient, "for a conzideration." The old eyes gleamed greedily.

They explored both stories of the house. The rooms, one each as the old man had said, were minute but adequate. It would be an unaccustomed pleasure to sleep in a proper bed for once, the first time since Toymerle, and in quarters that were not open to the stars.

"My squire and I will stand sentry duty tonight," said Tallis to Foxy. "We'll do turn and turn about as before."

Dando cooked them a fish supper.

Tallis took first watch, sitting just within the front door, and then, having woken Dando who in fact had been only pretending to be asleep, went to his couch. Dando lit a candle and waited impatiently until he was sure that the other two men were comatose. To lock them into that state he performed the sleeping spell in each of their rooms. Then he went in to Ann and was surprised to find her sitting in a chair fully clothed, stuffing things into her back-pack.

"What are you doing Annie," he whispered.

She jumped guiltily and moved to conceal the carrier behind her body.

"Nothin'," she said.

"I've worked the magic," he told her. "Come on, let's go up the hill, these beds are too small for two."

She shook her head refusing to meet his eye.

"Don't you want to? At last we've got a chance to get away. I can't wait any longer. I'm going bonkers."

"No," said Ann, "no. Anyway you be on watch."

"What could possibly happen in the middle of a village? There's plenty of other people around and *they're* not keeping watch."

"No," said Ann again.

Dando, breathing hard through his nose, seemed about to speak, checked himself and then in a penetrating whisper protested, "All right then – it's because you don't love me any more, isn't it?"

Ann shook her head.

"You don't want me."

"O' course I do."

"No you don't."

"Yes I do."

"No you don't!" The words came out through gritted teeth and the agonised expression on his face made it look almost ugly. In response Ann finally got up and without further ado took him by the hand and led him out of the house. Ralph rose from where he was lying and followed them up the road before going off on his own affairs.

Once they got past the village and into the wood that lay above the houses they turned aside, and as soon as they were well within the trees Dando seized Ann and practically threw her onto the ground with himself on top of her.

"Be gentle! Be gentle!" she gasped, terrified that the baby would be harmed. "Go slowly my love."

She tried to push him away and Dando saw genuine fear in her eyes. This brought him to his senses; the last thing he wanted to do was to frighten or hurt her.

"Yes, yes – I'm sorry." By a supreme effort of will he reigned himself in. He concentrated his mind as Tom had taught him to do and forced his body to obey him. Then he began again, slowly, slowly, step by step, making each stage last as long as possible, letting her take the lead, sensitive to her needs. When finally the climax was reached and they both came at the same moment in perfect harmony it was the best it had ever been, better than all the other times put together. Dando lay panting, staring up at the stars between the contorted branches.

"That was great," he said, "we'll have to do it that way again soon – sooner than soon!"

Later, when she was snuggled against him in the crook of his arm, he asked, "So you really do love me Annie?"

"O' course, bonny lad."

"As much as I love you?"

"More."

He crowed triumphantly "I knew it!" and punched the air. She caught his hand and pulled his arm around her. Turning his head he buried his face in her hair whispering sweet nothings. In a little while he had fallen asleep.

There was a wizard, an itinerant necromancer, who had come out of the utmost west long ago. He advertised himself as Gubbo, the Great Gubbo, but that was not his real name. His feet had been on the road for so long that he had forgotten where he hailed from or what his mother had called him. When he was not putting on a show, he went by the name of Gammadion. From his earliest days he had clung to this life, having no faith that there could be any other beyond death, so that now he was ancient past telling and his heart had grown black and shrivelled with the years. Far to the north, secreted in a place known only to himself, lay a purloined talisman, the source of his longevity, hidden securely away, he hoped, from both gods and men. At first he had carried it with him on his endless journeyings, believing that if he held it long enough it would grant immortality, but after several years of close contact found he was unable, any longer, to bear its presence. He had concealed it and left it behind. Even now, though, it called to him and however far he wandered the connection was unbroken – it still ruled his existence.

He was no charlatan, for his powers were genuine, but he used them always to his own advantage, duping and cheating the gullible he met along the way, battening on the naïve and weak. For vast ages he had been in the lands north of the Middle Sea and had only recently returned to the southern continent of Terratenebra in answer to a call from the city state of Pickwah. According to the proclamation, broadcast by a wandering crier, the tender, which sought those skilled in magic, had something to do with the ambitions of the town's leader and the fear its citizens had of some man-eating trees. The offer had been so generous that he thought it might enable him to set himself up in wealth and luxury, something he had singularly failed to achieve throughout all his long centuries of roaming. He had landed at Tagnaroque, was making his way westward along the coast road and had almost reached Pickwah, when he awoke one morning with an idea revolving in his head – a simple sentence that kept returning. *The streets of the Delta City are paved with gold* were the words that would not leave him alone.

"Where's the delta city?" he asked the landlord of a tavern whose plague of mice he had promised to charm away, having been instrumental in directing the little creatures to the hostelry in the first place.

"You mean Drossi," said the man. "'Drosnia Poule 's what it says on the signs. Down by the Kymer River – way you've just come. 'Portant place – lots of famous people – some very well off."

So, the streets of the delta city were paved with gold – this required thought.

The next morning there was a different phrase gnawing away at him. *Fortune to be made in Drossi* was the gist of it. Could this be a prophecy and if so whence or from whom had it come? Wary and suspicious he mulled over the words for a day and a night until at first light a further message replaced it – *Look to the road between here and the Delta* was how it went. Three times in a row – maybe one of the Great Ones was taking an interest in him. Wherever it came from such a foretelling could not be ignored. Assuring the innkeeper that his infestation had been dealt with he packed up, collected his money, and followed the highway eastward towards the great metropolis. This place of resort was obviously where he stood the best chance of getting on in the world – he must have heard of it when he was in these parts back in the dim and distant past. And now the prospect of personal gain had lodged in his mind and was prompting him to take that road because, as he understood it, something awaited him on the way, something to his advantage...

In the early hours of the night a slim virtually-invisible vessel prowled the coast off the Middle Sea's southern shore looking for rich pickings. The Panther's sea-wolves, secure in their base's immunity from invasion were going on the offensive, intent on a lucrative raid soon after midnight. When they returned to the Dark Island as dawn broke it would be with riches and prisoners, one of whom would be sacrificed to the trees, and maybe there would be some juicy specimen of womanhood amongst them that they could pass around amongst themselves. The pirate captain had a good idea of his destination – a small town grown wealthy from trade - an exception in this region of impoverished settlements. But then... *Hard a-starboard!* The command was imperative and impossible to ignore although it had come out of the blue and reverberated solely within his own skull. "Hard a-starboard!" he echoed and his crew obediently swung the ship round and headed in towards land where a straggle of houses climbed a wooded combe.

"All right boys," he shouted, "we're going to strip them to the bone. These dirty fish-mongers'll curse the day they were born. We'll root out their trove – they'll be only too glad to tell us where it's hidden. Get the torches ready!"

Yes, that was it, he must have heard something about this particular place from one of his previous captives. He must have been told that it was not just a collection of poor hutments, that the inhabitants had something of value, some heirloom, stashed away. Otherwise why should he have felt the need, the irresistible need, to alter course and attack somewhere so insignificant...?

Ann sat up and looked down on Dando. She would probably never see him again in this world if her plan of escape was successful, so it behoved her to fix this last image of him in her memory as he lay fast asleep, defenceless, child-like, without guile. It was time to leave. She would go up to the main highway and turn either left or right. Then she would take the first side turning along the road and lie low so that when the others came looking for her as they inevitably would they would pass by and she would remain undiscovered. After an interval, when she was completely confident that the coast was clear, she would set out again, but for what destination she had no idea. All her thoughts were of *coming from*, she had not began to consider the reverse direction of *going to*.

She took out her scissors and cut off a lock of her hair. This she plaited and wound in and out between Dando's fingers. Because, beside the track just before they entered the wood, she had seen an unseasonal clump of forget-me-nots flowering, she went and picked one of these and placed it in his other hand. Once this was accomplished she realised she had nothing of his. She snipped one of his curls and dropped it into her cleavage. In taking herself out of his life she realised she was going to stab him to the heart, but hearts have a way of recuperating from such wounds and he would recover, in time he would recover, and then he would be free to fulfil his destiny, whatever that might be, far from her fateful presence. She bent and touched his face with her lips, planting butterfly kisses on his mouth, his nose, his cheeks, his eyelids. She half hoped that he would wake, thus preventing her from departing so that they might have one more night together, instead he slept on but smiled in his sleep.

Going down the hill she wondered why she did not weep. In fact she felt completely numb; her sorrow too deep for tears. She entered the cottage and peered in at Tallis and Foxy. Both men were unconscious, under the influence of the enchantment that Dando had woven. Well, she no longer had the power to break the spell – the baby had seen to that - they would have to wait for the boy's return. By the light of the candle she held she examined Foxy. Whereas Dando in sleep had looked younger than his actual age Foxy appeared much older: writ large on his face could be read the whole history of Nablan suffering. She would be missed by her long-time protector and he would spare no effort in trying to track her down; it was imperative that she be well away before he woke. She went to her room, gathered her things together and then searched for Ralph, wanting to say goodbye to at least one of their number, but the faithful hound was nowhere to be seen. Climbing the hill once more she passed within feet of the spot where Dando lay sleeping but continued on until she reached the mouth of the combe. She stopped and looked back one last time. She had finally done it - she had broken away and perhaps *all would be well, all manner of thing would be well.* In reality, did she but know it, it was far too late to mend matters. As she quitted the top end of the valley a predatory ship with a black-cat flag at the cross-trees came nosing into the harbour at the bottom. At the same time an old, old man with a timeless, almost fossilised, face was following the coastal highway, drawing closer minute by minute.

"Tu-whit-tu-whoo, tu-whit-tu-whoo."

Owls again. Ann's blood ran cold; she turned quickly and hastened up the road. Surely this was just two local birds singing a love duet. Nevertheless in her ears the cry had a mocking, taunting quality. She made the sign that the country people use to ward off evil before hurrying away.

Dando woke once it was light to find himself alone. For a few moments he was completely adrift. Where was Ann? Why had she not roused him? Had last night's events been just a dream? Then he discovered the strand of hair between his fingers and the flower whose name he did not know. She had left him a message but he was unable to read it. Perhaps she had gone back to the house, but why without him? He should have woken Tallis hours ago; the knight would want to know the reason he had not kept to their arrangement. He tried to think of a good excuse for his dereliction. Something was bothering him, something that had dragged him from sleep in the first place. There was an acrid, dangerous smell on the wind that rang all kinds of warning bells in his head. With a growing sense of unease he scrambled to his feet, hastily knotting the plait of fair hair around his neck, and hurried to the edge of the wood. There he was met by a sight that was to haunt him for the rest of his days. Great billowing clouds of smoke were ballooning up towards him from the comb and within the cloud he could make out a sullen angry glare. This was no dream as the childhood nightmare that had once held him in thrall had been, this was real and worse than he could have possibly imagined. From what he was able to see through the enveloping smother, flames were shooting high into the air above the house tops and, below him, the whole village was ablaze!------------

An odd unnatural crop -
Nourished by blood.
Who will bring in the harvest?

Chapter thirteen

Dando rushed down the road towards the houses but was driven back by smoke born on a wind blowing from the sea. Sobbing with frustration he circled round trying to penetrate the smouldering streets from which issued a breath straight from hell. In the end, slipping and sliding, he climbed the almost vertical side of the valley to get past the flames and then descended again to arrive at the other end of town by the waterfront. It was all too obvious that the conflagration had not been started by some accidental house fire, it was far too general: the settlement had been put to the torch and now the perpetrators were already well away with whatever miserable booty they had managed to loot from this impoverished place. Dando dropped his jacket, pullover and pack onto the beach outside the harbour wall and plunged into the sea. Emerging he stripped off his wet shirt and holding it over his nose and mouth ran up the main street. What possessed every fibre of his being was the thought that he had left Tallis and Foxy spellbound, helpless to defend themselves. And again, where was Ann? The possibilities were too terrible to contemplate. Nausea gripped him but there was no time to stop and be sick.

Although the heat was tremendous, hardly to be born, he managed to make it as far as the cottage in which they had been spending the night. There he stopped appalled. The roof had fallen in, also the upper story. He stared through the gaping hole that had once been a window at the glowing, crackling, snapping interior. Collapsed beams, burnt and sooty, were propped at odd angles inside and there were less identifiable charred shapes with rims of fire which might be bedsteads or other pieces of furniture. He was scarcely able to admit to himself that what he was looking for was some remnant of a human body. He had only been there a few minutes before his damp hair began to smoke and his bare torso to scorch – he had to retreat. Running back down the street he caught a glimpse of something up a side alley and turned towards it. There was a prone figure lying between the houses still moving feebly. Coming closer he saw that it was a man whose clothes had been completely burnt away while his skin was blackened and split, the raw red flesh showing through. Blood bubbled from his lips as he spoke.

"Why us?" he moaned, "why us? We have nothing... less than nothing..."

"Where did they come from?" asked Dando urgently.

"The Dark Island... the Island..."

"Did they take any prisoners – anyone alive?" But the man had ceased to breath.

Back at the quayside he saw that the fishing boats in the harbour were half submerged, they had obviously been scuttled. The sailing dingies on the stony beach beyond the wall were still intact however. Retrieving his things he made his choice: a boat just a little bigger than the one he had sailed on the Wendover in another more fortunate existence. He dragged it down to the water's edge, launched it, threw his pack and clothes aboard and then climbed in himself. He had no trouble hoisting the sail but great difficulty in getting away from the shore as the wind was blowing dead on land. In the end he had to row several hundred yards out to sea before setting a course which took him roughly nor-nor-west. Dando had absolutely no experience of sailing on the open ocean and initially he faced enormous problems in steering the little craft as it was tossed around among white-crested waves that broke over the bow in fountains of spray. Afraid at first of capsizing he gradually got the hang of what was required and began to make slow but steady progress towards his goal - the long baleful-looking island that yesterday he had seen rearing up against the sky. The distance was more than three miles and as he tacked into the wind he had plenty of time to contemplate his guilt and follow a tormented and desolate line of reasoning.

He realised now that he was in the grip of some kind of hex - there must have been a bad fairy at his birth - and he seemed to have a talent for passing on to others the ill-luck which had been gifted to him; so many had been infected, contaminated, by his mere proximity. In fact nearly everyone he cared for, nearly everyone he had ever loved, had met with some kind of misfortune or adverse destiny. His animals, Puss, Asbo and Chocky, had all died before their time and Attack, the magnificent black stallion, had been maimed as a result of his negligence. Of his servants, Doll had been severely punished and Potto dismissed. His father had actually been killed while in the act of pursuing his errant son. He could hardly bear to think of Tom, dear Tom, the finest and wisest man he had ever known, who had suffered a terrible fate because he had defied the goddess on this miserable sinner's behalf. And now there were his three companions who might, or might not, be still alive but whose ill luck could be laid without question at his door. Whatever had happened to them was his fault entirely, because as a result of his revolting lust he had deserted his post and betrayed those who were depending on him. If the boat sank beneath him it would be a fitting reckoning and would remove a blight from the earth, not before time; it would be doing the world a favour.

The boat did not sink however and eventually the island metamorphosed from a vague outline into a place of rocks, breakers, hillsides, woods and the cries of a great host of birds. Somewhere there was probably a landing stage where larger vessels could tie up but Dando's little craft was small enough to sneak into a minor creek where he lay for a while before disembarking, waiting to see if his arrival had been noted. Nothing transpired - the corsairs obviously felt secure enough on their tree-protected isle to consider lookouts unnecessary. But where were these carnivorous trees? All the vegetation within sight looked perfectly normal and unthreatening. After a while he went ashore, beached the boat on a convenient pebbly bank and made his way inland. He walked up through woodland until he came out onto a bare hillside and could get a view along the coast. A bit further east a small promontory stuck out into the sea and beside it a fair-sized ship was moored. More cautiously now he worked his way along until, level with this feature, he found himself looking down into a hollow where there were huts, people moving about and smoke rising. He had found the pirates' lair! Inching closer he sat down to watch what was happening below.

There were some slatternly-looking women preparing food in the open air and a queue of men with plates in their hands waiting to get their share. Most retreated into the huts with the meal they were given or joined a group gathered round an open fire, but two dishes were carried to the top of a ramp which disappeared into the bowels of the earth. Here the plates were handed over to a man who seemed to be on guard duty and this individual took one down the slope, vanishing for some time. Dando's heart leapt and part of the great weight bearing down on his soul lifted slightly. Prisoners! There were prisoners there below ground! Perhaps it was his comrades! He set himself to wait for nightfall – for long after nightfall until the hour when the bandits had stopped drinking, singing and occasionally bursting into roars of laughter and had finally retired to their beds. Then he crept down to the huts. Slipping from one shack to another he got as close as he dared to the underground prison. The guard, although not the same man as earlier, was still sitting on what looked like a packing case smoking a cigar. Dando blanked his thoughts and, as he had been taught, brought his concentrated mind to bear. He stretched out his hand and, moving his lips, sang soundlessly in his head -

Everybody, have you heard,
She's gonna buy me a mocking bird...

For a moment his sight failed. When his vision cleared he immediately became aware that the man on watch had dropped his cigar and had rolled off the packing case onto the ground. He realised he had cracked it! - he could work the sleeping spell on someone even when they were still awake as Ann had once explained was possible. In his moment of triumph his first impulse was to share his success with his lover and it took him several seconds to remember that she and her fellow travellers might well be dead for all he knew. His heart turned to ice within him and then seemed to fracture into a million pieces. With swimming head he tried to recall what he had been intending to do - oh yes, the underground prison, it was just possible they might be there. He looked carefully round to make sure nobody else was about before venturing out into the open and over to the ramp. He picked up the guard's lantern and walked down the slope. At the bottom he came upon a door that was solid oak apart from a grill at eye height through which he could see nothing. "It's me – it's me, Dando," he whispered and waited for a reply but was met by complete silence. Back at the top of the ramp he searched the guard and eventually ran to earth some keys. Descending once more he experimented and eventually found the right device and so let himself in through the barrier leaving the keys in the door before holding up the light. In the dimness he saw a low-ceilinged largish space with earthen walls and floor that at first appeared unoccupied. It was not until he walked forward a few paces that the lantern picked out a pile of straw in one corner and on it a small inert figure. The sleeper was young, a child no more, and completely unknown to him. There was no-one else about. Dando bent down and pulled the boy up into a sitting position. By his clothing he was probably some poor fisher lad.

"Wake up," he commanded, shaking him. "Come on, wake up!"

The boy's eyes opened slightly and then widened in alarm. He stared fearfully at this stranger who had apparently materialised out of nowhere.

"Where are the other prisoners?" demanded Dando intensely, "The ones you came back with last night. For heaven's sake don't go to sleep again."

"Wha' other prisoners?" slurred the boy.

"The ones you came back with."

"Oy din come las' night – Oy bin yere a long time..."

"Well – when the robbers came back last night did you see what happened? – did they bring prisoners with them? – a woman...?"

"No – no."

"How do you know?"

"Oy heard one o' t' men say t'were a lean time for t' 'ostage business."

"So there aren't any other prisoners?"

"If there were they'd be yere."

"Are you sure?"

"Yes – yes. Let me be," pushing Dando away. "'Oo be 'ee anyway?"

Dando stood up and drew back, very pale. He felt as if he was going to faint and put his hand against the rough wall to prevent himself from falling. At that moment the final flicker of hope that, since the fire, he had nurtured within his breast guttered and went out and he was left in stygian darkness, the dark night of the soul.

"'Oo be 'ee?" asked the boy again of his white-faced visitant. "Why did 'ee come in yere? Be thee a ghost... or an angel?" All of a sudden he was greatly animated. "I've bin prayin' real yard. Hev 'ee come in answer to my prayers?"

"No – I'm no angel," said Dando, "but I can help you escape. The door's open and the guard's asleep. There's a boat along the coast, that way," pointing west, "in an inlet. You can sail a boat, can't you?"

"The boss come to see if I were zuitable, zee" said the boy as if needing to get something off his chest and for the moment ignoring Dando's offer. "If I weren't right they would hev done me in there an' then."

"Suitable for what?"

"You know - the trees." The child shuddered. "My da tol' me not to fish near the Island."

"Come on," said Dando, "get going. The boat's not far away. They won't know you've gone till first light. By that time you can be out at sea."

"But what about 'ee – don' 'ee be a-comin'?"

Dando shook his head. The boy rose and with an expression of incredulity stared up the ramp at the comatose guard. Hurriedly he donned a shabby denim jacket and boots with holes in the soles, seeming now in a lather to be gone before he awoke and found it all a dream. Dando walked with him to the top of the slope where the guard lay curled on the ground.

"Go on," he said, "you're free."

"Don' 'ee be a-comin'?" asked the boy again. Again Dando shook his head.

"Remember me," he said with a note of yearning in his voice. "Tell your father about me. I don't deserve his thanks but if he'll just spare me a thought now and then..."

When the lad had shown him a clean pair of heels he replaced the lantern, then went back to the cell. He pulled the door shut behind him, sat himself down on a box in the centre of the room, the only piece of furniture apart from a bucket, and prepared for a long wait.

About a year earlier the town of Pickwah, a member of the league of city states known as the Seven Sisters, had experienced a change of regime. The Old Prince had died and there had been no-one to succeed him but a weak-minded nephew. It was not long before the reins of power were in the hands of a self-serving military man and the Young Prince, so recently installed, ceased to be seen around the citadel. It was announced to the general populace that their head-of-state had a degenerative mental condition and was no longer fit to govern. In his place his loyal subject had been self-sacrificing enough to take over responsibility for the running of the city; for convenience sake he would henceforth be know as the Great Leader. The citizens were treated to many incendiary speeches urging them to put their shoulders to the wheel and support the Supremo in his bid to establish a unified rule and strong governance in the country round. A few months later most people had conveniently forgotten that up until fairly recently their overlord had been nothing more than a lowly lieutenant in the Old Prince's bodyguard; he had even had a name – Jory Trewithik.

Squatting with elbows on knees and head in hands Dando must have dozed off because, as he became conscious of his surroundings once more, the faint dawn light filtering through the grill seemed to have crept up on him unawares. He rose, walked to the door and was just about to go and break the sleeping spell when he saw movement. A dark shape dressed in loose robes and holding a staff with a light at one end was bending over the comatose watchman. This person touched the guard's face, apparently pulling back an eyelid, after which he began to make a thorough examination of the body. Then he shuffled down the ramp, pushing open the unlocked door, before discovering, with surprise, the cell's new occupant.

"Who are you?" he said, "where's the other boy?"

"I let him go," said Dando.

"But it's time," replied the elderly man (he seemed to be some sort of priest), "It's time for the purification."

"I'm here," said Dando, "won't I do?"

The cleric stared at him in concern. "Where have you come from?" he asked. "Was it you who cast the spell and unlocked the door?" He looked back fearfully over his shoulder "You're in danger, you know. The camp will wake soon - the Panther's men are totally ruthless and if they find you've used sorcery to release their prisoner they're quite capable of killing you – you could die."

"I know," said Dando sombrely.

"Who are you?" asked the priest again.

"One who deserves to die."

"That's foolishness – not even the lowest of the low deserves to die." He paused as if assessing the situation. "You know what they were keeping him for?"

"Yes," said Dando.

"He was to be the messenger – the next sacrifice – you realise that?"

"I do."

"But you can't understand - you surely don't mean you'd take his place - you'd go willingly to the trees?"

"Yes I would," said Dando his features stiffening and his eyes swivelling sideways as if, despite giving an affirmative, he almost wanted to deny what he was saying.

The man's face took on a strange look of reluctant eagerness mixed with incredulity.

"In the old days they always did – they always went willingly."

"I must go and lift the charm," said Dando and, ascending the slope, cancelled the enchantment, although the guard slept on. When he returned he found that the other was busy preparing for his rite.

"It's performed every morning over the messenger until the day of the offering. You appear to have cast a spell, does that mean you're a priest?"

"Sort of..."

"Well then, you should be able to understand."

The man went through a simple ceremony of prayers and chants ending with a blessing while Dando stood silently before him. When he finished he looked up at the boy with concern.

"You're too young for this," he said. "There's still time for you to change your mind. If you go now you might just get away. This is your last chance unless you know a bewitchment for unlocking..."

Dando shook his head. "I'm older than the other one," he said.

As no-one else had yet put in an appearance, the cleric, seemingly reluctant to leave, sat down heavily on the box in the middle of the room and they conversed. Dando learnt that his visitor had been living on the island since before the pirates' arrival. There had been an unbroken succession of celebrants there, he was told, virtually from the beginning of time. In the great days when the trees covered all the country round the victims had always gone voluntarily. Because of that the people lived in harmony with the trees and the trees protected them. The relationship had begun between the time of the first turning and the female immortal's discovery of the Treasure.

"Within recent memory sacrifices have continued to be made but it's usually been just a cony or two or a wild cat that was caught in a trap. Now the bad men have gone back to the old ways but it's not the same – the miserable scapegoats they select are given no choice."

"When will it be?" asked Dando, his gut suddenly churning.

"Always at the dark of the moon. That's about two weeks away. They picked up the boy just after the last time."

So, thought Dando, he had jumped off the top of the mountain but it was going to be an age before he hit the ground. This was a blow – he did not know if he had the courage to hold out for so long.

"Where are the trees?" he asked.

"There aren't that many now; the grove's up on the flat area in front of the sgurr."

"And do they really walk and eat people?"

"When they're hungry."

The priest had gone, locking the door and replacing the keys with the sleeping guard leaving Dando on his own. The boy had disarmed, had laid his sword, dagger and bow on the ground beside the entrance and was now sitting once more on the box. The light strengthened and pretty soon he heard an exchange at the top of the ramp. The guard came in bearing food, muttering about the god-botherer not having turned up that morning. He walked right past the weapons, laid the plate and mug down and retreated. It was only when he was at the door that he paused, looked back and did a double take. Then he came forward and squinted closely at Dando.

"'Oo are you?" he said.

Dando did not reply. For a long minute the man stared at him and then backed away in superstitious awe. He went and put his head out into the light.

"'Ere Fred, come an' take a butchers at this!"

A second man appeared and they consulted together

"I woz on watch all night, 'ow can this 'ave 'appened?"

"Wot are you worried about? - your prisoner's still 'ere."

"But 'e's different. This isn't the kid 'oo woz 'ere las' night. It's unnatural I tells you. Wot's 'appened to the other one?"

"Ask 'im."

The guard looked warily at Dando. "Where's the other fella?" he demanded with sudden ferocity.

"I let him go," replied Dando calmly.

You let 'im go!" The man stood stock still as if outrage had temporarily deprived him of movement and then, galvanised, raised his fist causing the boy to duck away. "Go an' get Bill," he muttered. A third man joined the other two and, on entering, noticed the discarded weapons and retrieved them. All three bent over Dando.

"What will 'is nibs say?" asked the guard.

"Don't tell 'im. 'Ee won't know no different. This one's as good or better."

"But it's unnatural I tells you. 'Ow could it 'ave 'appened? An' me on guard all through the night. 'Ow could 'e 'ave got pas' me unless I woz in some sort of trance? This one's a slippery customer – 'oo's to say 'e won' jus' vanish again the way 'e come?"

"Well we c'n make sure 'e don't. We c'n use a bit of belt an' braces like. Go an' get the stone."

While one man remained on guard the other two went out and pretty soon Dando heard a trundling and rumbling noise coming down the slope. With some difficulty a large torus-shaped rock was rolled through the doorway and moved into position near the pile of straw. It took both men to manhandle it. Dando realised he was looking at a grindstone, probably ballast from some ship that had come to grief on the Island. Fred also had a length of rather rusty chain over his shoulder that had a cuff at either end.

"Stan' up," he said to Dando. "Come over 'ere. Now just 'eave that up a little." The boy stooped and took hold of the stone. It was all he could do to raise one side a few inches as the man threaded the chain through the hole in the middle and locked the cuffs onto Dando's ankles.

"There you are Bob," he said to the guard, "'Ee won't get far draggin' that aroun'. Let's see 'im magic himself out of that one!"

The men quitted the cell carrying Dando's rucksack (he never saw it again) and he was left alone to eat the meagre breakfast he had been given and think thoughts that were comfortless to say the least.

The citizens of Pickwah soon felt the effects of the new dispensation. Heavy taxes were imposed and those who refused to pay were summarily dealt with. The tourist business came to an abrupt halt as the state's borders were closed except to locals and millitary personnel while the marine hot springs were handed over to the army for their exclusive use. This meant hardship. Since the fishing industry's collapse – the large shoals had completely deserted the south side of the Middle Sea – many people, from shop keepers to hoteliers to cottagers with just a spare bed or two, had come to rely on visitors from the wealthier cities as their sole source of income. But now a new way of making a living presented itself. The army was growing: after a recruitment drive in the country roundabout; young men from distant provinces were arriving in the city, some appearing extremely outlandish to the indigenous inhabitants. These trainees had to be housed, fed, clothed and armed. Crews were needed for the new ships that were being built and fitters were required to prepare them for sailing. The coffers in the treasury began to run dry. *More money* came the cry and the Great Leader promised that soon untold riches would be heading in their direction. His aim was to do away with what he described as the anarchy that existed along the coast to the east. The Seven Sisters League was weak, corrupt, he said, it had had its day. He intended to institute a new order under his benevolent dictatorship. But first there was a minor irritant to be dealt with, a nest of vipers, a gang of pirates who were preying on communities and legitimate shipping along the nearby seaboard. The outlaws thought they were safe in their island lair where flesh-eating trees protected them, but if those loyal to the town could summon up the resolution to attack this place of ill-repute with the aid of a cohort of magic-workers that were being assembled from far and wide they would be rewarded beyond their wildest dreams. Such a crusade would be a fine exercise for the novice forces to cut their teeth on and when they laid hands on the ruffians' ill-gotten gains they would acquire the wherewithal to finance future campaigns which in their turn would enrich everyone involved. In such manner the most westerly city in a confederacy of seven, an ally so the others thought, put itself on a war footing and prepared for action.

Now Dando's life had become all about waiting, waiting in the corner of the underground prison where he was pinned to the earth by the stone, unable even to cross the room. The minutes and hours dragged like the chain dragged at his ankles, but the days went fleeting by. The guard seemed to delight each morning in telling him, "fourteen days to go," "thirteen days to go." Mostly he could bear this with equanimity, impervious to the man's cruelty, but it was in the bleak reaches of the night that he sometimes woke in a sweat of terror, gasping fearfully, his poor confused flesh stiffening into a state of tumescence. This was the worst time, when he lay shivering, unable to think coherently and wishing desperately that it could all be over. Since his incarceration a veil had descended between himself and the everyday world; he was no longer a member of the general run of humanity who, although they were going to die, had no idea of the time or place of their demise and could therefore live their lives as carelessly as the immortals. Now he was one with the condemned and knew the measure of his days. Sometimes, even during daylight hours, he found it hard not to dwell on what was to come and it was then that, in order to confront the fear head-on, he asked the priest for more information concerning the history of the trees. He was told stories of wandering groves, men enmeshed and swallowed whole, dells of unseen evil, spirits who went hunting when night came. The forest, harbouring malice, had to be placated and so in times past folk of both sexes had been strung up, volunteers offered as an oblation; they called it *feeding-the-trees.*

"Those that the trees accepted died almost at once," the cleric informed him.

"And those that they rejected, were they taken down again?"

"Take back a gift once offered? – that would be utter folly."

"Did any of the victims escape?"

"No, why should they? They had given themselves to the Old Ones. It conferred merit on those left behind."

The tales came out of the distant past, pre-second-age. For Dando, sensing their antiquity, they seemed to echo a primitive terror of the wild-wood and all that it stood for.

He gained solace from the visits of the priest. After the man had performed the ritual of purification he took time to sit and talk, treating the boy with kindness and respect and not a little awe. There was also a young woman who sometimes brought him his meals. She rarely opened her mouth to say anything but gazed shyly at him with eyes full of pity. He always thanked her for the miserable fare she was forced to provide. One night she spoke at length for the first time.

"His brother has sent him a letter," she murmured in a cultured voice referring to the Cheetah. "The go-between's boat is down by the jetty. There's nobody watching."

To his amazement she produced a key and bent to remove the gyves around his ankles.

"The guard's gone to the latrine," she whispered.

Dando gripped her hand preventing her from releasing him. He shook his head.

"No, no," he whispered back, "the outlaws might do something terrible to you."

"I'll lock the cuffs up after you've left," she replied. "They don't know I've got this (holding up the key), they'll think it's been done by magic."

"No," he said again, "I can't go, although you're very good."

"What about your friends – what about those who care for you?"

"It's because of what I did to them that I'm here."

"But your girl friend – you've got one I'm sure."

"She's gone – gone before me - we didn't even get to say goodbye. All I can do is follow her into the dark."

On one particular day as Dando lay on the straw staring towards the light a small grey and white cat, on the prowl for food, materialised between the bars of the grill in the door. He remained perfectly still and the little animal who, by its thinness and the engorged state of the glands on the underside of its body, appeared to be nursing young, jumped down and sneaked a few minute scraps from his virtually empty plate. The next day he left at least half of the revolting mixture of gristle and bone he was being offered in the hope that it would return. The cat became a regular visitor and by the fourth day it had allowed him to touch it. Shortly after that when it had eaten and as he lay supine, it climbed onto his chest and settled itself beneath his chin. He stroked it absently and the scrawny little thing burst into a rhythmical purring before stretching out its neck to lick his face in a motherly kind of way. The warm, moist, rough little tongue gave him the feeling that he still had some connection to an indifferent planet.

In Pickwah Town the word had come down from the citadel that the time for the fleet to sail was almost at hand. The date for the invasion of Hungry Island had been set for the night before that of the new moon which the troops had been told was the most propitious time and was also thought to be when they could achieve maximum surprise. Pickwah's force would put to sea early in the day so that by the time they were approaching the island it would be dusk and hopefully the alarm would not have been raised. A small fishing smack had already spied out the land. About a week before the planned invasion the Leader's recently appointed seer sought an audience with his overlord in his private apartments.

"I must warn you my master that the squadron will be in grave danger if you sail when you intend. According to my new observations a great tempest is due to arise sometime during the hours of darkness on that date. I foresee shipwreck and drownings, the ruin of all your plans."

The Great Leader looked at him incredulously. Outside the window the view from high in the keep where they stood was of a completely tranquil scene, the blue sea reflecting the blue sky and the early spring sunshine lighting up distant vessels as they lay practically becalmed on their way to the great ports further east.

"Do 'ee be zerious?" he said. "'Ow come 'ee be so sure?"

"My conclusions were initially speculative," replied the soothsayer, "but the signs all point to what I've just told you - there's little doubt. I would advise that the invasion be delayed until the following day. By that time everything will have changed – changed to your advantage."

The presumptive despot was a superstitious man and the seer's predictions had been bang on the nail on previous occasions.

"Oy'll conzider it," he said.

Almost before he was aware, the day that had seemed so far off arrived. Now that the hour was upon him Dando felt completely calm and in control; he was just grateful that soon he would be able to write finis to his existence and lay down his burden of guilt. Before it got light the priest brought him a bowl to wash in and a comb, things he had been in dire need of. He made himself as presentable as possible but could do nothing about his filthy clothes.

"I'm afraid you're not allowed to eat anything."

"I don't feel like eating."

"The sacrifice is made as the sun rises, but you must give the signal if you are to go of your own free will. It's done from the edge of the sgurr. As I said, that's where the trees are situated – in front of the cliff. It takes a while to get there from here."

The purification ceremony having been performed, three men came into the room, one of them with a handcart. They freed Dando from the grindstone but then loaded it into the barrow. It looked as if he had not yet said goodbye to his granite gaoler, an unwelcome companion in his solitude during the last two weeks. As he left the prison he was surprised to see that, despite the early hour, the whole camp was already up and doing. Setting out, the men with the cart led the way, then came the priest who preceded Dando and two of his keepers, while the rest of the outlaws, both men and women, fell in at the rear. They climbed up the steep hillside until they attained the long bare shoulder from which both north and south coasts of the island could be viewed. Then they turned westward, eventually reaching a large rocky crag – the sgurr as it was known - that stood proud of the main ridge and provided the highpoint of this small island. Their approach took them up a steady ascent to a flat summit which soon ended abruptly as the land plunged about a hundred feet towards a small plateau. It was on this level area, in front of the drop, that the notorious trees grew, some of them tall enough to o'er-top the cliff.

Dando walked forward and stared down in the dim pre-dawn light. Nobody tried to stop him; it seemed he was to be given space to examine the stage on which his last hours would be spent. And there they stood – the trees. He realised immediately why they were thought to walk. They had not yet come into leaf so their basic anatomy was clearly visible. The pearly-grey surface of the great muscular branches was as smooth as silk – as smooth as a baby's bottom. The trunks, also flesh like, rose from bases that seemed to be composed of several columns only lightly fused together and looked as if they could have moved independently like the legs of an animal. The upper limbs ended in a fuzz of thorny twigs designed to enmesh passing wildlife and, even in the totally calm conditions prevailing that morning, they were in continual slight motion. Dando gazed for some time as if sizing up an adversary before retreating.

Turning back towards the spectators he saw that the bandits had spread themselves out over the summit of the hill and were settling down to a pleasant outdoor repast. Walking up through their ranks came a latecomer to the revels, a figure who was instantly recognisable to Dando although they had never met. This must be none other than the pirate captain, the brother outlaw of the one who ruled Rostan's shrine. As was fitting, taking into account his soubriquet, the bandit was wearing a black panther skin over his head and shoulders, his thin eremitic visage looking out from beneath the creature's upper jaw. The animal had presumably been caught somewhere beyond the sea - the species was not indigenous to the southern continent - and therefore its pelt would be virtually priceless in Terratenebra. Approaching Dando - he overtopped him by more than three inches – the man gazed inquisitively into his prisoner's face.

"What are you doing here? You're not the one I saw before. In what godforsaken hole did they dig you up?"

Anger leapt within Dando's breast and his hands flew to his empty sword belt. One of the outlaws, thinking his master was about to be attacked, grabbed the boy from behind and pinioned his arms.

"You k-killed my friends!" panted Dando, struggling to free himself.

"Did I?" The man shrugged. "I've killed so many people. It doesn't seem to matter any more. Sooner – later – what difference does it make when they die? But I won't kill you – the trees will do that for me."

"W-why did you attack the village?" cried Dando passionately. "They were poor folk – they had n-nothing worth stealing as far as you were concerned!"

"I suppose you mean that wretched rookery down by Trincomalee – that's over two weeks ago now. To tell the truth I have no idea," he smiled thinly, "it was a whim – a mere caprice."

"You kill people – you burn people – on a whim?!"

"Have you got a better reason?"

Dando stared at the other, his eyes misted with fury. The Panther turned away and with an weary gesture towards the priest indicated that things should proceed. A diminutive man puffed up carrying a small chest which when opened displayed a glistening, glinting treasure-trove of jewellery within. The priest pulled Dando aside and spoke to him under his breath. "Here are the gifts."

The boy blinked at him uncomprehendingly, still outraged by what he had heard.

"You are the messenger," the priest explained. "You must carry the community's offerings to the Old Ones. These are the people's tributes – costume stuff for the most part - I'll help you put them on."

The coffer appeared to contain a fortune in precious stones in all sorts of settings: bangles, pendants, anklets, necklaces, headbands; the piracy business obviously paid well. Dando looked at them horrified. This was something he had not bargained for. On the solemn occasion of his self-sacrifice he was going to go to his death decked out like the Queen-of-the-May. He could have shed tears at the prospect of being made to look so ridiculous. But then perhaps that was what he deserved; perhaps just dying was not considered sufficient punishment by whosoever administered justice. He bowed his head and meekly allowed the priest to deck him in the finery.

A rope was already stretched from the cliff edge to a branch of one of the trees and then back again, the two ends temporarily anchored to a stake driven into the thin soil. Dando was made to sit on the ground and then his wrists were tied together with one end of the rope. His old enemy the grindstone was rolled forward and another stout rope was threaded through the hole and bound round his ankles. Joined once more to the rock all his fears came flooding back and his blood ran cold. He remembered Rhys' words – *He ties weights to the poor wretches he sacrifices to make it impossible for them to escape.* This was going to be no picnic he realised grimly, hoping against hope that he would be one of the victims accepted by the trees and so would die quickly without fuss. He looked towards the priest for guidance.

"Now we wait," said his counsellor, "we wait for sunrise. When a beam strikes that islet," pointing to a skerry out to sea, "it will be time. After that, if you are to offer yourself willingly you must give the signal."

More delay. Dando gazed at the wrinkled blue-grey sea crawling below, at the happy birds winging overhead towards their daytime feeding grounds, at the sky dotted with tiny pink fleecy clouds and at the green island all around, its grasses and early spring flowers stirred into motion by a clean cold wind that had suddenly arisen. *How beautiful the earth is*, he thought. He turned his head and inspected the onlookers behind him, staring greedily into the faces of his fellow men. Rogues and villains they might be, but they were the last of his kind he would set eyes on in this life. With a silent farewell he faced forward again and looked towards the horizon. For a while he was lost to himself, his mind floating in an ocean of non-being, at one with the sea and the sky, until, brought back to this world by feeling the priest's hand on his arm, he saw that the water-girt rock which had been pointed out earlier was already illuminated. The two guards pulled him to his feet and, because he could not walk with the rope hobbling his legs, dragged him forward by main force and then held him upright so that he stood on the very brink of the cliff. For a moment or two his breath was taken away and he did not think he would be able to do what was required, but then, turning to look full into the priest's face, he found his courage. "Remember me," he said and gave the briefest of nods. The priest raised his hand and brought it sweeping down; the men holding Dando let go and stepped back. He fell forward into space as the grindstone was pushed over the edge and a roar came from the throats of the spectators. A row of pirates, a tug-of-war team, simultaneously hauled on the other end of the rope to ensure he would not hit the ground but would hang suspended in mid air in the midst of the trees.

As he fell Dando gave voice involuntarily, but the cry was abruptly cut off as the rope became taught and the weight of the stone yanked his body downwards with a power strong enough to dislocate limbs. He was swung in a long arc, the branch above creaking in protest, towards the massive trunk of the selected tree. The grindstone hit and bounced away, following which Dando met the tree head on. The rope tightened once more, the branch dipped and he swung back, penduluming to and fro, until equilibrium was established. But of this he had no knowledge. Mercifully, in cannoning into the tree, he had been knocked out. The outlaws lining the cliff waited for who-knows-what, but if they had been expecting yells and groans they were disappointed; everything remained quiet; it looked as if the spectacle was going to be far less entertaining than they had hoped. Eventually, becoming bored of waiting, they picked up their things and melted away one by one leaving the sgurr deserted. Very soon a few bold gulls put in an appearance and began searching for scraps left over from the pirates' breakfast.

Sometime later Dando drifted back into consciousness, back into a nightmare world where his limbs no longer belonged to him but were being ripped apart by opposing forces. Hung up like game in a butcher's window the ropes around his wrists and ankles bit into his flesh while between the two extremes, the UP and the DOWN, he was stretched like a prisoner on a rack. He became aware that he was still able to think and more to the point feel. Why was he alive? He had intended to cash in his chips as quickly as possible and get the horrible business over with, but his body was insisting on continuing the fight for survival, apparently prepared to sustain a battle for life over many hours despite his heartfelt wish to die. It persisted in its struggle to exist, to carry on breathing. Up there in the cool shadowy spaces beneath the resin-scented canopy he became a pupil in a new and bitter school, the first lesson of which was that pain is not constant but comes in waves: ride the crests, survive the crisis points and the rest can be born. Meanwhile the bright day hummed on its way, the hum provided by insects, attracted to the tree's rising sap. The branch from which he was suspended complained in a gradually strengthening breeze and he was turned gently round as if to admire the view from his exalted station. *I won't kill you, the trees will do that for me,* the Panther had said, but it was not the trees, it was the earth, the great round world he had been snatched from, which, in trying to reclaim him, was going to take his life. Surely the Mother must hate the living creatures that spring from her chosen element since she is never able to rest until they are dragged back down and ground to dust. But for the time being Dando was one with the unburied dead whose grave is the air.

As if to remind him of this fact he had a companion in his vigil. There were others further off, black shapeless bundles, previous sacrifices, but this one was quite close and still recognisably a man despite bones bursting through pathetic rags of flesh and the ravages of carrion eaters. The wind blew past the place where the dead thing hung, making it stir and turn one way or the other, before, picking up a whiff of corruption, it moved on to Dando, revolving him likewise, swinging him round to face in a new direction. Whatever measure the corpse trod Dando was perforce compelled to do the same, and throughout the day he followed this grisly dancing master, imitating its movements to perfection. As the hours wore on a dreadful suspicion grew on him that the torment was to be for always: that, caught in some moment outside time, death was to be forever withheld. If there had been anyone nearby at that moment he would have begged for mercy without shame; instead he cried out - a long wailing howl that echoed against the rocky walls and roused a blackbird into sounding its alarm.

Dando's head had fallen back during a moment of blackness and it seemed already beyond his powers to lift it again. He gazed dully up into the canopy of the tree from which he was suspended watching it slowly revolve. After a while it came as no surprise to realise that a figure was occupying the centre of his field of vision. Moreover the figure was one that he recognised – his servant Potto was sitting decorously on a stout branch high overhead and looking down on him.

"Be you all right Lord m'dear?" the strangely situated old man enquired.

"Help me Potto," he cried, or thought he cried. "Get some shears and cut the rope. Or come down here and make a hole, just a little hole. It's the skin, you know, that keeps the life in."

The figure on the branch became harder to distinguish in the gathering gloom and changed strangely. It was not just Potto after all but Damask, his sister Damask, who was sitting astride the bough and showing her knickers.

"Help me sis," he pleaded.

"You idiot," scolded his twin, "how did you get into this mess? I might have known you'd come to a bad end. What are they going to say back home when I tell them what a complete cock-up you've made of things?"

But now, next to Damask, a third had materialised above him.

"You are a pathetic excuse for a son!" roared his father.

"Help me," Dando groaned. Even as he spoke all three shapes darkened and rushed together until they became something black and menacing which acquired two cat-like eyes and bent on him a look of glaring malevolence before slinking away like a shadow into the heart of the tree. At dusk an anonymous compassionate soul came with ladder and club in order to break bones and bring his suffering to an end, but the coup-de-grace on the head was not final and he was left still conscious despite being barely aware of the blows or of the damage they inflicted.

Daylight had finally left the sky and a fierce, inimical current of air blew from the cold places between the stars. A voice said **"THIS WAY"** and obediently Dando slipped sideways out of his body and turned to view the pathetic strung-out scrap with which he seemed to have little connection any more.

"He is dying," he whispered in awe, for the fact was written plain in the still face.

"DEATH IS NEAR,"said the voice, **"BUT IT WILL PASS HIM BY."**

"Oh no," cried Dando in sharp distress, "let him die."

"IF HE HAS SINNED, LET HIM NOT ADD ANOTHER BUT LIVE AND ATONE FOR HIS FAULT. THE TASK IS INCOMPLETE AND IT IS NOT YET TIME FOR HIM TO GO THROUGH THE CHANGE."

"Who are you?" said Dando weeping.

"YOU KNOW WHO I AM, DAN ADDO... SLEEP NOW CHILD. I WILL WATCH OVER YOU."

"Ann is dead," Dando wailed, "because of me."

But although the manifestation faded, a joyous laugh seemed to ring in his ears - Annie's laugh - the delicious girlish giggle that, once upon an idyllic time, he had helped her relearn.

All day a great storm had been hatching, building its strength over the wide watery expanses that lay far to the west. It had been born at the very moment that Dando fell forward off the cliff and now, grown to maturity, it came rushing eastward along the trough of the Middle Sea, leaving devastation in its wake, carried on the jet stream that eternally circles the globe. As evening approached the Master-of-Winds began stirring the pot, adding just a soupçon of malice to the brew. He had been instrumental in bringing about this tempest in the first place because, not long before, he had awoken to his consort's intention to deal now rather than later with the miscreant who was causing them so much concern and that, unknown to him, she had already brought the boy to the very brink of extinction This was surely a mistake. He had a gut feeling that, at present, their possible nemesis would be far more use to them alive than dead. Because of this he brought it about that an intense whirlpool of air gradually manifested, picking up moisture as it swept across the surface of the sea. It was midnight by the time the gale reached its maximum strength, and it was at this witching hour that the water spout he had created struck the Dark Island with deadly force. It roared ashore bearing weeds, fishes, even rocks within its vortex, tore into the woods as if they were matchsticks and then passed on. When morning came not a single tree on this isolated piece of land was left standing and the man-eaters had not been spared: they had been felled along with the rest.

Pickwah's invasion fleet with its compliment of military - the Axemen as they jokingly called themselves - cruised along the coast of their objective, crews and soldiers staring incredulously at the shattered vegetation. After a wild night during which the ships had lain snugly in harbour at Trincomalee, the seas were judged to have relented sufficiently to allow them to set sail. A collar of foam still marked the place where ocean met land, but the wind was favourable and the conditions were moderating. On the foremost vessel Lord Trewithik, as he was now often known, gazed up at the high plateau in front of the cliff. The feared grove, the thicket of insatiable hardwoods who were the last of an ancient line going back to the dawn of history, no longer dominated the skyline. A conviction was born in his heart that the island's defences had been breached and that the pirates' stronghold was his for the taking. He walked forward to join the select band of maguses and conjurers that he had assembled when he thought he had a supernatural menace to deal with. They were a sorry-looking bunch at present, somewhat green about the gills, and, because of this, he was prepared to risk the possibility that, through vexation at his words, their magic would be turned against him.

"Genn'lemen," he said, addressing them, "Oy'd better tell 'ee that we don' require thy services after all. Oy'll distribute a moderate recompense before reaching port to zee you don' go empty handed – but that be that I fear where 'ee be concerned."

As the vessels made their way along the southern shore of the island they reached the small promontory against which the pirates' ship was normally moored. The boat was missing and a short way out to sea the upturned hull of a wreck could be seen stuck fast on some rocks. It looked as if the privateer had been cast adrift in the storm. Cautiously the fleet closed with the quay and the fighting men disembarked. A short way inland they came upon the buccaneers' camp. Every building of which it was composed had been either smashed or tipped on its side and the hollow in which the settlement was situated appeared deserted. Then at the top of the hill they made out a row of figures, a tall man wearing a panther skin in the centre. The pirates, although drastically depleted in number, were preparing for battle. The Axemen advanced up the slope and a short fierce engagement followed of which the outcome was a forgone conclusion: despite their belligerent appearance the outlaws had lost the will for combat after experiencing the atmospheric catastrophe that had overtaken their refuge during the night. Within a very short space of time some had been killed, a few had fled and the rest were taken prisoner, among them their captain. The Leader set about extracting information on the whereabouts of the hoard he believed lay concealed nearby while most of his men scattered across the surrounding country in pursuit of the fugitives. Inevitably a morbid curiosity led the boldest to the plateau in front of the sgurr. Here their hopes turned to certainties - they found that the notorious trees were no more. The famed man-eaters lay uprooted on the ground in magnificent ruin or stood propped at crazy angles against the cliff.

The bravest of the explorers, venturing amongst the splintered branches, came upon half-rotted bodies in the wreckage with sparkling prizes wound around the whitening bones. Pocketing these trophies they searched further, greedily snatching up the pretty trinkets wherever they found them and scattering the pitiful remains without a second thought. Inevitably someone made a curious discovery.

"Hoy! Come an' look at this! We've got a breather here – this one's still with us."

His companions gathered round and gazed down in astonishment at the prone figure huddled with eyes shut, almost as if asleep.

"'Ere – cut those ropes. We'll take 'im back with us. Maybe the boss'll get a kick out of a live'n an' reward us or sompfing. It's not often you comes across an 'uman sacrifice wot's cheated the grim reaper."

"I don' know Con – could be bad luck – 'e's bin given to the trees after all."

"Oh don' be such a molly. The trees 'ave 'ad it – look at 'em. I never knowed such a blighter for worryin'. Next thing you know you'll be shittin' yourself at the sight of your own shadow."

"Well orl righ' then - Krull c'n carry 'im. But I think 'e's gonna snuff it anyways - 'e looks pretty near the end."

"Give us a mo' – I've jus' got a bit more groun' to cover."

Eventually, when the scavengers had satisfied themselves that there was no further booty to be gathered, Dando's body was lifted onto the shoulders of the largest and strongest soldier amongst them and the group, toting their ill-gotten gains, made their way back to the ships. Later in the day the fleet put to sea loaded up with chests of treasure (Lord Trewithik's search had been rewarded), a bunch of dispirited prisoners in the hold of the flagship and, on the lower deck, one unconscious, cruelly injured young man hovering momentarily between life and death. Hungry Island – its sting drawn – was left deserted.

Unborn and in peril,

A dark future in prospect,

Perhaps death would be preferable.

Chapter fourteen

On the night of the pirates' attack Foxy had awoken when a glowing flake of ash fell on his face. That the enchantment he was under had lost its enabling power would have been no surprise to any devotees of the occult that happened to be nearby, for, as Ann had once explained to Dando when he was being slightly obtuse, the sleeping spell could be broken if danger threatened. Sitting up the Nablan brushed the burning ember away and at the same time saw that the room, situated on the first floor of the fishing village's cottage, was lit by a ferocious glare. The light was coming in through the window but also from chinks between the walls and ceiling. He realised that the roof of the house as well as the roof-beams and roof-tree were on fire! Leaping up he grabbed his pack and jacket – fortunately he had not undressed – and rushed to wake his companions. Dando and Ann's rooms were empty; it did not take him more than a moment to discover that they were nowhere in the vicinity. Going in to Tallis he found him dead to the world, as yet unaware of the threat and therefore impossible to rouse. Bending, he picked the man up and carried him bodily downstairs and out of the house. A couple of glances told him all he needed to know. The upper part of the village was in flames and lower down he could see silhouetted figures apparently torching the cottages closer to the sea. A beam came crashing down through the ceiling of the house they had just quitted and a storm of sparks enveloped them, landing on their clothes and burning their skin. Sensing pain, Tallis awoke with a gasp. "What's happening?" he cried.

"The town be on fire," replied Foxy urgently. "It be a raid – we mus' get away."

Tallis, back on his feet, turned towards the cottage.

"Where are the others? Where's my squire?"

"They be gone the rascals – run away I reckon. Come on – we can't stay here."

"But my things – the kuckthu!" He went to re-enter through the door. Foxy grabbed hold of him.

"You can't, the roof be collapsing. Come on – there's no way out of the village upwards – we mus' go down." Pulling a reluctant Tallis along with him he set off towards the harbour at the same time reaching into his inside pocket for his gun. About a hundred yards further on a couple of the arsonists swung round at their approach. One of them raised his hand and a bullet whizzed past, almost parting Foxy's hair. He fired in reply and dragged Tallis into the doorway of a house where the flames had not yet taken hold. He peered out and saw a number of men creeping up against the walls. Then a voice spoke behind him.

"Quick – this way – out t' back!"

He realised there were other people inside this particular dwelling and they were beckoning him urgently towards the rear. Already any escape route into the street was a non-starter as the gang members were arriving outside. Foxy made a split second decision, a decision on behalf of both of them as Tallis seemed somewhat dazed and dilatory. He followed their half-seen guides through to the back entrance of the cottage into what appeared at first to be a dead end – a tiny dark yard right up against the steep hillside. But someone took his hand, he tripped and stumbled down some steps and before he knew it was within the rock. A door slammed behind him; he groped around and found Tallis' sleeve, then grasped his arm in the darkness.

"Where are we?" he cried.

"Shhhhhhh," said a voice, "tub-runners tunnel - take 'ee down t' beach in t' next cove. Follow me – mind yer 'ead."

One of the fugitives had kindled a tiny light and by this flame they were able to get an idea of the dimensions of the hole in which they found themselves and to make progress of sorts. It seemed to Foxy that they spent an age shuffling through a succession of airless passages punctuated by caves, sometimes bent double, sometimes wading waist deep in water. Then, suddenly, he was out on a beach in the cool night air and the sound of waves came to his ears. He saw that there were at least a dozen people standing between themselves and the sea while many more had already started up a steep hillside path, for it was quickly apparent that no boat was on hand to take them off and that the only way out of this cove was to climb.

"It be about four mile over to Praa from yere," a man told them in passing. "We'll maybe get help. But it be too late to zave the village curse 'em. Forwhy did they pick on us?"

Despite this gloomy assessment the fisher-folk were not going to waste time. They set a cracking pace, leaping up the ascent like mountain goats. Even for Foxy it was a gruelling challenge, Tallis found it physically killing. Nevertheless he had no choice but to keep up, for once left behind in the dark he could have gone completely astray. Before long his breath was coming in laboured gasps and his heart was beating nineteen to the dozen. By the time they started their descent into another coastal comb he was in a wretched state.

Praa was a larger, slightly more prosperous-looking place than the ravaged settlement they had just left behind whose name they discovered, rather tardily, was Gweek. It took a while to alert the sleeping inhabitants of this small port to the present situation and then they showed a marked reluctance to get involved.

"You zay it were they divils from Hungry Island? Be they there still? It don' do to be too hasty. We'll yave to zend for more men from Pentarwen and Looe. Mayhap it'd be better to take a peek from offshore once it gets light – zee what the zituation be. While you're waiting we'll put you up yere at the institute – the wives'll look after you."

Ann reached the coastal highway a few hours before dawn and waited there until light began to creep into the eastern sky. Then she looked left towards Tagnaroque and right towards Trincomalee and Pickwah. Which road, if either, were her companions most likely to take she wondered? Whichever one it turned out to be she must go in the opposite direction. In the end she decided on the right-hand way. She would find a refuge from where she could watch the track.

If no-one appeared inside a day she would presume they had either put to sea or gone east. She walked for about an hour and, once morning had truly established itself, searched for a suitable hideaway. She was just about to cut up through the woods on her left-hand side when she saw a solitary figure coming towards her. Here was someone she could ask – someone who might know the local geography. As the man approached she saw he was of medium height with a thin rangy build. Although his face was palish-grey and deeply lined - the wrinkles seeming more like miniature crevasses - her general impression was of agelessness and a kind of ancient vigour. His clothes were loose and strangely patterned, rather like vestments. He did not seem to be carrying any luggage. When they came within speaking distance he nodded in a friendly fashion and held out his hand.

"Good-day to you sister," he hailed her in greeting.

Ann was about to reciprocate when she noticed what he wore around his throat. Just below his chin hung a large pendant, probably of antique silver, in the shape of a jointed manikin. Its wrists were attached to the neck chain so that when the man moved it jerked and gesticulated as if trying to escape. Its left foot, the foot on the right-hand side, was missing. Ann, suddenly on her guard, went to withdraw her hand but by now she had left it too late, the stranger grabbed hold and pulled her towards him, placing his other hand on her forehead.

"Gubbo the Great," he continued, "pleased to meet you. And you are...?"

Ann had no intention of revealing her name. As soon as the man touched her she understood that he was in possession of power equal to or greater than that which she had recently possessed. In such a case identifying herself would be asking for trouble, the last thing she should do. Yet, contrary to her intentions, she found herself answering in a small sad voice, "Hilda Hannah Arbericord."

"Ah," he said, "Hilda Hannah Arbericord," and she felt the noose tightening. "I think we should step aside and sit down on that pleasant stretch of grass over there while we continue the introductions and get to know each other better."

"I have to travel on," Ann meant to say, but because he still had hold of her hand she was compelled to go with him whether she would or no.

As she sat on the ground the wizard (not actually named Gubbo the Great, although he often styled himself as such, but Gammadion, the Key stealer) knelt beside her and, gripping her wrist, began stroking her hair, meanwhile cocking his head to one side as if listening intently.

"Ah Hilda," he said, "you and I are two of a kind, or were before you lost your cherry, you stupid girl. Now you have a little one on the way and are consequently no more gifted than Mary from the dairy or Doris the drudge. Was it worth it I wonder?"

Again he placed his hand on her forehead and stared into her eyes. Looking back at him she saw how he radiated darkness despite his pale skin and the bloodless flesh beneath. She sensed the ancient abyss that lay within, the hollow man, but realised he was still capable of great evil.

"So why are you alone?" the wizard continued. "Did he desert you? No, it's you who decided to leave – how strange. Come on Hilda Hannah Arbericord, tell me about it."

Every-time he used her name she sensed her ability to withstand him weakening. It was not long before, in answer to his questions, she began to speak in a dull monotone, conveying at first in fits and starts but soon fluently what he wished to hear.

"And who are these people you were with? And where did you all come from? That far away! And what are you doing here? This so-called knight – you tell me he is on a quest – a quest for what? A Key? – how curious. And the boy – the one who deflowered you – you say he is this knight's squire? Where are they to be found? A village on the coast? Show me." So for the rest of the morning Ann retraced her steps along the highway, walking ahead, the wizard following.

"You take the lead my dear – you know where it is, this village. Allow a poor tired old man to lean against your shoulder. The legs are weary and the way is long."

To any one passing them going in the opposite direction it must have looked as if Ann was supporting her companion as she had supported Tallis after his seizure. Only she knew that his bony fingers, digging into her flesh, compelled her onwards giving her no choice but to obey. Midday was approaching as they turned down towards the sea and entered the combe in which the village of Gweek was situated. They were met by a low-level smoke-haze, trapped between the hillsides and hanging amongst the trees.

"Hello," said Gammadion, "this isn't right. Something's been happening since you were last here. It wasn't like this when you left, was it?"

The flames had not reached the wood; it was still intact. As they emerged from its lower limits and looked down on a devastated settlement, they saw that nearly every dwelling was roofless with murky fumes still rising from the blackened interiors. Ann gazed in horror. Could this be real or was it just a figment brought about by the powerful spell she was under? If what she was seeing was the true state of affairs then the implications were immense – she could not take them in – she only knew that something dreadful was hovering on the margins of her consciousness.

"Where were they staying?" said the wizard, "show me the place."

Her heart cold and empty, Ann walked down the high street and stopped outside the cottage that had provided their night-time shelter. Like Dando a few hours earlier she stared with unbelief through the window at the wreckage within, aware that the small house looked even smaller now that its upper floor and roof had collapsed. Gammadion stood silently beside her. Eventually he said as if to himself, "They're not in there."

To remain within that polluted atmosphere for long was impossible. They climbed up to the wood where the air was cleaner. The wizard glanced slyly sideways.

"Do you have anything of theirs?" he asked.

Ann summoned up all her rapidly diminishing powers of resistance and managed to shake her head.

"Oh Hild," said Gubbo, "I don't think that's being very honest, you naughty girl. Come here."

He searched her pack and then went through her pockets, confiscating her meagre valuables, eventually bringing to light a small object which he held up between thumb and forefinger.

"This isn't yours, is it?" he said. "This belonged to the knight."

Ann recognised a button that had come loose from Tallis' jacket and which she had been intending to sew back on.

"But there's something else, isn't there?" went on the wizard, "something precious that you're trying to hide."

Brutally he plunged his hand into the neck of her blouse and brought forth a few strands of lustrous black hair.

"Oh excellent, excellent!" he exclaimed.

"No!" Ann managed to croak. The wizard laughed.

"Sit down there," he ordered, indicating a tree stump, "and I'll give you a lesson in how to curse."

Standing within the wood, almost on the spot where she and Dando had lain in each other's arms, the man tucked the button into the palm of his left hand and then delicately took hold of the silver manikin's head. With his other hand he began describing circles in the air almost as if winding a ball of wool, meanwhile moving his lips in a muttered incantation. Beneath his fingers a roiling, whirling sphere of darkness formed a few feet from the ground and spun before them with no visible means of support. Gammadion picked up a stout stick lying nearby and took the smoky globe into his left hand. He tossed it upwards and as it floated down dealt it a sharp whack with the stick for all the world like someone going for a boundary in the game of cricket. There was a loud crack, the missile soared into the air and then, abruptly altering course, shot off over the horizon. "And now for the other one," he said with a smirk, twisting the curl of dark hair round his finger, "perhaps the more dangerous of the two. I don't think the head spell will take, he's still too young, but we can slow him down a bit. It may be a while before the conditions are right for this to work but work it will, sooner or later."

He went through the same routine, only this time gripping the figurine by its truncated left leg while he recited the charm.

"What do you think of that then?" he said once the spell came to an end, apparently full of conceited self-admiration. Ann felt the constraints binding her suddenly relax. She could have spoken if she had wanted but instead turned away, silently weeping.

That night Gammadion availed himself of her quiescent body. You could not call it making love – love had nothing to do with it. You could hardly call it rape, although, under normal circumstances, that is how it would have appeared, because it was not done against her will, her will had been totally abrogated, she no longer had a will of her own apart from the one the wizard imposed on her. Afterwards he seemed inclined to talk – a rambling monologue incomprehensible to any but himself.

"There – I've dealt with them – they'll never find it now – and they won't understand why – they'll *never* understand, they'll never know. And those other slippery customers – those imposters who've pulled the wool over humanity's eyes and made themselves out to be gods – they're no gods I can tell you – they think they can manipulate me, but what I do, I do of my own free will – they'll find out soon enough that if I go along with them it'll be on my own terms..." He went on muttering to himself in this vein for sometime until he become aware once more of Ann's presence.

"Oh Hilda – do you realise that you remind me of someone I once had dealings with – a girl I had to persuade to retrieve something. That was hard I can tell you because it was necessary she undertake the task without any conjuring on my part - I managed it in the end."

"Tomorrow we'll set out for Vadrosnia Poule. You'll come with me – you'll be my entertainment on the road. But the child – that's a different matter – if he's born with inherited power that boy could be very useful. Oh, didn't you know? It's a boy – I'm sure I'm not mistaken."

For the rest of the hours of darkness Ann remained in a half-conscious stupor, awake and yet not fully aware. Gammadion had transferred the pendant from his neck to hers and it weighed her down making it impossible for her to slip away while he slept, which he did noisily with much snorting, snoring and smacking of lips. He had made no provision for her bodily needs and she suffered the consequences. In the morning she got to her feet when he released her, deathly tired, with the prospect of another day of enslavement ahead. She understood all too well that she had been trapped like a fly in amber, that her plight could probably be traced back to the Mother's original vindictiveness towards her and that as a result she might not survive. But this concerned her less at that moment than the cold terror that gripped her when she thought of her three companions and what might have happened to them, and the even more abject fear she felt on behalf of the fourth member in the equation. *What about the baby,* her soul cried, *the babe who is blameless? What will become of the child?*

Foxy and Tallis, as outsiders, were not required to join in the fierce arguments for and against intervention at Gweek, intervention which the Praa citizens thought - taking into consideration the pirates fighting prowess and the fact that the damage had already been done - would be quite pointless as well as dangerous. Those from the ruined village, on the other hand, pleaded that it still might be possible to save a few precious items in their shattered hamlet if the invaders were driven off. Our two travellers hung around at a loose end until lunchtime arrived when they drifted, in company with the women and children, to a largish hall where an impromptu meal was being provided. Here they were handed tin plates and queued up to take their share. Foxy addressed a few remarks to Tallis but received no reply. He noticed that the knight was screwing up his face as if in pain and had started to sway slightly on his feet. Every so often he put up a hand to touch his brow. It was just after his dish had been piled high with food and he was turning away from the serving hatch that Foxy heard him utter a surprised little, "Oh," and watched as his legs buckled and he collapsed in a limp heap. The platter went clattering to the floor scattering its contents in all directions. Exclamations and consternation filled the hall.

A crowd immediately gathered round the motionless figure and Foxy found himself gazing at a solid wall of backs. He pushed his way through and picked Tallis up in a proprietorial manner but then stood at a loss, unsure where to take him. Plenty of advice soon came his way: there was a speaker's chamber at the end of the hall, it had a couch on which he could lay the poor man down; the ge'nnelm'n must have had a fainting fit, he needed time to recover. Foxy was ushered into a well-furnished sitting room where, indeed, he found an old velvet-covered sofa big enough to accommodate Tallis' lanky frame. A woman opened a drawer and produced what looked like a heavy duty tablecloth. This they spread over the invalid while another woman offered to fetch a warm drink to which she would add something that she insisted would revive the sufferer. Foxy was left temporarily alone as they bustled off and, with nothing to do for the moment, gazed down nonplussed at his fallen leader. As he had never known a day's sickness in his life anything concerning ill health was completely foreign to him. He became aware that the knight was not actually unconscious, that in fact he was trying to speak, but all that emerged was a sort of strangled gargling sound. There was something wrong with his face, it looked only half alive; the left side of his mouth and his left eyelid had both developed a pronounced droop. The animated side wore a startled, scared expression as if he did not fully understand what was happening to him.

One of the females returned with a brimming beaker which she handed to Foxy. He lifted Tallis and began to tip the liquid between his lips only to find that it dribbled back out of the sides of his mouth; it seemed his patient had lost the ability to swallow. Foxy laid him down again and requested a towel to clean up the mess. As he mopped and wiped he asked himself what the hell he was doing. This was not a job for him, this tending of the sick, this was women's work, or more properly a task for the knight's bondsman who had vowed himself to the wanderer's service. Rage boiled up inside him as he thought of Dando and Ann. He and Tallis had been within minutes of being burnt alive in that little house because there had been no-one to warn them of the threat to the village. The Glept, who he now realised he should have dealt with long ago, had deserted his post and was probably already well down the road with the girl in whom all Foxy's hopes had been invested. What price his virgin priestess now - what price the glorious uprising of his people? Well, whatever the outcome, the runaways need not think that they had seen the last of Captain Judd or his deadly little equaliser. He would track them down and exact retribution, most definitely against the boy and maybe even against his protege who had betrayed him by absconding, despite everything he had done for her benefit. Having for the moment completely forgotten his promise to Ann, he smiled grimly, a smile with more than a hint of menace, and then applied himself anew to the chore of attending to Tallis.

Eighteen days earlier, down on the Kymer flood plain, two riders on horseback and the occupants of a showman's caravan came face to face along a minor road near the town of Thrubwell - a road that began near the Great River and ultimately led to the mountains.

"Dando? I don't know where he is. I thought he'd be with you," replied Damask in answer to Milly's initial greeting, her surprise causing her thought processes to seize up for a moment.

"I di'n't find 'im," said Milly sorrowfully. "I foun' 'im instead," dismounting and indicating Jack who was also just getting down from his horse. "'Ee's seen 'im. No I mean..." She hesitated, then confided in a whisper, "I mean 'e *can't* see, you see, an' 'e's one of them," she made an effete gesture with her hand, "but 'e's orl right."

By the time she had got to grips with the situation and recovered from her amazement at this unexpected meeting Damask realised that she was overjoyed to be reunited with Milly. It was only now as she set eyes on her maid once more that she finally admitted to herself that she had been living with a constant undertow of worry and a thoroughly guilty conscience as a result of her past actions. In a delayed response she grabbed hold and practically squeezed the breath out of the little girl. Then she switched her attention to the other new arrival, a boy in dark glasses who was walking towards her, his hand held out. She proffered hers in return and waited for him to grasp it. Instead he missed her by at least a foot and was about to pass by, bringing home the fact that he was indeed blind. She caught hold of his arm and gripped his hand. He turned to her with a smile.

"Hallo, you're Dando's sister I understand. I've been hearing a lot about you."

"Not bad I hope."

"Oh, terrible... terrible..."

"You've seen Dando? I mean..."

"At Toymerle. He and his master, along with Foxy and Ann, rescued me and the other prisoners."

"His master? I don't understand."

"Tallis – Tallisand the knight – the one who's looking for a key."

"But Dando doesn't have a master."

"No – that's what I thought when we first met – but he does – he's the knight's squire."

"Squire? What does that mean? What pile of manure has the idiot landed in now?"

Damask and Jack were soon deep in conversation, learning about each other, exchanging information. Meanwhile Milly stood beside them feeling slightly left out. Then she noticed another who was being totally ignored. Pnoumi the Mog had gotten down from his van and was hovering a few yards away gazing anxiously at Damask.

"'Allo Mister Cat Clown," she said. "She foun' where you woz 'idin' then?"

"She plomise to be my rittle wifie," replied Pnoumi mournfully.

"You'll be lucky."

Pnoumi looked back towards his wagon.

"You rike to see my pussies?"

"Not really."

A while later, standing shoulder to shoulder with Jack as if they had known each other for years, Damask made an announcement.

"OK," she said, " we're going back to Drossi. Jack says he can fix us up with accommodation and show us how we can earn some dosh. Here's Pnoumi Jack – he's got this really weird show with hundreds of cats – it's really something."

"Thirty-thlee," said Pnoumi.

"I'll ride with him but there's no room for more than two up on the box. You'd better stay on the horse and come behind with Milly."

Damask had automatically assumed command of the little band and under her direction they headed towards the road beside the Great River and then turned left along it into the flow of traffic making for the Delta City.

"I'd better tell Damask that the caravan won't be allowed through the gates," Jack remarked as he and Milly trailed along at the rear. "They can probably leave it on Parker's Piece as the Solstice Festival will be over by now."

However when they arrived at the show ground they found a new attraction was in the process of setting up. A very large circular tent covered most of the area, from the top of which flew a streamer proclaiming *Quatre's Corybantics – alpha acts – entertainment for young and old.* There was the noise of much hammering coming from within, mingled with the sound of a band rehearsing, while round the outside were scattered trailers and vans of all descriptions.

"It's the circus!!" cried Milly in a frenzy of excitement, "the Colonel's circus! I mus' go an' let them know I'm 'ere." But when she reached the gate she found it barred against her.

"No members of the public allowed in 'till tomorrow," barked the man on duty.

"But I comes from 'ere," protested Milly, "I b'longed to the Colonel."

"The Colonel's no longer in charge. Are you a performer?"

Milly had to admit she was not. The man looked past her at the cat circus caravan.

"How about you, are you one of the new acts?" he called to Damask and Pnoumi.

"That's right," exclaimed Damask, suddenly finding herself presented with a unique opportunity and seizing it with both hands. "Where do we go?"

"Round to the right of the big top – try-outs tomorrow morning, bright and early."

"Give me ten minutes," Damask called to Jack and Milly, and then to Pnoumi beside her, "come on the Mog – here's your big chance."

It took quite a bit of persuading to inveigle the clown into driving his wagon through the gate and round the side of the tent where they were met by another man who pointed out a parking space.

"But my pussies not part of big circus," protested Pnoumi, "this my circus," waving his hand towards the rear of the vehicle.

"Why shouldn't they be?" replied Damask, "what could be better? Guaranteed audience – much larger than you're used to – roof over your head when you perform – share of the profits – someone else to do all the worrying – and before you know it you're the star of the show."

"But you say we go sma' town – you say overnight sensation."

"I've changed my mind," replied Damask, "don't worry, I'll help with this."

"You be my rittle wifie?"

"Yes – for the moment – but not tonight. I must get back to Jack. I'll see you first thing in the morning."

"Don't reave me," pleaded Pnoumi.

"I won't – I'll be back tomorrow. But I've got to go now. Bye-bye my soul." She gave him a quick peck and hurried away.

Just as it was getting dark Jack and Milly settled the two horses into a livery stable at the town end of the Green Dolphin Avenue then they all headed into the urban sprawl. Jack had a map of the city in his head and the girls followed his directions as he reeled off a list of streets.

"Turn right into Kinlet Road, left down Plum Lane, keep straight on through Nightingale Vale, cut across Beresford Square..."

"Where are you taking us?" demanded Damask.

"My home from home - should be in full swing at the moment – chance to say hello to a few old friends."

Their final destination turned out to be a small close at the end of a quiet residential street. At least it would have been quiet if it had not been for an insistent thumping beat coming from below ground level. They saw that there was a doorway in the square which did not appear to belong to any of the houses on either side. In front of this a small crowd had gathered, smoking and drinking. Above the door hung an illuminated sign; it read *The Green Goat*.

"What's going on?" asked Damask.

"Oh it's just a club where you can have a meal or dance if you want to - somewhere with good music where you can hang out. Most of my friends come here – live here you might say." Jack seemed a trifle nervous now that he was back on familiar territory.

The crowd parted to let them through but then a burly man barred the way.

"No juveniles," he said pointing at Milly. "Go on ducks, off home with you. It's past your bedtime."

"Come off it Bruiser," said Jack, "don't be such a spoil sport – she's with me."

"An' you are...?"

"Who do you think?"

The bouncer stared hard at the dark glasses after which his jaw dropped.

"Howgego – Jack Howgego - by all that's 'oly! We thought you'd snuffed it!"

"No – not yet. Are you going to let us in?"

The interior of the club, reached down a flight of steps, was cavernous and dimly lit. On the left Damask and Milly could make out an array of tables occupied by diners who appeared to be in the middle of an evening meal; on the right stood an illuminated bandstand beside an open area intended for dancing, although so far no-one had taken the floor. As Jack, plus the two girls descended the stairs Bruiser followed them and had a word with a man just inside the entrance. This individual's mouth formed into a silent O of astonishment, then into a whistle, before he overtook the newcomers, mussing Jack's hair in passing, and made his way to the stage, holding up his hand for silence. The band, which had been playing *Raz*, the innovative jazz style that synced with the latest dance craze, broke off and the speaker was able to make himself heard.

"Ladies and gentlemen," he proclaimed, "a prodigal has returned to us – the Chancer is once again in our midst. Let's give him a right royal welcome!"

The drummer, quick on the uptake, played a roll ending with a stroke on the high-hat. All eyes turned towards the stairs and Jack immediately became the centre of attention. The occupants of the night club crowded round, slapping the young man on the back, punching and manhandling him amid a general din. Then one of the enthusiasts' voices rose above the rest.

"Where 'ave you sprung from fella? We got tol' you woz a write off – least that's wot came down from above. Howgego Associates put out a statement – regrets an' orl that. *Mr John Howgego, grandson of the Chairman of the Board, has unfortunately*

---

met with an untimely end at the 'ands of a criminal element with which he was known to be associating."

"No," said Jack, "it wasn't quite like that."

"Well that's obvious man, cos 'ere you are, alive an' kicking. 'Ere, Dotty, go an' tell Tony that Jack's back."

"No," said Jack, "I'll tell him myself later."

"Oh – that's all orf, is it? Wot 'ave you gorn an done? Found a new boy friend?"

"Maybe."

There was a babble of voices. "Why are you 'idin' your pretty face?" piped up another party-goer. "Wot you doin' wearin' those shades?"

He reached forward and plucked Jack's glasses from his nose. There was a universal intake of breath and the people closest to the young man actually recoiled. After a pregnant pause most of the males in the room suddenly melted away leaving the women to coo and cluck and usher their old friend to a table where they installed him next to his two companions. Jack demanded his spectacles back and eventually they were tracked down and reinstated.

"Whatever's happened to you, honey chil'?" asked a glamorous middle-aged woman in a voice of hushed concern. Damask stared in amazement at her incredible hour-glass figure which at her advanced age must surely be aided and abetted by some cast-iron underpinning in the corsetry department.

"Oh, it's too sordid to go into," replied Jack with a tired sigh. "Is there anything to eat in this place?"

A meal was brought and their new acquaintance sat next to the boy as if she doubted that he would be able to feed himself.

"Don't fuss Becca," Jack scolded, "I can manage perfectly well. This is Becca," he said to Damask and Milly, "professional name Miss Peepo – star of stage, screen and singer with the Lazy River Band. She'll be able to put you up – she's got a rooming house – and she can probably help you get a part, Dando's sister, if you want to tread the boards. She comes from Armornia."

Damask regarded the woman with interest. So this was what someone from *Across-the-Brook* looked and sounded like.

"So, are y'all fixing on coming to me tonight?" asked Jack's friend a while later in her languid drawl. "How much?" demanded Damask, immediately getting down to practicalities.

"Two and sixpence per day, three dollars – no I mean fifteen shillings - for the week."

"We haven't got much money between us," said Damask, feeling that this time she had better lay her cards on the table and get things straight right from the start. "We need jobs – can you help us?"

"Sure, any friends of this guy I'll give it my best."

By the time the meal ended Milly was yawning and her head had started to droop.

"This chil' needs her bed," said Becca, "Maisy can take my spot tonight." And to Jack, "are you coming kiddo?"

"I've got people to see," said Jack, "and the night's young. Don't wait up."

"Where will you sleep?" Damask asked him.

"I'll bed down wherever I end up – don't you worry. It's what I'm used to. No fixed abode – that's Jack Howgego."

"But can you find your way?"

"Oh, I'll latch on to somebody."

Becca's lodging house, which was not far distant, proved to be a neat well-kept establishment in a street of modest but prosperous-looking houses. The showgirl demonstrated a natural curiosity regarding her guests and by the time they reached their destination she had learnt all about Damask's ambition to go on the stage and Milly's love of the circus.

"The thing this year has been musicals - plays with music and songs if you know what I mean," she explained. "I guess I might be able to see you right if you can hold a tune."

Damask filled her lungs and gave voice.

"*I'd like to bomb you from above,*

"*With a crossbow bolt of love...*" she sang.

"Mmmmmmm – good enough for me – in fact more than good enough. Say, d'you know who wrote that little number? None other than yours truly. It was part of my act until the Fanatiks stole it from me and then other groups stole it from them. Here's a suggestion: howbout you get up in front of the band at the Goat tomorrow night an' we'll see what you're made of – then we can take it from there. And you say you've got a date at Quatre's in the morning? I'll give you a call."

Early the next day Damask set off to keep her appointment with Pnoumi, accompanied by Milly, whose desire to renew her acquaintance with the circus had been enough to persuade her to tag along. As they walked through the gate, their right to be there unquestioned this time, the child looked around eagerly for people she recognised, but her search for old acquaintances was doomed to disappointment.

"Well," said Damask, "it's sometime since you were last here isn't it? I expect most of those you knew have moved on."

Pnoumi was waiting for them, wound up into a state of nerves.

"We next ones to do our act. Need help to cally cats and stuff into tent."

"Have you got enough baskets?" asked Damask.

"All leddy in basket. They good pussies."

Taking two baskets each they were able to transport all thirty three cats to the side of the ring. Pnoumi went back for his equipment.

"The setting up of properties will have to be done in full view of the audience," said Damask to Milly, "That can be my job. You had better handle the cats – let them in and out of the baskets and suchlike."

"I don' know about that," objected Milly.

"Come on, you said you were friendly with a cat at the Spread Eagle. You can talk to cats you said – do it now. Go on..."

On further urging a reluctant Milly was prevailed upon to do her cat impression and was immediately rewarded by a chorus of mews from the baskets. In fact, once their try-out got under way in front of a critical ringmaster, Milly proved to be a brilliant assistant to the clown. There was something about her that caused the cats to treat her as a friend. She had only to chirrup and they would come running; they seemed to regard her as a slightly larger member of their own species and her presence gave them confidence. Consequently she was invaluable in rounding them up once they had finished one part of the performance and positioning them to begin the next. When their act reached its climax there was a smattering of applause from other entertainers who had gathered to watch. The ringmaster, who was also the new owner, shook Pnoumi's hand.

"Needs some work," he said, "but you're definitely on the books. Start tomorrow. I can only take one of the girls – the little dark one. Seven and six each a day. I'll give you an advance so you can buy some suitable clothes."

"But where you go now?" cried Pnoumi, almost weeping, as he and Damask walked back to the caravan carrying four of the baskets, leaving Milly to pick up the other two along with the props. "You say you be my wifie – you say you stay with me."

"Don't worry," replied Damask, "I'll come and see you often – I mean it – tonight if you like."

"Reary?"

"Yes, I promise."

Pnoumi looked slightly mollified but unsure whether to believe her.

"You velly fine woman – you not reave me prease."

"There you are Milly, now you've got a job and you'll be working in your beloved circus," said Damask as they made their way back towards town. Milly did not reply but pursed her lips into a sulky pout.

"Aren't you pleased?"

"It woz you 'e wanted, not me."

"But you're much better as his assistant than I could ever be. Animals and I just don't seem to mix it."

Milly held her peace.

"What's wrong? You look as if you've lost a pound and found a sixpence."

The little girl glowered and then suddenly burst out "Sposin' 'e tries sompfink on?"

Damask exploded into laughter.

"Is that what you're worried about? Come off it Milly – show a bit of gumption. You're made of sterner stuff than that. He's a cream-puff - you could twist him round your little finger - in fact you could knock him over with a clothes peg. Don't be such a wet week girl – give it some welly!"

Milly smiled wanly.

The next time they saw Jack, which was that evening at the Green Goat, he was transformed. His hair had been cut and styled, his skin looked suspiciously unblemished and he was dressed in cutting-edge clothes which his fashionable thinness set off to perfection. He had acquired a new and expensive pair of sunglasses.

"Jack, you look... amazing!" gasped an impressed Damask.

"Thanks," the boy replied. "I managed to get an appointment with Cyril – not always easy – he's usually pretty booked up. Can't go around Drossi looking like last week's leftovers you know. I'll recommend you if you like. Becca tells me you're going to sing with the band tonight – good luck an' all that."

He reached out and she let him trace her features with his hand.

"No," he said, "you're not much like him, but I envy you being with him so long. I only had him for four days."

When the time came for Damask to do her turn on stage her heart was in her mouth. Nervously she gave the band-leader the time signature, hummed the tune to the keyboard player who was to be her main accompanist and then turned to face the curious onlookers.

"My first date," she warbled tentatively,

"The wretched boy came late.

I asked myself was he coming at all,

You could hardly call it a ball."

"My first hug," with greater confidence,

"Snug as a bug in a rug.

What started off as a mammoth smooze,

Quickly turned into a snooze."

"My first kiss,

I thought it was going to be bliss.

My two front teeth got stuck in his braces,

Talk about red faces..."

This ditty had originally been written by Dando for one of the Dans' Yuletide entertainments. Later it became a matter of pride for him to have composed a new verse every time she took to the stage which meant that in the end it got so unwieldy that it lasted almost half an hour. She gave the crowd an edited version, thinking that these sophisticates would probably pronounce it poor infantile stuff at best, but in fact they laughed and applauded and called for an encore. She wished Dando could have been there to share in the approbation.

The band had begun a new set and she had slipped back into the crowd when a scruffy looking type, with a hint of the avant-guard about him, grabbed her elbow.

"Can I have a word?" he asked urgently, "I run a small experimental theatre company up town which is hoping to stage a satirical take on the latest trend: these musicals everyone's into this season. We've got a brilliant young writer/composer – clever lyrics, catchy tunes. Now we're looking for good voices with acting ability and you seem to fit the bill. Would you like to come for an audition tomorrow? I can pretty well guarantee a favourable outcome."

Damask accepted with alacrity. When Becca, alias the ex movie-star Peepo, had finished her number and come off stage she passed on the good news.

"Oh swell," replied the Armornian, "that's what I thought would happen, but I didn't want to raise your hopes too much. So now you've both got jobs. I guess you'll be able to pay me at the end of the week!"

Damask and Milly became bread-winners. Each day they rose early, ate a hasty breakfast, and started, Milly for Parker's Piece in order to share in preparations for the circus's evening performance, Damask for the little converted warehouse doing service as a theatre where she was handed little more than a pittance as recompense for her abilities but was rewarded ten times over by the satisfaction she got from helping to create a partially-improvised play with music. She spent the occasional night with Pnoumi, more as a duty than a pleasure. Pleasure was currently to be found elsewhere, for the two girls were extremely pleased with themselves, due, mainly, to the fact that they were both earning money and had a permanent place to live. They were in the happy position of knowing that their futures were secure for the moment and felt they were taking their first steps on the road to becoming Drossi citizens. Milly would have had not a care in the world except for the fact that she remained intensely worried about Dando and was still feeling her way in her professional relationship with Pnoumi. Meanwhile Jack drifted in and out of their lives having returned to the rackety existence he had been leading before his kidnapping. He flitted from one seedy hangout to another, frequently under the influence of an insidious local brew known as Jitta-Juice which he carried around in a flask in his hip pocket. Damask had recently become aware of a radical mood change on his part and sensed that he was now deeply unhappy about something despite being the focus of enormous concern and solicitude from those surrounding him. She was mightily puzzled as to the reason for this as she did not think that the obvious one entirely fitted the bill. In his soberer moments he often took her aside to hear accounts of her and her brother's upbringing in Deep Hallow.

Drossi, the city, was all about trade. Goods flooded through the port from the hinterland and onto ships at the docks, while other commodities were imported from abroad, offloaded and sent up country after the townsfolk had skimmed off the cream. As a result of this commerce the metropolis wallowed in the lap of luxury and got richer by the day. Protected, as they thought, by their treaties with the surrounding states, the city's authorities made no attempt to create a local standing army or even a metropolitan militia, relying on a rather shambolic police force to maintain law and order. The ruling council governed with a light hand, knowing, from experience, that this encouraged enterprise. However in recent months it began to be recognised that a standing navy might have come in useful. The shipping heading in and out of Drossi harbour was being preyed upon by a voracious band of pirates rumoured to be holed up on Hungry Island where they had reached some kind of arrangement with the local ambulatory flora. The city was helpless before their depredations which were affecting business. The citizens rejoiced greatly therefore when they heard that the buccaneers had been routed.

"It was an army from Pickwah wot done it – they call themselves Axemen. Evidently they crossed from Trincomalee on purpose-built boats. The story is that they killed all the pirates and cut down the trees. We won't be bovvered no more."

"Well, good-luck to the Pickwah Army – bully the Axemen. We ought to give them an award or sompthin' to show our appreciation."

The most westerly member of the Seven Sisters alliance basked in an approving glow emanating from the other communities along the south coast of the Middle Sea. It was just a few cautious pessimists who poured cold water on the enthusiasm by questioning why Pickwah should have found it necessary to build up their army to such an extent in the first place.

"It can't be just because of a few sea-faring bandits – Pickwah isn't a trading nation – their wealth depended on tourism – they wouldn't have suffered as we have. This has all happened since the coup that toppled the old regime. There's a new man in charge – Trewithik's his name I believe - come up from the ranks so they say - seems an ambitious sort – I'd be a bit wary if I were you."

As Damask had predicted, King Pnoumi's Cats became the star turn at Quatre's. When the circus reached the end of its run and was getting ready to set off on a tour of the towns farther up river she urged Pnoumi and Milly not to abandon their burgeoning careers.

"You're doing so well it would be a pity to give up now. I hear the show will be back in the autumn and after a successful progress you're sure to return in a blaze of glory. It'll put my little theatrical effort thoroughly in the shade."

Milly was nothing loath to go on the road. By this time she had the clown completely under her thumb – no funny business was her rule – and was enjoying herself. She had developed quite an affection for the cats. As for Pnoumi, his initial passion for Damask had had time to cool. Since their re-acquaintance there had been too many rivals for her affections to suit his taste and her promiscuity was beginning to get him down. The big top was struck, all the gear loaded into wagons, the trailers and vans queued before the gate and our two performers hitched up a rather out-of-condition Shingai and prepared to depart. Damask stood at the end of the Green Dolphin Avenue to wave them goodbye.

It was about this time that Jack disappeared off her radar. When she tried to make contact he was unreachable and his usual haunts knew him no more.

"Where's Jack got to?" she asked of one of his less-disreputable friends.

"Oh, ain't you 'eard the news? 'Is grandfather's 'ad a change of 'eart - ol' Hiram Howgego - mainly cos folk were startin' to boycott 'is business. See the story goin' roun' is that the kidnappers up at the Oracle sent a ransom demand on behalf of his grandson as was usually the case with those in the money but 'e wouldn't pay it, the ol' man, an' that's why... well, that's why they did wot they did to poor ol' Jack. Quite a lot of folk are really up in arms about it an' 'ave started movin' their goods elsewhere. So Hiram gets in a panic an' puts out a statement that orl is forgiven and forgotten. The Chancer's bin taken back into the bosom of 'is family an' the Chairman is promisin' to provide for 'im an' cater to orl 'is needs which will be consider'ble now 'e's so 'andicapped."

Damask enquired of Becca as to the accuracy of this statement and she confirmed what the man had told her. "I heard the other day that Jack was up at his grandfather's place – that gin palace on the grand canal – living in the lap of luxury I shouldn't wonder."

"Is that the truth? Lucky old Jack. But why haven't we seen him? He wouldn't just abandon us – he wouldn't just walk out on us, surely?"

"He may have had no choice - his granpaw's a very strong-willed old man you know."

"Well, Jack's no shrinking violet. Isn't that why he's called the Chancer? – everyone round here calls him that."

"I guess he was always up for the main chance and prepared to take risks – from what I hear he's been that way since he was a kid."

"Yes, that figures – he certainly seems the sort to chance his arm if the opportunity arises even if he could be riding for a fall. Anyway, I hope he won't just cut us off completely, even though he might have reached the top of the ladder as you say an' we're still down around the bottommost rung."

Poisonous thoughts bug me.

What's the solution?

Time to colour me gone.

Chapter fifteen

The truth of the matter was that Jack, far from being a free agent and able to please himself as to his comings and goings, had been kidnapped for a second time. It had happened in this manner. Spending most nights after his return on the fringes of the Drossi underworld he and his cronies gravitated to wherever the action happened to be: private parties, open-air raves, jam sessions, the latest stage-shows. At the last mentioned they usually ended up by being ejected as a result of their unruly behaviour. On one particular evening they were at a bash in somebody's house which was threatening to get out of hand with consequent damage to property. A couple of newcomers who stood out like sore thumbs because of their age and outdated attire pushed their way through the minor riot to where Jack was ensconced, holding court, surrounded by a number of hangers on.

"Mr John Howgego? Your grandfather Sir Hiram Howgego requests the pleasure of your company at his domicile where a small function has been arranged in your honour. We've been sent to escort you."

The hour being late Jack was in no fit state to form a coherent reply, although he was compos-mentis enough to know that he recognised the voice, but the other party-goers made their views perfectly plain:

"Fuck-off you traitors! 'E wants nothin' more to do wiv that slime-ball!"

"Crawl back into yer 'oles!"

"The Chancer's not interested."

"Leave 'im alone scum-bags! 'Ain't you done enough orlready?!"

But this was not to be the end of the story. Almost twenty-four hours later, shortly after dusk, the blind boy happened to have left one of his fellow-revellers' squats in order to go out on the streets alone en route for a nearby tobacconists'. He was constantly challenging himself in this way although there were always plenty of acquaintances willing to run errands on his behalf. He had nearly reach his goal when without warning something or somebody cannoned into him from behind and he was knocked to the ground. He was aware of being surrounded by at least three men and in a trice his hands and feet were bound. When he opened his mouth to yell for help a gag was rammed into it. In those first few minutes he almost died of fright as he imagined that history was repeating itself. But then he felt himself being carried down some steps and onto a boat and again he heard that familiar voice. These were not the gangsters from Toymerle, he realised, these were his grandfather's men. They were only afloat for a brief period before the gondola came alongside a landing stage that seemed to be under cover. He was lifted ashore and into an enclosed space where the acoustics spoke of a stone floor surrounded by walls on three sides with a ceiling overhead. From there he was hauled, with little ceremony, up a carpeted stair and into a room with the smell of money about it. Here he was dumped onto what was either a bed or a sofa. He heard his grandfather's voice.

"Nice work lads – I'll see you're properly rewarded. Wait outside the door. In a few minutes you can take him to his quarters. Make sure they're ready to receive him."

This was followed by silence. Jack sensed that the old man was standing close by looking down on him. During the manhandling he had lost his dark glasses. He turned his head aside.

"It's about time something was done about that disfigurement," Hiram remarked, "I'll arrange that for you. Where are you staying?"

Jack shook his head, unable to reply.

"Well wherever it is you're to move here – I've had some rooms readied. In your present condition you're not fit to be seen in civilised company. You should have come to me straight away when you got back from wherever you've been, instead of attempting to go it alone and consequently bringing the family name into disrepute."

Jack groaned and tried to speak. He felt hands at his face and the gag was removed. As soon as he was free to articulate, words came bursting out of him.

"Untie me!" he cried, "you can't keep me here! You've no right!"

"You're to have a suit in the west wing. You'll lack for nothing. Once a month you'll accompany me to one of my public functions where you'll act as a suitably grateful dependant. Any misbehaviour and I'll have you committed."

Jack could scarcely believe what he was hearing.

"You must be kidding!" he exclaimed in fury.

"Don't imagine I can't do it. We'll say your experiences have driven you over the edge. We've got plenty of evidence, gathered during the last few weeks, which could provide proof, besides the fact that you are a well-known deviant and therefore obviously mentally unstable."

"It's because of you I'm in this state!" shouted Jack.

"Now you really are sounding thoroughly unhinged."

They carried the boy up to rooms on the fifth floor and released him into a sort of luxurious captivity. He was provided with every comfort and given two male members of staff to wait on him exclusively. He had nothing to do all day but eat, sleep and think his own thoughts, the sort of thoughts he had been trying to avoid ever since he began to negotiate the intricacies of a dark and unfamiliar Vadrosnia Poule. Damask had been right about her friend's altered state of mind but, as previously mentioned, had not known the reason for his volt-face. What had brought about the change, as she found out eventually, was a piece of news he had received soon after his return, which had knocked him for six. On arriving in Drossi he had set out to visit his mother and, reaching her doorstep, had rung the bell. His intention was to resume an alliance that had been very important to him over its comparatively short existence. Due to his grandfather's possessiveness he had seen nothing of his one remaining parent during his early years. In his teens, when he was old enough to rebel against the harsh strictures by which his life was governed, they had made contact and quickly formed a bond of mutual dependency, finding that each fulfilled a need in the other. As Jack was nearly grown when they re-met the relationship was not that of mother and child but of equals, an intense friendship which became very close. Now he waited nervously, half looking forward to, half dreading, encountering the woman in his sightless state. Someone answered the door but it was not her.

"Lisa Godophin?" enquired Jack, (In recent years she had reverted to her maiden name).

"Don't live here no more," said a man's voice. "Perhaps you'd better enquire at Cemetery Island." He laughed unpleasantly.

"Where's my mother?" Jack asked his friends and associates. They were evasive but, through persistence, he dragged the truth out of them. It seemed no-one had seen fit, or maybe had had the nerve, to tell him that she was dead. The account he was given of his grandfather's actions was similar to the one Damask was regaled with later. The story went that soon after his disappearance the old man had received a ransom demand from the criminal who was occupying the shrine at Toymerle, but he insisted it was a fake. He produced witnesses to prove that his grandson had been seen enlisting on an outward-bound ship. Jack's mother had gone to her father-in-law and pleaded with him to pay the money. Her son, she said, would never have left on a voyage without bidding her farewell. Hiram turned a deaf ear and shut the door against her. Then, following the delivery of a small package at the shipping office, came the announcement of Jack's death. She had suffered from bouts of depression ever since losing her husband twenty-two years earlier and this proved to be the final straw. Howgego Associates paid for the funeral.

As he idled the hours away in his grandfather's mansion, the palace of Non-Pareille, Jack was forced to come to terms with his loss. It was a hard thing to countenance, as were also his memories of the time spent in the robbers' lair. Toymerle had been a place of both hell and heaven for the boy but it was its hellish aspect that was uppermost in his mind now. During his incarceration, there had been two or three very wicked men in the gang, bloated with rage and hate, and the rest took their colour from them, for they were strong and the others were weak. Under their tutelage the rank and file preyed upon and terrorised one another until a sort of hierarchy evolved with the prisoners at the bottom of the pile. It had been his misfortune to be a recipient of this persecution as the outlaws set about degrading their victims in both body and spirit in order to bring them down to the general level of iniquity to be found in that place. Only when you were one with them, indistinguishable, would they leave you alone. Some of the captives did actually go over to the other side and start ill-treating their fellows. The Cheetah found this amusing.

Now, marooned on the fifth floor of the palace, Jack ducked and dived trying to hide from the horrors that were imprinted on his brain. In the mad hedonistic whirl into which he had plunged on his return to Drossi he had managed to keep the bad thoughts at bay right up to the point when he collapsed from exhaustion in the early hours and won himself some welcome insensibility, but that was no longer possible. To act as a distraction he set about making imaginary journeys through the city with which he had been having a love affair ever since he was small. This however turned into another kind of nightmare because his recollections became overlaid by fantastical images which had little bearing on reality. Drossi metamorphosed into a gloomy and inimical limbo, home to hallucinations and fugitive apparitions. Through sleepless nights he flogged his tired brain while the place that had always smiled on him became full of shadows and menace. He began to imagine that once sight has been lost visual memories also start to fade and after a while you go blind in your mind as well. His mutilation was never so great a burden than at this time although often before and after he needed sight more.

So wrapped up was Jack in hating his grandfather that it came as quite a surprise to discover that the old man was nursing an equally burning resentment of him. The two servants delegated to serve him appeared to have been picked mainly for their warped sense of humour. Once they realised that it pleased the Chairman if life was not made too easy for his young captive the boy was fair game for any little spites or frustrations they needed to work out. One pastime they played inexhaustibly was a sport known as *moving-the-furniture*. If he left the main room even for a few minutes to wash or relieve himself, he was sure to find, when he returned, that things had been rearranged and a table or chair placed where he was likely to fall over it. This was hilarious it seemed and as time wore on they got very ingenious at setting booby traps. It was thoroughly unnerving to know that if he put out his hand to get his bearings he ran the risk of touching a naked flame or something equally ghastly but anonymous. The furniture game constantly destroyed his points of reference so that he became lost within an area of a few square feet. In the end he was so disoriented that he shrank from taking more than a pace or two across the room for fear of meeting a further hazard; he who, with Milly beside him, had come through miles of wilderness on his way from the shrine!

Being spied on and tormented week in week out in an atmosphere of malevolence eventually wore him down. Somebody, and a lot of the time he felt sure it was his grandfather, always seemed to be peering in at him from behind half-closed doors. He could not even cry into his pillow at night without the feeling of being watched. As a refuge from this persecution he turned his thoughts towards Dando, his saviour and provider at Toymerle who had turned the place into a temporary heaven, and the recollection of their time together comforted him and even helped him to avoid a complete breakdown. He knew that if they were ever to meet again he must find a way to get out of Hiram's palace. Also, if he wanted to dodge going round the bend in grim earnest, he had to discover some means of escape not just from the mansion but from Vadrosnia Poule in its entirety so that he could begin a fresh chapter and start to experience life in a new way.

Equinoctial gales blew in from the sea. The wind howled around the Poule and up and down the Grand Canal, shrieking in the rigging of ships and rattling windows. Jack loved the sound; it was a reminder that there was a larger world outside his shut-in restricted existence. With the storm at its height he would fling open the casement and lean out in order to feel the rain in his face and the taste of salt on his lips. But this was frowned upon: it was dangerous, the carpet was getting wet, it was making the whole house cold. He contested the issue with his minders for several days until they settled the matter by having the windows nailed shut.

As he became more determined to get away he began to ask himself how he was to leave the city behind without being detected. The land-gate was out of the question, far too public, and although there were footpaths along the east and west dykes there was no way he would be able to negotiate those without going astray.

No, Vadrosnians were not born with webbed feet for nothing; it would have to be by water and he thought he knew how. Off to the east of the delta the coast mutated from marshes to a sandy peninsular sparsely dotted with pine trees, and the currents had sculpted this ever-changing heathland promontory into a spit that grew steadily northwards year on year. It was a desolate place, useless and barren, and was normally given a wide berth because of the smell. Twice a day the city sluices were opened and the tide came up into Drossi and cleansed it. The filth and muck had to go somewhere and that was where it ended up - on that cape. It was not uninhabited; there were people who made a living off the rubbish and anything else that washed up such as boats gone adrift, the odd bale or barrel from the docks, even dead bodies. Jack could imagine nothing for it but to purloin some old dinghy, turn himself into a bit of flotsam and go and join them. First though he had to solve the problem of the nailed-up windows. Here he had a stroke of luck. The means by which water was supplied to the bathroom in his apartment had been discovered to be faulty and a workman was employed to install new piping. While the man was off buying some necessary component Jack managed to filch and hide a medium-sized pair of pliers that he discovered by touch. After that he had to decide on a suitable time to make his escape.

Each year the merchants and traders of Vadrosnia Poule vied with each other in the staging of sumptuous banquets at the Customs House. The one organised by the Howgego Corporation, which always took place in the spring, had the reputation of being the finest and most lavish. Preparations went on for weeks beforehand, the best chefs were employed and every member of staff was roped in and dressed up in order to make the occasion more magnificent. Jack discovered, by listening in to conversations between his two attendants, that they were going to be required to act as footmen on the night in question and that the dwelling on the Grand Canal would be virtually deserted. Moreover the tides would be right. (How did he know the times of the tides? In Drossi they were the breath of the city – everybody lived by them – you could not help but know). So that was it – that was when he would make his bid for freedom - but first of all he had to make sure he was not required to be present at the festivities himself. He did this by behaving thoroughly badly when his grandfather took him to an informal get-together of his business friends a week or two before the significant date. He enjoyed himself so much and was so rude to the poor innocent traders that in the stony silence that prevailed on the way home he wondered if he had overdone it and was heading straight for the loony-bin. But instead it meant bread and water for a few days and a withdrawal of privileges (what privileges?), which under the circumstances proved to be no great hardship.

The night of the feast arrived and everyone cleared off leaving Jack locked securely in his suit of rooms with only an old caretaker and his wife downstairs to keep an eye on the place. Now that the time had arrived he was shaking with fright at the thought of what he intended to do. The doors were fastened but that was not going to be his way out. He took the pliers he had purloined and a bronze figurine of none other than old Kymer himself, the river god, to show him the way, and set to work on the battens nailed across one of the windows. With much tugging and leverage, the noise of which brought his heart into his mouth, he got them off one by one until he could push the sash up and lean out into the cold evening air. Sounds of bells and horns came to his ears; the night was foggy – an added bonus. Five floors below, the waters of the Grand Canal lapped gently against the walls of the house – or did they? This was the fact of which he was not certain and was why he was having kittens. Some houses plunged straight down into the water while others had quite a wide paved area between the footings and the canal-side. As far as he could remember the walls of Non-Pareille Palace were washed by the tides twice a day but the more he thought about it the more unsure of this he became. He took the bust of the god and, reaching through the opening, dropped it out of the window. Nothing! Neither a clatter nor a splash. Why was that? He put on a jacket, buttoning it up to his chin, took off his boots in order to hang them round his neck and stepped onto the outside sill. Head first or feet first? Head first would bring a quick death if there was solid ground below, feet first and he might end up with a crippled body to add to his sightlessness. Heads it must be then. He stood there for so long and got so chilled that eventually he had to clamber back into the room to warm up and the first thing he did was trip over a chair and measure his length on the carpet. He lay cursing fluently, thinking at the same time - *is this what the rest of my life is going to be like – stumbling around rooms falling over furniture? Surely even smashing into the ground would be better?* He went back to the window, climbed outside and launched himself into space.

Once in mid-air his body took over. When it came to diving off high places he had always prided himself on being pretty good at it even by Drossi standards, and despite his blindness he found he had not lost the knack. Missing a hanging basket by a fraction of an inch, which was where the little statue had ended up, he entered the water, clean as a whistle, and with hardly a splash, just as he had intended. Coming to the surface he shook the wet out of his ears and listened. Mournful hoots and toots echoed up the canal in the queer distorted way you often get in a fog. Nearby he could hear the slap of wavelets on the roof of a culvert and sensed masonry looming above. He swam quietly along beneath the walls looking for the landing stage where he had been brought ashore after his capture, which in Vadrosnian mansions was usually let in under the dwelling so that guests could disembark almost straight into their host's living rooms. He found it without much trouble and was just starting to feel his way round the hulls of the various moored craft in order to pick out a good one when he was startled by the sound of a door slamming a couple of floors above. Deciding that discretion was the better part of valour he slipped the painter of the nearest boat and beat as hasty and silent a retreat with it as he could manage. When he got it well out into the canal and scrambled in over the side he discovered he could not have chosen a better. This was the heavy flat-bottomed old tub that the housekeeper used to ferry supplies, and was safe and as steady as a rock. Moreover it contained two pearls of great price: a tin of biscuits and a large rug. He wrapped himself in this last and was grateful for the warmth it provided as he sat there, not attempting to unship the oars or guide the boat in any way, but listening, with all his ears, for sounds from moorings and from the shore.

Fairly soon it became clear that, as he had anticipated, the tide was ebbing, meaning that he was drifting down the Grand Canal towards the Poule. Ships' bells, at first ahead came abreast and then passed to the rear. Voices, eerily loud across the water, shifted their positions as he revolved in the current but eventually died away. He kept himself alert ready to fend off if necessary, but nothing came near. He was slipping out of Drossi as sweetly and silently as in a dream, and she let him go without a murmur - *Goodbye old dame, nice to have known you*. One after another he must have left behind the storm sluices, the dock gates, the harbour defences, until the shore sounds withdrew to a great distance and a lonely little breeze with salt on its breath came and ruffled his hair. But it was not until much later that the boat woke to life beneath him and he knew he was out at sea.

Now he was cast away on the face of the waters, at the mercy of the currents wherever they chose to take him. He should have been terrified but instead felt extraordinarily happy. He ate a few biscuits and then curled up under a thwart as comfortably as was possible. How long he drifted he did not know; it may have been days and he may have been swept to and fro along the coast several times. After a while he remembered suffering from thirst until a storm of wind and rain brought too much water and he bailed with the biscuit tin for hours on end until he was exhausted. Looking back, this period seemed like an interval outside time, an epic odyssey across uncharted oceans towards new and undiscovered lands. In actual distance gained he may only have travelled a few miles, but to get to his destination he felt he had been to the uttermost ends of the earth. He had enough faith in his little craft to fall soundly asleep on several occasions and he woke from the last of these slumbers to the noise of waves running up a beach and the awareness that the barque was no longer in motion. His voyage had ended for good or ill and he had been brought safe to shore. By the pungent stink on the wind he guessed he had arrived at the refuse strewn headland.

It was when Foxy's money ran out - the reward money he had received in Toymerle for routing the bandits - that he began to feel that he and Tallis had outstayed their welcome at Praa. The citizens of the fishing village were already playing host to most of the inhabitants of Gweek and after some time they began dropping hints that they could do without the extra strain on their resources imposed by the two impecunious strangers. Normally Foxy would have moved on much sooner - he had at least one pressing reason for resuming his journey - but Tallis' condition acted as a stumbling-block. The Nablan had imagined that a few days rest would see his companion back in good health. As far as he understood it maladies usually lasted not more than a week or two at most. During their escape from the fire he and Tallis had been showered with flying embers and had received multiple burns to their exposed skin. These had soon healed, the scabs were shed and only pink scars remained to provide evidence of what had occurred. Foxy had expected the knight's inner hurts to mend just as quickly, but this proved not to be the case. When Tallis continued helpless and totally dependant on others he was left bemused and at a loss as to what he should do. While he tried to decide on a course of action he was occupied with the strange, unfamiliar task of nursing his companion. He had some help from the women of the village when they could spare the time but as for the rest Tallis was left to the mercy of his clumsy care. He found he had to deal with all the knight's most intimate needs. *Who would ha' thought when I set out,* he complained to himself, *that I would ha' ended up wipin' a grown man's arse. It be whooly beyond belief!*

Not long after their arrival at Praa he returned to Gweek, to the ruined house in which they had spent the night, in the hope of bringing to light Tallis' coin-stuffed purse which had been abandoned when the roof caved in. He rooted around amongst the debris, shifting charred lumps of wood and heaps of ash in his search, but found nothing. Either the heat had been so intense that the money had been destroyed or else someone had been there ahead of him. He realised now that it was by a sheer fluke that they had been overlooked during the raid. If the pirates had known of the cache of gold lying beside the knight's bed the travellers would have probably ended up with their throats cut. These extra funds, had he acquired them, would have tempted him to leave Tallis in the settlement, having paid in advance for his care, with the intention of returning for him later, but as it was this was not an option.

"Where be you intendin' to go from yere?" asked the head man one day in a meaningful way.

"My gaffer be still poorly an' I don' hev money for transport" retorted Foxy. "I reckon it be unlikely that we be a-gooin' anywhere soon."

"Well, I might be able to zee zomeway out for 'ee there. Come wi' me."

Foxy followed him to a large shed at the back of the village hall. The mayor attacked a huge pile of junk and odds and ends in the interior, eventually unearthing an ancient and very dirty bath-chair that looked as if it had fallen out of use at least fifty years earlier.

"Belonged to my granzer before 'e passed on. Bit of greaze on t'axels an' t'will be good as new."

Foxy examined this mechanical methuselah with incredulity.

"You c'n push him," explained the head man unnecessarily. "get along like a houze on fire, if that don' be too much of a touchy zubject at present."

Knowing that the Praa citizens would be only too glad to see the back of their two guests Foxy had no option but to accept the offer with as good a grace as he could muster, after which he set about putting the contraption back into working order. No amount of lubricant could rid the chair of a persistent squeak, the origin of which he was unable to determine. However he cleaned it up, acquired some cushions to make it more comfortable and introduced Tallis to his new conveyance.

"I be a-gooin' to make for the Delta City. When we get there we c'n maybe find an honest quack who'll set 'ee to rights. There be no mileage to be gained in stayin' here."

Tallis could neither stand nor walk but he had made some progress during the time Foxy had been looking after him. His swallowing reflex had returned to normal, although at first, to prevent regurgitation, all his food had had to be mashed or pulped. He could use his right arm fairly well and there was some restoration of movement in his left. For a long while his attempts at speech were no more than an incomprehensible gabble until one day he produced a clearly articulated word.

"Hil-da," he mouthed awkwardly.

Foxy looked up in surprise. "Hil-da," repeated Tallis.

"Gone," said Foxy. "She be gone along wi' that wicked scallawag who near had us burnt to a cinder back in the village. That duzzy rascal – I got a bone to pick wi' he."

His fury had settled into a slow-burning resentful anger that fed on itself. But by this time he had remembered his promise to Ann and consequently his mental threats were not quite so implacable. *I won't kill he – nor she. But I'll teach they a lesson they won't forget in a hurry!*

"North," was Tallis' next intelligible utterance, "north... Key..."

"When we get to 'Drosnia," Foxy reassured him, "an you be on your feet agin', you c'n get some trader type to take 'ee narth. You c'n get to near anywhere you want from the Delta City."

Through sunshine and showers, wind and rain, Foxy pushed the bath-chair along the coast road. At night he and Tallis took shelter in barns and outhouses, pigsties and stables, sometimes with permission, sometimes without. The food they took with them was soon exhausted and the Nablan, leaving Tallis undercover, set out to hunt and forage. But, since the collapse of the fishing industry and the advent of a virulent corn blight that had severely affected local agriculture, the area had become an impoverished region and other needy scavengers had already cleared the woods of edible plants and game. The two travellers grew progressively more hungry. The long hours spent being pushed over rough roads were taking their toll on Tallis' health. It was an ordeal that set back his already uncertain recovery and the lack of nourishment enfeebled him still further. Even Foxy, usually indifferent to others' weakness, could see that the knight was failing. He came to the conclusion that if he could not supply their needs by fair means he would have to do so by foul. All the same he was loath to steal from those in as bad or worse state than they themselves. But needs must when the devil drives and he was on the verge of casting his scruples aside when, looking along the coastline one morning from a high vantage point, he noticed, in the distance, a beam of sunlight picking out a substantial mansion standing atop a terraced hillside which ran down to the sea. Despite the totally different landscape in which it was set this castle-like structure had a certain familiarity about it - it reminded him of the Gleptish manor houses that he had known in Deep Hallow, the habitations of his hereditary foes. Here was somewhere he would not think twice about robbing.

Almost five miles farther on, the road took them past the estate's rear gates which were set into a substantial wall. Foxy examined the barrier critically, calculating the degree of difficulty to be met with in climbing into the grounds after dark. But then he caught sight of a hand written notice fixed to the right-hand side. His reading skills were pretty basic and he rarely had cause to use them, but in this case he was curious enough to take some time to puzzle out the wording:-

Under-gardener required -

Strong, young, willing.

Experience not essential – training given – adequate remuneration.

Accommodation available free to the successful candidate.

Apply at the side entrance.

There was an arrow pointing in the direction that interested parties should take. Foxy read the advert aloud to Tallis.

"What do 'ee think?" he asked. "How 'bout if we stop here for a bit. You need a rest – I need money – better 'n starvin' to death on the road."

Tallis seemed to be trying to say something but then gave up and shut his eyes as if resigning himself to fate. Foxy, assuming this to be an assent, set off in the direction of the arrow, prepared for the moment to humble his pride and take employment with those he normally regarded as his bitter enemies – the landed gentry.

As day followed day and then days turned into weeks Ann began to show signs of infirmity. There was an ethereal quality about her, and, while her belly swelled, the rest of her body became gaunt and wasted. It was not that Gammadion starved her, although he was not exactly generous when it came to sharing food, it was more that no human being can stand being constantly in the power of so great an enchantment as the wizard imposed on her without suffering the consequences. Eventually even he noticed the change and realised that if she was going to bring her baby to full term, something he greatly desired, he would have to remove the spell for at least part of the time. His solution was to maintain the magic when they were under observation, so that she appeared to others to be his willing helper, but to remove it when they were on their own and to use physical restraint instead. He found a pair of handcuffs in one of his bottomless pockets and employed these, when they stopped for the night, to shackle her to any convenient stationary object that happened to be nearby, and to chain her to his own wrist when they were on the move. Although set mentally free for a large part of the twenty four hours Ann showed no marked improvement when subjected to this new regime. She felt his control of her relax, but by this time her spirit had been entirely crushed, and she was bound by an overwhelming despair. Any hope of escape had virtually disappeared and in her worst moments she believed that from now on she would be merely the wizard's plaything to be used or abused according to his passing fancy.

Gammadion by contrast was in a cheerful mood. He knew that they would reach Vadrosnia Poule in the next few days and he was dwelling on the prophecy he had been vouchsafed which had assured him that he would make his fortune there. He conveniently banished to the back of his mind his suspicions as to its source.

"Wait 'till they see my act," he enthused, "they'll have witnessed nothing like it before in these parts, I warrant you. First I conjure a fetch from beyond the grave – a spectre you know – or at least that's what I tell 'em it is. They know no better the poor fools. It's impressive – scares the living daylights out of them. Then I invite them to ask the apparition questions about things that concern them – *Is my Billy happy in the after-life* and so on. Did they but know it their Billy has probably been reborn as a flea and has already been splatted. Meanwhile, my dear, as I perform, you will go among the crowd accepting contributions, the giving of which I tell them will bring luck and good fortune, whilst also selling amulets and phylacteries."

He stuck his hand into his robe and brought forth a collection of tawdry-looking trinkets intended for sale. Ann had already learnt that he could produce virtually anything he wished from his pockets as long as it was of no great value.

"You'll bring in the customers, I guarantee it – such a beautiful and fragile-looking assistant. I'll tell 'em you're my daughter and have been impregnated by an angel. We'll say that the baby when it's born will right all wrongs and be the saviour of the world. They're always looking for a saviour. The fools think that such a one will deliver them from their self-created predicaments and that he'll bring an end to war; that's always part of the bargain. You'd think that war was something imposed on them from without instead of being entirely of their own making."

So Gammadion bragged to his captive, enjoying the opportunity to indulge in self-aggrandisement, but when they reached Drossi he was in for a big disappointment. The audiences that gathered on the street corners where he chose to perform were thin and critical – he was even heckled. What he had not realised was that others had got there ahead of him. The redundant magic workers that Lord Trewithik of Pickwah had assembled to accompany his invasion of the Dark Island had been put ashore near the Delta City just over a month earlier when their skills were no longer required, with the result that Drossi was now overrun by a plethora of magicians all trying to make some money to compensate for the huge reward they had been promised but which had not materialised.

"The town's crawling with flimflam artists!" the wizard exclaimed in disgust, "we've got no chance against such hucksters. We'll try our luck further east and come back in the autumn when maybe people'll be more in the mood to appreciate a true miracle-worker when they see one. Come Hilda Hannah Arbericord, we're going to shake the dust of this place from our feet."

Wearily Ann fell into step behind him, her shoes dragging, her head bowed and one hand laid protectively over the bulge below her waistline. *Oh Dando my love*, she cried inwardly, *where are you? Why haven't you come looking for me? I don't deserve to be saved – but the baby – let not its existence be ended before it's begun.* In her misery her mind turned back more and more frequently to her soul-mate, and after that to Foxy, her protector and defender, and then to Tallis, the leader of their small band. Surely they would not all have abandoned her? Although Gammadion was adamant that her companions had not succumbed to the fire or been captured, because of their continuing absence she feared that every last one of them might have met with some calamitous mischance on the road as a result of the necromancer's maledictions. In addition, where Dando was concerned, she could not dwell on thoughts of their lovemaking without returning, inexorably, to its life-changing outcome - the unborn infant - whose survival had become, for her, the most important thing in this whole wide world of broken dreams.

The bones are tossed
And their pattern on landing
Reveals a strange outcome.

Chapter sixteen

"How dare you come between me and the chosen one! How dare you!"

"You are a fool wife to try and do away with him so soon. Originally I backed you up when you decided to neutralise him, but now I realise that if we let him live he will lead us to the place where the treasure is hidden. And why have you got your knife into the girl who's been accompanying him? I thought it was through her we were going to be able to trace his whereabouts."

"That's my business, husband, my business entirely."

Dando awoke from three weeks of fevered delirium and opened his eyes onto a totally strange and unfamiliar scene. He shut them again immediately and sought to escape back into the darkness from whence he had come. To find himself in the land of the living once more was a thoroughly unwelcome surprise and he was going to try to deny the fact for as long as possible. But if he could negate sight by keeping his eyes tight shut he could not prevent his other senses from operating. For a long spell he was aware of the wind howling - it was the season of gales – and the sound of rain beating against glass. Then, when the tempest passed, mild air brushed his cheek. A window had been opened and he listened to the distant noise of marching feet and shouted commands. The clang of ships' bells came to his ears and the tang of the sea to his nostrils. There were sea birds somewhere in the vicinity, he could identify them by their distinctive cries, first heard during his time on the Dark Island, and not far away footsteps were climbing and descending stairs accompanied by heavy breathing. People, mainly men, paid visits to his bedside and, despite all his efforts, words penetrated the mental barriers he threw up.

"...the Island..."

"...Trewithik...the Panther..."

"...incredible escape...the boss...bad luck..."

"...don't like it...come to no good..."

While the other gawpers, of whichever gender, came and went there was just one woman amongst them - an old woman it seemed - who remained near to him at all times. He felt the touch of her hands but tried to ignore what she was doing. Often as she approached he smelt the nauseating smell of food. A vessel was put to his lips and moisture trickled onto his skin. He compressed his mouth into a hard unforgiving line and the liquid ran across his face before wetting the pillow. "Just a sip, just a sip," said a cracked old voice hoarsely. "If you don't eat and drink, my lover, you won't survive. Let me give you just a spoonful of soup."

Dando turned his face to the wall and sank back into insensibility.

"Zo, this be the one they zaved," remarked another voice in vibrant peasant tones which contained the ring of authority. "How long zince they bring him yere?"

"The army bring 'im up as zoon as the ship dock, zir," replied someone in a more deferential manner, "as you instructed. Nance be caring for 'im but 'e don' be like to thrive zofar."

"Hey you!" Dando was poked in the ribs by some sharp object. "Who be 'ee? Where do 'ee hail from? How come 'ee be given to t' treez?"

Dando kept his eyes closed and stubbornly refused to acknowledge that anything was happening. If he tried hard enough he was positive he could bring to an end all this useless chatter that was attempting to tear him away from what he most desired. It just required an effort of will, a strong enough determination, to write finis to his existence for good and all.

"Zome of the boys be none too 'appy at him bein' yere," the second voice added timorously, "on account of it bein' ill-luck 'im 'avin' bin given like."

"If oy zay he should be yere, then yere is where 'e stay. Oy makes me own luck!" But a slight note of uncertainty accompanied this last statement.

"It's plain we can get no further with the present treatment, that's for sure," another authoritative voice opined sometime later in an entirely different accent. "We've got no option now but to operate. Will you be a pal and scrub up? You will? That's great!"

Something unspecific was done to Dando's hands which caused him to pass out and he fled, gratefully, back into a state of temporary non-cognisance far from the danger of having to face intolerable truths.

Time moved on. Since his return to consciousness Dando had refused all nourishment, and a grey curtain was beginning to descend between his awareness and the unknown environment surrounding him. But once again words penetrated the mists and interrupted his pursuit of death.

"Where did they fin' him – the Panther's mob I mean? 'E don' look like a local lad."

"They zay 'e were picked up in one o' they coastal raids. That time the head man lost 'is marbles an' decided to turn Gweek inside out for no good razon. They were on their uppers that lot – not even a couple of farthin's to rub together."

"Well then – they're no worse off – an' they moz' all ezcaped I year."

"Well – not all. But a lot did get away – down the zmugglers' tunnels. Gweek were a great place for that in the old days."

"Courze the houzen'll hev to be rebuilt."

The voices faded away and a door slammed. Dando heard feet descending stairs. For only the second time in that place he opened his eyes and saw an ancient dame coming across the room towards him. He presumed that this was the one in whose care he had been left and who had been trying to persuade him to eat.

"Gweek," he croaked in a dry rusty voice, "where is it?"

The gammer sped to his side. "Heaven be praised," she cried, "you've decided to return to us at last. I'll get some broth – it just needs heating up."

"No," demanded Dando impatiently, "Gweek – where is it – describe it!"

"Gweek? That's one of the last places the Panther raided. It's where the east road from the mountains comes down to the coast – a very poor little anchorage. Bide still, my sweet – don't go back to sleep. I'll have some food ready in a trice," and she hurried away as fast as her poor bent old legs would carry her.

Dando was left with his head spinning. The end of the road from the mountains! That must be where he, Tallis, Foxy and Ann had ended up – where the fire had taken hold! And most of the people had escaped they said! Suddenly Dando had a reason to go on living, a motive for putting his shattered body back together again. It seemed they might not be dead after all, his three companions, and if so it was imperative that he find them in order to atone for his wickedness. He would kneel before them and say "Please..." No, he could not beg for forgiveness – not after what he had done. He would throw himself on their mercy: his master, his beloved and the one whom he had learnt was his half brother. They would be free to exact whatever retribution they chose. Only then would he find peace.

No sooner had Dando embraced life once more, no sooner did he turn from the dark towards the light, than that very life reared up and dealt him a severe and admonitory blow. His body, which had been virtually insensible during his pursuit of oblivion, began once again to feel and, because of the condition it was in, to suffer. He became aware that his movements were severely restricted. His arms and legs were in plaster and attached to slings and hoists; he could neither sit up nor lie full length and was just as much a prisoner as if he had been chained to a wall in an underground dungeon. His muscles and joints - heaven knows what damage had been done to them - throbbed and ached, giving him not a moment's peace. His skin which had become dry during the high fever he had endured itched intolerably and there was no way he could scratch. His hands were bandaged and hurt like hell; his feet also hurt – everything hurt – and he had no choice but to put up with the pain for hours, days, weeks on end.

All he wanted now was to get moving, but instead he was totally helpless in the web of ropes and pulleys attached to his limbs with no means of breaking free.

"Excuse me," he called to the old woman whose back was, at that moment, towards him, "I'm afraid I don't know your name. I need to leave as soon as possible – I need all this stuff taken off me," indicating the plasters with which he was encased.

She swung round and came limping over.

"Well my sweetheart, I don't know yours either. You can call me Nance if you like, though I'm Squinancy to the lads. No respect for their elders and betters those boys. I was part of this place long before they were born."

"This place?" asked Dando.

"Don't you know where you are, my lover? You're in Pickwah fortress – up in the very topmost tower. You were given to me to bring back to life."

The truth was that when the fleet returned to its home port and the army piled onto the quay and began to make merry, a small detachment had wended its way through the town in order to ring the bell at the gates of the stronghold built on the summit of the rock and demand an interview with whoever was in charge. The Great Leader had not yet returned to his base, being still occupied down by the harbour with the results of their expedition, so, after a delay, the door beyond the gates swung slowly open to reveal a small bent figure, leaning on a stick.

"Look what we've brought you, you old hag," cried the captain of the band, and the enormous soldier known as Krull, head and shoulders above the rest of the men, stepped forward with an inert body in his arms. This he laid carefully down on the threshold, while old Squinancy, for it was she of course, stared for a moment, then hobbled greedily forward. She would have picked Dando up there and then if she had had the strength. Instead she called for assistance from a couple of other castle retainers and the boy was taken inside. No one really knew why Squinancy was one of the few women permitted to live permanently within the fortress and allowed many liberties, when apparently more worthy citizens were excluded. Her presence had been established through custom over a long period and was no longer questioned. Some said that once she had been a great beauty, a mistress to the Old Prince's father, and it was whispered that she may have been the Prince's real mother, the other woman, his father's wife, having proved barren. Alternatively there was a story going round that she was a veritable witch and that her spells kept the place safe. Perhaps both tales were true. Whatever the facts of the case she was now subjected to a barrage of anxious questions from her charge concerning his situation.

"How long have I been here? Who put these things on me? How far is Gweek along the coast? I need to leave immediately."

Squinancy laid a pitying hand on his shoulder.

"My poor baby – don't you realise the shape you're in? You're in no fit state to go anywhere. Not for a long time yet."

"But I m-must," replied Dando almost frantically, "I c-can't stay here. I need to find my friends."

"If your friends are genuine enough to be concerned they'd say the same as me. They'd tell you to bide still until the healing has had time to take effect. At least you've decided to stop starving yourself to death – that's a start."

"But who did all this? Who put me in plaster? It wasn't you was it?"

"That was the Armornian – comes from across the water. He's a doctor of sorts. Said we had to move fast if we were to get you back into any kind of working order."

"Well, can I speak to him?"

"He'll be coming on his rounds in the morning but he'll tell you just the same as I have."

As it got light Dando surfaced from a fitful sleep to find a large person standing just inside the door, leaning against the wall with his hands in his pockets, examining him with interest.

"Howdy," remarked this individual, " Raymond Spoon at your service. You want to ask a question?"

"Are you a doctor?" enquired Dando.

"Surgeon. Bit of an oversubscribed profession where I come from. Decided to take a powder - didn't like what they were asking me to do. Went on my travels and crossed over the Middle Sea. The big man here offered to employ me to treat his troops. Lots of minor wounds even when they're just training. Needed funds. Been here ever since."

This stranger was well over six feet tall, large limbed and fleshy. There was a glossy sheen about him, a sleekness, like that of a well-fed cat, that suggested he had never know a day's privation in his life. The eyes in the smooth unlined boyish face sparkled with intelligence. Was he a typical example of someone from across the Tethys Dando wondered?

"I need to leave here," he said emphatically to the man, "as soon as it's possible to do so. When can I get out of these casts? I must be gone in the next few days."

The other stretched, knuckled his eyes and yawned.

"Not getting enough sleep," he said. Then he laughed somewhat bitterly. "I guess you're joking, ain't that right? You've been through the wringer, boy. You were strung up – on the rack – for probably more than twelve hours so they tell me – barbaric – utter savagery. It's not something you're going to recover from overnight. We've had you in plaster for two and a half weeks. Fractures usually take about six weeks – the other injuries probably much longer. All the organs of your body have been affected. Do too much too soon and you'll prejudice your recovery; you could even end your life."

Dando stared at him in complete dismay. He was struck dumb and at a loss. Raymond smiled and patted him on the head.

"Patience fella, patience. Are you a reader? I'll find you some books."

The next day he returned with some rather tattered-looking volumes in soft covers.

"I brought these with me," he said somewhat shame-faced. "They're by my favourite author – Ertinger Cumberland. They're a sort of cross between fantasy and sci-fi I reckon - an acquired taste."

"Sci-fi?" enquired Dando.

"Science fiction. They're easy to read – all of 'em translated into in the common tongue. This one's set on a planet where the land's not all in one place – different to ours. It's about this guy called Chris who sails three ships across a vast ocean and discovers another country called the New World. *New World* – that's the book's title. And this one takes place in the future and is about a guy named Neil who travels to the moon and back – gee wiz, does this fella have an imagination! This one tells the tale of a little kingdom that conquers a huge empire and then has to give it all back, and this one's about a prophet who starts a religion, gets put to death and becomes a god. Here – take 'em – enjoy. I'll prop them up here – Nancy can turn the pages if your hands ain't up to it. That reminds me – I'm going to have to have a word about your hands – nothing too terrible, but you cain't loose circulation for so long without some damage being done."

Dando was acutely embarrassed at being unable to do anything for himself and having to rely on Squinancy for every intimate necessity.

"I'm awfully sorry to give you all this trouble," he apologised, blushing furiously.

"There, there my sweeting – I've brought up seven children, it's second nature to me."

He realised he was wearing nothing under the bedsheet.

"Where are my clothes?" he asked the old woman.

"Clothes?" she repeated. "My lover, when they gave you to me you were mother naked, and none the worse for that. I'll find you something when you finally get back on your feet."

"No boots? No purse?"

She laughed. "Boots! Purse! They'd be the first to go. No, the only things you were wearing when I set eyes on you were that ring on your finger which they probably thought not worth bothering with and that raggedy bit of hair round your throat."

The blood fled from Dando's face. He tried to put his hand to his neck but discovered that that was impossible.

"Can you show me?" he asked.

"I'll have to cut it."

"No, don't cut it."

He relapsed into silence, lying flat on his back, while his eyes welled up and two tears oozed slowly out of the corners and ran down into his ears.

About a week later the physician unwrapped most of the bandages from Dando's extremities, leaving the casts in place.

"You must realise," he said, "that we've saved as much as we could. Might have been a lot worse. You'll be able to manage."

When he was on his own Dando examined the ruin of his hands with melancholy interest and suddenly became aware of what he was seeing. A host of early recollections crowded his mind. Still too small to peer over the edge of the kitchen table he had gone running into the great, warm, sweet-smelling cookhouse bellowing *Show!* in his childish treble, drunk with the unexpected power he had found it was his privilege to wield. Also, at about the same age, on the occasions he played with a group of nibbler children, if the game went against him, if an unexpected buffet took him unawares, *Show!* was his retaliation. And he remembered his father, when some unfortunate groom of the same race had forgotten an important piece of equipment or failed to round up the pack to his satisfaction, yelling the word down from his vantage point on the back of the hunter *Warrior*, while the man, expecting the blow or cuff that was bound to follow, cringed forward, arms held out and face upturned. Two fingers - the middle and index - lost from his right hand, one – the little one – lost from the left. These were nibbler hands now - strange, unnatural, incomplete. In the future he would no longer merit the epithet *Glept* if it was hurled as a curse against him. In the quiet of the empty room he stretched his hands out as far as he was able in the *Show* gesture of submission, which in this context could be taken as an appeal for clemency or a reaching for human contact. Then slowly he relaxed as much as he was allowed by the restrictive hoists and, accepted his situation, breathing out a long weary sigh. For the time being he was content – he closed his eyes.

The great day for the removal of the casts, and all the paraphernalia associated with them, came at last. Dr Raymond Spoon and another man set to work chipping and sawing until they were able to discard the plaster that had been moulded to Dando's limbs.

"Don't try and move yet," he was instructed, "wait until we've finished."

Dando was only too happy to oblige. The work went forward cheerfully enough until they began on his lower body. Then as they pulled the hollow die away from his left leg he heard the medic give vent to what sounded like a suppressed expletive. The man and his assistant exchanged significant glances across the bed.

"Have you got any numbness in this foot?" Raymond asked, putting his hand on the boy's ankle.

"A bit," replied Dando with a grimace. He squinted down his body and noticed that his left shin seemed to be of a darker colour than his right.

"We'll give it a few days, some exercise might get things moving," said the surgeon. "Strange," he added to the other man under his breath, "I made sure that the blood supply was good, otherwise I would never have opted for immobilisation."

"Ok, lets get started," he went on, addressing himself to Dando as if attempting to be upbeat. "We'll check out whether your muscles are working. Reach up and clasp my hand."

Dando went to stretch upwards, yelped and shrunk back into stillness.

"Try the other one."

The same thing happened.

"Swing yourself round till you're sitting on the edge of the bed." Dando gritted his teeth and with a stifled groan did as he was bidden.

"Good, good – you've still got strength in your arms."

"But it hurts."

"It's bound to hurt a bit - at first."

"It's more than just a bit!"

"Look – let me explain – you're a bright guy, you should be able to understand. For a normal healthy person pain acts as a warning, not to put their finger into the pretty flame, not to draw the sharp edge of a knife across their hand. But for you pain is a barrier which you've got to work your way through, you've got to try and ignore it and carry on as if it wasn't there. For the moment pain is your default setting."

"What does that mean?"

"It's an expression we use when talking about machines – it means that that's what's normal for you."

"But I'm not a machine."

"No – but some people think the human body is."

"You say I've got to expect to be in pain?"

"For now – yes - despite the fact that I c'n provide some locally sourced analgesics. What the future holds I couldn't say, but things will probably improve. Now see if you can stand up."

Dando took a deep breath, steeled himself and made an attempt to rise from the bed. He teetered upright for a moment until his legs gave way and he would have fallen flat on his face had not the two men caught him and helped him to lie down again.

"That's enough for today," said Raymond encouragingly. "No use trying to run before you can walk. I'll come back tomorrow."

"But I can't even stand!" cried Dando despairingly.

"Patience, my man, patience."

That night, Dando's muscles, roused from their long period of inertia, refused to go back to sleep but kept contracting in vicious contorting spasms that seemed to be passed from one part of his body to another. He lay and endured, moaning, "Oh, oh, oh!" under his breath as quietly as possible to avoid waking Squinancy who slept close by. In the morning she found him hollowed-eyed and ashen.

"Why didn't you call me?"

"There's nothing you could have done."

"Let me be the judge of that."

"I'm sorry, fella, there's no easy way to say this." The Armornian had come to a difficult decision and his normal bouncy manner was in abeyance. "That foot will have to come off."

"Off?" repeated Dando in a small voice.

"Yes – the lower half of your left leg below the knee is gangrenous. I've done all I could but I'm afraid it was too little too late. If we want to save the rest we'll have to operate straight away."

What's the good of a leg without a foot? thought Dando, but held his peace.

"If it's OK with you we'll set a date for tomorrow morning."

At first light the soldier Krull appeared and carried Dando to the surgeon's quarters where a room had been prepared. The medic's assistant and Squinancy were in attendance. Raymond smiled down on him where he lay on the operating table.

"This won't take long. I'm afraid the anaesthesia is going to be rather unconventional. At home I could have put you out with a single jab, but here the only thing available is this snake-oil," he held up a bottle, "which to our eternal shame we export to the Dark Continent. Beads for the natives – something to get them hooked so they'll continue trading. However it seems to work remarkably well as a pain-killer, although it's extremely addictive so don't make a habit of this, will you!" He laughed mirthlessly.

Dando held out his hand and took the bottle. *DR GOOD'S SUPER-STRENGTH ELIXIR,* he read on one side, *highly effective against deep wounds and amputations.* Wordlessly he gave it to Squinancy who poured some of the golden liquid into a tumbler and held it to his lips. In only a matter of minutes after swallowing, his perception was radically altered. The ordinary domestic ceiling above him seemed to have retreated to a great distance, he got the feeling he had shrunk in size, everything around him appeared enormous and the light from the huge windows, which he had not even noticed before, was shot with all the colours of the rainbow. He was vaguely aware of something being put in his mouth and of the doctor beginning to operate. There was pain, yes, terrible pain, but it did not feel as if it belonged to him; he had been lifted high above it and for a period walked in elysian fields on two good legs while his omnipresent guilt shrank to the size of a love-bite on the side of an elephant. He must have briefly lost consciousness for, when he recovered, Squinancy was smoothing his brow, Raymond was telling him it was all over and displaying the imprint of teeth-marks on a leather strap which had been almost bitten through.

"You've certainly got a strong jaw on you kid!"

Once more Dando was bedridden in a helplessly invalid state, with just the solace of the doctor's books to curb his impatience. In his dependency he began to appreciate the small comforts Squinancy provided - a hot water bottle tucked into his side; clean sheets; a warm moist cloth against the skin – but it was only occasionally he was afforded what he most desired – a night of oblivion. Sometimes, however, it would come to him, the sweetest of sleeps - he was young after all - and in that sleep the marks of attrition that were beginning to appear on his face looked like nothing more than the traces left by a tired child's too-eager play.

The Great Leader, otherwise Jory Trewithik, was in the process of giving one of his rabble-rousing speeches on the steps of Pickwah's town hall, surrounded by his cohorts.

"The time ha' come!" he yelled. "The Master-of-Winds ha' granted us great favours! He stretched forth his han' and they were conquered! In the heart o' darkness he sent forth his ztorm an' the tabernacles o' our enemies were laid low! He's callin' for us to take the next step and follow him abroad on a great adventure! We'll bring peace and justice to these troubled lan's. We'll slay the idolaters and their issue will flee away! We'll lay waste their fields, their crops will wither an' the place of their habitations will know them no more. Wi' God on our side no man c'n stan' agin' us. Our reward will be great an' their ill-gotten gains will come into our han's. We'll take back what be rightfully ourz!"

A huge cheer greeted these words but as it died a lone voice shouted, "If God be wi' us then how come the deaths?" Another voice chipped in, "Three gone in the las' week – there be misfortune in the town," and a third added, "An' zurely we know forwhy!"

The Leader had a word with a couple of his henchmen and pointed in the direction of the speakers. The minders began pushing their way through the throng towards the guilty parties while he turned back to the crowd.

"There be no ill luck," he shouted, "there ha' been deaths but it weren't that. A few of the lads got too enthusiastic an' a friendly wrestling match turned into a fight in grim earnest. But that just shows what our boys are made of. Their folks will be comp'nsated when we c'n find 'em."

There was an uneasy murmur. Anyone level-headed enough to look at things dispassionately would have realised that there had been no more fatalities among the troops – a large number of men living in close contact with one another - than would normally have been expected, but the army was in a state of keyed-up excitement and any unusual events: a duel in which a popular officer had been injured; a walk-out by the shipwrights; the birth of a deformed baby among the camp followers, were taken as bad omens and someone was sought on whom to heap the blame. Trewithik's men laid hands on one of the hecklers and started to drag him off but, resisting all the way, the man managed to get in a last word.

"You can't cheat the treez! If they c'n walk who's to say they won't pick themselves up from the groun' an' go on the war path! They'll come for their own, you mark my words!"

"You're doing well, kiddo," said Dr Spoon enthusiastically. "Things are on the up and up. Carry on at this rate and your stump will be ready to be fitted with a prosthesis in about six months time."

"Six months!" cried Dando appalled.

"Of course we can get you moving far sooner than that, but we need crutches. Do you think..." turning to Squinancy, "Is it possible...?"

"Leave that to me," said the old woman. "There's a carpenter down in the town who owes me a favour."

"You'll have to get him to come and measure the boy."

The crutches when they finally arrived were works of art: varnished oak wood, with brass ferules on the bottom and green padded-leather armpit supports at the top. Dando was anxious to get started straight away, but to his utter frustration his muscles would not obey him and his joints let him down. Day after day he struggled, ignoring the agony, but with little sign of improvement.

"You need some means of exercising your limbs that doesn't involve load-bearing," said Raymond frowning. Then his face brightened. "Ah!" he exclaimed, "I know just what we'll do."

The next morning Krull was once more co-opted to transport the invalid. He picked Dando up as effortlessly as if he were lifting a baby and carried him through the narrow streets towards the sea, accompanied by the surgeon. A few hundred yards to the right of the quays, along a well-made road, they came upon a large water-filled rocky basin divided from the ocean by a narrow breakwater and bordered on the shore side by changing rooms and other leisure facilities, mainly deserted. From the surface of the gently rippling mere rose curls of steam.

"This is one of the hot springs," said Raymond. "From what I've been told I believe they were all the rage with the wealthy from the towns of the Sisters' League up to about a year ago. Then Pickwah closed its borders and turned them over to the army. They're salt. The tide flows over into the pools twice a day and mingles with what comes up from underground. They're supposed to have healing properties if you immerse yourself for long enough."

"But I can't swim," said Dando.

"Can't you? Well it won't take you long to learn. This is just the sort of exercise you need."

At a nod from the doctor Krull leaned out over the pool and, without any preliminaries, dropped Dando into deep water. The boy yelled with fright as he fell, following which he disappeared into the depths. Coming up he thrashed for a moment in terror and disappeared once more. Krull stripped off his clothes, reached upwards, allowing his huge body to tip forward and entered the water like a plunging whale. When he surfaced he had Dando in his arms. Raymond shouted instructions from the rocks above.

"Turn over on your back! Stop freaking out! Put your head back, arms out to the sides. There you see, you're floating – the water's holding you up."

Dando coughed and spluttered, his heart rate slowed, the water, hotter than blood heat, was indeed supporting him and the shock of his submersion seemed to have temporarily driven all thought of aches and pains away.

"Turn over onto your front - kick your legs! - paddle with your hands! That's right – now you're swimming." But Dando's nose had gone under the surface, he breathed water into his lungs and reverted to panic mode.

"Ok, we'll have another session tomorrow – bring him out Krull."

Four times now Krull had acted as Dando's beast of burden, carrying him on instruction to various locations, but so far they had not exchanged a word. The boy felt it was high time they established some form of communication.

"This is a bit of an imposition," he apologised as he was taken back to the fortress, "asking you to cart me around like this."

"Nein, nein," replied the big man.

"You don't mind?"

"Nein, nein."

"Am I taking you away from more important duties?"

"Nein, nein."

"And you'll come again tomorrow?"

"Ya, ya."

And when they had nearly reached the door:-

"Do you have a family here?"

"Nein, nein."

"Where do you come from?"

The giant shook his head but forbore to speak.

"Do you like being in the army?"

"Ya."

"Well anyway, I'm very grateful."

Krull nodded and there was a slight softening of his granite features that might have been his version of a smile.

If Dando did not exactly take to swimming like a duck to water he nevertheless soon lost his fear and made rapid gains. He always had the springs to himself. If there were any soldiers in the pool they quickly returned to dry land and made themselves scarce when they noticed his approach. He began to appreciate the benefits of submerging himself in the warm bath. The kindly element cradled him on its bosom and for a few precious minutes tricked his idiot body into thinking it was hale and hearty. This was far from the case, but things were improving. He began to find, even when not in the water, that he could stand on his one remaining foot and achieve a few tentative hops with the aid of the crutches. It was a red letter day when he actually managed to descend the flight of stairs outside his room in the fortress and so was no longer a prisoner on the top floor of the castle. Raymond was pleased with his progress but was still talking of recovery in terms of months if not longer.

"I must leave," Dando told Squinancy, expecting opposition. He was taken aback when she actually agreed with him.

"The army doesn't like you being here. They think your presence is bringing them bad luck. That upstart is a credulous man. If there are any more setbacks he may come round to their way of thinking and then I'm afraid of what he might do. Where do you want to go, my lover?"

Dando explained about Gweek and what had taken place there.

"I must search for my friends. Perhaps if I ask in the villages round about someone will know what's happened to them. Then once I find out I'll go looking, however long it takes."

"All right – I'll help you. But first I'd like you to talk to a very wise man I know who lives locally. There's something about you my dear; I've had this strange intuition ever since you came to me. They say I'm a witch. Well, perhaps any woman who's lived as long as I have gets a sense for things that are hidden. I think this man, Trewithik's seer, may be able to tell you something you ought to know. I'll make an appointment for you."

The next day she came back with news.

"He'll meet you tomorrow but first he wants details of where and when you were born."

"Deep Hallow – the Lap of the Mother they called it once - in my father's castle. I was born in the Year of the Cat, not the last one, the one before – on the twenty-fifth day of the ninth month – I'm seventeen."

"Time?" asked Squinancy.

"Er – just before midnight I think."

Dando understood that this soothsayer was some kind of astrologer, a species which he had been taught to distrust from the cradle. He was extremely sceptical about the forthcoming consultation but was prepared to go along with it purely to please Squinancy because of all she had done for him. When he found his way to the correct door and knocked he discovered that the seer in question was a bony dark-skinned man with a scalp covered in tiny blond plaits. His cheeks were tattooed with some sort of totemic symbols and he wore a loose gown of rusty red. He was surrounded by the tools of his trade: alembics, crucibles, glass retorts and a working model of the solar system. The air was heavily and exotically scented.

"Come," he was ordered, "sit there. Hold my hands."

Dando's pale damaged hands rested for a long time in the man's lean brown ones while the prognosticator gazed keenly into his face.

"Yes," he said at last, "I cast the bones earlier but now I understand."

"Understand what?" said Dando.

"The Great Ones are at loggerheads because of you - and you have other enemies, one of whom will do anything to stop you. Yet the storm was created purely to bring about a rescue."

"Sorry?" said Dando. This made no sense at all.

"No-one has told you? Well, here is the plain truth. You are a child of destiny; such a one is born every millennium or so – they step down onto a path already laid."

Dando could not restrain a slight snort of disbelief.

"Maybe you've never heard the call. Maybe someone has blocked your ears - one of the immortals perhaps - but it is a fact nevertheless."

Dando gripped his crutches and made as if to rise. "I'm sorry, I must be going. I'm afraid I've wasted your time."

"There was a priest, a brother sorcerer. He saw a glimmer of the truth. He sacrificed himself for you."

Dando froze - sat back down again.

"You've made a vow to a man to act as his servant, but he is deluded – the quest for the all-powerful Talisman is yours, not his, and the end will be utterly at odds with what he believes should happen."

"You know about my friends?" cried Dando passionately "Are they alive?"

"Yes. But the woman..." he shook his head, "she is in the power of your enemy."

"I must find them."

"Your task is to go north towards the place where the Object is hidden – north - *Across-the-Brook*. That is your duty – your duty to the world."

"But I must find them first."

"I cannot help you there."

Dando, Squinancy and Krull descended the main street of Pickwah Town towards the harbour, Dando not in Krull's arms any more but walking independently with the aid of the crutches, things having progressed thus far in recent days. This was supposed to look like a normal swimming expedition but it was hard to disguise the fact that Dando was wearing a new outfit - clothes suitable for a journey - and that Krull was carrying a backpack much too small for his massive shoulders. As soon as it had been decided that Dando should leave, Squinancy had been in a fervour to see him gone.

"The army, the Axemen as they call themselves, are starting out on their grand campaign of conquest the week after next. Osh is to be their first target I believe. The fleet will keep pace with the troops as they march along the coastal highway and invade from the sea as they launch attacks from the land. Everything is prepared; the men are ready and eager to go; any delay now would be fatal to their esprit-de-corps and the eventual outcome of the expedition. But you, my love, must leave even sooner. I've booked you a passage on a cargo ship that operates between here and the Delta City. The captain has agreed to put you ashore at Gweek then wait two days for your return. That should give you time enough to enquire after the fate of your companions. Then you must go on to Vadrosnia Poule and, with the money I'm going to give you, employ someone to act on whatever information you've gathered and hopefully run your friends to earth. When you find them get them and yourself well inland or alternatively over there," pointing out to sea. "Yes, over there would be best. This coastline won't be a healthy place for the next few months."

"I must tell Raymond what's happening."

"No, by no means. He'll try and stop you. He's quite capable of informing Trewithik. He doesn't understand the danger."

"Well, I must write to him then."

Awkwardly, with his crippled right hand, Dando tried to put his gratitude down on paper but was thoroughly dissatisfied with the result.

"Tell him... oh, I don't know... I owe him everything I spose... I owe him my life."

"He's a doctor – he's just been doing his job."

"But what about you? Won't you be in danger?"

"Don't worry about me, my lover, nobody will believe I would want you gone."

"And how about Krull?"

"He'll be all right; he won't be held responsible. The majority don't even consider that he's got any brain worth speaking of."

Squinancy handed him a small bottle of golden liquid.

"Something to see you through the bad nights my dear." The old woman had gotten into the habit of offering Dando a dose of Doctor Good's on the frequent occasions when he suffered from night cramps, her heart ruling her head in pity for his misery.

"Don't attempt to do too much at first," she added, "remember you still need rest – you mustn't overtax yourself."

When they reached the water's edge they came upon a modestly sized carrack lying against the outermost quay, the concentrated activity all around indicating that she was about to set sail that very day. A tanned stocky sailor in working clothes but wearing a gold-braided cap came down the gangplank and bowed ingratiatingly to Squinancy.

"This is the master of the Cormorant, bound for the Delta and all points east," she told Dando, meanwhile handing the man a money bag, at which he touched the peak of his cap deferentially and indicated that the boy could go aboard. Dando's heart sank – it was time to part and he hated goodbyes. He could think of nothing to say. Instead he stooped and kissed the old woman on the forehead. She put up a hand and touched his cheek.

"Well my darling, when you came I had a feeling you wouldn't be with me for long. I'll miss you more than words can say. Perhaps we'll meet again after all this is over. That is if I last."

Dando nodded and smiled wretchedly.

"I hope so," he said, giving her another peck before turning and hurrying, as fast as he was able, onto the ship. Squinancy and Krull remained in situ, with the intention of waiting on the quayside until they saw the Cormorant put to sea.

It was late afternoon by the time the ropes were cast off and the vessel moved away from the quay. The strip of water between ship and shore rapidly widened and in a matter of minutes she was well out to sea. Looking back from his position on board Dando realised that the small figure of Squinancy had melted into the background, but Krull, standing with raised arm, was still distinguishable, motionless as a monolithic statue, and could easily have been mistaken for a colossus placed on the outermost limits of the harbour to greet ships or speed them on their way.

The Cormorant lay a course to the east, following the coastline, but only an hour or so later turned in, once more, towards the shore. She anchored off an isolated beach below a group of cottages, all apparently deserted. A boat was lowered. Dando watched with interest, presuming this was a trading stop, but he was in for a shock. The captain ambled casually along the deck to where he stood.

"'Ere's where you get orf, sonny," he said.

"What do you mean? This isn't Gweek," said Dando.

"No – but I ain't 'avin no Jonah aboard my ship longer 'n I c'n 'elp," (Jonah Benallack was the name of a sailor, infamous in those parts, who had survived five wrecks in which all his shipmates had drowned).

"You want me to disembark?"

"That's the idea."

"But you took her money!" cried Dando with great indignation. "It's cheating!"

"You might call it that, but, if she hears about this, she won't dare incriminate me for fear of incriminating herself." The man gave a grin, revealing that he had lost most of his front teeth.

"You can't make me leave!"

"Oh, can't I?!" and, taking the boy by surprise, he neatly whipped one of Dando's crutches out from under his arm and threw it down to the crewman waiting in the dingy below. Dando grabbed hold of the rail, at the same time realising that three burly matelots were standing behind their captain, one of them carrying his pack.

"Come on sonny, get on the ladder. Here's your things and some cash – I'm not really trying to rob you."

"Yes you are!" replied Dando hotly, despite having no choice but to obey.

The seaman who rowed the boat ashore and helped Dando out onto the cobbled ramp which was all this lonely place could boast by way of a jetty seemed to have some sympathy for his plight.

"Coast road's up thataway – not very far. Turn right an' you'll soon be back in Pickwah town. Should be able to do it in a day or two." He glanced doubtfully at the gap between the boy's left knee and the ground. Dando nodded grimly and performed an awkward balancing act as he slipped his arms into the straps of his rucksack. Then he settled the crutches in place and started up the steep incline from the beach.

The man was right, the bypass was no distance, although it still took him the best part of an hour to reach it. Once having gained the thoroughfare he looked both ways, on the face of it presented with a hard decision. Should he go right towards Pickwah or left towards where he believed Gweek and the Delta City lay? If truth be told he had already made up his mind. He knew that if he made for the place he had quitted only a few hours earlier he could be walking straight into the arms of an army to whom he was persona-non-grata and who considered him a jinx. On the other hand if he went in the opposite direction each difficult step he took on his crutches and one remaining foot might bring him nearer to his heart's desire: a chance to rendezvous with the three people he had betrayed and to whom he longed to make reparation. As far as he was concerned there was no contest - left it must be. He faced away from the setting sun and, turning east, followed his shadow up the road.

A solitary vagrant
With no refuge behind or before,
Just the lonesome road beneath.

Chapter seventeen

The evening was already far advanced by the time Dando set off in the direction of an approaching darkness, swinging himself forward between the two crutches and resolutely ignoring his protesting limbs. The highway, quite empty of other travellers, stretched into the distance in featureless monotony like a pale undulating ribbon with nothing along its length by which to gage his progress apart from the occasional run-down cottage set among small stony fields with a sad air of neglect about them. His stomach was telling him it was well past his normal mealtime and he was already beginning to wonder where he was going to spend the night. It was not long since he had slept out in the open in the harshest of conditions but then he had had the other travellers around him. The prospect of bedding down al fresco totally on his own was an entirely novel proposition.

After a while he began to creep past barns and outbuildings surrounding a substantial farmhouse which, although apparently uncared-for and somewhat dilapidated, appeared to be occupied. Despite accusing the Cormorant's captain of robbing him he was still fairly comfortably off thanks to Squinancy's generosity, the money hidden in a belt at his waist. If he passed by this possible refuge he might not find another inhabited dwelling before nightfall. He decided to turn aside and try his luck. His nose caught a promising smell of cooking as he approached the building. He knocked and waited. Eventually a tiny woman opened the door and stood on the threshold peering up at him.

"I'm trying to find somewhere to stay," said Dando diffidently. "There doesn't seem to be an inn along this stretch of the road. Could you put me up? Perhaps we might come to some arrangement," patting his belt, "I'm not looking for charity."

The woman seemed to have been struck dumb. She gazed at him in horrified fascination, not saying a word, until he began to ask himself if she was wandering in her wits.

"If not," he continued, "I would be very grateful if you could give me a meal – sell me a meal," he clarified hastily.

The little woman was abruptly swept aside and a big man stood in the doorway gazing at the boy with cold hostility.

"No spare beds," he grunted, gesturing behind him. Dando became aware of several other men further back in the extensive interior staring challengingly in his direction, all with a strong family resemblance. Could the tiny silent female possibly be the matriarch of this enormous brood he wondered? He was about to explain that he would not mind sleeping on the floor or in a barn if necessary when he suddenly realised that he did not trust these people. There was something off-putting, even threatening about them which made him regret ever having advertised his presence.

"Sorry to have troubled you," he said, "I'll try further along. Goodbye," and limped quickly away.

As expected he came across no hostelries or even private houses before dusk began to encroach upon the land. While there was still enough light to see by he explored the margins of the road and discovered a pleasant sheltered dell where he felt he could be comfortable enough wrapped up in the warm cloak Squinancy had thoughtfully provided. The night looked as if it was going to be clear and already the first stars were creeping into the sky. With a stab of sadness he remembered other nights when he and Ann had lain in each other's arms gazing up at the heavens in wonder. He composed himself for rest trying to forget the fact that he was going to bed supperless. After taking a sip from the bottle Squinancy had provided he soon fell asleep – he was very tired.

An instinct for self-preservation tore him back into consciousness at some unknown hour after midnight before there had been any noise or physical contact to wake him. In an instant he became aware of several dark figures close by and knew immediately that he was in trouble – deep, deep trouble. As they descended on him he grabbed a crutch and swung it above his head, hitting one of the intruders on the brow. That was the first and last chance he got to defend himself. The crutch was wrenched from his grasp and stamped upon, after which he was entirely at the robbers' mercy. Two men held him down while others went through his pockets. Then they rolled him over, tugged his cloak out from under him, stripped him of his jacket and pullover and unbuckled the money-belt, the stealing of which was obviously their main aim. Notes were extracted (paper money was used among the towns of the Seven Sisters) and the empty belt thrown contemptuously back across his body. Then, pulling off his single boot which they immediately discarded as being useless on its own, they administered a sharp kick to the ribs and melted into the night taking his pack along with them. All this was accomplished in total silence apart from heavy breathing and the sound of Dando's panting struggles to free himself.

For a long time after they left he lay shaking and hiccuping unable to pull himself together sufficiently to appreciate his predicament. When at last he managed to collect his wits about him his first thought was that these had been the men from the farm, there was no doubt about it; someone must have shadowed him along the road and told the others where he was lying. He sat up, found his boot and put it back on. Then in the light of a waning moon he picked up the crutch which was broken in two places. He stared at the sections stupidly and tried to fit them back together as if there were some way to remedy this catastrophe. An idea occurred to him and he looked wildly around for the other crutch, in dread lest the robbers should have carried it off. With great relief he found it whole and undamaged at his side. But that, and the boot, were the sum total of his assets. His pack was gone, his money was gone, his warm outer clothing had also been taken and the bottle of Dr Good's that he had been relying on to help him through the dark hours had vanished along with the pack. He could have wept in despair but instead set out to put as much distance between himself and his attackers as possible.

Making progress with just one crutch was a far harder task than with two. It involved a sort of precarious acrobatic trick in which all his weight was committed to balancing on the wooden support while his good leg parted company with the ground in order to hop forward. If he did not get this manoeuvre exactly right a fall was inevitable and several times he ended up sprawled at full length on the ground; he gave up counting his bruises. Such a means of locomotion was exhausting but he would not allow himself to halt until the sun had climbed high in the sky the next day and the den of thieves, as he now believed it to be, had been left way down the road. Then for an hour or two he lay just off the highway and napped uneasily, jerking fearfully awake at frequent intervals, until he gave up trying to rest and continued his journey. When night came and he finally called it a day he could not sleep. He was hurting a lot, having pushed his body far beyond what it should have attempted at this stage of his recovery. He was frightfully hungry and, besides the absence of his wooden crutch, he was also missing the chemical crutch he had come to rely on.

For two more days he struggled on in this fashion until in desperation he nerved himself to go and knock on another door.

"Please," he said, too ashamed to look the person that answered in the eye, "could you spare some bread or something? I haven't eaten in three days."

He heard the householder (was it a woman?) turn back into the dwelling, followed by the sound of running water. As he stared resolutely at the ground something round and wet was pressed into his hand. He nodded his head and muttered, "I'm very grateful," before turning away and beating a hasty retreat. When he looked to see what he had been given he found it was a large raw potato. Having once overcome his scruples about begging he was emboldened to try again, despite the fact that each time he made his plea for a handout he got the feeling he was descending into a mire of degradation. On the second time of asking the door was slammed in his face, on the third a man threatened to set the dogs on him. His fourth attempt, however, produced results. A kind-hearted girl took the trouble to make him a pack of sandwiches. He thanked her fervently for her generosity but when he had finished eating he discovered that what he really longed for was not just food but the golden liquid that had been able, for a limited period, to make all his suffering, both physical and mental, completely disappear.

On the whole his requests were refused far more often than they were granted. As day followed day he realised that if things went on this way, he was not going to be able to keep body and soul together. One home-owner, after impatiently telling him to move on, shouted after him, "Osh be the place for 'ee – outzide the gates. That's where all the scroungers like 'ee hang out. Can't be arrested there."

It had not occurred to Dando that he could be arrested for what he was doing.

"Where's Osh?" he asked.

"Next turning t'wards sea. Thataway."

He followed these instructions and eventually came in sight of both the sea and the walls of a town. The track swung right towards an imposing gateway through which traffic was continually coming and going. And yes, he could make out a group of huddled figures crouched by the roadside, holding out their hands to passers by. With a total sense of unreality he took himself across to them and settled himself amongst their ranks. The other beggars waited until he had hunkered down, then rose up as a man and drove him from their midst. Harassed, set upon and astonished he ended up at the top of a grassy slope against the city wall, a fairish distance from the road. The alms-seekers smoothed their ruffled feathers and settled themselves back into the hard-won positions that in the past they had fought tooth and nail to establish.

Although there was little chance of any money coming his way in the remote place to which he had been banished Dando did have a bird's eye view of the various donors as they passed by. Carriages came to a halt and a servant was sent to distribute largess to those beggars nearest the road, some even taking the trouble to reach across to those further back. There were very few who completely ignored the petitioners; quite poor-looking people managed a coin or two. It seemed to be the custom among travellers entering the environs of the town to hand something over, as if the new arrivals were paying their dues. Perhaps such giving conferred good luck. Not many quitting the town bothered to donate, apart from one mounted youth who, galloping hell for leather through the archway, put his hand in his pocket and, as he passed the suppliants, sent a silver fountain flying through the air. There was a mad scramble among the crouching figures and during the scrimmage a tiny coin was impelled all the way to where Dando stood. He did not pick it up immediately for into his mind had come a picture of another young man astride a magnificent black charger who in a different world had been too impatient to stop at a town's limits and had similarly showered the needy with money which had meant little or nothing to him. It had been that day in High Harrow when he had been playing truant from his studies, the day after his seventeenth birthday, only eight months, or rather vast ages, ago.

Eventually he bent and retrieved the coin. It was a sixpence. He was rich! He left the group of unfriendly beggars behind and propelled himself through the city gate into the town proper where he found the reason for all the activity on the road: it was Osh's market day and trading was in full swing. All manner of goods were on display including a wide range of food stuffs. What should he spend his windfall on? In the end he bought himself a crisp buttercup-yellow pasty almost too hot to handle and retired into a side alley where he sat on a stone block in order to eat without interruption. When the turnover was consumed he sucked every last crumb from his fingers and even licked the paper it had been wrapped in, temporarily feeling he had never tasted anything so good. However the next moment his craving returned and he was dissatisfied once more. It was when he came back into the market square that he caught a glimpse between the stalls of something that would have provided the perfect ending to his meal. In the distance he could see a booth advertising patent medicines for sale and on the high counter at the front of the kiosk, bottles were displayed that drew him irresistibly. He slipped through the throng, trying to merge into the background as much as possible until he was standing just below the objects of his desire. Yes, he was right, the flasks were made of clear glass with labels on them in blue lettering proclaiming *DR GOOD'S ELIXIR, STRENGH 5, see back for details*. Someone had marked them up at one shilling and sixpence a bottle. Dando waited until the vendor was busy serving another customer and then, stretching out his hand, quickly hooked a bottle from the end of the row and stuffed it into his trouser pocket, before sidling away, making as if to lose himself in the crowd.

"All right lad – I'll 'ave that!"

Dando, almost at the far end of the market, swung guiltily round to find a square-shouldered thick-set man in some sort of uniform planted, arms akimbo, behind him.

"Have what?" he asked but could not prevent the blood from flooding his face.

"What you just put in your pocket. Come on – 'and it over."

Slowly Dando produced the bottle of Dr Good's and held it out. Someone reached across from the side and tried to grab it.

"That's my property," said the stall-holder who seemed to have materialised out of nowhere. The policeman, if that is who he was, quickly took possession.

"Evidence," he retorted. "Come to the station and put in a claim if you think you've got a case. OK lad," he continued, turning to the boy, "follow me. There's at least three constables in the vicinity should you decide to try and escape."

Run away! That was a joke!

"I'm sorry," Dando said out loud, "I'm afraid I forgot to pay." It was a feeble excuse and deserved the contempt it received.

"You can tell that to the beak. I'm sure 'e'll be extremely interested. This way – it's not far."

On reaching the police station the bottle of Dr Good's was placed in a prominent position on the Chief Inspector's desk, a silent accuser and witness to Dando's guilt. It seemed that when minor malefactors were brought in for questioning this exalted individual - head of the constabulary in this small city state - acted as both judge and jury in addition to his other duties.

"First offence? I'm inclined to be lenient. Just the regulation punishment for vagrancy I think plus a night in the cells. That should do it. And," to Dando, "I want you beyond the city limits by twelve midday tomorrow – understand? Take him outside."

"OK boy," said the sergeant - the one who had brought him in - "you'll find this won't be too bad. Just sit there for a few minutes while I go and arrange things. Keep an eye on 'im," he added to a constable standing nearby.

"W-what are they going to do to me?" asked Dando of this man who did not seem much older than he was.

"Pickwah handshake," said the grinning tyro with a flick of the wrist more eloquent than any words. Dando tumbled to the fact that he was going to be whipped, a realisation that hit him like a sledgehammer and filled him with an urge to flee which almost had him leaping up and making a break for it there and then despite his crippled condition. That he did not do so was due to a sudden flashback. Into his mind came an image of the Punishment Yard at Castle Dan and the column he had seen in that hell hole with a hook a foot or two above head height. His good kindly Doll must have been tied to that post when she suffered a totally undeserved beating after the child of the house died. It was his family, and by association he himself, who had been responsible for that atrocity. He was well aware that the way Doll had been treated was a crime more serious than the stealing of a bottle, and penance was long overdue. Resigning himself to his fate, he tried to prepare for what was to come, and when the moment arrived made an unsuccessful attempt to turn himself into an unthinking, unfeeling block of wood. Afterwards he was put in a warm dry cell which even had a thin mattress on the sleeping shelf and offered a meal which repelled him so thoroughly that he could hardly bear to look at it. Infantilised by shock he lay wide-eyed with thumb in mouth for most of the night, his mind a demented jumble. The next morning he left town as fast as one leg and a single crutch would allow, heading back towards the coastal highway.

Part of the reason for his haste was down to the fact that something remarkable had occurred. On discharge he was handed his meagre possessions by some junior clerk who seemed to have his mind on other things. However, accompanying these - he could scarcely believe his luck – he was presented with another item - the bottle of Dr Good's Elixir that he had stolen. He almost cried out in astonishment but then buttoned his lip and made a getaway before anyone realised their mistake. "Thankyou, thankyou," he muttered to his guardian angel as he set off along the track.

Back on the road he resumed his slow and painful journey towards his goal, dragging himself along at what felt like the pace of a half crushed snail. The highway was no longer deserted. At first there was a normal morning flow of traffic up and down the track but this was soon augmented by a larger crowd all going in the same direction. Riders on bicycles and on horseback, riders in carriages and carts, people afoot pushing or pulling barrows, people carrying bundles over their shoulders and dragging reluctant children by the hand, all came rolling up from behind and forged ahead of him leaving him to eat their dust. He listened in to the mutter of conversation as they passed and realised that, taken as a whole, the voices were conveying one single urgent message:- "The Pickwah army! They're coming! The Axemen are on the warpath! Heaven help anyone who gets in their way! They're burning and looting! Nobody's safe!"

Dando watched as the refugees disappeared into the distance until eventually their numbers dwindled to nothing. The hairs on his neck began to prick and the silence surrounding him took on an unnatural, ominous quality. He kept looking nervously over his shoulder. But the sight he feared most to see - a marching host growing larger every minute - never materialised. This was because the Great Leader's force, with its cavalry and foot-soldiers, its cannon and siege-engines, its wagons, comfort women and camp followers, had taken the turning that earlier had brought him back to the highway and, as Squinancy had predicted, was now heading for the unsuspecting city of Osh, the first port of call in a campaign of conquest.

While he had been lying sick in the Pickwah fortress, spring had crept up on winter, burgeoned and then passed by, before morphing into high summer. Now there were times when the sun shone from dawn to dusk, the blue sea sparkled, birds sang and everything seemed right with the world. But there were also days on this treacherous coast when the light suddenly went out of the sky leaving the sea grey and angry as foam-capped waves piled in towards the shore. The whining, moaning wind which had arrived from nowhere, gradually strengthened, carrying at first just a few drops of rain on its breath but, in no time at all, bringing a lashing, driving downpour that drenched anything or anyone who happened to be within its orbit. Such storms sometimes lasted for over twenty four hours before dropping as quickly and as inexplicably as they had arisen. As well as stirring the sea into a rage the tempest was often strong enough to upset Dando's precarious stability sending him tumbling into the mud. On occasions he had to give up trying to make progress of any kind and find what shelter he could. He would crouch shivering under some bush or overhang, soaked to the skin, waiting for the bad weather to pass and thinking sheepishly of the time when, talking to his sister, he had advocated the pleasures of walking in the rain.

Never in his life had Dando been so completely anonymous as he was now. Alone on the road he was treated as a nobody, a nonentity. Always in the past he had had a name to live up to, certain standards of behaviour that had to be maintained. Now nothing was expected of him, no-one was watching him to see that he conformed. He realised his innominate status conferred a kind of freedom; he was invisible now to all but himself and he had only his own principles to guide him. It was a great responsibility.

He was also learning some hard lessons along the way. In the past he had been a gregarious, sociable youth cordially disposed towards those he encountered on his voyage through life. He imagined that the bulk of humanity felt the same way towards him. But now, in his present situation, he was finding out that this was not necessarily the case. An unwashed young tramp with no more than the shirt on his back to pay his way was treated quite differently, he discovered, from the wealthy son of an influential clan chief, a son whose father had the power of life and death over those under his sway. His helplessness and vulnerability seemed to attract mockery and worse from certain elements. Gangs of boys in the small towns through which he passed would shout abuse after him - "Gimpy! Lame duck! Raspberry ripple!" - and one or two would brush past in the narrow streets, surreptitiously trying to kick his crutch out from under him; stones were thrown. Up on the bypass, carriages - usually the richer equipages with a couple of high-stepping thoroughbreds in the traces - swerved towards him as if to run him off the road. Made wary by this treatment Dando began to avoid close contact with passing strangers and to skirt the hamlets that lay in his path. This was unfortunate because it was in these little towns that he was most likely to find food, the sort of nourishment that came in the form of left-overs dumped at the back of cafes in the small hours or perishable market produce that the stall-holders could not be bothered to carry home at the end of the day. In the coastal villages that he came to, occasional fish heads, tails and guts were available, for the possession of which he would have to compete with gulls and feral cats. Learning, through bitter experience, that in his defenceless state he could no longer trust people, Dando cut himself off as much as possible from his fellow men and went his own way, but as a consequence felt incredibly lonely. Physically his condition was deteriorating. His right hand, foot and armpit were blistered from continual chafing and he was in almost constant pain. Ruefully he remembered Potto's words, spoken in the comfort of the ancient house in High Harrow, which now came back to haunt him: *It be a great sorrow to be out alone in the world with no roof over your head and no bed and no one to know your name – a fearful thing.*

In his extremity Dando did not turn to prayer. Such piety did not seem fitting in this particular situation because, after all, which deity would he pray to – would it be to the Sky Father who had disowned the Gleptish race, or the Mother who, as far as he understood it, wanted him dead? But often he stared yearningly heavenward neglecting the track in front of him with the inevitable consequences. Up above his head all was serene and peaceful; the cloud country promised succour and a surcease from suffering. If only he had wings to fly he could spread them and soar up and away from this bad karma that seemed to have taken over his life. His existence would have been insupportable - he would have given up long before, resigned his purpose and lain down in the road to die - had it not been for the bottle of Dr Good's that he guarded obsessively and rationed so carefully and parsimoniously. All day he thought of little else but the moment when he would allow himself just one mouthful of the miraculous nostrum that had the power to work transformational magic. After swallowing it he would lie gazing upwards and if the night was clear his consciousness would expand exponentially until it encompassed the stars, the spaces between and, rushing outwards faster than the speed of light, the whole universe in all its glory. Sometimes he laughed aloud for the sheer joy of it. At the next stage of intoxication his awareness of place disappeared entirely, he existed neither here nor beyond but everywhere and nowhere at once. After that he moved into the realm of trance, or rather hallucination, and remained in that state for the rest of the night.

One vision occurred quite frequently but was hard to recall after he had awakened. It started with blackness and cold that extended all around and on and on forever. After a while, in the darkness, he saw a small light, pinkish in colour, not illuminating anything, just suspended before him softly glowing. This little light was like a comforting word spoken gently, caringly and he felt, at first, that as long as he could see it he needed nothing else. Gradually, time became meaningless, his attention reached for the light while the rest of his mind resembled a blank and empty cave. There was a sweetness and loveliness about that little light and at the same time a homeliness and familiarity. He began to long towards it with all his being, experiencing an exquisite ache of separation. Then, in a fraction of a second, the light was within him, yet not within because he was no longer extant, he was part of the light and everything was all right forever. "Annie?" he murmured and woke, and, in the waking, stretched luxuriously, only to be shocked into a more acute consciousness by a sharp stab of pain that warned him in this brutal fashion that all was not well with his body. Often, as he returned from such a drug-fuelled pipe dream, his heart would beat a jittery and reverberant drum roll for fear of he knew not what.

Not every hand was raised against him; there were some kindly-disposed folk in the world. Drivers of the more humble sort would occasionally stop and offer him a lift.

"Come on sonny – get up on the cart. Oy be goin' two or three miles down t' road. Zave 'ee a few steps."

One bright afternoon Dando had just fallen over for the umpteenth time and seemed unable to summon the energy to rise. To tell the truth it was quite pleasant lying there in the dirt with the sun warm on his back. The wheels of a vehicle rumbled to a halt beside him and he heard creaking as someone climbed down onto the road. Footsteps approached and a hand gripped his shoulder. He tensed, not knowing what to expect but fearing the worst.

"What's wrong lad?" said a voice.

"Tired," Dando muttered.

"Here, let me help you up – Oy can take you on a bit if you're goin' my way."

And so Dando found himself sitting on the driving bench of a farmer's dray next to a middle-aged capable-looking man whose calloused hands gripped the reins of a grey broad-bottomed cart horse.

"Where ha' thee come from lad?" this samaritan enquired, "are 'ee goin' far?"

Dando knew that, if only for politeness sake, he ought to frame some sort of reply but somehow, just for the moment, it seemed beyond his capabilities. His chin dropped onto his breast and he swayed drunkenly. The driver put out an arm to steady him.

"Hang on fella – you seem a bit woozy like. When did you last eat?"

Dando shook his head. All he wanted to do was sleep.

"Well sonny – I'm on my way yome – Oy think p'raps you'd better come back wi' me an' we c'n maybe give 'ee a bite." A mile or two along the road the wagon swung right into a lane which eventually reached the gate of a large farmyard overrun by a menagerie of chickens, ducks, geese, cats and of course the ubiquitous dogs. On the gate was a sign reading *Chysauster Farm*. Once on the other side of the barrier, the dray rolled to a halt and the man gave a shout:- "Mother! - Hoy, Mother! Come out here!"

A fat jolly-looking woman enveloped in a huge rather dirty apron appeared at the back door of the house.

"Ah – there you are Glad. This young man be fair done in. He need a meal an' a bed for the night."

Dando was helped down from the wagon and the farmer supported him across the yard. The wife held out her hand and, after a moment's hesitation, the boy clasped it.

"I'm afraid this is a terrible imposition," he husked.

"Not at all, not at all. One more at my board won't make a haypeth o' difference. Come in lad."

Inside the kitchen a large table almost filled the room, covered with a bedsheet-sized cloth on which several places had already been set. At the corner stood a great oven-proof dish holding some sort of pie covered in pale crumbs. Poking out round the sides of this concoction Dando saw a ring of small fish heads staring goggle-eyed at the ceiling.

"Cloud-Watcher's Crumble," explained the wife proudly, "made for special occasions. It's the man's birthday today. Just about to go in the oven. Be ready in less than an hour. Zit thee down at the table me dear – Oy'll bring thee a glass o' Zyder."

"What sort of fish?" Dando croaked.

"Fish?" replied the farmer's wife in surprise, "oh – you mean in the pie. They're mackerel."

"Is there a sauce?" Dando was showing more animation than he had for several days.

"No – but we stuff 'em with parsley and onions, then bacon an' egg are put in between. Is it not to your taste?"

"No, no – it sounds delicious – but what's the crumb made of?"

"The usual – flour, butter an' I add oats if I've got 'em."

"Mmm," said Dando, storing this away, " and why do you leave the heads on the fish?"

"My word," said Gladys laughing, "you're a nozy-parker an' no miztake. That's just the way we've allus done it. Here lad – have a drink – from our yown orchards."

She busied herself about food preparation and a few minutes later turned to find her guest sprawled forward over the table with his head in his arms. Smiling she deftly removed the empty glass.

Nearly an hour passed, then a hand on his shoulder brought Dando back to consciousness. He blearily raised his head to see several shadowy faces on the other side of the table and realised he had been committing an unforgivable faux pas.

"I'm terribly sorry," he whispered hoarsely, "You must think I'm awfully rude."

"Nonzenze lad – you're not the first one I've had azleep at my table by a long chalk. Here you are – tuck in to this."

The fish pie was followed by trifle, concerning which Dando was almost too weary to do justice. After the meal, leaving the rest of the company to celebrate, he was shown upstairs to a little room containing a soft bed where, despite his weakness and exhaustion, he was again plagued by the chronic muscle spasms that had been with him sporadically since before he left Pickwah. To counter this he swallowed a mouthful of Dr Good's and eventually, listening to the sound of singing coming up from below, drifted into insensibility.

The next morning, having spent a night under a roof in a place of safety, he felt he had regained sufficient courage and resolution to carry on. The farmer's wife served up a hearty breakfast and kept tabs on him while he ate it.

"Oy be a-wonderin' what a nice lad like 'ee be doin' out alone on the road in such a condition," she remarked.

Dando opened his mouth to reply but, in casting his mind back, was suddenly swept by a surge of emotion. Gladys, sensing his distress, squeezed his shoulder.

"All right me dear - oy c'n zee that it's a long story, an' mayhap a zad one. Don' tell me if 'ee don' wan' to."

The farmer came in having already been up and about for several hours.

"In a week or two I be goin' to Trincomalee. You be welcome to stay here till then an' come wi' me," he offered.

"Gweek - how far is it from here?"

"Is that where you're headed? It's a fair ztep. I'll be passing that turning on the way an' I'd be happy to drop you off. Do 'ee wan' t' wait?"

"No, no – you're very good but I must carry on. I can't waste time. How long will it take me to get to Gweek?"

"It be a fair ztep."

Dando prepared to depart. The wife disappeared for a few minutes and came back with something draped over her arm.

"Oy couldn't help noticing the state of your clothes lad. They barely cover 'ee. This b'longed to my great-granzer, he wore it when he served cross the sea under General McLoy in the Madderhay Wars. It's mayhap a bit heavy for zummer but you might be glad of it later on."

The garment she held out was a military greatcoat in a sort of camouflage green, dulled and faded with age, but still in reasonable condition although it was obvious that at sometime the moth had been at it. Dando tried it on. It reached almost to his ankle but was, on the whole, a good fit. The lining had parted company from the main fabric in places and it smelt both ancient and musty, yet in its warmth and solidarity it promised protection against bad weather and a hostile world. "It's just what I need," he replied gratefully, "but isn't it precious to you?"

"Oh no," she said, "you take it. And here's the scarf that goes with it. I don't know why we hang on to these old things."

The couple came to the gate to wave him off under the curious gaze of those working nearby.

Gladys: - "Go safely my dear."

Her husband the farmer: - "I'll keep an eye out for 'ee on the road."

Dando: - "Thankyou, thankyou. You've been so very good to me. I won't forget."

He gathered his forces and tried to give the appearance of moving effortlessly as he set off down the lane to rejoin the highway once more.

Although renewed and energised by the kindness he had experienced, two meals and one night in a proper bed were not enough to restore him to the degree of fitness necessary for his self-imposed mission; the weeks of virtual starvation and exposure to the elements had taken their toll and he was no nearer to finding a reliable way of feeding himself. Within a very short space of time he was feeling nearly as debilitated as he had before the farmer picked him up. Also he was apprehensive about what awaited him in the future. His bottle of Dr Good's, his comforter and sole support, was now less than a quarter full. When it ran out the terrible nigh-time contortions that he dreaded would pounce like a stalking cat.

About three days due east of Chysauster Farm he heard galloping hooves behind him and quickly shrank to the side of the road. A rider came flashing past shouting as he did so, "Osh has fallen! Osh has fallen!" Dando heard him pass on the same news to other travellers further down the track. On reaching the next village he found a crowd of people on the street talking their heads off at the top of their voices.

"Osh has fallen! The Axemen have taken Osh! They zay they be movin' on to Lamorna. Trewithik's Horde be a-comin'! What'll be their next target? We mus' get ourzelves organised! Surely the other Zisters will zend help."

People were running to and fro in panic.

Each community he passed was similarly affected, swarming like a disturbed ants' nest, frantically trying to raise citizens' armies, volunteer militias and bands of vigilantes to counter the perceived threat. Dando was frequently stopped and questioned - treated with suspicion.

"There be spies about," he was told, "you mus' account for yourself before we let you through."

On each occasion he eventually managed to persuade the frightened townsfolk that he was harmless enough and received permission to continue his journey. Once more the road was thronged with refugees and once more they left him in his wake.

Dando did not deceive himself when it came to his physical state; he knew his time was running out. Every morning he asked himself if this was the last day he was going to be able to get back up onto his solitary foot, or was it perhaps the second to last day. Maybe he could keep going for another three days, or even a week, but two weeks seemed out of the question. As for the elixir, he estimated that he had enough to last for another five or six days, and this lulled him into a false sense of security, but in fact the end arrived far sooner than expected. Gladys, the farmer's wife, had given him a small knapsack in which to carry essentials and this was where he stowed his precious bottle. One evening when he went to retrieve it he found the flask on its side without its lid; he could not have screwed the top on tightly enough the previous evening and it had worked loose. Disaster! He held the bottle up in the desperate hope of finding something left at the bottom but every last drop had vanished. All the same he put it to his lips and sucked on empty air before throwing it angrily into the ditch as if it had betrayed him. He sat staring into space, a hollow feeling inside. What was he going to do? How could he cope?

The first day following his loss was not too bad, and he even managed to get some sleep after dark, but the second was a nightmare. The weather had turned hot and the sun beat down on his unprotected head. Sweat ran off him in rivulets and his heart hammered; he was shaking like a leaf. Twice he stopped to retch by the side of the road but as he had nothing in his stomach there was little to show for it. That night he lay and writhed in torment, moaning and sobbing, before getting up before dawn and rushing back onto the road as if trying to outdistance his suffering.

When the sun finally rose he found himself in one of the small seaside towns with no idea as to how he had gotten there. He was standing by the harbour wall and below him floated row upon row of fishing smacks, moored side by side. Whereas normally, at this time of day, there would have been serious activity as the fleet prepared to set sail, instead everything was quiet and still. All he could hear, over the sound of blood pumping in his ears, were the silvery notes of a pipe on which someone was playing a well known sea shanty. The musician was standing on the bridge of the nearest vessel leaning on the rail in a relaxed attitude, seemingly absorbed in his performance. He was a very smart sailor, this piper, decked out in a red and white striped top, red scarf and a skimpy denim lugger jacket over tight blue trousers slightly flared at the hems. Covering his eyes were mirror-lensed sun-specs while on his head he wore a shiny black boater tipped at a jaunty angle, to the brim of which was fixed a red flower. From his wrist hung a slender cane painted in all the colours of the rainbow. Dando shut his eyes and then took a second look. He shook his own head trying to dismiss this chimerical illusion from his brain, despite which the young man remained in his field of vision. Miracles do happen after all. He opened his mouth and tried to shout. The name that he intended to cry was *Jack* but his voice came out as an almost soundless croak. The sailor went on playing. Dando coughed, cleared his throat and took a deep breath. "JACK!" he yelled with all his might. The music stopped. "JACK!" Dando shouted again. The boy turned in his direction then, deliberately doffing his hat, he stuffed it down his shirt-front and thrusting the pipe and his glasses into a side pocket descended to the foredeck of the ship and, from there, jumped into the harbour. Dando - shocked and amazed - hurried to the top of a flight of steps leading down to the water.

"Over here – this way!" he cried to the swimmer but the other already seemed to have a good idea of direction. As he mounted the steps onto the quay he was muttering, "ruined, ruined," having given his boater the once over, then, gaining the top, he reached out and made contact. With a cry of, "My little bird!" he grabbed Dando up into a fierce, rough, wet embrace. In response, the boy gasped with pain. Jack started back.

"What's wrong?" he asked, in sharp concern.

Rapidly his hands flew to and fro over the other's body, lingering for a moment at the crotch, discovering the gauntness, the wooden support, the missing foot.

"Whatever's happened to you my love?" he demanded, "Explain!"

Once again he hugged Dando, but more gently, and the boy clung to him, burying his head in his shoulder, while his prop went clattering to the ground.

"Oh Jack," came the muffled response.

"All right, all right, I'm here," comforted Jack massaging the other's back. "Don't cry - I've got you. Everything's going to be all right now – everything's going to be quite all right."

"Jack," muttered Dando once more, completely unmanned, his face hidden. His one and only desire at that moment was to tell the intricate baroque tale of his misery, to pour out the story of his continuing misfortunes, but instead all he felt able to do was to repeat his friend's name over and over again.

"It's ok lad," reassured Jack, "take your time. Now that I've found you we've got all the time in the world – all the time in the world."

Banners,
Ragged and bloody,
Fly above the fiercest fighting.

Chapter eighteen

The Commander in Chief of the Pickwah Army, alias the Great Leader, alias Jory Trewithik was dissatisfied with the progress of his campaign of conquest despite his troops' early victory. After his success at Osh he had sought to establish his headquarters in the centre of the city but nowhere came up to his demanding standards. He had had to use the government's cabinet chamber as his office, a cramped and inconvenient place, and the mayor's parlour for his overnight accommodation which harboured a fusty, musty, dusty smell redolent of dirty furnishings and unswept rooms. Pickwah's next-door neighbour was a mean second-rate town he realised, yet it had been surprisingly hard to take. When the walls were finally breached and the gates thrown open he got his own back by punishing the inhabitants severely for their stubborn resistance. The rank-and-file fighters, he dispatched to fend for themselves out in the cruel, hard world, while he executed their leaders in a variety of inventive ways. The campaign, which he had always imagined would climax with his troops, himself at their head, marching triumphantly into the Delta City was proving, at the outset, to be a lot tougher than expected. Perhaps he had acted too precipitously when setting the date for the off, perhaps in launching the invasion he should have waited until he had more men at his disposal.

He heard a clash of weaponry outside his closed door as someone presented arms and a voice shouted, "Party to see the Supremo!" A murmur of conversation followed and then Lieutenant Moyle, his secretary and general dogsbody, knocked and entered. "A group of men ha' been intercepted on their way from the mountains, Lord. They be wi'out. They claim to have been zent by the one who calls hisself the Cheetah. They be asking for an interview."

"The Cheetah, eh? That's the gangster that's gone to earth in that holy pot-hole that folk down south set so much store by. Ha' they brought me a message from the Voice – a prophecy?"

"They just zay they need to zee 'ee."

"How many?"

"Zeven, Lord."

"Ha' they been disarmed?"

"Oh yes, Lord."

"Zearch them again thoroughly – then zend 'em in."

The deputation duly presented itself, their spokesman a tall fussily-dressed man who looked vaguely familiar to the Head of State.

"Who be thee?" asked Trewithik.

"My name is Thomas Merrick. The reason I'm here is because you have my brother, Nicholas Merrick, in custody. This is unacceptable. I have a proposition to make."

"Nicholas Merrick," said Trewithik turning to his secretary, "who he?"

"He be the chief of the pirates that we defeated on the Dark Island, Lord. He be in the cells wi' the rest of 'em."

The Great leader's eyes widened slightly and he turned back towards his visitor.

"Your brother? Zo you be...?"

"Some call me the Cheetah, some call me far worse than that. I can offer you a substantial sum if you'll release this particular prisoner. However, if you're interested, I have a far better idea for an exchange, something that would be to our mutual benefit. I could bring you reinforcements, extra manpower, which I believe you're in desperate need of. I could enlist a thousand volunteers or more to your cause, and my brother would be able to match that. It will take a week or two to recruit them but I believe I could provide sufficient incentives."

"Criminals, guttersnipes, lawbreakers..."

"Desperadoes I grant you, but good fighting men who would be happy to follow you if they felt it worth their while."

"An undisciplined rabble..."

"Not so. I know how to rule such people – I have experience."

Lord Trewithik stood cogitating, staring past his petitioner, pulling at his lower lip.

"Leave it wi' me," he said at last, "I'll have an answer for 'ee by morning. You say you would take part yourself? You would acknowledge my authority?"

"Me and my brother."

The upshot of this was that over the next few days messages went winging their way through the towns bordering the Middle Sea and into the back country along the Kymer River. They percolated down mean alleys and via waterfront bars, passed from tavern to wine cellar, from whorehouse to knocking-shop, handed on from slum to stew to ghetto until they reached those ears for which they was intended. The ones who listened, the ones who owed allegiance to the two brothers who had once been legitimate businessmen but whose names were now suffused with the lurid glamour of outlawry, abandoned whatever nefarious schemes they happened to be engaged upon and directed their steps westward in expectation of promised plunder and booty.

Foxy stood before the pair of men, one middle aged, one elderly, whose task it was to interview candidates for the post of under gardener. He had no idea who they were and would have been surprised to learn that the more senior of the two was actually the Lord of the Manor, the landowner himself. To Foxy he seemed a pleasant enough old cove but there was nothing to mark him out as a grandee. It was the other man, vigorous, in the prime of life, with a direct and critical gaze, whom he felt he had to impress. He had left Tallis in a safe place up the road; time enough to introduce him into the equation when he had secured the position.

"An' why do 'ee wan' to join the Witteridge Estate?" the younger man asked.

"I needs a job," replied Foxy bluntly.

"Do you know anything about horticulture?" asked the older man. Foxy had never heard the word before.

"I can learn," he said.

"What's your past employment history?"

"In hort... you mean in hort...?" puzzled Foxy.

"What other posts have 'ee held?"

"I did inn work – looking after horses – fetching an' carryin' – helping in the kitchens. I be good wi' the bow."

"Manual labour?"

"What?"

"Did you work with your hands?"

"O' course."

"You look a fine strong lad – have you had anything to do with plants?"

"I spen' mos' o' my life among plants," replied Foxy cautiously.

He was asked several more questions and then told to wait outside. Maybe his prospective bosses had been presented with little choice; maybe there were no other applicants. Whatever the reason, when he was called back into the room Foxy knew immediately by the interviewers' manner that he had got the job.

"The wages be fifteen shilling a week wi' midday meals provided. There be a two room cottage. One day off a month."

"I got my ol' father along wi' me – he be no trouble – you'll scarce notice he."

The men held a whispered conference, the younger apparently raising objections, the older making light of them.

"Well – I don't think that will be a problem but you must remember that this is a private estate – your father should realise that he can't come and go as he pleases. He'll have to remain in the cottage except when given explicit permission to cross the grounds."

"That be all right," said Foxy, " he ha'n't got the use o' his legs – he won't be gooin' a-wanderin'.""

They shook hands.

"This is Mr Witteridge, your employer," said the head gardener, "I be Murdock. An' you are...?"

"Trooly," said Foxy, "Everard Tetherer Trooly."

The next morning he began the apprenticeship that soon ignited so great an enthusiasm in his breast that it eventually supplanted all previous passions, even his revolutionary ones. Murdock took him on a tour of the grounds, leading him from the topiary and parterres of the formal gardens at the front of the mansion to the extensive lawns at the back edged by herbaceous borders and rose pergolas, on past a herb garden, a water garden, a scented garden intended for the use of the visually impaired to the walled kitchen garden with its fruit cordons and neat lines of vegetables. Just inside the back boundary they reached an orchard and grazing for the estate's herbivores. By the end of the day Foxy was already dirtying his hands weeding rows of young carrots with the aid of a small fork he had been given for his exclusive use. Murdock showed him what should be pulled up and what left. He gained satisfaction from the work.

In less than a week he was getting up earlier than necessary and setting out before the time appointed in his eagerness to become more adept at this new craft to which he was being introduced. All his life he had been accustomed to living cheek by jowl with wild nature; now he was being taught what man and nature could achieve when they worked in harmony with one another. Because there were only three permanent gardeners – Murdock, himself and a boy – he found he was expected to turn his hand to a huge variety of tasks and this meant he was absorbing new facts every hour that he laboured between sun-up and sun-down. By the time his day off came around Murdock paid him the highest compliment he was ever likely to bestow.

"You be a pretty handy fellow," he remarked dryly.

Meanwhile Tallis sat alone in the cottage that went with the job, empty hours crawling by on leaden feet, unfitted to occupy himself or do anything useful. To say that he had lost the use of his legs was not strictly true any more. He was able, by this time, to make his uncertain way to the privy when necessary or to bed at the end of the day as long as he had something to hold on to. His arms were both functioning adequately and the occasions when he vomited after eating were getting fewer. His speech was becoming more intelligible. However he still required help with washing and dressing and he relied on Foxy and the bath chair when travelling any distance. Foxy administered to his needs with a bad grace, often grumbling under his breath or muttering, "I don' hev time for this," while ineptly trying to stuff Tallis' arms into his filthy shirt or the shirt into his stained trousers. Personally provided with substantial ready-to-eat meals in the middle of the day, the Nablan made a mere perfunctory attempt to feed Tallis when he returned to the cottage. Bread and jam, bread and cheese, bread and dripping, sometimes accompanied by small beer if fortune smiled, made up the whole of the limited menu that the invalid was being offered. If Tallis objected to this spartan fare his carer pleaded pressure of work, and indeed the sum of Foxy's energies at that time was directed towards the estate and the steep learning curve which his employment involved; his obligations towards Tallis were just an extra burden he could have done without. Because of his inattention he did not realise the depths of despair into which his companion had sunk.

Tallis' mind dwelt continually on his quest. Finding his people and after that the Key, thus enabling the restoration of the Land-of-the-Lake to take place, had been the sole purpose of his existence, a pursuit to which most of his life had been dedicated, and now, because of his bodily frailty, his ability to complete the task he had been set seemed to have gone forever beyond his reach. Without assistance he was never going to progress any further towards his goal and he was well aware by now that Foxy was not the type to cast his own ambitions aside in order to aid someone who meant little to him; he was beginning to feel that his life had been totally wasted in following after a phantom that had always been out of reach. While he sat through the long days and lay sleepless through the interminable nights his thoughts kept returning to his young squire, the boy that he had treated with such disdain at the start of their journey mainly to compensate for his own feelings of inadequacy. Despite this the lad had supported him quietly and uncomplainingly during their long weeks on the road but had now disappeared to goodness-knows-where. Too late, Tallis yearned for his gentle efficiency, for the tempting meals he provided, for his self-effacing patient service. He had finally awoken to the truth of the saying – *you don't know what you've got till it's gone* – and knew he had been stupid not to value him more. Despite evidence to the contrary he did not share Foxy's suspicions of Dando's behaviour on the night of the fire. In fact, taking into consideration his previous conscientiousness, he clung to the idea that the boy must have had a good reason for his defection. In connection with his squire he also brought to mind the messages he had received from the Voice at Toymerle: - *Over-the-Brook... the old man is not the one... he that speaks must turn it.* At the time he had thought that this last gnomic utterance applied to himself alone but now he remembered that it was Dando who had actually been speaking at that precise moment, or rather that the god had been speaking through him. Could it have been he rather than Tallis that the Voice had meant?

Foxy was also thinking about Dando and Ann, or rather realising that in actual fact he had not thought about them for quite some time. It was a chance remark of Tallis's which brought home to him the realisation that, because for the past few weeks all his attention had been directed towards understanding fascinating techniques such as hoeing, fertilising, mulching and composting, he had allowed his desire for revenge to drain away until it barely existed. He had begun to consider his situation here as permanent and was even looking forward to following seasonal changes in the gardens throughout the year. The possibility of a return to the valley of Deep Hallow which had been his hope for the greater part of their journey, had been virtually forgotten.

"My squire always brought me a drink before I slept."

So Tallis had grumbled one evening and with a shock Foxy became aware that his quarrel with Dando was no longer uppermost in his mind; it seemed like an age since his one desire had been to catch up with the fugitives and exact retribution for their treachery. How could he have allowed himself to grow so cold? That night he lay awake trying to fan the flame of his resentment back to life but the embers were well and truly dead, the fire was out. What had happened? This place had changed him, that was plain. All the same justice must be done and be seen to be done. If he ever got the opportunity to encounter the high-born Glept once more there would have to be a reckoning. Yet he no longer felt the desire to go chasing off after the boy along the road. *Let him come to me*, was his prophetic thought, *and I'll show him the error of his ways.*

Meanwhile, although rumours of distant fighting occasionally reached the ears of the estate's inhabitants, and it was noticeable that there were an unusual number of people passing eastwards along the high-road, as yet the employees of the manor did not feel that such events impinged on their own existence here in the house and gardens. Their day to day routine, therefore, continued on in its normal tranquil way and, when summer finally arrived, it was Mr Witteridge himself, the Master of Witteridge Acres, who suggested to Foxy that Tallis might like a change of scene: "A nice day like this, why don't you bring your father out in his chair and park him near to where you're working? I'm sure the old gentleman would appreciate an airing. I'd have no objection."

"There's a fifth column operating here in Drossi – the council has incontrovertible proof!"

"They say that Trewithik's just the front man for a consortium of nobs who were plotting to overthrow the Old Prince – the fellow's merely a common soldier after all."

"Osh wouldn't have been taken if a faction who were in league with the Axeman hadn't opened the gates at the dead of night."

"Now that the underworld's joined up with that pretender we're all going to be murdered right here in our beds before the army even arrives!"

"They're transporting ships overland to the Kymer and are going to come down on us from up river. We're totally defenceless in that direction."

"I hear that the Kingscauldie troops are getting ready to march to the rescue – I don't know who to fear most, them or the Axemen."

"They've reached Trincomalee!"

Rumours such as these had been flying around Vadrosnia Poule all summer. Damask paid them little heed. Her theatre company had just launched its second play of the season, having achieved a modest success with the satirical cabaret it had put on in the spring. She had a leading role in the new drama and consequently could spare little time or energy on the current political situation. She was vaguely aware that a few of the richer and more influential citizens were closing their town houses and retreating to dachas up country; also that muddy tent cities were sprouting like mushrooms on various nearby islands. She had heard that Jack was no longer at his grandfather's palace; the word going round was that he had at last fulfilled his ambition to go to sea. Sometime during the summer the news came that the Ixat Instipulators had arrived in Drossi and had spent a frustrating few days trying to find a venue for their productions. In the end they had had to give up and go away. Damask was flooded with a delightful sense of schadenfreude at their discomfiture and felt that it served them right for not appreciating her talents more. Well she was doing fine now, she had no further need of them. In the early autumn the circus returned to the Delta City and Milly put in an appearance at Becca's door, a small cat with a cream body and dark extremities perched on her shoulder.

"This is Meena – although Pnoumi used to call her Lotus Blossom. She's my 'ittwl mate."

"But where is Pnoumi?" asked Damask.

"Oh, 'e's gorn back to 'is own country – 'e's got a woman there an' a family so 'e tol' me."

Damask gazed at the cat's Nablan eyes, a vivid cornflower blue, and felt thoroughly put out. It had never occurred to her that the clown, who had professed such devotion towards her, might have had a partner in another part of the world.

"Oh well," she said bitterly, "good riddance to bad rubbish."

"The circus are willin' to keep me on," announced Milly proudly, "they say I'm a good worker."

One of Damask's jobs as a member of the ground-breaking company of players she belonged to was to put up posters around the town advertising the opening night of the coming production, now that the rehearsals had been brought to a successful conclusion. She roamed widely, looking for suitable sites, mingling with the busy life of the city. There was always plenty of street theatre around to tempt her away from her task and occasionally, when she happened upon something unusual, she would stop and watch, aware that these were her fellow performers and that the only superiority she could claim was that she acted under a proscenium arch. In a small square one day she noticed an illusionist conjuring up pocket-sized atmospheric phenomena for the delectation of a meagre crowd. There were clouds, flashes of lightning, rumbles and bangs, a minuscule rainstorm, a rainbow - it was all really rather clever. The magician had an assistant, a young girl, heavily pregnant, her fair hair bunched in a violet ribbon, who was passing among the onlookers with a hat, a blank look on her face. Eventually she stood in front of Damask waiting for a coin. Damask stared and then stared some more. She could hardly believe what she was seeing.

"Ann!" she exclaimed. "It's Ann, isn't it? Dando's Annie?"

The girl looked back stupidly with not the faintest flicker of recognition. She shook the hat making the money chink. "Of your kindness pliz," she said in the voice of a talking doll. A miniature thunderclap came from the other side of the square; the show had ended. The prestidigitator loomed up behind the girl and put an arm possessively across her shoulders. Damask saw a face of extreme pallor criss-crossed by dark and dirty lines. *He looks only half alive*, she thought. There was a vast contrast between the angry suspicion burning in the man's eyes and the insinuating grin that played upon his lips. Damask got the feeling that she had been noted and filed away as someone to watch.

"Come on Hild, my precious," he said, "time to move on. Make your excuses. Oh, by the way, I'll have that," (appropriating the money).

His minion picked up a large canvas bag marked with the words *Gubbo the Great* and walked away, the burden weighing her down. Damask watched the couple leave and dithered for a moment totally conflicted. Was this really the little nibbler she had known when they were both children together at Castle Dan? Surely she must be mistaken? Yet her immediate instinct told her that she had indeed encountered her old playmate and first impressions are often the most reliable. As the couple rounded a corner she was released from paralysis and, coming to a decision, set out to follow.

The pursuit took her eastward onto an area of reclaimed land and into a district of storage sheds and junk yards. Because there were so few people about she had to hang a long way back from her quarry for fear of being spotted. Consequently she eventually lost sight of them. When she cautiously advanced into the region where the magician and his assistant had vanished they were nowhere in the vicinity. It seemed probable they had gone into one of the buildings, but which one? The only thing to do was to wait for them to reappear. She lurked round a convenient corner and was eventually rewarded by the sight of the illusionist emerging alone from a narrow path between two warehouses and making off towards the city. This was a stroke of luck: his passive minion had been left behind and should be not far away judging by the time that had elapsed; she had only to hunt. She walked into the alleyway and came upon the sliding door to an enormous depository on her left hand side. It was shut but not locked. She pushed it open and entered, finding the interior crammed with what looked like redundant pumping engines.

"Ann, Annie!" she called and held her breath to listen. Everything was quiet – so quiet that she could hear the sound of the town's clocks striking twelve in the far distance.

"Ann – Ann!" she called again. She waited, but when there was no reply decided that she had come to the wrong place. She was about to leave when she remembered the girl's total unresponsiveness, her glazed empty expression when at the beck and call of the street-performer; perhaps it would be as well to conduct a search. She walked up and down the lanes between the huge machines and had almost given up hope of finding anything when she saw a pale gleam on the other side of an intricate tracery of metal. She walked round into the next aisle and there she was – Ann – sitting on the ground with one arm pinioned above her head, her wrist shackled to a horizontal pipe, an untouched plate of food and some of the magic-worker's effects beside her.

"Ann," said Damask, "it *is* you!"

The girl gazed up. The vacuous stare had gone from her face but had been replaced by a look of abject terror. As Damask watched she placed her unfettered hand protectively over her distended abdomen. Damask squatted down in front of her.

"Ann," she said, "don't be afraid. It's me, Damask, Dando's sister. You remember me – we used to play together – you took us to see your father's workshop. I've come to rescue you. Who's that man who's got you under his thumb?"

The prisoner tried to rise, was prevented, and then, apparently involuntarily, let out a whine of distress from deep in her throat while her eyes filled with tears. Damask examined the handcuff locking her to the machine and then tried ineffectually to shift the metal pipe which seemed to be made of cast iron. It was far too robust a construct to be moved.

"The pipe's hopeless," she said. "I'll have to get something to saw through the cuff – a file or something. I'm going to leave you for a while, but I'll be back, never fear – I'll be back in two shakes of a lamb's tail."

It seemed to take an age to cover the ground to the lodging house where she discovered Milly in residence, the little girl having just returned from her morning's rehearsal.

"I've found Ann, Dando's Annie," Damask cried as she came through the door, "it's incredible! What on earth is she doing here? Some man's holding her prisoner. I need something that will break through handcuffs."

Milly's eyes grew huge with surmise until they were almost popping out of her head.

"Annie?" she said. "The Lordship's sweetheart? Where is 'e then? Where's my Lordship?"

"No idea," replied Damask, determined not to be diverted from her main purpose and, for the moment, uninterested in her brother's fate. "I need some cutters - we need to be quick – he may come back for her – he may take her away and then we won't know where to look."

Milly's one track mind ran quickly through a sequence which ended in an obvious conclusion: Ann was here in Drossi, Ann had been travelling with Dando, Ann would probably know where Dando was to be found. Realising that rescuing the girl might be the key to discovering her beloved's whereabouts she focussed on the problem at hand.

"I know 'oo we c'n ast. 'E's stayin' just up the road – Alfonso the esc'poligist – 'e undoes locks an' stuff – 'e's a good bloke - 'is name's really Ted – 'e'll 'elp I'm sure."

This local Houdini was fortunately at home and readily agreed to lend a hand. They hurried back to the warehouse, Damask watching out for any sign of the sorcerer, and when they got there found Ann still imprisoned beside the machine. Ted crouched and for a few moments was busy with a small device. Then the cuff round Ann's wrist snapped open and she was free. Damask and Milly bent down and helped her to her feet.

"We'll take you to the place where we're staying," said Damask. "Becca will take care of you. Will he come to find you do you think?"

Milly stared almost rudely at the fair-haired girl. This was the first time she had had a chance to view her much-loved hero's inamorata and she could not help but be sensitive to the contrast between this wan silvery-coloured lady and her own dusky looks.

They returned to the rooming house, Ann stumbling like a sleep-walker in their midst, to find Becca within doors. The situation was explained.

"Lan's sake! Who'd 've thought it! An' her with a young 'un on the way. Not far off by the looks of things."

"Where's your sweet'eart?" asked Milly urgently of Ann. "Where's the Lordship? Where's Dando?"

"Heavens to Betsy," protested Becca, "leave the poor chil' alone. Can't you see she's like to collapse any moment? She needs something warm to drink and then rest, lots of rest. She doesn't need to be bully-ragged by you."

A slight flush crept beneath Ann's transparent skin. She looked gratefully at Becca.

"My Dadda used to use those words," she whispered.

Becca shepherded her upstairs while Milly and Ted went off to take part in that evening's performance. Damask, for whom curtain-up was sometime later, became aware that half the posters that she had promised to display that day were still in her shoulder bag.

The next morning there came a thunderous knocking at the front door. Becca went to open it. A figure whom she had never seen before but whose identity was not hard to guess at stood on the threshold. The wizard had come for his own.

"I believe you have my daughter under your roof."

"I don't take your meaning."

"A fair-haired, blue-eyed girl. You brought her here last night. My daughter."

"Under my roof? Related? Oh no, mister – tell that to the marines The lady upstairs is no daughter of yours. No-one would treat a daughter the way you've treated her!"

"And you are...?"

"Do you take me for a fool? You're not getting me with your ju-ju spells. I've met your sort before. Scram! Vamoose!"

She slammed the door and listened as the sound of footsteps faded away. Then Milly appeared at the top of the stairs.

"Quick Milly," said Becca, "go to the market and buy some garlic, several bulbs, and visit that herbalist, the one on the corner of Mereworth Drive. Get some Lady's Mantle and Agrimony, Angelica Root and Green Aniseed. If you can't get them there try the apothecary's. Here I'll write you a list. Oh," as Milly was going out the door, "and call in at Sophie's on the way back and ask if I can borrow her Cats Eyes."

Becca went to the summer house in the back garden and rooted out an old tin of paint. She brought it back inside and commenced dabbing hand-prints round all the doors, while at the same time persuading a bemused Damask to sprinkle salt on the thresholds.

"Arrow-heads at the windows would be good but we don't have any. However I know what I do have. It's in my room."

Damask followed her into the bedchamber and waited as Becca dove into a bottom drawer and brought out a black shiny-looking object that made a noise when shaken.

"Got power to ward off the Maluka. I'll put it in the girlie's bed."

"What is it?" asked Damask.

"Rattlesnake's rattle. Had it since I left home. It brings good luck."

That afternoon Gammadion tried, for a second time, to persuade Becca to give up his protege. When he was again turned away he issued a veiled threat - "You'll regret this" - and retreated. After dark, a few hours later, he returned incognito to the scene and stood, half concealed, in a doorway on the other side of the street. If you had been present and watching closely you would have seen his lips moving but would have heard no sound, and you might have noticed his left hand, round which was wrapped a violet ribbon, tracing circles in the air while his right gripped his manikin pendant just below the waist. In the dim light it was hard to make out the smoky sphere he created, but then, as he stretched out his arm beneath a street lamp, a palpitating black ball was clearly visible, resting on his open palm. Very gently he impelled it into the air and in the manner of a helium-filled balloon it bobbed, gradually rising, across the road. Gammadion then turned away and backed off with a could-not-care-less kind of swagger, but on his face, as it caught the light, you might have detected, if you had been close enough, an expression of mixed fury and regret.

The dark swirling globe washed up against the upstairs windows of Becca's lodging-house like a piece of flotsam against a breakwater but was immediately repelled. Again and again it sought to find a gap through which it could enter but fell back each time as if stung. Eventually it seemed to lose buoyancy and sank lower, exploring below the lintel of the front door before drifting round to the rear. It was Becca's boast that she had a downstairs' lavatory, accessible from within the house, which was a luxury greatly valued by her tenants, but this privy had been built onto the back of the building and therefore had an external wall into which several air-bricks had been set in order to keep the atmosphere in the little room sweet. The sphere tried the window of the closet with the same result as before but then for several minutes lodged itself against the wall, adhering there like the dense sticky tangle of a spider's nest. It was only as it grew smaller and less distinct that it became clear that its substance was gradually oozing through the holes in the bricks until eventually nothing was left to show that it had ever had substance in the outside world.

As Ann began her sojourn in Becca's house several hours passed before the ex movie star would allow Milly and Damask to spend any time in the bedroom where she had installed the expectant mother and even then she hovered in the doorway in order to monitor what went on. Milly, scorning to beat about the bush, jumped in impetuously with both feet.

"Is it 'is?" she demanded. "Is it the Lordship's?" pointing to Ann's bump.

"Milly!" scolded Damask. Even she, not usually sensitive to other people's feelings, realised that this was grossly intrusive. Ann did not seem offended however; she just smiled wanly and nodded.

"Jack's told us about meeting you at Toymerle," Damask offered hurriedly, "but what happened after that, how did you end up in Drossi?"

"Where's the ol' geezer," asked Milly, "an' the red-headed bloke? Where's the Lordship?"

In a weak voice Ann began to give her version of events, but the more the girls heard the less they understood.

"Possessed - wot do you mean possessed?" puzzled Milly.

"And you say you *raised* the Mother," added Damask. "What does that mean? Surely what happened is you *prayed* to the Mother. But that can only be done back in the valley, isn't that right?"

"You left 'im? But I fort you two woz sweet'earts for life?"

"It seems unlikely that a wizard could lay a curse on Dando and Tallis if they weren't even there. It all sounds a bit far-fetched to me if you don't mind my saying so."

Milly was profoundly disturbed to hear of the attack on Gweek.

"'E woz asleep at the top end you say. Are you sure 'e di'n't wake up an' go back down?"

"I know they don' be there," wept Ann.

"That's enough," interjected Becca. "Y'all leave her alone now – she's not to be upset. You can visit her again tomorrow."

When the two girls had gone back to their rooms she put things straight around Ann's bed, washed her face, combed her hair and brought her a milky drink. Then she helped her to lie back on the pillows and sat stroking her forehead.

"Poor chil' – you're plumb tuckered out – they don't realise what it's like. I know – I've been there."

"All summer he wouldn't let me be," whispered Ann. "First of all he got stuff together for his act and then we jus' keep gooin' from town to town puttin' on shows. At the end of last month he say we mus' come back to Drossi – he say something be a-waitin' for he here."

"Well you're free of him now," Becca reassured her. "I sent him packing and I guess he won't come back a third time."

Ann gazed sadly at the show girl as if wishing she could believe her.

"I be a-feared for the child," she murmured, " an' I be a-feared for the father. Dando don' know – I din' tell he I was in the family way but I should hev. Please make sure the baby be properly looked after when it come."

Becca shot her a penetrating glance.

"It's your baby, honey," she said. "You'll look after it yourself, of course, and we'll help you."

"Mmm," said Ann with a sigh.

Several times while within Gammadion's power, she had been haunted by disturbing and monstrous dreams. On one occasion she imagined she was back in the valley playing the part of a helpless and abused chattel, and on another she seemed to have a bird's eye view over an open plain on which raged silent and bloody battles. Frequently she found herself in a great low-ceilinged cave with a dark smoking pit in the centre of the floor which she knew indisputably led down to hell. Once she saw a small figure in the middle distance, pitifully familiar, hobbling along an endless winding road on one foot and a crutch as if condemned to travel unceasingly.

Now, because she could not tell how far along her pregnancy had progressed, being uncertain as to the exact date on which she had rescued Dando from the Voice, Becca immediately sent for a local midwife to look her over. This woman, who obviously considered herself the fount of all knowledge where gynaecological matters were concerned, gave it as her opinion that the child's arrival was still some way off.

"It's being carried high," she said after questioning Ann and physically examining her, "she shows none of the signs as yet. I would say two or three weeks at least. She needs to build up her strength."

Becca felt relieved.

"You stay in bed this evening and have a nap," she told Ann after the woman had left, "I've got to be at the club until ten but I'll look in on you when I get back."

Damask and Milly were also both working that evening, Damask at the theatre, Milly at the circus. Only Meena, Milly's little foreign-looking cat, was on hand to keep Ann company. During her mistress's absences, she had begun to gravitate to the girl's bedroom where she curled up under the coverlet next to her legs. Ann guessed that Becca would bring her a night cap as soon as she returned. For the moment she felt warm and cosseted. The baby seemed to have fallen asleep. She gradually drifted into a doze, grateful for the comfort with which she was surrounded. She woke sometime later to the sound of a soft hiss. There was a lamp alight in the hall downstairs and by the faint illumination that filtered through the doorway she could see that Meena had emerged from under the bedspread and was standing near her feet, her back arched, her fur on end, her whole body rigid. She seemed to be staring at something in the gloomy recesses of the room just below the ceiling. The hiss changed to a low angry snarl and then, galvanised into action, the cat streaked out the door which slammed shut behind her leaving the room in total darkness. Ann raised her head. She sensed that there was some presence close by, some malignancy that did not wish her well. Something touched her face between nose and lips and for a moment blocked her nostrils. She recoiled, slapping at the empty air. Then she waited with baited breath for what felt like an age until gradually the tension in the room eased. She relaxed slightly and as she did so felt a gush of fluid between her legs. At the same moment pain gripped her. Ghostly fingers were suddenly wrenching at her lower torso and she sat bolt upright, clutching the sides of the bed. Two, three, four times the spasms were repeated - agonising spasms - then for a brief period the contractions eased and she was granted a short respite before the pangs returned worse than before. This was hardly to be born. She panted, alone in the blackness, soaked in sweat, hugging her body. Surely such torment was not how it was meant to be? - treatment such as this would kill both her and the baby before the night was out. She wanted to shout for aid but knew that, without exception, everyone was away. Instead she prayed with all her might - prayed to Tom whose presence had sometimes seemed so real to her during their long journey northwards: *Help me Dadda, don't let he die. I don' care what happen to me but don' let the baby die. Help me protect him, help him to have a life. Please don' let he die.*

When Becca arrived home and found her charge in the first stages of a cruel and violent labour she cursed the midwife with every imprecation under the sun, then sent a message to a doctor who was highly regarded amongst the Drossi elite. This message, carried by a frightened Milly, who had also returned, stated that there was a lady in dire distress, that it was a matter of utter urgency and that he must come at once. Next she searched the room for the rattlesnake's rattle. She found it tucked away on a high shelf where it had been placed and then forgotten by the daily woman when she had done the cleaning. Putting it on the pillow beside Ann's head she sat down close to the girl, took her hand and, accepting that soon she might be involved in a conflict to the death with whatever was threatening the two lives under her care, readied herself for battle.

I climbed the mountain
To be at your side.
See, touch, enfold and the healing follows.

Chapter nineteen

"Jack, you've got eyes!" cried Dando, astonished, noticing for the first time a glint of green behind the dark-blond lock that always flopped over his friend's forehead.

"Glass," replied the other, tapping his nail against one of the orbs in question. "The old man arranged it – he didn't want me to appear too hideous – bad for the image. He had them specially made. They look ok don't they? I wasn't sure."

The two of them were squatting close to the road, shielded by a screen of trees, not far from the small port where they had met about an hour earlier. Dando, at Jack's urging, was sipping milk from a bottle while another container, holding ale, sat on the ground between them.

"You're nothing but a bag of bones," Jack had told him as they embraced on the quayside. "You need feeding up. Wait there a moment."

Appearing well acquainted with the layout of the little coastal town he disappeared into a nearby alley, his cane sweeping the ground before him, and re-emerged in a matter of minutes bearing the two bottles.

"Show me how to get to the highway," he instructed as if in a hurry to be gone.

"Y-you're ship?" Dando stammered, the first words he had managed to utter since their meeting apart from his friend's name.

"The ships aren't going anywhere, they're locked in. The Pickwah fleet's patrolling up and down the coast, imposing a blockade. If anyone dares put to sea their vessel is impounded and the crew pressed into service – it's worst than in the days of the Panther. No, I'm coming with you."

"B-but you're soaking wet!"

"It's summer - who cares. Find us a place out of sight of passing traffic – I want to see you get these down you, and then you can tell me how you came to be on your uppers."

Although his teeth were chattering and he could not stop shaking, Dando felt a slight alleviation of his symptoms now he had the comfort of another's presence. He imagined that he might even be able to put words together in order to give an account of his experiences if he could summon up sufficient resolution. They sat side by side on a piece of old rusting farm machinery, Jack's hand proprietorially on Dando's knee, while the dark-haired youth made an attempt to explain to the fair one, with many stumbles and embarrassed pauses, some of his recent history.

"I thought they were all d-dead. I decided I couldn't t-take any more. It wasn't too nice what happened. I didn't really come round until I was up in the tower in Pickwah fortress."

"And you say you could have escaped but you passed up the chance? You're crazy – you know that?"

"This chap – Raymond Spoon – he c-cut my foot off. Then I was supposed to be getting a lift all the way to V.P., stopping off at Gweek on the way in order to find out about the others, but the c-captain put me ashore the same afternoon and then I was robbed – they cleaned me out."

Dando imagined he was spinning a sad and cautionary tale. He was surprised and indignant when Jack doubled up with laughter at this last detail.

"You're telling me you lost everything on the very first night?" The boy slapped his side and wiped tears from his cheeks. "Well, you know what they say – *a fool and his money are soon parted* – and you are a fool, my sweet, some sort of holy fool I think."

Dando brooded for a while and then asked, "Have *you* got any money Jack?"

"Not a sou," - Jack flung his arms wide - "but we can remedy that – take me to the nearest town." They stood up, Jack putting his arm around Dando's waist to help him walk while Dando gripped Jack's shoulders, partly in order to support himself and partly to act as guide. Thus linked they climbed back onto the highway.

"This is a joke," remarked Jack, "the blind aiding the halt and the halt leading the blind. But all the same we'll do all right – we'll go the distance."

The next settlement along the road was more of a village than a town in size but boasted a large main square which, judging by the crowded pens and folds on the periphery, was being used for livestock transactions. A number of buyers were milling around; there was apparently going to be an auction later in the day.

"Find me a tin," instructed Jack.

"A tin?"

"Yes, a tin can out of a waste bin. A clean one if possible."

There were one or two receptacles for rubbish in the square. Dando searched and found what Jack required. The blind boy bent down and, running his hand over the ground, picked up two small stones which he dropped into the can. Then, taking out his realistic looking eyes, he tied them in the corner of a handkerchief before thrusting them into his pocket to join his penny whistle and sun-specs.

"Point me towards a group of women," he ordered.

Making great play with his cane and rattling the stones in the tin he walked across to where he could hear people talking, Dando following just a short distance behind.

"Give to the poor war-orphans of Osh," Jack cried. "Their daddies all were heroes, their mummies victims of atrocities by the Pickwah Army – as was I," indicating his face, "although I don't like to talk about it. And here's my friend (gesturing theatrically behind him) who was wounded in the battle for the town and since then has been reduced to penury. He's hard put to it to know where his next meal is coming from."

There was a murmur of concerned surprise from the assembled company.

"Poor young man," a voice was heard to say and people began reaching into their pockets and bringing out their purses. Coins clattered into the tin. Dando stood looking on in stupefaction.

"What the hell do you think you're doing?!" he cried. Spurred into action, he brought his crutch into play, heaved himself forward and grabbed hold of Jack's arm, attempting to drag him away.

"Stop it," whispered Jack, "I'm just earning our bread and butter,"

"But you c-can't do that - you can't get money by false pretences!"

"You want to eat, don't you?" and Jack turned back towards the prospective donors determined to demonstrate how he had earned his nick-name. Dando went to limp away, waving his hand as if bidding a final farewell.

"You can count me out," he cried, "I'll have no part of it."

"Don't be an idiot."

"No way, Jack, no way – I'm leaving."

Jack raised his own hand. "OK - see you later," he called, and then to the crowd, "The poor lad's embarrassed – he comes from a good family – he's too ashamed to beg."

After that donations came in thick and fast.

About two hours passed before Jack emerged from amongst the houses, feeling his way forward with his cane. "Are you there little bird?" he called.

Dando, sitting by the roadside, watched him approach, and when he had drawn level and was about to pass by said quietly, "I'm here."

Jack stopped and held out one of a pair of greasy packages.

"You're not going to turn your nose up at good food are you?" he said.

They sat and ate the fish and chips, not saying a word, thinking their own thoughts, until, still unspeaking, they got up, linked themselves together as before and continued on down the road. It was as they approached yet another small settlement that Dando at last broke silence.

"Is there any money left?" he enquired.

"A tidy sum – why?"

"I need some medicine."

"What sort of medicine?"

"Oh just something to help me sleep."

Dando tried to speak casually but he was not good at dissembling and a hint of desperation accompanied the words. Jack was immediately on the alert.

"What sort of medicine?" he asked again.

"Oh you know – the kind of stuff that comes from abroad with blue labels and a blurb on the back."

"Dr Good's?!" exclaimed Jack incredulously, "that satan's syrup? What strength?"

"Five," replied Dando shamefaced, turning away.

There was a long pause and then Jack gave another shout of laughter.

"Well munchkin," he said after he had recovered himself, "who'd have thought it! Kicking the gong around - and you such a Goody Twoshoes! I'd never have taken you for a junkie. It's poison that stuff, unadulterated poison. I should know, I was hooked on it for two years."

"But I need it Jack," pleaded Dando piteously, "I c-can't sleep without it."

"Yes and one night you'll sleep a bit too soundly - you'll find you're sleeping your very last sleep of all. I've seen it happen to a lot of good kids. The lead singer with the Posse, that time they were still doing their own thing – you've heard of him? He was one of them."

"I need it," repeated Dando as if stuck in a groove. "It's a nightmare when I haven't got it. Please Jack."

"I thought you lost everything weeks ago – it's expensive stuff. If you've been taking it recently where did it come from?"

Embarrassed, Dando confessed to his crime. Again Jack was doubled up with laughter.

"A fine crook you must have made sweeting, but by some miracle you got away with it."

"No Jack, I was caught. I was whipped. But they gave it back to me when I left."

This sobered Jack up.

"And you've been without it for two days? I suppose you're feeling rotten?"

"Awful," said Dando.

"Well, you're going to feel a lot worse before you're done cos you're going on the wagon my love, I can assure you of that."

"Oh no, Jack – I just couldn't – if I don't take it I get these awful pains."

"Really? Well, I'm sure there's remedies for dealing with those that don't involve killing yourself. I'll help you through it I promise - we'll do this together - I'll be with you every step of the way."

Jack had collected enough money to buy them beds at an inn for a few nights. Dando was persuaded to stay in one place for a while and take some much needed rest although he fretted at the delay.

"I must find Annie, I must – and Master Tallisand and Foxy of course. And there's something else - this man told me it's my destiny to go over the sea."

"Destiny? That sounds a bit creepy to me – you don't believe all that fortune-telling mumbo-jumbo do you? We're a bit more enlightened in Drossi than to give elbow-room to that kind of stuff."

"I don't know – all I know is I must keep moving."

But in a couple more days Dando was in no fit state to go anywhere. When Jack had offered to break him of his addiction he had not been aware of his true physical state and now he was horrified to witness the extent of the boy's suffering. The withdrawal symptoms he was experiencing due to the absence of Dr Goods aggravated his physical debility and the trauma his limbs had undergone intensified the drug induced dysfunction. If he sat or lay still for more than a few minutes he sweated, shook and vomited while his muscles began to clench and tie themselves in knots causing him intense agony. He was forced to leap up and drag himself to and fro across the room keeping his body in continual motion; it was the only way he could gain any sort of relief. Jack lay listening to him in appalled silence throughout two long nights. On the third he had to intervene.

"Stop it, stop it!" he cried. "You're not doing yourself any favours! Come back here – let me try something." And when he sensed Dando was within arms reach he pulled him down onto the bed and crouched above him.

"I used to help my mother. She was a martyr to her legs. I massaged them to relieve the pain – let me try that."

At first Dando was terrified. "You'll make it worse," he whimpered.

"No I won't – just let me try. Tell me where it hurts."

"Everywhere."

Jack's hands seemed to come with some sort of magic attached; there was a lightness and delicacy present when they made contact. He explored Dando's body from head to toe noting the overstretched ligaments, the displaced cartilage, the partly dislocated joints. He discovered muscles twisted and contorted, hard as iron, and set about kneading them back into malleability. Dando breathed shallow and quick, in panic mode, but did not attempt to escape. He looked up into his friend's face out of some sort of private hell, his eyes, pits of darkness, clinging on as if to a life-line. Slowly he began to recognise something healing in the other's touch; he began to trust and as a consequence to unwind. Smoothing, stroking, squeezing, pummelling Jack persuaded the stubborn knots to loosen and as he worked he sang, a bawdy lullaby with lyrics made up on the spur of the moment. Miraculously the pain eased and Dando began to drift off and away, released for a time from his torment (for seventy-two hours he had had no rest at all). As he hung on the cusp between waking and sleeping he became aware that Jack was going slightly further than mere massage.

Dando's companion was true to his promise. He stayed with him throughout every passing moment, comforting when necessary, persuading him sometimes to be still and sometimes to exercise, talking and getting the boy to talk back in order to take his mind off his miseries.

"You must avoid being hungry, angry, lonely or tired," he advised as if reciting a litany, "and relax, my bird, relax, always relax."

They went out together, arms round each other's waists and walked to the cliff top where they sat watching and listening to the ever-changing sea. Jack played on his pipe and repeated the massage whenever Dando's cramps returned. It was on the fourth day of their stay that a knock came at the door of their room and Jack opened it to find the innkeeper standing outside.

"I've 'ad complaints," he said. "I'm afraid I must ast you to leave my establishment by this evening at the latest."

Dando was surprised and totally mystified at this summary dismissal but Jack knew immediately what was up.

"This young gentleman is in my care – our relationship is purely that of doctor and patient," he lectured haughtily, "he's recuperating from a serious accident. It was thought beneficial that he should convalesce in a marine environment. His condition requires daily manipulation. He's not fit to be moved."

"I'm sorry," said the innkeeper, "I've got to think of my other guests. I can't put up wiv pervert practices under my roof."

When the man had gone Dando looked to Jack for an explanation.

"Did he mean..." he began, then faltered.

"Yes, you've got it in one," Jack laughed bitterly. "Queers - that's what they think we are. If two men share a room it's enough to raise their suspicions. Well, in this case they're half right. Come on birdy, the money was about to run out anyway. It's summer, it's warm – how about a night under the stars?"

That evening after it got dark they made their bed in a small secluded dingle. Soon Dando began to move restlessly and require Jack's administrations once more. The other obliged, but this time, having eased his friend's discomfort, he made no bones about admitting to his intentions regarding the one who had stolen his heart.

"Let's give them something real to complain of, eh my sweet?"

Dando, initially alienated and repelled, pushed him away.

"No Jack, no – I don't want to."

Jack desisted and did not try anything more for several days, but meanwhile Dando gave the matter serious thought. He realised that it was within his power to furnish something that his friend devoutly desired and that up to now, since their meeting on the quayside, all the giving had been on Jack's side. He asked himself why he should mind and where was the harm. No one would know and he was sure the blind boy would be careful not to hurt him. This was something that it was in his power to grant in return for the other's care. And so, through gratitude and the pity that had played a part in his feelings for Jack ever since their first encounter, he came to a decision and on the next occasion that the young man made an advance he allowed the intimacy and in this almost casual way became his friend's catamite.

To give Jack his due, after some time had passed he offered to reverse roles and proffered his own body for the other's use.

"Now it's your turn my love - there won't be any problems – I've been well broken in – you could drive a horse and cart up me," but Dando declined with thanks.

"Well how about I give you a blow job? - Or we try our hand at soixante-neufs," offered Jack, determined to be generous, but again Dando declined. Apart from the occasional night-time erection, born out of some confused erotic dream, his own libido had fallen asleep on the night of the fire and showed no sign of reawakening. He made himself available to Jack and felt a faint twinge of regret that he could not join him in his transports when the climax arrived. He did not question or raise objections to the other's demands, however strange he found them. Sometimes during their lovemaking Jack would remove his belt and gently bind Dando's wrists together as well as blindfolding him with his red scarf. He seemed to get a kick out of having his paramour apparently helpless and completely in his power.

Meanwhile, during the day, their ingenuity was exercised in finding something to fill their bellies. In deference to Dando's scruples Jack did not try the war-orphans scam again, but to his chagrin found that other clever and inventive ways of making money were also frowned upon. Selling raffle tickets that he had *acquired* from a stationers' in one of the larger towns they passed through was not allowed; taking bets on a local horse race with the intention of absconding with the proceeds was greeted with horror; persuading school-children to give up their dinner-money by playing the highwayman-game with a make-believe pistol was strictly off limits.

"You're determined we should starve, aren't you spatzi," he grumbled ruefully.

As Dando had done before they met they were reduced to knocking on doors and begging for their bread but with a marked lack of success even when the younger boy was sent in alone.

"You look more up against it than me," Jack decided on volunteering his friend for the job, although he had only his sense of touch to inform him of Dando's mien.

On one occasion, despite their empty stomachs, they were both lying dead to the world in a camp they had established at the base of a small hillock. It was the night of the full moon and a great golden orb was just rising behind the rim of the mound. Earlier Jack had lulled Dando to sleep with rhythmical caresses and, once he knew the boy had drifted off, begun gently exploring his face. He ran his fingers over his friend's immobile features, conjuring up the beloved visage in his mind's eye, the one he had never seen. He imagined it worn and wasted but beautiful still, an exceptional face, a face that might move multitudes. If only he still had his sight! He sat and brooded over what had been taken from him and, a rarity for him, wallowed for a while in self pity before making a dismissive sound in his throat and stretching out beside his lover.

A short while later it was Dando's turn to become fully awake and, pushing his hair out of his eyes, he looked around wondering what had disturbed him. The round glowing disc of the moon was resting on the top of the hill as if its weight was too great to heave itself up any higher into the sky and against it, sharply delineated, he saw the pitch-black immobile silhouette of a large wolf-like animal. He raised himself on his elbows, his eyes fixed on this manifestation. What he imagined he was seeing was one of the Old Ones, those spectres he had been plagued by as a child but which in later years he had learned to deal with so effectively that he had almost stopped believing in their existence. Only when he was on his way to the Upper Valley to exorcise his dream and then later when he had been hung in the tree and had come close to death had he sensed the nearness of that thaumaturgic world. Was this the Gally Trot, the Hell Hound he could see up on the hill and if so what did it want with him? The shape in front of the moon suddenly vanished but there was just light enough to detect a dark shadow coming swiftly down the slope towards him. He groped round about for something he could use as a weapon but neither he nor Jack was carrying even a knife between them. His hand chanced on the other's slender cane and for want of anything better he picked it up and held it before him at the ready crying as he did so, "Keep away – avaunt, avaunt!"

What had he learnt to do back in the day? Oh yes, of course, he had to recite – that was it – rattle off some piece of doggerel which would act as a kind of spell and set up a counter-magic to that of the creature's. He rapidly dredged something from childhood memories:

> *"Hark, hark, the dogs do bark,*
>
> *The beggars are coming to town.*
>
> *Some in rags and some in tags*
>
> *And some in velvet gowns.*
>
> *Wait, wait, don't lock the gate..."*

The shadow came to a stop a few yards away. It crouched down and Dando thought he could detect a tail tentatively thumping the ground. Then it began squirming forward on its belly, a faint whine in its throat. Dando rubbed his eyes and looked towards Jack as if needing confirmation from the blind boy as to what he was seeing, but the other remained totally comatose. He faced towards the approaching apparition and croaked in a voice of unbelief, "Ralph?" The animal, much more obviously a flesh and blood dog now it had come out from under the shadow of the hill, was seized with an ecstasy of tail wagging but hung back as if uncertain of its reception. Dando dropped the cane he had been holding and shouting, "Ralph!" at the top of his voice flung himself forward to embrace his old friend – it was a moment of unadulterated joy.

"Ralph, where have you been? How did you get here? Are the others close by? I'm so glad to see you."

The dog twisted and turned in his arms, his tongue licking any part of Dando's exposed flesh that presented itself.

"What's going on?" The noise had finally woken Jack and he rolled over, drowsily running his hand down his face.

"Jack – its Ralph – I told you about Ralph – Tallis' dog. Heaven knows how he found us. Praps he's brought the others with him. No Ralph! - this is a friend!" for as Jack sat up the dog growled softly and the hair rose on his neck.

"Here," said Dando apologetically, "let him smell you, then he'll know you're not a threat."

Jack held out a hand and felt Ralph's fur and his undernourished body.

"One more mouth to feed," he grumbled.

The hope Dando nursed that Ralph would lead him to Tallis and his other companions was quickly dashed. The next morning when he commanded, "Where's Tallis? Find Tallis Ralph, find Ann, find Foxy," the dog stared off into the distance for a moment then turned back sadly while both his head and tail took on a defeated droop. He was saying as plainly as he was able, *Sorry master, no can do.* It was clear when they examined him in daylight that Ralph had been on an odyssey of his own and had been alone for some time: his paws were sore and his coat matted and filthy.

"He followed us that night when Ann and I went up to the wood," Dando explained. "I think he may have been frightened off by the fire. Perhaps by the time he came back everyone was either dead or gone. That he's found us now is really amazing."

Having come across one of his own people, maybe by some sort of psychic direction-finding, Ralph was not going to let him out of his sight. He settled himself by Dando's side each night and was never more than a few feet away from him during the day. He treated Jack with profound suspicion, sensing a rival for his master's affections and a hostile one at that. Once camp was set up Jack had a tendency to trip over the dog when he came upon him unexpectedly which caused him to let rip with a string of oaths under his breath. This did not improve their relationship.

The food situation was getting desperate; a remedy was required and soon a short-term solution presented itself. When they arrived at one particular sea-side town and learnt that a wedding reception was to take place in the community hall that very evening Jack pleaded with Dando to relax his standards slightly.

"Weddings are a good thing to gate-crash; one lot have no idea what the other lot looks like. If you act like you belong everyone just thinks you're part of the other side. Come on birdy, be a bit adaptable for once – after all you're a hardened criminal – you and your Dr. Good's - why should you object?"

Dando blushed and reluctantly allowed Jack to try and smarten him up.

"We must look a right couple of scarecrows," regretted the former dandy. "Have a good wash and let me comb your hair – and get rid of that ratty old coat – its much too warm for this weather anyway."

"I'm not getting rid of the coat," said Dando.

In the end they had no need to dissemble. When they presented themselves at the door having left Ralph to guard their temporary campsite a man put plates in their hands.

"Come on in lads, its a free-for-all tonight. Bride's from across the brook – brought a fine dowry with her."

They ate until they were fit to burst, Dando carefully stowing away items to offer to Ralph, and then found seats round the edge of the room from where Jack could listen to the music and Dando watch the dancing that followed. Jack got out his pipe and played along, thoroughly enjoying himself. It was when he passed a remark to Dando about the familiarity of one of the tunes that he realised that his companion was no longer at his side. Faintly worried he went out into the salty night air and called but it was only on his third attempt that he received a reply from a short distance away. Dando was sitting on the sea wall across the road, his back to the bright lights of the hall. Jack put his hand on his friend's head and ruffled his hair.

"What's the matter, mon ange?" he asked.

"I used to like to dance," said Dando, "I was good at dancing." His voice held a profound note of regret. Jack realised that this was no laughing matter, was in fact a serious issue.

"You can still dance," he said.

"How?"

"You can make up your own kind of dance. Look at me, do I let this stop me from doing what I want?" pointing to his missing eyes.

"I'm not like you Jack."

"No, you're like yourself and that's not to be sneezed at. You could do it if you tried - if you set your mind to it."

Dando sat silently, staring into the darkness.

"Come on," said Jack playing a run on his pipe, "get up – give it a go."

Dando remained where he was.

"Come on," repeated Jack, "show some chutzpah – let's see some moves."

The boy lent on his crutch and slowly pulled himself upright. He tucked the support under his arm. The music from the hall was clearly audible. Jack put his pipe to his lips and began to harmonise. Dando assayed one or two tentative hops which were accompanied, as always, by small shooting twinges of pain. Suddenly he was flooded by a feeling of intense anger. Why shouldn't he do this? What right had circumstances to rob him of all the best things that existence had to offer? What did it matter if it hurt or even if it shortened his life? Lifting the end of his crutch from the ground he held the grip with both hands and then slammed it down hard. At the same time he kicked off with his one remaining foot and swung his body round in an almost horizontal arc using the crutch as fulcrum. Three times he did this, landing safely, until on the fourth attempt his foot came in contact with the wall he had just been sitting on knocking him off balance. He lay in the road panting and laughing weakly, testing his limbs to make sure he had not made things worse for himself.

"What's up?" demanded Jack. "Don't stop when you've only just begun."

"Enough, Jack, enough."

"Well – I promise you – you're going to practice every single day from now on until you're the best bloody one-legged dancer this side of the Middle Sea."

They came to Gweek. Dando stood below the wood at the top of the comb in which the village was situated looking downwards while Jack hung a yard or two back respecting his friend's need for solitude at this moment. He wondered what the boy was seeing. As far as he was concerned he could hear the sea in the distance and detect a faint scorching smell on the wind. In fact Dando was thinking how it would not be long before he would probably know the unvarnished truth concerning the fate of his companions. In consequence he was feeling coldly apprehensive. The scene below remained one of ruin and desolation, the pitiful blackened interiors of the roofless houses still open to the sky, but in two areas there were signs that the place had not been completely abandoned. The undamaged stone walls of a couple of cottages were being used as bases for the construction of fresh upper stories built of timber which, along with other materials such as slate for roofing and glass for windows, could be seen piled nearby. All was quiet – there was no evidence of activity – but then he detected a small movement. A man was standing within the frame of a half-constructed doorway eating a sandwich.

"There's somebody down there," he told Jack. "I'm going to go and see if he knows anything."

Dando descended the main street followed by his friend. He realised that the lone inhabitant was standing quite close to the site of the cottage in which the travellers had taken refuge on that fateful night, the place where he had succumbed to his desires and abandoned those who were depending on him. Payment had yet to be made for that treachery.

"Excuse me," he called to the man as soon as they came within hailing distance, "I'm looking for three people. They were here on the night of the fire, the night the village was attacked. I'm looking for two men and a young girl. You might have noticed them because they would have been strangers to you – they didn't come from this part of the world."

The man gave Dando a searching look and then nodded.

"We 'ad to bury a few 'oo weren't quick enough off the mark but they were our own folk; there weren't no furriners among 'em. Those as did manage to get away went over to Praa for the most part."

"But did you see any strangers – two men and a girl?"

"I 'eard tell o' two men – that's all – one none too lusty – they left back in t'spring."

"We must go over to this Praa place," Dando said to Jack and then asked the man, "how do you get there?"

"There's a path but it's zteep – you'd do better to go back to t'road and take the second turning on the left."

"Thank you very much, you've been most helpful."

At Praa they heard the same story. Yes, two strangers had come on the night of the raid – one had been taken ill – they had left three and a half weeks later. No, they had not seen a young girl. "I mind there be a new man over at the big houze," piped up a woman, "in the gardens. My Mary tol' me – she works at Witteridge. He be a furriner – not from roun' here – red-headed fellow. Praps it be he that you're lookin' for."

"Yes," said Dando eagerly, "and did he have a girl with him – a blond girl?"

"No – no girl."

"How do we get to Witteridge?" asked Jack.

"Back on the road and then head towards Drossi, it's a fair ztep; take you a while on foot."

The Praa folk had presumably registered Dando's crippled state but no-one seemed prepared to offer them a lift.

"Course you may find 'em packed up an' gone – a lot of the quality are gettin' out ahead of Trewithik's army."

"An' zo should we," someone remarked.

"Oh he won't be botherin' his head with zmall places like this."

The road was becoming more and more crowded, the whole country being on the move it seemed. Entire communities overtook Jack and Dando, baggage wagons piled high with domestic impedimenta, youngsters, oldsters and small livestock perched on top, the vehicles hung round with every conceivable size and shape of container. A few men were to be seen travelling in the opposite direction, desperate-looking characters armed to the teeth, but whether they were going to join the invading army or to fight against it there was no way of telling. Villages they came to were either almost deserted or were throwing up barricades in order to defend themselves in case the invaders got that far. There was a feeling of lawlessness and anarchy in the air. Jack and Dando minded their own business and tried not to draw attention to themselves. When they camped they chose secluded places well away from the road. On one particular evening they had bedded down in a hollow that seemed pretty much out of harm's way: it was well screened and about a mile from the next settlement. Jack took his pleasure as he did most nights and then they both fell asleep. It was in the dark hour before dawn that the blind boy came to himself and sensed that Dando was awake and tense beside him.

"Are you in pain, my love?" he asked.

"A little."

"Here, let me help you."

Jack worked his usual manual magic and then the two of them lay and talked, neither feeling they needed to go back to sleep.

"What's this scar on your arm?" asked Jack, running his fingers over a slight imperfection in the otherwise smooth skin.

"Oh it's a tattoo – it's the double D," replied his friend, "that stands for Dando and Damask – something my sister did for me when we were kids – it got us into trouble. How about you? You've never said how you came to be aboard ship."

"You really want to know that?"

Jack had already explained what had happened after his return to Drossi and told of his escape from his grandfather's palace but now he continued the story.

"I made my way to Dermody and hung round the docks. There was a merchant I knew there whose vessel had just come into port and some of his crew had gone awol. He was one of the many independent traders who are at daggers drawn with my granddaddy's corporation. He took me on just to spite the old fossil I think but once aboard I found things to do. I began learning my trade and showed him that a blind man isn't totally useless. I'll go back to it someday. How about you birdy? Are you clean now – or will you make a beeline for the candy man as soon as I turn my back?"

"I think I can get by Jack, but I won't know for sure till I'm on my own. I couldn't have done it without you, it's having you here that's made all the difference."

"Well, I'm not thinking of heading off anywhere just yet lad. You're going to have to put up with me for a while longer – at least until we get to this Witteridge place and find out if this red-headed guy is your friend Foxy, though if it were me I don't know if I'd call him a friend at all considering the way he took away your lay at Toymerle."

"He's more than just a friend Jack – he's my half-brother."

"What!?" Jack raised himself abruptly and turned towards Dando in astonishment. "Your actual brother? You're kidding me!"

"No – it's almost certainly true," and Dando recounted the tale of his father's illicit love affair and its outcome.

"And then I went and did the very same thing – fell in love with a Nablan girl. Anyway he doesn't know anything about what I just told you – Foxy I mean – and you mustn't let on because..."

"Because of what?"

"Well, I promised Ann – and there's something I missed out when we talked at Toymerle."

"What's that?"

"Well I found out that when I left the valley my father came after me; he meant to take me back home I suppose, but he never got to do that because somebody shot him – shot him dead with an arrow on the Northern Drift. A long time later Annie told me about what happened and who did it - it was Foxy - he was the one."

"My god! No wonder you're at daggers drawn!"

Dando shook his head.

"At first I wanted to kill him – not now."

"Stap my vitals cully! And he doesn't know he shot his own father? Someone ought to put him in the picture!"

"No Jack – not you – let it be."

They relapsed into silence for a while until Dando said, "You know I really think that even if it wasn't addictive, every time I saw Dr Good's on sale I'd be tempted to buy some. I had the most amazing dreams."

"There are other techniques for tripping my love that don't involve risking your life."

"Yes I know; I used to get sort of high sometimes when I was on my own in the valley without taking anything, but I'm not sure that that would work any more. I made a big mistake after I left Gweek and I feel that's why so many bad things have been happening."

"Mistake? What do you mean by mistake?"

"Well, I thought Annie, Tallis and Foxy had been killed an' that it was all my fault so I decided I wanted to die too. I set out to commit suicide on the Dark Island and I know now that that was wicked. However badly you've behaved you have to stay alive and make up for what you've done, not try and do away with yourself – to do so is cowardice."

"You think you're being punished?"

"Yes."

"And I suppose this is my punishment for being on the hur," pointing to his face.

"Don't be stupid."

Jack put both arms around Dando and drew him into an embrace.

"All right, birdy," he said, "I won't try and shatter your illusions but I'll let you into a little secret – you couldn't do *wicked* even if your life depended on it," and he kissed him full on the lips.

"Tch, tch, tch, tch," interrupted a voice, "wot's goin' on 'ere?"

A man was standing on the edge of the hollow where they had camped holding up a lantern and with some sort of weapon, a primitive blunderbuss it looked like, over his arm.

"Obscenity in a public place; unnatural acts; corruptin' civic morals. We can't 'ave that kind of thing I'm afraid – you'll 'ave to come wiv me."

The two boys, who had thought themselves well hidden, shrunk away from each other while Ralph leapt to his feet and stood in front of them a growl in his throat.

"Control that dog," ordered the night-watchman, if that is what he was, raising his gun.

"Stop it Ralph!" cried Dando grabbing his protector and pulling him out of the light, terrified that he might be shot.

"Come on," said the man again, waving the firearm, "get up. I'm taking you to the command post."

"No," said Jack struggling to his feet, "just take me - it's not what you think – he's perfectly straight."

"Is that so? Well, we'll discuss that when we gets to 'eadquarters. Let's see you both come to attention – smart-like."

Dando also climbed back onto his one leg with the aid of the crutch and then looked down at the dog. "Stay Ralph," he ordered. "On guard. I won't be long."

The vigilante pointed them towards the road making great play with his weapon. They were marched eastwards until they came to a large hut on the right hand side. It was already getting light. Within were a host of men, some sleeping, some eating breakfast. They had apparently just returned from night patrols in which they had been on the watch for the Pickwah army.

"Look what I've found," cried Jack and Dando's captor as he came through the door, pushing the miscreants ahead of him with the barrel of the gun. "Two fairies 'avin' it orf in the bushes – they were surprised to see me I c'n tell you."

This was greeted with jeers and laughter accompanied by one or two wolf whistles.

"It was me," repeated Jack again, "he had nothing to do with it – you've got to let him go."

"Oh ok," said the man who had already arrived at a decision concerning the two boys' immediate futures, "it's the pillory for you then mate, dawn to dusk." Turning to Dando he added, "You c'n spend the day 'ere wiv us while you waits for 'im to complete 'is sentence."

"No!" cried Jack sharply, suddenly seeing where things were heading.

"Oh yes," replied the man and to two of his sidekicks, "take that one outside."

"No!" cried Jack again, contending with his captors, and then as they dragged him away, "Be brave, Dando! They're nothing, nothing. They can't hurt you!"

"'Oo's a lucky fellow then?" said the militia man to an uncomprehending Dando after the door had closed and hidden Jack from sight, "'is boyfriend gets stuff chucked in 'is face all day long which could be quite unpleasant, while 'e 'as the chance to go to a party and make lots of new pals."

To forgive an enemy
Is easier than to forgive a friend
Unless atonement follows.

Chapter twenty

The light was fading and it was well on towards nightfall by the time Jack was released from the pillory in which he had spent the day. He was bruised, filthy dirty and hardly in control of his body after being in one position for so long but fortunately most of the missiles hurled at him had been fairly soft: bad eggs, rotten fruit, dung for the most part; the town-folk's hearts had not been totally committed to the assault; they had had their minds on other things.

"Where's the lad who was with me?" he rasped as the two men who had been sent to free him lifted the plank from his neck and, rather surprisingly, handed over his cane along with a few other items that had been removed from his pockets at the start of his sentence.

"Oh, your rent boy – 'e's gorn," pointing down the road. "We gave 'im a good seein' to – 'e won't forget us in an 'urry."

There was an ache in Jack's chest as if his heart had been spitted on a stake as he stumbled through the settlement calling and calling again with what was left of his voice, not caring about the spectacle he was making of himself. When he got no response going eastwards he turned and retraced his steps through the dark streets leaving the little burg by the way he had entered it.

"Birdy, birdy!" he cried, "Dando, Dando!" listening all the time for the familiar loved tones but hearing nothing but the lonely sigh of the wind. The chest pain spread upwards to his throat and down to his gut until he felt on the verge of collapse as his desperation grew. He walked, shouting his friend's name, until he was sure he had passed the place where the patrolmen's hut was located, then came to an indecisive halt, having reached a complete impasse with no idea as to what to do next. In that moment of desolation a remote noise was carried to him on the breeze, the faint complaining whine of a large dog.

"Ralph!"

Jack turned off the road in the direction of the sound and after blundering into trees, getting caught up in bushes and falling over roots came at last to the hollow where they had spent much of the previous night.

"Ralph," he cried, "are you here?"

He groped forward and his hands made contact with a rough coat, pricked ears and a long wolf-like muzzle. The faithful hound was still standing guard as he had been told to do over twelve hours earlier. It was time to bury the hatchet.

"Ralph, I can't find him," said Jack, a catch in his voice. "Where's Dando? Where's your master?"

Ralph whined and shifted uneasily; he seemed to sense that something was totally amiss.

"You'll have to track him down fellow, I can't do it. Find Dando Ralph, find your master!"

The dog wriggled his body, his tail tucked between his legs. He was obviously perplexed. His canine thoughts, if they could have been put into words, would have run something like this: *Here's the place where I've been told to stay by the one I worship and who can command me in all things. Yet now the other hairless one, the usurper, is telling me to neglect my duty and go elsewhere. This is completely out of order. But conversely I'm also being instructed to find Dando, the master I'm missing more and more with every passing minute and who, through some strange animal intuition, I sense is in trouble.* As if trying to decide on a course of action he paced to and fro for several minutes, rumbling and growling in his throat, before coming to a decision and starting for the road. As he brushed past Jack the boy grabbed at his coat and managed to seize hold of his tail. The dog shrieked and turned to snap, then pulled away, but Jack hung on so fiercely that he was towed out of the hollow, up onto the highway and along it.

Eventually Ralph came to a stop and refused to go any further. Jack tumbled to the fact that Dando must be in the vicinity, that he could actually be quite close by, and, if this was the case, then he had probably passed him more than once during his search. He released the dog's tail and the animal bounded forward in order to be reunited with the master he loved, the master who, in fact, was sitting on a low wall less than five feet away, only to give an astonished yelp as he was roughly repelled. After that the Glept froze into a corpse-like stillness until Jack, making contact, attempted to put his arm about his shoulders. Dando immediately swatted his hand away as if it were a fly, muttering as he did so, "Don't touch me."

Jack waited for a few minutes and then, saying gently, "Come on lad, it's time to make a move," tried unsuccessfully to lend the boy a helping hand. Having again been rebuffed he stood irresolutely on the highway in the chilly night air while Ralph whined almost silently beside him.

"Are we going to stay here all night?" he asked eventually. "Don't you want to get away from this wretched town? Come on, let's go and find somewhere where we can wash off the filth."

This seemed to be the catalyst which broke through Dando's ossified trance. Jack became aware of his friend making an attempt to rise, he was still apparently in possession of his crutch, although he seemed to have some difficulty pulling himself upright and Jack thought he heard a suppressed groan. He could not prevent himself reaching out towards the other but once more his aid was spurned and again the boy croaked, "Don't touch me."

Forbidden to make physical contact, all Jack could do was take his cue from the noise of Dando's dot-and-carry-one footsteps and follow the sound down the road. After a mile or two another voice, musical and watery, interposed itself and grew louder as they approached. A small rivulet was singing a song as it ran through a culvert under the track's tarry surface. Jack's sharp ears detected a similar but more urgent strain coming from somewhere off to the right.

"Try following the watercourse upstream," he said to Dando. "There may be a place out of sight where we can bathe."

His companion silently obeyed and within a few minutes they came upon a pool before a low cliff over which the stream was cascading. Without apparently stopping to think Dando waded fully clothed into the water and stood under the fall as it poured down over his head and shoulders. Jack, more circumspect, disrobed and felt his way into the pond where he washed both his garments and himself. Then, climbing out, he dressed in the wet clothes before trying to locate Dando.

"Where are you, my bird?" he called and by listening carefully noticed that the changed voice of the fall indicated that something was interrupting its flow.

"Come on, leibling," he said, "the water's freezing. You'll catch your death if you stay there much longer. Let's get going – if we start walking we'll warm up and then we'll begin to dry off."

There was no response; Dando still stood with the fall breaking over his head. When Jack re-entered the pool and tried to seize his friend's arm the other fought so frantically to free himself that he had to let go. He walked downstream towards the road thinking that if he put some distance between the two of them the boy might relent. After a few yards he stopped and stood dripping.

"This is all my fault," he moaned to himself, "my fault entirely - I'm to blame! Merde! Merde! Merde! Merde!." After each profanity he slashed at the air with the cane, the cane that had been restored to him on his release, only for it to snap in two as it came into contact with a waterside willow. He threw the piece he still held into the stream shedding accusatory tears.

A long while later Dando returned to the road and turned eastward. As before Jack followed the sound of his boot and crutch through the night until, sometime in the small hours, the young man sank onto the verge as if he could go no further. Jack lay down as near to him as he dared. Neither of them slept.

Without his cane, which had acted as a substitute eye, Jack was greatly handicapped. The next day when they resumed their journey he walked with his hands held out in front of him but this told him nothing about the track beneath his feet. Almost inevitably he stepped on a piece of road that had gone missing and took a tumble. It was a bad fall. In landing he sprained both wrists and, what was worse, hit his head on the far side of the pot-hole knocking himself out. When he regained consciousness a little later, someone had their arm about him and was dabbing at his forehead with a scarf. It was Dando.

"I'm sorry," the boy whispered.

"It's all right, lad," said Jack, "trust me to go arse over tit."

When eventually Jack got to his feet ready to continue Dando put an arm across his shoulders to guide him and allowed the other to encircle his waist so that they were once again linked as they had been throughout their journeying together. They continued on in this fashion, normal relations to all appearances having been restored, but for the whole day Dando uttered not a word. In the evening Jack managed to beg some bread and cheese from a friendly cottager before making camp. They sat eating, or at least Jack did; Dando seemed unable to face the thought of food. Ralph came and nuzzled the young man's shoulder, begging for a caress, but was pushed away. Jack, who had relapsed into a silence almost as complete and prolonged as his friend's finally decided that the situation could not be allowed to continue in this fashion. The abomination had to be brought out into the open; the unspeakable must be spoken of.

"I may as well tell you" he said quietly, " that the same thing happened to me - once in a back-alley in Drossi and more than once up at the Cheetah's hideaway. You probably won't believe it now but you get over it. No – I mean things are never the same afterwards but you learn to cope – to live in a different way."

He was not even sure that Dando had heard him, there was absolutely no response. Jack took a risk and broached a subject that he was almost sure would elicit a reaction.

"You're going to have to come to terms with it lad. It won't be long before you'll be back with your Annie – you want to be right for her, don't you?"

Dando's breath caught and his face was momentarily distorted by an ugly grimace.

"That's all over now," he mouthed, the words coming out in a hoarse whisper.

"Over? What do you mean?"

"I'd only make her dirty."

"Dirty? - Don't talk nonsense. We're going to find her, you can be sure of that, and then you'll be like the cat who got the cream."

"No, I'll make her dirty too."

"Look lad, it's not you who are dirty – it's them, those dirty old men. Dirty minds – dirty hearts."

There was a pause, then Jack, trying a different tack, said, "Tell me about that cottage in the place that you come from. You used to go there with Ann you said."

Yet another long silence ensued. Jack thought his companion had reverted to a state of frigid vacuity until the young man stirred and began speaking in a low tone as if communing with himself.

"She'd help me sometimes," he said, "when she wasn't doing her garden. We'd prepare vegetables together – bent over the same bowl – her head almost touching mine – just the two of us," and he began to weep.

"Good, good," cried Jack; this was progress. "Keep going, keep going!"

When the sobs subsided he urged, "Describe the first thing you cooked up there – and then what was the next thing you tried? Yes, and after that - what then? Now how about that priest fellow from Drossi you told me about – Father Adelbert – what did you cook for him...?"

As Dando became absorbed, despite himself, in the subject dearest to his heart and began tearfully to explain his culinary techniques, the blood started to creep back into his face, which for the past few hours had been as white as a sheet, and he began to look a little healthier. At last he yawned. Jack hid a triumphant grin.

"Go to sleep now, caridad," he said, "but remember, you've got a lot more to tell me in the morning."

Day followed day and Dando's behaviour settled into a simulacrum of normality; he even managed the occasional wan smile when Jack acted the fool for his benefit. At night though their former intimacy and its accompanying emotions which had been so terribly mocked and degraded, had inevitably become a thing of the past. The tender affection that had played a major part in their intercourse was forever compromised by the layers of insupportable memories that had been superimposed over it in Dando's mind. Jack realised that they were never going to be partners in the physical sense again. It did not seem to matter. All that concerned him now was that the boy should not suffer any more in body or spirit. When the cramps returned as they inevitably did he found he was allowed to remedy them with massage as before but he had to be careful, oh so careful: it was like stroking a half-wild cat which up to that point has known only blows and abuse from man. Jack felt he was walking on eggshells.

In due time they came to the Witteridge Estate. The road took them past the demesne's rear entrance, the pair of wrought-iron gates that had been the focus of Foxy's attention five months previously when he had taken the trouble to puzzle out the wording on a sign advertising the position of under gardener. To the right of the gates hung a chain, obviously a bell-pull. Jack discovered this with the stick Dando had picked up along the roadside and given him as a replacement for his cane. He raised his hand to give it a tug but then desisted.

"These people," he asked Dando, "what are you expecting to happen when you meet?"

"That I'll make reparation for my fault," replied the other.

"Your fault? You mean the time you went absent without leave in order to get it on with your ride?"

"When I betrayed them," said Dando.

"And what will you do to *make reparation* as you call it?"

"That will depend on them."

Jack frowned and shook his head.

"Not good," he said, "not good little bird. That red head's a bully if ever I saw one. I could tell it a mile off."

"Jack," said Dando, " I think you'd better let me do this my way."

"I'm not leaving you," replied his friend – the very same words Dando had uttered on the day they first met.

"Well, don't interfere."

It was Dando who pulled the chain, setting off a sonorous tolling that probably carried for more than a mile. They had a long wait before a small figure approached on the other side of the gates. A boy of about thirteen spoke to them through the bars.

"Mr Murdock be up by the house. 'Oo do 'ee wan' to zee?"

"I'm looking for a man called Trooly," said Dando, " or he may be going by the name of Judd."

"Everard – do 'ee mean Everard?"

"Has he got red hair?"

"Red as a ztormy zunrise."

"I'd like to talk to him if I may."

The boy looked back in the direction of the mansion and then up in the air for a minute or two as if searching for inspiration.

"I don' zee why you shouldn't,"he said. "The man you wan' be down within the walls along o' his da. Mr Murdock's busy so he wouldn't want me to interrupt what he's doing an' there's no-one else about, far as I know. I don' zee why you shouldn't go there if I comes along wi' you."

They were let in through the gates and were then conducted down an avenue of trees for some distance before turning right towards an opening in a red-brick wall. Passing through this barrier they found themselves in an extensive enclosed space criss-crossed by narrow paths which marked out rectangular beds filled with row upon row of neat well-tended crops. Planted against the encircling brickwork were fruit trees bearing apples and pears for the most part, almost ready for picking. The place was beautifully sheltered and the air within seemed a degree or two warmer than that to be met with in the rest of the gardens. Over in the sunshine on the far side Dando could see two figures, one busily turning over the mould with a spade, the other sitting nearby in a wheeled chair. Jack, constantly attuned to ambient sounds, heard the chink of metal on gravel.

"Is it him?" he asked.

"It's *them!* Foxy and Master Tallisand!" replied Dando.

"And your girlfriend?"

"No, Annie's not there."

Jack, who, as usual, had his arm around his friend's waist to support him urged, "Come on then – let's go and introduce ourselves."

"No Jack, you stay here. I must do this by myself. Please Jack," and to the dog, "stay Ralph."

Reluctantly Jack agreed to remain near the door. Dando set out for what was to be a decisive encounter, a feeling of inevitability spurring him on. He had covered half the distance across the garden before the man at work noticed that anything was afoot. Realising that someone was approaching he stopped digging and rested on his implement, looking towards the newcomer. Dando halted and they stood staring at one another for several minutes. Eventually Foxy, for indeed it was the red-headed Nablan that awaited him, put his hand into his jacket as Dando began to limp slowly forward, not breaking gaze, until he reached the trainee horticulturist. Using his crutch to steady himself he sunk down onto his knees and knelt before his half-brother, his eyes locked with the Nablan's vivid blue ones. The two young men understood one another in that moment and shared a common purpose, maybe for the first and last time in their lives. From an inside pocket Foxy pulled out his gun – it was his most treasured possession and he carried it with him wherever he went - and held the barrel against Dando's temple. Sixty seconds ticked slowly by, neither moving, while the threat of death hung between them; then, drawing the weapon back, Foxy smashed it across the other's face with all his might. It was just one solitary blow but it knocked Dando sideways onto the ground where he lay unmoving, making no attempt to rise.

Tiny sounds - birdsong, a distant mowing machine - began to make themselves heard once more, and the nearby terrain which had virtually ceased to exist during the two protagonists' confrontation slowly rematerialised. Tallis, who had been watching events unfold, was making futile attempts to rise from his chair; Jack, breaking his promise to remain at a distance, began to hurry across the garden feeling the way with his stick; their guide, the boy who had let them in through the gates, appeared to have vanished. Foxy carefully wiped the gun on his trousers and put it away. Then bending and placing his hands under Dando's armpits he began to raise him. Dando came back onto his knees and with blood and mucus streaming down his face managed to shuffle across to Tallis' chair. Bowing down to the earth he lifted his master's foot in both hands and placed his head beneath it.

"No, no!" cried Tallis. He groped in his pocket with shaking fingers and brought forth a grubby rag. Leaning forward he reached down and putting his palm under Dando's chin raised the boy's face towards him while with the cloth he attempted to staunch the blood. But by this time Jack had arrived and found that something insupportable had been done to his companion. He roundly cursed both Foxy and Tallis with every expletive in his extensive multi-lingual vocabulary, retrieved Dando's crutch and set about helping him to stand. At this juncture two more people appeared on the scene. The gardener's boy, taking fright at the sight of a gun, had run to the big house for help and had cannoned into none other than the owner himself, Witteridge of Witteridge Acres, who had been taking a walk by the goldfish pond. Now the lord of the manor, hurrying to the kitchen garden on the understanding that he was needed there to prevent a crime of the first magnitude, came upon a very confused situation indeed.

There was no sign of the weapon he had been warned about. He recognised the under-gardener Trooly and the invalid that he had been told was his employee's father although he had often remarked to his butler that there was absolutely no physical resemblance between the two of them. But in addition he saw there were a couple of strangers present who should never have been allowed into the grounds without his permission. One was a fair-haired young fellow who seemed to have some problem with his eyesight and the other, maybe even younger and also somewhat disabled, had suffered a recent traumatic injury to his face; how and by whom it had been inflicted was not at all clear. The three older men all seemed to be solicitous for the boy's welfare. The fair-haired chap had his arms wrapped around him in a most inappropriate manner, Trooly was brushing the lad down, the lad who was balancing uncertainly on his one remaining leg and the old man was waving a blood-stained handkerchief and trying to stand. Of the four the dark-haired cripple was the only one who had noticed his, Witteridge's, approach and was making an attempt to push the others aside in order to greet him man to man as was right and proper. The country gentleman walked forward and held out his hand to the boy, for in Dando he recognised someone of significance. He ignored the blood-smeared dirty features, the unwashed hair, the emaciation, the moth-eaten overcoat muddied around the hem. He disregarded the air of having been used, of brokenness about the young man and saw that this stranger possessed something with which he was totally familiar. What he identified was a certain kind of face, common among his own kind, which only appears after generations of selective breeding. The owner smiled a greeting and, ignoring all the aforementioned impediments to such a presumption, acknowledged a fellow patrician.

"You appear to have been in the wars my dear sir - you appear to need medical attention," he said. "Have you anywhere to lodge or can I offer you a bed?"

Dando looked at Foxy.

"He be agooin' ter stay wi' us," said Foxy in a surly manner.

"But, as I thought everyone was aware, the gardener's cottage is only big enough for two. You must come up to the house where we can do what's necessary for your injury. If your man," glancing uncertainly at Jack, "can help you we could go there now."

Dando looked again at Foxy and the two appeared to communicate without words.

"I'll stay down here," he mumbled with some difficulty.

"Really? Well, if that's your choice I'll send my old nurse, Nan Burrington, to attend you – she's very experienced. Come and see me tomorrow if you're able. I'm shutting up the house in two weeks time and travelling to the Delta City. By then, if you're feeling better, you could accompany me and the rest of my household – we're going to stay there until this present trouble blows over."

A small procession made its way back to the cottage, Foxy in the lead pushing the knight in his chair followed by Jack with his arm around Dando who, at present, seemed mentally stupefied, while Ralph brought up the rear. A buxom female in a starched white apron came bustling from the direction of the mansion, her bounce and vigour belying her advanced age. Once indoors Dando was made to lie on one of the beds while the woman examined his nose and sent the gardener's boy on various errands to gather the medical supplies she required. Straws were pushed up her patient's nostrils to keep his airways open and the broken bones pinched back into place around them as accurately as possible. She did her best to restore his face to normality but, after weeks had passed and the wound had finally healed, his profile no longer displayed the clean straight lines that had once contributed to his physical beauty.

Presently, the treatment over, Dando, although feeling extremely groggy, managed to stand upright and cross to Tallis who had been sitting forgotten in a corner. He again knelt before him in order to bring their heads on a level and gave voice to what he had intended to say earlier.

"Master, I c-can't ask you to forgive me for what I did but I will try to m-make amends. I am yours to command."

Tallis reached out and touched the boy's hair.

"I must go north," he whispered.

"We *will* go north – across the sea. I'll help you. We'll find a ship. But master, where is Annie?" Foxy's ears pricked up and he began to pay attention.

"Annie? You mean Hilda? We thought that she was with you. We thought you'd run away together."

"I haven't seen her since that night – the night that I..." Dando bit his lip. "I'm afraid for her. I'm afraid something really bad may have happened."

"We'll find her," said Tallis, "she can't be far away. But what happened to *you* my boy after we parted?"

Fighting the pain in his face Dando stumbled once more through the sad tale of his misdeeds. To Tallis, however, the account was far from an indictment.

"You sailed to the island, the pirates' lair, because you thought we might have been taken there as prisoners? All on your own? My goodness that was brave. You're a good boy, a good boy." Foxy turned away.

That night Tallis and Dando were given the use of the beds in the cottage because of their indifferent health while Foxy and Jack slept on the floor. With four men in the little dwelling it felt as though it was about to burst at the seams.

"You an' the boy should 'a' taken up the gaffer's offer to goo up to the house," Foxy reluctantly admitted to an initially unresponsive Jack the next morning. "If he asks you again I should say yes. I don' be objectin'"

Life went on. Dando, on Jack's eventual urging, paid a visit to the mansion as he had been invited to do and in no time at all both of them were being offered lunch in an elegant dining room. After this, having learnt that the arrangements at the cottage were unsatisfactory, Mr Witteridge opened up a fine suite of rooms for their use.

"This place is far too big for me nowadays; I rattle around in it like the last biscuit in a barrel. I'd be pleased for you stay here until we leave. You're going to accept my offer of a lift I take it?"

The man was obviously very glad to have someone to talk to; he seemed a lonely old cove. Soon disabused of the idea that Jack was Dando's factotum and that in fact the blind boy was related to the famous Hiram Howgego, he eagerly set about questioning him regarding the current situation in Vadrosnia Poule.

"According to the news that has reached us in this out-of-the-way place the invaders have passed Trincomalee and are coming in this direction, meeting very little opposition. That's why I've decided to close up and move everything, bag and baggage, down to the Kymer. Surely it's inconceivable that this Trewithik could take over Vadrosnia Poule – he's only a jumped up lieutenant after all. I understand that the Council are raising an army with help from some of the other towns. Kingscauldie already had its own force I believe. No, the Delta City could never fall – we'll be safe enough in my house on the Broadway."

Jack and Dando agreed to travel with him when the whole enterprise took to the road. For Dando, the idea of again serving Tallis, now that he had found him, gave what had become, over a single traumatic day, a completely pointless existence some purpose, while Jack could not bear the thought of leaving the love of his life to fend for himself, especially now when he seemed most in need. All the same he was somewhat apprehensive about putting himself, once more, within reach of his grandfather's power base.

Foxy, in consultation with Murdock, voiced his disquiet about abandoning the estate at such a vital time. "Everything within the walls be jus' comin' up for harvest an' the flower gardens need lots of attention at this time of year. I be whooly chooked if we leave the place to goo to rack an' ruin. Surely, even if the gaffer move out, we could stay on until he return an' see things are kep' ship-shape?"

"It be all right for thee," replied Murdock, "thee be a single bloke. I got a wife an' childer to think of. The master zes he'll take 'em wi' him to Drossi - that he'll take all o' uz an' give uz employment when we gets there. Don' look a gift horse in the mouth zay I."

Dando, who really should have been bedridden in order to give his broken nose, and other more profound wounds, a chance to heal, came down to the cottage each day to wait on Tallis. During their time on the Northern Drift he had spent many evenings surreptitiously watching Ann as she went about her self-imposed tasks and as a consequence had unintentionally learned quite a lot about washing, mending and domestic duties in general. He now turned his hand to similar chores as well as he was able. Besides spring-cleaning the cottage which he discovered was in a shocking state he laundered Tallis' clothes and helped him to dress and undress. He cooked the knight nourishing meals and even gave him a bath. It upset him that he could not push the invalid-chair when Tallis wanted to go out, but, as he was totally dependant on his crutch when walking and had only one foot to give him purchase, it proved quite impossible. He tried to set Tallis' mind at rest about the direction they would be travelling in.

"Even if we went to the nearest port we wouldn't be able to get a boat from here," he said. "According to Jack there's a blockade in force - nobody's putting to sea. When we get to the Delta things may be different. We'll find a ship – don't you worry."

Foxy handed over his responsibilities regarding Tallis with relief - he was frantically busy seeing that the garden was left in as good an order as possible when they quitted the manor and had no time to devote to elderly dependants. He and Dando had symbolically signed a peace treaty now that the issue between them had been settled to the satisfaction of both, the evidence for which was written large on the younger man's damaged face. From this point on they treated one another with a careful formal courtesy. As for Tallis he was in some kind of seventh heaven, realising, more now than ever, that he had a jewel in this assistant who had sworn an oath to serve him, a jewel who had hidden his light so efficiently under a bushel that it had taken Tallis several months and goodness knows how many accumulated miles to recognise his qualities. There was something that disturbed him however. Dando's nature appeared to have altered - this was no longer the bright, eager, naive young man he had met in the King's Head Tavern in the town of High Harrow; there was a sadness about him now and he rarely spoke except when spoken to. He was also as jumpy as a cat on hot bricks; unexpected sounds had him spinning round ready to defend himself. Tallis wondered which of his experiences since leaving the valley had wrought the change.

Jack spent his time exploring all the dusty neglected corners of the ancient mansion. He made friends with the staff and kept Mr Witteridge company. During their conversations they found they had several acquaintances in common. The landowner gave him a new cane and even dug out a pair of crutches to offer to Dando ("I broke my leg out hunting one time") but they proved too short. Jack and Tallis also occasionally fell into conversation and Jack found that the knight was mourning the loss of the ancient kuckthu.

"What was it like?" asked the blind boy. "I know an instrument maker in Drossi whose arm I could probably twist to make you a new one if you describe it accurately enough. There's always a way to get what you want if you put your mind to it."

Once a day Jack produced his penny whistle and insisted that Dando do some dancing practice now he appeared to be on the road to recovery. The partially disabled young man had recently learnt how to manage a spin with the aid of his crutch, as well as attempting various other ambitious moves - splits, handsprings, backdrops and pikes - that he was gradually incorporating into the routine he was creating. It was something of a miracle that he could manage such athleticism in his present condition but it was steely determination that saw him through. He did not admit to Jack what the effort cost him or what effect he suspected it was having on his body. He just grimly set about becoming *the best bloody one-legged dancer this side of the Middle Sea.* The gardener's boy was greatly impressed by these terpsichorean demonstrations and always managed to be on hand when they took place. He watched with his mouth hanging open and applauded enthusiastically at the conclusion. For Dando the dancing was something affirmatory to bolster his fragile self-esteem, something positive to counter the feelings of worthlessness which these days swept over him in regular waves and dragged him down into an oozy quagmire of despair.

Three enclosed carriages and one large open wagon waited by the rear gates of the estate for the household to clamber aboard. The cart was already piled high with treasured items that Mr Witteridge and members of his staff could not bear to abandon. Into the carriages climbed the Lord of the Manor himself, his butler, his nurse, his cook, two parlour maids, two kitchen maids, one footman, one stable boy, the three gardeners and various members of their families. In addition room was found for Tallis, Jack and Dando – it was a tight squeeze. Tallis' chair had been hoisted onto the wagon which was also accommodating several dogs. Ralph however insisted on staying with Dando and travelling in the carriage. Other animals belonging to the demesne were left behind and let loose in order to fend for themselves as best they could, apart of course for the horses which would be needed to pull the carriages and wagon. Eventually, after several false starts during which things that had been forgotten were hurriedly retrieved, the whole convoy lurched up onto the thoroughfare and joined the stream of refugees fleeing the fighting and heading for what they hoped would be sanctuary. Once the journey had begun, progress proved to be extremely slow: the road, although comprising the main coastal highway, was narrow and there was little opportunity to overtake. The wheeled traffic was reduced to adopting the pace of the slowest vehicle. Frequently there was a snarl-up ahead: perhaps a load had shifted somewhere along the line or an axle on one of the ancient carts had broken. Everything came to a halt while the bottleneck was sorted out. Each day Mr Witteridge sent his footman on ahead to book accommodation for the coming night but, because of the high demand, even those only used to feather beds up to now found themselves in some pretty rough billets. At Tagnaroque the road left the coast and turned south-east in order to make for Vadrosnia Poule via Urgun. Tallis fretted at being forced to go inland once more; he seemed unable to accept that this might be a roundabout way of achieving his desired end.

The road-users greatest fear was that they would be overtaken by the Pickwah Army - that the Axemen would come marching up from behind ready to start laying about them in order to clear a path. The Witteridge contingent caught the contagion and spent a lot of time poking their heads out of the carriage windows and looking rearwards. It was with complete incomprehension therefore that, trapped in yet another hold-up, they saw the traffic ahead of them splitting apart and being pushed to either side of the track like earth before a plough. When it came close enough to be distinguished they saw that the plough in question took the form of a great host of marching men swinging down the centre of the road towards them. To see an army coming from this unexpected direction was quite a shock. They drew the carriages and wagon onto the verge and sought an explanation from the forerunners of the horde.

"Who are you?" shouted Mr Witteridge. A small man in some sort of ancient outfit that was far too big for him took the time to stop and reply.

"Don't you know about us? We've come to your rescue. We're the Kymer Volunteers – all good fighting men. The towns up river - Ixat, Sassanara, Rishangles - have combined with Dermody and Kingscauldie to send troops – I'm from Toocumcarrie myself. We've been quick off the mark, unlike Drossi – they're still faffing around. Trust the money-bags to get cold feet when they're afraid there might be a drain on their purses. Oh well, I s'pose we'll have to save their necks for 'em - we'll send those Axemen packing – you bet your life!"

The motley crew was dressed in a weird selection of uniforms that looked as if they came straight from amateur-theatrical productions. There were short men and tall men, fat and thin, old and young, a few very young. The weapons they carried were a mixture of everything under the sun from firearms to pokers. Spirits seemed to be high and they were shouting, laughing and singing popular ballads as they swung along. The refugees, who had no choice but to wait for them to go by stood on the bank and applauded.

"Come and join us!" cried the untried soldiers, "the more the merrier! There's fortunes to be made. Trewithik's carrying the pirates' treasure in his van!"

The ground shook from the tramp of their feet and the air rang. Foxy swung himself out of the carriage and clambered up onto the roof in order to get a better view. He had his massive bow over his shoulder and they heard him exchanging banter as the wayfaring cohorts urged him to bear them company. Jack reached out to make sure Dando was still opposite him and had not followed Foxy into the road only to discover with a shock that the boy was sitting stiff with fright. He understood immediately why this should be, but could do nothing to comfort him apart from taking Foxy's vacant place at his side and surreptitiously squeezing his hand. In so doing he rediscovered the missing fingers, and, of those that still existed, the fragile bones beneath the skin, and was swept by such a rush of protective emotion that he was hard put to it not to scandalise his host by flinging his arms around the young man. Instead he whispered in the other's ear, "Be brave little bird, they'll soon be gone."

In fact the Kymer Volunteers, whose numbers were divided into several separate detachments, took nearly an hour to pass. As the last stragglers came abreast and confirmed that no-one else was following Mr Witteridge stuck his head out of the window.

"We're about to move on, Trooly," he shouted. "We'll have to make up for lost time if we're to have a hope of getting to Urgun by this evening."

Foxy jumped down onto the road but shook his head when the door was held open for him.

"I be gooin' along o' they," he said, pointing after the disappearing troops. "They could do wi' my help. I don' be a-gooin' ter miss this!"

Nothing they could say would dissuade him. He dug out his possessions, such as they were, from amongst the goods in the wagon and then, taking bow in hand, pulled back the string and aimed into the distance, miming the loosing of an arrow for the benefit of the watchers in the carriages. "Bang!" he cried incongruously before, with a wave and an insouciant grin, he set off to overtake the amateur army.

"Well," said Mr Witteridge, "I hope he knows what he's doing. We can't wait for him. If we get no more hold ups we should reach V.P. in the next day or two."

The other refugees both behind and before regained the carriageway, horses and oxen were persuaded into motion and the whole cavalcade began to creep forward towards the plains once more and a hoped-for refuge beside the Great River. What sort of a welcome they would receive from the indigenous population of that region remained to be seen.

Such a dance was danced
Once death had been conquered,
That love must be held accountable.

Chapter twenty-one

On the rooming house's upper landing stood a chintz-covered chaise-long. Damask and Milly sat there, side by side, listening to Ann's cries. They were not allowed to go in to her. As soon as the doctor arrived and had been gratefully welcomed by all three carers Becca conducted him to the sick-room and when the two girls fell into step behind she had made a dismissive gesture as she disappeared through the doorway, indicating that they were to remain where they were. The night hours ticked away but neither of them could face the prospect of going to bed; they knew without the shadow of a doubt that there was nowhere they could retreat to, however distant, that would put them our of earshot of that dreadful clamour. All the same weariness eventually won out and they both cat-napped, leaning against one another, Milly's head on Damask's shoulder. Dawn crept through the windows and the younger girl opened her eyes onto the vague realisation that Becca and the doctor had come back into the hall and were talking together.

"I've never seen a case like this before," the man was saying in a lowered voice. "This is not a normal labour; you'd think she was being torn apart by wild beasts."

"But you sure must do something," insisted Becca, "the poor lamb can't go on this-a-way."

"No, you're right. We must bring it to an end somehow. A decision has got to be made. I'll save what I can but it'll have to be one or the other – if I don't act it will be neither."

"Mercy," said Becca, "is that the truth?"

"I need a decision within half an hour," and the doctor went to re-enter the room.

"It ain't our part to decide," Becca called after him, addressing his retreating back, "it's hers - she's got a right to know – if you don't say anything I will," and she stepped forward in order to pursue the physician.

"No, no," cried Milly, struggling out of the throes of sleep, "you can't do that. It's not fair!" For the first time Ann had become a real person to her rather than just her beloved's adjunct and her whole being revolted at the idea of getting her to decide who would survive.

Damask had also come partially awake by now. "Hasn't it been born yet?" she yawned.

"They fink they oughta ast 'er oo's life to save," said Milly indignantly. "That's not right - poor mare!"

Damask, once she had been apprised of the situation, quickly made up her mind.

"What if it were you," she said, "wouldn't you want to be given a choice? I would."

"But you know wot she'll say – wot any mother would say."

"All the same, we can't not ask her."

"Enough already," chided Becca and vanished through the doorway. They heard the murmur of speech but could make out nothing of what passed. It seemed an age before the showgirl reappeared and when she did she had obviously been crying. She spoke just two words, "The baby," and went to hide herself away.

"You can come in now."

Becca's moment of weakness had not lasted long and she soon returned to the fray. With great efficiency she assisted the doctor in his life-saving operation and now the thing was a fait acomplis. The medic, a man in great demand, departed on another urgent call, promising he would return as soon as he was free. Damask and Milly peered timorously around the door. The curtains had been drawn back and bright early morning sunlight streamed into the room. In a hastily improvised cot (a laundry basket on a trestle table) a small bundle was placed, a tiny wizened face protruding from one end, half obscured by a blanket. Ann lay on the bed, her features ashen, her glorious almost-white hair spread out over the pillow. Eyes, the blue of a harebell, stared back at them and her lips moved but speech seemed to be beyond her. Milly took hold of her limp hand while Damask examined the baby.

"He looks ancient," she said and then added hastily, "ancient but nice. What are you going to call him?"

Ann attempted to say something. Afterwards the two girls could not agree on what they had heard. Milly thought she had caught *Tobias* while Damask was sure it had been *Horace*. Perhaps in fact it had been something completely different and nothing to do with the baby's name at all.

Milly squeezed the patient's hand. "The Lordship will be so pleased," she told her.

There was the faintest suggestion of a smile in reply.

Damask had not expected to find Ann alive. *So the doctor managed to save the both of them after all,* she thought, trying to convince herself, against her better judgement, that this was the case.

Out loud she declared, "We'll look after him till you're well. Becca knows about babies. All you'll need to do is feed him."

Ann gazed up at her with a speaking look but what she was trying to convey remained unclear. She shook her head very slightly and her eyes slowly closed until her lashes rested on her cheeks, the blue veins within the lids clearly visible.

"That's enough," cautioned Becca who was standing behind them. "Say goodbye now and leave her in peace."

Milly detected a hint of finality in the words. She looked sharply at their hostess, her brows puckered in a frowning enquiry.

"Say goodbye," repeated Becca gesturing with her hand.

Milly bent and kissed Ann's cheek and Damask, taking her cue from the younger girl, did the same. Nevertheless she felt impelled to add, "Have a good rest – you'll feel better later on. We'll see you when you wake up."

Once in the hall they exchanged glances but had nothing to say. It required greater eloquence than they possessed and harder hearts to put what they were thinking into words. They went downstairs and took themselves off to their separate rooms, not emerging until the day was well past its prime.

The ordeal had ended. She was no longer being tortured by every fiend in hell. The pain had gone, taking all sensation with it, but the price she paid for this and the saving of at least one life was the fact that her blood was draining away minute by minute. She knew she would soon be parted from the baby, the babe who had only just entered the world. Although her eyes were closed, some extra sense enabled her to see the room she occupied quite clearly; it was the living entities within it that were hard to distinguish. Beside the bed sat a misty presence that might have been a woman from beyond the sea named Becca, and next to her head lay a small animated opacity that up to a short while ago had been part of her own body, the body she was about to leave. Reaching out mentally she became aware of hollow chambers above and below the room she was occupying, and city streets beyond the house, full of shifting shadows. Further off there were other cities, other continents, other earths; she saw them parade before her inner eye as her consciousness expanded. The material universe had a solidity and sharpness because of its permanence, while the creatures inhabiting it, whose lifespans were so brief, seemed just insubstantial ghosts. Besides this awareness she intuited, very close and already almost a part of her own reality, organic matter: tissue, bone, entrails, cells. A womb was being prepared and her next incarnation awaited. This was the path most people naturally followed after death as they were drawn from one material envelope to the next. But a voice interrupted the inevitable transition, a well-loved voice out of the past. *"Sweetheart,"* it said with enormous solicitude. Ann sat up in mind at least and looked around. A figure was standing not far off, this time clearly visible, but occupying an entirely different dimension from that of the surrounding room. The ground on which it stood was not the floor beneath the bed, the air that it displaced was somehow finer and more rarefied than the common element being breathed by earth-bound creatures.

Ann also stood up and took a step forward.

"Dadda!" she cried with joyful gladness, "I always knowd you be close by – I hear you speak – often!"

Tom smiled and held out his hand.

"Your journey in the flesh be whooly ended, my maid," he said. *"Join me an' we'll take a new road together."*

"But the baby Dadda!"

"He cannot come with you my hinny – not for a long time yet – you mus' leave he to others, but you can watch over he."

Ann was aware of a great chasm lying between herself and her father: they stood on either side of a divide deeper than the deepest abyss, yet there was a passage across the pit for those who dared assay it. At the same time she saw the stark choice with which she was being presented: in one direction lay the wheel of life, a return to mortality and to an existence similar to that which she had so far known, in the other stood a portal to the eternal dance. She realised that by taking the second route she would be able to explore the infinite, clothed in a new immaterial body, but in so doing would eventually sacrifice all the familiar comforts of the flesh. She hesitated.

"I be afeared Dadda," she cried.

"Look into my eyes, darling," instructed Tom, *"don't look up or down. Reach out for my hand."*

"I be afeared," repeated Ann but took two more steps forward.

There be one in need," said her father, *"his road be hard – a journey to the depths. Come to this side and you can help him on his way – you can give he strength and protection."* He smiled and held out both arms as if inviting her into an embrace. *"Come over,"* he urged, *"come over sweetheart, come Over-the-Brook."*

Ann looked back into the room one last time. She saw, clearly, the skeletal snow-maiden on the bed, stretched already death-like beneath the sheet. She saw the baby in its cradle. Then, turning away, she took one further step and grasped Tom's hand. He drew her towards him and, facing neither to left nor right but straight ahead, she summoned up all her courage, broke the ties that bound her to this mortal life and passed over.

They put an antique wedding dress, taken from the theatre company's costume chest, on Ann's pallid body, and laid the corpse in a coffin of grey elm wood lined with ivory satin. They then paid a ferryman to row them across to Cemetery Island on a bright cool autumn day. Drossi citizens were interred in tiers above ground because of the prevailing waterlogged conditions, their remains locked for all eternity in row upon row of monumental filing cabinets made of white marble. Ann's full name did not appear on the plaque which closed the slot into which the undertaker slid her coffin.

"Hilda Hannah Arbericord - that was her nibbler name," said Damask, "it was part of her servitude. Dando always called her *Annie* and Tom called her *my hinny*. They were the ones she meant the most to and who meant the most to her."

So at Becca's suggestion the inscription simply read:-

ANNIE

GREATLY LOVED

DIED THE 21ST DAY OF THE 9TH MONTH IN THE 420TH YEAR OF THE HARE

"Four days before my birthday," said Damask. "and Dando's of course. Do you realise that what's happened to her also happened to her mother? That's the reason she ended up with Dando and Doll when she was a baby."

"How's the Lordship gonna feel when 'e finds out?" said Milly. "I won't be able to tell 'im - not in a fousand lifetimes."

They were all in a sombre mood as the boat carried them back to the city, none more so than Becca.

"That obi-man – he got to her after all," she murmured. "Despite everything I could do he worked her ill. But we rescued the baby, praise the Lord - at least the child's safe."

While Becca, Damask and Milly had been dealing with matters of life and death, other similar events, if not quite so fundamental, were happening in the world around them. The latest rumour was that Tagnaroque had fallen and Trewithik's men had turned south-east and were less than a week's march from Drossi. Word reached the city that a force had been raised up river in order to make a stand against the Axemen. Many of the town's younger citizens equipped themselves with weapons and, without asking permission of their families, crossed the causeway known as the Green Dolphin Avenue and set out to join this army. Becca tried to find a wet-nurse for the baby but most of the lactating females in the town had gathered up their children and headed for greener pastures; those that remained were not prepared to take on extra responsibilities at a time of such uncertainty. The apothecary sold her a dried formula that he swore would supply all the baby's needs, but Horace or Tobias, or whatever he was going to be called, (Damask got in the habit of referring to him as *the little horror*), did not thrive. Hour after hour he whimpered and grizzled, refusing to swallow when they attempted to feed him. In the end Damask cried, "Oh for pete's sake!" and, unbuttoning her blouse, put him to her own breast. He latched on, sucking greedily, and for the first time in nearly three days all was quiet. After this he went to sleep and when eventually he woke and started to complain she repeated the performance and continued to do so. About twenty four hours later Becca was standing watching when she noticed a revealing rim of white between the baby's lips and Damask's skin.

"Lan's sakes, you're producing milk girl!" she said in astonishment.

"Of course," said the Glept, "after all he *is* virtually mine. We're very closely related – what did you expect?"

Those were the days when it felt as if time hung suspended. Although the air in the Delta City was full of an electric expectancy, none of the townsfolk spoke of the forthcoming battle that would ultimately decide their fate. They thought of virtually nothing else however, especially those whose loved ones had gone to join the fighting. They waited for word but no word came. Meanwhile Horry/Toby flourished under the new regime and put on weight at a phenomenal rate. Every few hours the three women noted some new development, some fresh example of his progress.

"He's a real healthy little guy," said Becca uncertainly, looking down at him with doubt in her heart as he lay on Damask's lap. "I hope he doesn't outgrow his strength."

One morning Milly met her at the front door as she returned from the hairdresser's.

"The majesty says come an' 'ave a look," she invited as Becca put down her bag, "the nipper's learnt to smile an' now 'e can't stop."

"Oh, that'll just be wind," replied their landlady. "They don't smile until six weeks or more."

"That's not wot the majesty finks – you come an' see."

The baby was lying in his improvised cot which he had nearly outgrown. Damask stood beside him with an air of proud possessiveness.

"You watch this," she said as Becca came through the door, and bending over the crib crooned, "hallo you little horror – who's a big strong boy then?"

The child waved his arms and legs enthusiastically and gave an unmistakable grin, wicked and mischievous. There was something extremely knowing in his expression.

Becca took a step backwards and put her hand to her breast.

"Mercy," she gasped, "the Longval Curse!"

"The wot?" demanded Milly and at the same time Damask exclaimed, "I beg your pardon?"

Becca stood for several moments unspeaking then seemed to get her breath back.

"No," she cried, "no," flapping her hands. "Shut ma mouth – forget I said it. It cain't be, it jest cain't be," and after that would give no further explanation for her outburst.

Damask, who had been aching to show off her charge's brand new trick, was thoroughly put out by its reception. All that day Becca kept silent and avoided approaching the baby. It was not until late in the evening when the child had been asleep for some time that she ventured near the cot and stood looking down, a sombre expression on her face.

"What did you mean this morning?" said Damask who had followed her into the room. "Long something you said – the long something curse?"

"Come into the lounge," replied Becca in a whisper as if she was afraid the baby would overhear. When they were well out of earshot she spoke in her normal voice.

"The Longval Curse," she repeated. "It was something I was told about when I was just a chil'. It was a curse that cuckolded husbands were said to arrange to have placed on their pregnant wives if they suspected that the baby they were carrying was another man's."

"And did the baby die?" asked Damask.

"No – worse than that. The baby grew old – once born it grew up so fast that when it should have been just a youngster it was already adult and by the time it was twenty or so it appeared to be an old, old man or woman."

Damask screwed her face into an incredulous scowl.

"That sounds pretty far-fetched to me," she said, "I find it hard to believe."

"My mother saw a case once," said Becca, "she told me about it: a boy of fifteen and he was already bald and wrinkled and walking with a stick. Nobody can lift the curse except the one who cast the spell in the first place or except that one dies."

"And you think that Horry...? Surely not!"

"It was not a natural labour – you knew it – Dr Grimwade knew it. And babies don't smile until they're six weeks old or nearer to two months in fact – I can vouch for that."

Damask was set to go on arguing. She opened her mouth with fresh refutations but at that moment there came a knock on the door.

"Who can that be at this hour?" wondered Becca.

Earlier that day a procession had turned into the wide street known as Broadway and come to a halt before the imposing town house that was Witteridge of Witteridge Acres' second residence. With great generosity the owner offered to accommodate Jack, Dando and Tallis whilst they remained in town. Jack accepted for all three.

"Always good to have a pied-a-terre," he muttered.

They were given a meal and invited to make themselves at home, but in the evening the blind boy suggested that he and his friend should visit the Green Goat. He was continually trying to take Dando's mind off what had happened to him back along the road and thought that this might prove the perfect diversion.

"Becca'll be there and maybe Milly and your sister too."

The squire went to ask his master's permission.

"You can go boy," said Tallis, who was starting to enjoy the luxurious living to be found at twenty-eight Broadway, "as long as you keep out of trouble. They're chancy places these local drinking dens. Watch out for shady characters and be home by midnight."

As they approached the club a thumping beat accompanied by raucous brass began to make itself felt, issuing from the bowels of the earth, causing everything not tied down to rattle uncomfortably.

"Sounds like a good night," remarked a cautious Jack. He was soon being greeted at the door as if he were some famous superstar and a passage was cleared through the scrimmage. The sheer volume of noise that assaulted Dando's ears as he entered took his breath away. Despite the war situation, or maybe because of it, the spot was packed to capacity and he looked over the heads of those on the stairs at a heaving swirling throng. The floor below, illuminated by constantly changing coloured lights, was crammed with a mass of young people all leaping up and down in unison, their hands waving above their heads. The pounding of the dancers' feet had a visceral impact on his body, bringing his heart into his mouth. Meanwhile Jack was surrounded by well-wishers who threw their arms across his neck or slapped him between the shoulder blades.

"Great to see you fellow," they shouted, "you've been away far too long."

"With good reason. Don't tell the old man I'm back," warned the boy nervously.

Dando was left to his own devices. He searched for Milly, Damask and the woman called Becca who he had been led to believe was a singer with the band, but saw no sign of them. He retired to a chair by the wall where he could get a good view of the action and sat looking on. Watching other people gyrate he began to feel envious, while the insistent rhythm called to the most primitive part of him, demanding that he move to the beat. He swayed and tapped his foot but felt left out and on the periphery. He wanted to get up and join in the fun or else go outside and take himself away from this reminder of what life had once had to offer. Eventually Jack caught a whiff of his unhappiness.

"What's the matter, birdy?" he yelled, (it was the only way he could make himself heard). "Is something up?"

"It's the dancing," replied Dando, "I wish I could join in the dancing."

"You want to dance? You shall dance."

"But there's no room."

"We'll make room."

Without more ado Jack barged into the revellers on the floor and began shoving them aside, clearing a space.

"My friend's going to dance – get out of the way or you'll get hurt."

Some of his cronies came to help and very soon they were holding the crowd back around an open area.

"Here you are birdy," shouted Jack, "quick – while you've got the chance."

The band, in bemusement, had stopped playing. Jack turned in their direction - yelled a title - "Rocket Roll-Down!" - and they dutifully broke into this well known number. Then, returning to Dando, he pulled him upright before giving him a push towards the dance floor.

"Go birdy go," he said, "It's your scene – show them how to do it!"

Dando limped forward on his crutch until he was in the middle of the cleared space. He felt horribly exposed. The crowd looked on with sceptical curiosity. He stood still for a moment, then did an experimental twirl. If it were not for the music, whose hypnotic beat had him in its grip and compelled him into movement, he would never have dared begin. Against his normal inclination he said a prayer to whichever unknown god might have dancers' interests at heart, screwed himself up to the sticking point and went into his routine. Some of the crowd danced with him but most stood and watched, first heckling then encouraging him. What they saw was a revelation. The young one-legged man seemed to float on air, defying gravity, weaving a sphere of action round the top of his crutch with his long body, the shaft of wood being the one fixed point in the midst of a flickering changing pattern of moves. The dance was acrobatic in the extreme but also supremely graceful. It had the character of being improvised on the spur of the moment, a joyful impromptu performance expressing the dancer's fleeting emotions. Dando became completely soaked in sweat as he carried on far past the point at which, for his own good, he should have given up. Eventually the band-leader, evidently concerned, wound up the session. Dando came to a halt and, gasping for breath, bowed low to the ground. There was a shout of acclamation from the whole room followed by cheering and applause. He straightened up and then staggered sideways. "Jack!" he cried and in the blink of an eye Jack's arm was round him. Dando bowed again prompting the other dancers to clap rhythmically and yell, "Encore!"

"Do you want to kill him?" shouted Jack, and then to his friend, "they want you to go again."

"I can't," groaned the young hoofer: the effort had completely drained his strength.

"No of course you can't," scolded his friend and he drew the other out of the limelight and found him a place to sit down.

Dando gradually stopped panting and began to breath normally but he was still shaking from the effort.

"Are you all right caridad?" said Jack, "you're absolutely dripping."

"I'm ok."

"Come on then champion – let's get out of here and go to Herbert Road – that's where Becca's place is. They'll give us supper."

When our ex movie star went to answer the late knock on the door it was with a certain amount of trepidation. Callers after eleven at night are rarely the bearers of good news. However as she opened up she found a pair of orphans on her step with their arms about each other.

"Jack!" she cried, "gee, what a surprise. But who's this?"

She did not recognise the other young man. Her initial impression was of a boy with dark hair and a pale complexion who seemed to have damaged his nose. She also could not ignore the crutch and truncated leg. On his face he bore the stubborn, slightly cussed look of one who has to contend with pain on a daily basis. The lad looked exhausted and extremely bedraggled as if he had been though some recent demanding ordeal.

"This is Dando, Damask's brother," said Jack. "Are Damask and Milly still with you?"

Damask's brother! The absentee father! Becca realised she had some very bad news to impart.

"Hi honey," she said, holding out her hand. "Damask's just gone into the lounge. No," as the girl appeared behind her, "talk of the devil – here she is."

"Don't make so much noise," cautioned her lodger, well aware of the priorities, "there's a baby asleep upstairs."

"But isn't it time to give him his evening feed?" asked Becca, turning away from her visitors.

"I will in about half an hour."

Damask and Dando stared at one another. It was their first encounter since leaving the valley. Damask took in her brother's appearance.

"It doesn't look as if you've been exactly leading a quiet life," she remarked.

Dando shrugged. "Oh, just a bit of bother," he replied.

Nothing more was ever said on the subject between them. Damask got the details of her sibling's recent history out of Jack later. A third person appeared in the hall. Milly had been woken by the knock on the door and had come down in a dressing gown from an early bedtime to investigate.

"Jack," she cried and then joyously, "it's the Lordship!"

She pushed past Damask but stopped with a gasp, grabbing hold of the other girl.

"You're 'urt!" she exclaimed as she became aware of the changed mien of her hero. The scarred wrists, the missing foot, the broken nose; she noted them instantly and through a perfect empathy immediately experienced the other's suffering in her own body. In that brief moment she felt the burn of the ropes, the cut of the knife, the blow to the face. If she had known about the stealing of the elixir she would also have felt the lash of a whip. At one and the same time she realised that Dando would have to be told the truth about Ann's death.

"Oh blimey!" she cried and rushed to hide herself away in the kitchen.

"Come in," said Becca to the two young men. "Have you eaten? Then I guess you're hungry. I reckon I can find you something on the cold shelf."

Dando turned to Damask with a puzzled frown.

"This baby," he said, "is it yours?"

Damask opened her mouth to reply but Becca hurriedly interposed.

"Food first," she said, "then we can talk. Where are you staying guys? Would you like to spend the night here?"

Soon Jack and Dando were sitting eating at the kitchen table while Damask went off to attend to her charge. Milly, partially recovered, perched on a stool, drinking in every aspect of her idol. Eventually Damask reappeared with the baby in her arms.

"He won't go back to sleep," she said looking questioningly at Becca.

Becca walked round the table and put her hand on Dando's shoulder.

"The baby's not Damask's," she said gently, "he's yours, honey chil'."

"Mine?" responded Dando, completely baffled.

"Didn't you realise she was expecting?" exclaimed Damask in her usual forthright manner, "typical man – doesn't notice something even when it's staring him in the face."

"Annie!" cried Dando, "Annie's here?"

"She was dick head."

"Where is she?" His chair scraped the floor as he got up and stared heavenwards as if expecting his sweetheart to appear through the ceiling.

"It was a difficult labour," said Becca, "we did all we could – the doctor did all he could."

"Is she ill?" said Dando.

"We saved the baby – it was her choice."

"Where is she?" asked Dando again.

"Oh, for heaven's sake!" cried Damask. She could not bear all this beating about the bush. "She's dead, Do-Do. She died so that the baby might live. The doctor was only able to save one of them."

Dando's hand flew to the tangled, filthy skein of hair round his throat. His sight darkened. As his head swam and his muscles turned to water he crumpled to the floor. Jack jumped up in his turn and then fell to his knees beside the one he loved.

"Little bird!" he cried.

Still clutching the plait Dando attempted to speak but his voice became indistinct and faded away as consciousness failed him.

"Wot you done?!" cried Milly, incensed. "You shouldn't 'ave let on! Wot did 'e say?"

Jack stroked Dando's hair and then heaved a deep sigh.

"I think he said, *So I killed her after all*," he replied.

When he came round a few minutes later Milly and Damask helped Dando to Becca's best bedroom on the first floor, a twin-bedded room, and Jack lay next to him for the rest of the night ready to provide human comfort or anything else he might need. To the surprise of everyone, by morning, despite the fact that his features seemed frozen into an expression of permanent sorrow, the Glept was ready to get up and face a new day. The initial shock had knocked him for six yet the news of Ann's death was not quite the blow that they had imagined it would be - it was almost as if he had been half expecting something of the kind and had prepared himself.

"Now it's been paid in full," he said to Jack. "I must go to her – I must go to the grave."

"Tomorrow," promised his friend, "we'll go tomorrow – I'll take you."

But by the time the following day dawned their circumstances had altered considerably; in fact the whole town had come under threat and people were hurriedly leaving; the ferryman who took passengers to Cemetery Island had gone with the rest and his boat was no longer at the quayside. As yet however that was in the future. It was still the morning of the eleventh day of the tenth month and Jack and Dando took themselves off to the house on the Broadway to collect Tallis and Ralph. Becca had suggested that the travellers and their friends should all be together under the same roof – hers - at this time of crisis and it seemed the most sensible arrangement. Tallis took some persuading. For one thing he was angry with Dando for not coming back the previous night ("You don't realise how I worry when I don't know where you are") and for another he had become accustomed to the sort of high life in which he had servants to wait on him and all his needs catered for.

"I'll take care of you master," said Dando, "I'll see that you want for nothing."

As soon as they entered the showgirl's house Ralph came nose to nose with Meena. A lot of spitting and swearing followed, after which the cat fled to the top of a tall bookcase while Ralph looked up with a disappointed whine in his throat; he would have liked to be friends, in fact his great plumed tail was demonstrating his amiability. Becca seized hold of Dando's arm and pulled him into the room which was being used as a nursery.

"Sit down," she instructed and put Horry on his lap.

Dando stared down at the child with an unreadable expression.

"How old is he?" he asked.

"Just over two and a half weeks."

"He looks a lot more than that."

Becca shot a meaningful glance at Damask who had arrived in the doorway.

"We've taken to calling him Horry because we believe Ann was thinking of Horace, but if you want something different...? Horry's rather a strange name..."

"I don't mind it," replied Dando.

"Horry was born four days before your birthday," said Damask, "we're three of a kind. I s'pose it's escaped your notice that you're now eighteen. Think what a fuss they would have made if you were at home and still in the Outriders – officer status at the very least."

The infant's hair was flaxen and he had bright blue eyes.

"He looks just like her," said Dando and all of a sudden his face was painfully convulsed. Thrusting the baby back into Becca's arms he stumbled blindly out of the room and took himself off to grieve alone.

That night a new noise wove itself in and out of the city-folk's dreams. CRUMP-THUD!....... CRUMP-THUD!........ The sound came from a great way off, almost like a distant electrical storm, but was far too regular to be natural. Dando raised himself on one elbow and stared into the darkness.

"What the hell's that?" he said.

"Cannon fire," replied Jack who was also awake. "They're coming."

He sat up and swung his legs out of bed.

"You know birdy, we made a big mistake returning to this place. If they've reached the Kymer there'll be no way out by land."

"How far away are they do you think?"

Jack listened intently.

"Eight miles - ten miles."

"All the same," said Dando, "it was good we came. Otherwise I would never have been sure..." his voice stumbled to a halt.

The following day, the twelfth, the citizens of Vadrosnia Poule witnessed the spectacle of a defeated army at their gates. The Kymer Volunteers had not been equal to the task they had set themselves and had consequently been overwhelmed. Numbers of battle-weary fighters streamed along the Green Dolphin Avenue and into the city. Once in the streets they did not spread out or disperse to their homes but made their way with great singleness of purpose across town and down to the docks. They were in a variety of physical states, these new arrivals, but with just one thought between them: to find a ship that would carry them to safety across the Middle Sea.

In the afternoon a member of the combatants arrived on Becca's doorstep. He was battered and bloody, with a cloth about his head, and his eyes were shadowed like those of a man who has looked on horrors. It was Damask who opened the door to greet him.

"They tell me at the big house," he announced, "that the knight be here along o' the Glept an' his pansy pal."

"I don't know what you're talking about."

"The top dog – we travel through the mountains together. He were taken ill an' I push he in a chair."

"Do you mean Tallis?"

"Yes – the knight as they call him."

The gentlewoman and the Nablan sized each other up. Although sharing a common birthplace they had never met. Both saw someone diametrically opposite to themselves in background and circumstances yet, at the same time, recognised a fellow-traveller guarding an almost identical independence of spirit. Each in their own way found this both disturbing and intriguing. Damask also saw someone who had recently been to hell and back.

"Are you Foxy?" she asked.

"Some call I that."

"Come in," she said. "You look as if you could do with a break. Come and tell us what's been happening."

Foxy was immediately taken to the bosom of the little family. Becca tended to his wounds, fortunately none of them too serious, while Milly fed him and Jack and Tallis attempted to draw him out about his time with the Kymer Volunteers. Dando remained silent. He knew it was his duty to tell the newcomer of Ann's death and the circumstances that had led up to it, but now did not seem to be the right time for a confession - would the time ever be right he wondered? If, when Foxy learnt the facts, he blamed Dando for the tragedy, as he had instantly blamed himself, then he would probably set out to kill him in grim earnest this time, and maybe that would be all to the good. Life was not so great that he felt any huge desire to hang on to it.

Foxy described his experiences. There had been a pitched battle just south of Urgun he told them and the Axemen, not numerically superior but better equipped and, by now, much more seasoned in war, had trounced the amateur army. Since then the defenders had been fighting a hopeless rearguard action, gradually retreating, waiting for non-existent reinforcements.

"The berserkers'll be here by tomorrow. I come to warn you to get out. When they take a town they don' shew no mercy. The only sure way now is by sea. Trewithik's fleet is launching an attack on Kingscauldie further east so the blockade is a lot less solid at the moment. Best to goo tonight."

"It doesn't seem real," said Damask, "I can hardly believe it's happening."

"Don' you hear the guns? You be believin' it when the shells start landin' on your head."

Becca came to a decision.

"I guess I'm going to go home sooner than expected," she said. "The harbour master's a pal of mine. I've got a notion that the Ry-Town mail-boat leaves tomorrow night. I'll ask him if, as a special favour, he can get us on board."

She set off at once but returned an hour later having met with mixed fortunes.

"A lot of boats have already taken their chance and left and the packet's been cancelled, but he says there are several ships putting in on the fourteenth that are prepared to take people off. He promised to give us priority." She held up some tickets that she took from her handbag.

At first light on the thirteenth day of the month a dark mass appeared at the far end of the causeway into the city. Trewithik's victorious troops, their goal finally within sight, were gathering on the landward side of the grand approach, equipped with cannon, howitzers and every imaginable kind of ordnance. And there, outside the city, they remained for twenty-four hours, waiting for the arrival of some of the larger guns that would provide the planned bombardment's backbone. This breathing space gave the town time to assemble a small group of defenders at the gate, ready to oppose the conquering force if it started to cross the causeway. Foxy refused to join them.

"They don' have a hope," he said pityingly. "I don' be a-gooin' to throw my life away for no good raison."

Whilst they waited for the main blitz to start the Axemen's sure-shots, employing the weapons already available, indulged in a little playful target practice. One by one the copper-clad dolphins that had lined the approach to the Delta City, time out of mind, were blown to pieces. When the last great statue had been toppled the artillerymen extended the reach of their cannon by raising the field pieces to a higher elevation and began to attack the city proper.

"I think they intend to reduce the whole town to rubble before they march in," said Jack. "Poor Drossi."

"Get your things together," instructed Becca. "I know the Diamond's not supposed to dock till tomorrow but if we get down there now we'll be ahead of the rest."

An hour later they set out, Becca leading the cavalcade, weighed down by two large suitcases, followed by Damask with Horry in a sling and Milly, close on her heels, carrying Meena in a newly-acquired basket, much to Ralph's fascination. Then came Tallis, Jack and Foxy, the two young men taking it in turns to push the older man's chair, while Dando brought up the rear feeling relatively extraneous. It had been a vain hope that they would be first in the queue. When they arrived near the water they found the area crammed with people, including many ex-fighters from up country. The good ship Diamond, plus the Amber and the Briar Rose, had already docked but the crowd was not being allowed on board. All night Becca's party stood there, pushed and jostled by those around them, while the sound of exploding shells crept nearer. At last a gate was opened in the fence across their path and the would-be passengers began to fight their way towards it. Becca waved her tickets in the air but nobody took a blind bit of notice. "First come, first served!" they heard a man shout. For almost half an hour they despaired of moving forward, then suddenly found their way unimpeded. The route to the ships appeared open until they came upon a turnstile filling a gap in a second barrier. Becca, Damask and Milly were permitted to slip through easily enough but when Tallis, Jack, Foxy and Dando presented themselves before the obstruction an official pulled a lever, temporarily stopping the device from revolving.

"Women and children have priority!" he barked.

"What!" exclaimed Jack, while Foxy pointed to some men already on one of the ships.

"How about they?!" he shouted indignantly.

"Women and children first," the man repeated.

The three who had already passed through the turnstile realised that their friends' right of passage had been denied and came back to see what had gone wrong.

"But I've got tickets," cried Becca, flapping them in the face of the official.

"No longer valid," he told her wearily. "Clear the way. Come along there," to some elderly matrons behind Dando.

The rest of the prospective evacuees were getting restless, wanting to know what was causing the delay. A couple of sailors intervened on the ships' side of the fence, pulling the women towards the gangplank while others in the crowd attempted to shoulder past. Milly stumbled forwards, looking back desperately over her shoulder.

"Lordship!" she cried in distress.

Becca also turned round.

"Rytardenath," she shouted. "Find your way to Ry-Town. Ask for Peepo – that's the name I go by on the coast. They all know me."

"I'll look after him for you," Damask yelled to Dando, holding Horry aloft, and then to the baby, "Wave goodbye to your daddy," but her eyes were fixed on Foxy. He stared back, totally bemused, not yet having been apprised of the baby's parentage. Who was she addressing? Who was the father of her child? For a moment longer it was still possible to shout something to the ones beyond the barrier but no-one took advantage of the opportunity, then there was a great surge as escapees of both sexes seized their chance to embark, and those who hesitated or tried to prevent them were swept aside. You might have noticed, if you were close enough to recognise faces, that a certain street performer, stage name Gubbo, was caught up in the panicky scramble. After various setbacks our necromancer had decided that this part of the southern continent was not to his taste after all and had made up his mind to return whence he came in order to seek out a talisman whose hiding place, chosen at random in a past age, he had begun to fear was no longer secure. He was the last to board one of the ships in the general frantic exodus from the ill-fated city (despite his magical talents the only way for an enchanter to cross salt water was, like the mass of humanity, by ship) and he only just made it up the gangplank before it was withdrawn.

The male members of Becca's party, having been roughly handled by the impatient crowd, were slow to join in the general stampede and by the time they made the attempt it was far too late.

"It was the bath chair, birdy," said Jack as they hurried through the mean little alleys inland from the harbour, " plus the dog and your crutch - that's what made them take against us. But never say die – I think I know what we can do. Wow! That was close!" as a shell burst just a couple of streets away.

For a moment the roar shocked them all into silence, then the blind boy found his voice.

"If we skirt round the west side of the docks we'll get onto the dykes. Farther down the delta there's a boat – an old barge – or at least there was last time I was here. It's tucked away up a side channel. I discovered it years ago and went aboard despite the fact that ships were supposed to be a no-go area where I was concerned. I've no idea who it belongs to. I reckon we could get away on that as long as we can avoid Pickwah's patrol vessels."

"Sail a boat?" said Tallis doubtfully. "What do we know about manning boats?"

"Quite a bit," said Jack. "For example I've been told that this lad had his own yacht," stretching his hand back in Dando's general direction.

"Only a little one," said the boy.

"How long be it since you las' see it?" asked Foxy, referring to the barge.

"Oh, a couple of years. As a kid I used to sneak down there when my grandfather wasn't looking. I took it out to sea once, all on my own."

"Two years is a long time if its been left to rot," said Tallis.

"Have you got a better idea?"

With Jack giving directions and the others obeying them they eventually passed an area of fishermen's huts built on stilts which was followed by a ramshackle collection of boat houses. In the midst of these they made out a grassy bank with a footpath along the top which wound off into the distance.

"The dykes are a real maze," explained Jack, "but keep to the one with a path, then you won't go far wrong."

"Mazes can be dangerous," warned Dando dreamily, apropos of apparently nothing.

"I come here before," remarked Foxy, "when I were in Drossi las' time. I set up camp a bit farther down."

"You've been here already?" Jack asked. He was surprised. To him Foxy appeared to be the very antithesis of a city dweller, a real backwoodsman. He had not imagined that the Nablan had been anywhere near a large town before.

"Keep your eyes skinned," he instructed, returning to the matter at hand, "I used to make for a lone tree, the only one remaining on the delta proper I believe. If you spot it and then look carefully you'd see the Gloriosa's masts right beside it."

In a very short time they were out under a large sky with salt marshes all around. From the city at their backs rose several towering plumes of smoke – Drossi was burning. Progress with the bath chair was difficult as it often had to be lifted over obstacles along the rough track. Foxy and Jack managed it between them although Jack was hampered by the fact that he could not see.

"What can I do?" asked Dando, disqualified from helping by his disability, yet feeling guilty that the other two young men were taking the lion's share of the work.

"You're our lookout spatzi," said Jack. "You must find the ship."

They were by no means alone on the marshes. Others had taken the same escape route from the town despite the fact that it led nowhere but out to sea. Seeing a group of people who appeared to know where they were going, these waifs and strays fell, one after another, into step until there was quite a little procession following along behind them.

Dando shaded his eyes with his hand.

"There it is," he cried, "the tree I mean – it's way ahead and off to the right."

"Good on you lad," said Jack, "and can you see the masts?"

"No, I can't. Maybe she's heeled over – it's low tide."

"Yes, we're going to have to wait for the water to come in and float her off."

After at least one wrong turn which took them to a dead end they reached the tree and discovered the barge. She was lying on her side just below the dyke on which they were standing surrounded by glistening mud. There was the sound of water trickling but whether it came from inside or outside the vessel they could not be sure.

"What does she look like?" asked Jack.

"Old," replied Dando, gazing at the barnacled and weed-encrusted hull.

"Are the masts still in place?"

"Yes."

"And can you see any sign of furled sails?"

"I think so."

High tide was not due until seven o'clock that evening. They had several hours to wait before they could be sure that the ship still floated. In that time some of their hangers on drifted away but new fugitives arrived, saw what was in hand and attached themselves to the party. Jack listened in to conversations, assessing their numbers. He was not sure if the old boat would be able to accommodate so many. Amongst the crowd there were one or two familiar voices.

"I know you, don't I," he remarked to someone nearby. "you're from the Posse. Are the others with you? Where's Primo?"

"There's only the three of us," said Winnie, the accordion player. "Where that big-headed bastard is I don't know and I don't care. Let's hope he got in the way of a blockbuster."

"I always thought you were better off without him. Is Matt back with you?"

"He's our front man now."

"That's a bit of a turn up for the book. Going to take your chances in Ry-Town?"

"If we can make it across."

"Well, you can come with us when we get this tub under way."

There also seemed to be a group of Roma present. He heard Dando exchange a wary greeting with two of them. Jack guessed that they must belong to the tribe who used to visit the boy's homeland and whose members had been his sister's friends.

Gradually the sea crept up into the backwater where the vessel lay and with much creaking of timbers the old ship righted itself and lifted off the bottom.

"Is there a plank? Slide it across the gap," instructed Jack. "Go ahead of me birdy – help me discover if things are still shipshape. Be my eyes."

Jack felt his way around the upper and lower decks and into the hold. He refamiliarised himself with the place that had been his secret refuge in his teenage years. Eventually he pronounced his verdict.

"I think she's sound. There are probably a few leaks but she's got a pump. If the sails are still in one piece I reckon we can give it a go."

He took Dando to the wheelhouse.

"You must be our steersman, patootie. I'll stand beside you and tell you what to watch out for. There are buoys marking the main channel – red to port, green to starboard going down river. We must get out to sea before it gets dark. I need some strong men to raise the sails."

The sails were stiff from neglect but had not yet disintegrated. It was hard to decide on their original colour as they were so faded, stained and dirty. Foxy and a couple of other willing helpers contended with disused and rusty mechanisms and eventually, with much shrieking of bearings, the canvasses began to creep up the masts. Eagerly the refugees came piling on board filling every available space while Jack anxiously sensed, through his feet, the effect this was having on the ship.

"I don't know if she can stand all this weight," he said. "Well, I spose we've got no choice. You'd have to be a better man than me to turf them off. Let's slip the moorings and get under way."

A light wind was blowing from the south-west. Slowly the Gloriosa, as the barge was named, moved out of the creek and into one of the delta's channels where she turned north towards the sea.

"Yo ho ho! Shiver me timbers! Heave ho me hearties!" sang out the ship's captain, elated at this apparent success.

"Shut up Jack," admonished Dando, clutching the wheel in a paralytic grip, terrified he was going to run the whole shooting match aground.

Dusk was rapidly approaching and in the dim light a lurid glow was apparent up river in the direction of Vadrosnia Poule. There were other areas of fiery luminescence, spreading into the sky from beyond the low horizon.

"The whool country be aflame," said Foxy.

"Well, we're leaving it behind," answered Tallis. "At last we're going north across the sea. At long last."

Two essences of pure energy came flashing out of the back reaches of space and hung for a moment above a tiny rocky planet orbiting an insignificant star in the outer regions of the arm of a minor spiral galaxy. They were living entities, these emanations, but the matter of which they were composed was of a different order from that of lowlier creatures who were still forced to creep on their bellies across the surface of material worlds; they had left their mortal bodies behind to moulder into dust and, mastering time, had embraced sempiternity.

"I took you to view the dance, sweetheart," said Tom, *"so you could see where your future lies – it lies among the stars."*

"It were wonderful Dadda, an' there be more like us – many, many more – they fill the whool of everything."

"Yes but be wary, my hinny – they be not all kindly. Now I bring you back because there be something to attend to here where we hail from. If you stay too long away - if you join the dance - you will forget those still bound to the wheel, those whom you loved and who also loved you. In the end you will even forget yourself."

"I do be forgetting Dadda. Shew me what I need to know."

"Do you mind that there were a young lord - the Lord Dan Addo? You share the same breast, you play together as childer although he were far above you."

"I mind he! He were my bonny lad! We lay together – I bore his chil'. The baby, Dadda - I mind the baby! Where be he?"

"I will shew you my maid, but first come back wi' I to before the now, to the time when you parted at the end of the road. I will let you see what happen, but you must be strong when you witness it, you must be stout of heart."

The events of the last few months, which, because of the nature of time, were apparently set to repeat themselves over and over again ad infinitum, played out before Ann's appalled gaze as father and daughter followed one particular line out of the past.

"Oh Dadda," she cried in deep distress, *"I never knew. This be all down to me. If I ha'n't left he asleep that night he wou'n't ha' thought we be taken prisoner – he wou'n't ha' gone to the island an' then he wou'n't ha' despaired and resigned himself to die. What can I do to make amends - what can I do to help he?"*

"You mus' do nothing my hinny," Tom said sharply, *"you mus' change nothing before the now – else there be all sorts of upsets in both heaven and earth. But you can be with he in that past time if you wish, long as you don' interfere – you can give he courage."*

"But will he know I be there?"

"He may do, in his dreams, and, coming back to the present, that which you gave him - the little plait he wound round his neck – could protect him from harm. Because you have passed over and become a dancer your powers have greatly increased."

"But why do all this hev to happen to he, Dadda?"

"Well pet, he hev powerful enemies, as you do too, even now."

"She from the Midda – he from the sky."

"An' remember the chil' of those immortals, the Dark Brother that dwells below. Also there be the one who stole the treasure – the one who aimed the curse an' held you in thrall. Beside that, I know of deeper reasons why he should be tested, reasons to do wi' who he is an' what he was born to do. Come wi' me now an' I'll shew you what be happenin' in the present moment. There be a great undertakin' goin' forward."

By the time the old barge reached the open sea night had fallen.

"Stay on the same bearing," Jack instructed Dando, "and keep an eye out for other ships. I must hang the lights out and then go below. I don't like the feel of her – there's something not quite right."

What was not right, he soon discovered, was that the hold was half full of water. A rota was organised to man the one and only pump but after about half an hour something broke inside the casing and nothing Jack could do would bring it back to life. As a substitute a chain of volunteers passed buckets to and fro but, however hard they worked, the water gained. In less than two hours the voyagers' initial euphoria evaporated and was replaced by fear. Eventually even Jack had to admit defeat.

"Sorry folks, we'll have to turn back," he said. "Stand by the boom," and to Dando, "bring her about."

Dando put the wheel hard over but at that moment the wind, which had been fitful at best, died completely and the ship answered sluggishly if at all. At the same time the deck gave a sickening lurch beneath their feet and the vessel slowly tipped sideways, listing well to starboard. The passengers let out a gut-wrenching cry of fear.

"There's some flares, we'll signal for help" said Jack, trying to sound reassuring. "They've been wrapped in oil-cloth – they should work." Sotto voce he added to Dando, "Our only hope is to be picked up – Trewithik's fleet would do – anyone would do who's nearby in this calm. Keep a constant watch – it would be easy to miss another ship on such a dark night."

Everyone, not just Dando, stared into the dimness, their eyes peeled for any sign of movement, but the harder they looked the less they saw. The little Gloriosa seemed to be totally alone on this stygian sea. Dando and Jack stood on either side of the useless wheel. Eventually Jack reached out and found Dando's hand.

"Who would have thought it would end like this, birdy," he said. "I was really looking forward to hitting Ry-Town. Well, one thing – at least we're together."

"There be danger," said Ann. *"I feel they be in danger. Yes, there it be - a ship, a ship near the lan' where the towns be a-burning. They're on the ship – the knight an' Foxy an' my own dear lad. But now I see it will goo beneath the water. Oh Dadda – what can I do?"*

"Look to the east," said Tom. *"Look to where the sun will rise."*

"I see another," cried Ann. *"I see another ship – a great ship wi' smoke comin' from its chimblies."*

"Yes," said Tom, *"that be their salvation. Go to that big ship an' find the lookout man. Whisper in his ear that he mus' watch for fires low down, just above the surface of the sea. Go to the steersman an' tell he to turn the wheel to a new bearin' – tell he to steer west-sou'-west. An' go to the captain an' say that there be folk in trouble an' he mun't leave they to drown."*

"Will they hear me Dadda?"

"Yes, they'll hear you sweetheart, but they'll think it be their own inner voice speaking. Go quickly now an' the people'll be saved."

The old work horse groaned softly and sank deeper into the water. She seemed to know that her hour had come. The passengers, apart from the ones who were still uselessly bailing, waited silently for something they could scarcely credit. On such a calm, tranquil, balmy night, surely death could not be hovering in the wings. Dando, who continued to look rather hopelessly beyond the prow, suddenly clutched Jack's arm.

"There's some lights!" he cried, "but it can't be a ship, they're way up in the air."

"Listen," whispered Jack. A new sound had joined the lapping and trickling of water. From afar off came a deep rumbling and pounding, almost below the threshold of hearing.

"Engines!" he said with suppressed excitement, "it's a steamer!"

The flares were standing ready to be fired. He touched a taper to the first and it shot into the sky.

"Thank god for that," he exclaimed. "I was afraid they were too old. But has anybody noticed? Quick – get some kindling together – light a fire."

"The whole ship may burn," cried someone.

"What does that matter – she's only got minutes to live anyway."

Soon flames were leaping upwards from a pile of planks that had been wrenched from the dry part of the upper deck. Jack launched his second flare. Everyone stared anxiously towards the lights which bore down on them remorselessly.

"It be a-gooin' to run us over!" cried Foxy.

The throbbing note changed and there was an enormous frothing and churning of water.

"They've put her into reverse," shouted Jack.

Slowly the great ship lost way and, by the time she reached the barge, had almost come to a halt. Like a huge black cliff her hull towered over them and above that her four impressive funnels scraped the clouds. Their vessel seemed minuscule by comparison.

"Can you read the name?" Jack asked Dando.

Dando stared upward.

"B-E-H-E-...." he spelled out.

"The Behemoth! We've hit the jackpot! She's a luxury liner - she'll be on her way back to Ry-Town after a round-the-world cruise. The Tethys Experience they call it - Tethys is the name the Armornians give to the Middle Sea."

For some time nothing happened whilst water began to creep over the barge's deck on the starboard side. Then very high in the beetling hull a door, a rectangular hatch, opened emitting a beam of light into the night. Slowly, from this opening, a companionway unfolded down the side of the ship. At the same time a rare puff of wind blew the barge towards the bottom of the steps.

"There's a way up," Dando told Jack.

"Quick," cried the Gloriosa's captain to the other passengers, "while you've got the chance – get on the ladder."

The refugees needed no second prompting. As fast as they could they made their way heavenwards, disappearing through the lit doorway.

"Come along," said Jack to Foxy, "we've got to get our invalid and his chair up there."

Between them they were soon fully occupied lifting Tallis to safety. Neither noticed that Dando had not yet set foot on the ascent. He hung back as everyone else took their turn and now stood alone on the Gloriosa's deck with only the faithful Ralph for company. If truth be told he was experiencing a great reluctance to take the irrevocable move that would lead him to the northern continent. Recently he had been through many trials which he had barely survived; he had been physically and spiritually wounded and had nowhere near recovered. But these tribulations were nothing, he feared, to those that lurked on the other side of the Middle Sea. The seer had told him that he had a destiny to fulfil there and he quailed at the thought of what might be demanded of him.

All I ever asked for was to be like everybody else, he anguished, *I just wanted to be normal, to be allowed to go my own way. Why should they have picked on me to perform their miracles for them?* Who *they* were he had absolutely no idea.

A man's head poked out from the hatch. Now that everyone had vanished within Dando thought he could hear, very faintly, music coming from above him. The brightly illuminated opening looked extremely inviting in contrast to the watery grave that awaited if he chose to remain below.

"All aboard that's coming aboard," sang out the sailor and was just about to retreat when, by the light of the fire that continued to smoulder on the deck, he noticed the two who still clung to the doomed barge.

"You're leaving it a bit late," he shouted. "The mutt'll have to stay behind - no animals allowed."

"I'm not coming without the dog," Dando called back.

The sailor withdrew but returned a few minutes later.

"They say they'll stretch the rules," he shouted, "but make it sharp – we can't sit around here kicking our heels while you decide whether to grace us with your presence."

And so, for Ralph's sake rather than his own, Dando climbed the ladder and, nerving himself to face whatever lay in store, entered the ship accompanied by his canine friend. The stairs were retracted, the hatch shut and, left deserted and no longer needed, the Gloriosa sank with quiet dignity beneath the waves. The Behemoth, black as the gloom that surrounded her, let off a great roaring blast from her bowels, a thunderous marine fart, as her screws began to turn. Getting under-way she proceeded slowly and majestically into the night leaving a long phosphorescent wake behind which gradually spread out and dispersed over the surface of the sea.

To be continued...